Jessica Blair grew up [...] teacher and now lives in [...] time writer in 1977 and [...] under various pseudony[...] *Distant Harbour, Storm Bay, The [...] The Restless Spirit, The Seaweed Gatherers, [...] Charlotte, The Locket, The Long Way Home, The Restless Heart, Time & Tide, Secrets of the Sea, Yesterday's Dreams, Reach for Tomorrow, Dangerous Shores, Wings of Sorrow, Stay With Me, Sealed Secrets* and *Secrets of a Whitby Girl* all published by Piatkus.

For more information about the author visit: www.jessicablair.co.uk

Echoes of the Past

Jessica Blair

piatkus

PIATKUS

First published in Great Britain in 2003 by Judy Piatkus (Publishers) Ltd
This paperback edition published in 2011 by Piatkus

A CIP catalogue record for this book
is available from the British Library.

ISBN 978-0-7515-4561-6

Typeset in ATTimes by Action Publishing Technology Ltd, Gloucester
Printed and bound in Great Britain by CPI Mackays, Chatham, ME5 8TD

Piatkus
An imprint of
Little, Brown Book Group
100 Victoria Embankment
London EC4Y 0DY

An Hachette UK Company
www.hachette.co.uk

www.piatkus.co.uk

For

A. G. J. and D.
With grateful thanks for their wonderful support
through everything

Acknowledgements

I am grateful for help from the men of Whitby Lifeboat Station, and from Dominic Hudson on sailing matters. As ever I thank my editor, Lynn Curtis, and all at my publisher for their help towards creating the finished book. My gratitude goes to my family for their help, constructive criticism, and advice – without their support this book would not have been finished.

Chapter One

John Chambers took the two steps in one stride, tugged at the bell pull and waited impatiently for an answer, but it was the impatience of one eager to impart good news. He turned with his back to the door to enjoy for one more moment the September sunshine on this beautiful afternoon in 1832, expelling his breath with a deep sigh of contentment.

The door opened. He swung round. 'Miss Katherine at home, Lizzie?' he asked eagerly.

'Good day, sir.' The young maid, neatly dressed in high-necked, well-fitting black dress, was used to opening the door to this likeable young man but today her usual cheerful greeting was missing. Holding the door wide, she moved to one side without a word.

It was only as he stepped past her and sensed a different atmosphere in the Kemp household, on the boundary of the fashionable area of Newcastle-upon-Tyne, that he realised something was different. He turned back and was struck by the sombre expression on Lizzie's face, noticing that her eyes were red from crying. She did not wear the usual white apron and cap, and with her hair drawn back tightly into a bun at the nape of her neck, the severity of her appearance was marked compared to her usual bright and cheery aspect. The five members of staff of the Kemp household liked this young man and were pleased that their

1

beloved Miss Katherine had found such a personable and friendly suitor who always had a kind word for them too.

'What is it, Lizzie?' he asked in a tone that assumed she was troubled and at the same time offered help.

She did not answer but led the way across the hall to the drawing-room. Mystified by her reaction, he took it as an indication she did not want to enlighten him, not at least for the moment, and followed without a word.

She opened the door and in a voice that was scarcely above a whisper and had a catch in it, said, 'Mr John, miss.'

It was at that moment that he knew something was dreadfully wrong. Confirmation came as he entered the room. Katherine was sitting on the sofa with Mrs Nicholls, the cook-housekeeper, sitting beside her. She was holding Katherine's hands in hers and both of them had tear-stained cheeks and expressions that spoke of tragedy.

'What's wrong?' John's questioning glance moved from one to the other. He saw that the utter despair on Katherine's face was mixed with bewilderment as if she was far from understanding what had happened.

He saw that Mrs Nicholls' sombre countenance also carried the strain of someone coping with loss while at the same time trying to support and comfort another.

'It's the master, sir,' the housekeeper replied in a faltering voice. John's puzzled expression and obvious desire to have none of the truth held back drove her on to utter something she would rather not have. 'He's dead.'

The blunt words hit John hard. He immediately wanted to doubt them, though he knew they would never have been uttered if they were untrue. Then the moment of disbelief was submerged in concern for Katherine. He was on his knees beside her, taking her hands in his.

'Oh, Katherine, I'm so, so sorry.' His voice was filled with sympathy and love for her, and desire to take the pain away. 'What can I say? What can I do?' He held her eyes and from his poured an immense love that she accepted

2

with gratitude, knowing it was for her, offering a strength on which she could draw.

'Be here for me,' she replied quietly.

'Always.' He glanced up at Mrs Nicholls who had risen from the sofa, knowing that the young people needed to be alone. 'What happened?'

'As you know, Mr Kemp has been sleeping in of late but has generally been down by ten or ten-thirty. He didn't appear at that time this morning so we thought he must be taking an extra rest. When he hadn't appeared by twelve we became concerned. Miss Katherine went to see if he was all right and found . . .' Her voice faltered.

'He was still in bed.' Katherine took up the story in a voice which came weakly but with a determination not to shrink from what she had to say. 'When I went to him I thought at first that he was asleep, then I realised he wasn't.' The picture she was seeing caused her voice to falter.

Mrs Nicholls took over. 'The doctor and the constable are with him now.'

'Constable?'

Katherine glanced at Mrs Nicholls and in the look she gave the housekeeper read the desire that she wanted to impart the rest of the information on her own.

Mrs Nicholls gave an almost imperceptible nod of understanding and said, 'Call me if you want me.'

'Thank you,' replied Katherine in a whisper.

Mrs Nicholls left the room. As the door clicked shut Katherine flung her arms round John's neck, buried her head against him and wept.

He held her tight, stroked her hair soothingly, said nothing but let her sob the initial distress out of her shuddering body.

When the crying stopped she eased herself from him. His hands slipped to her arms and held her while they looked deep into each other's eyes.

'I love you, Katherine, no matter what.'

3

She drew immense comfort from the sincerity in his voice. 'And I love you too, John. Help me through this. You know that Father has been depressed since Mother died six months ago?'

He nodded, knowing Mr Kemp had been shattered by the unexpected loss of his wife. They had been a mature couple full of good will and vitality with a tangible bond between them. Then tragedy had struck and Katherine's father was bereft.

'The doctor had given him something to try to counteract his low spirits. The bottle was empty on the table beside Father's bed.'

'Oh, no!' The implication brought confusion to John's mind. How to cope with this? How to help Katherine accept what she was implying?

Before he could reply a knock came at the door. John glanced at her, rose to his feet and hurried to answer it. He opened it to see the doctor and the constable standing there.

'A word with Miss Katherine, please?' said the doctor, a short, rotund man with a florid face whose kindness extended to all classes of society. The constable standing behind him was, in contrast, tall and thin, with sharp, serious features seemingly forever gripped by a severity that precluded any frivolity. The letter of the law seemed to be written all over him but that was a false impression. Though more often than not he would enforce it, he was not averse to bending the rules if he thought fit.

'Please come in,' said John and stepped to one side.

The doctor crossed to the sofa and sat down beside Katherine. The constable stood a few paces inside the room. John came and stood beside her, his hand resting comfortingly on her shoulder.

The doctor hesitated only a moment. He knew of the relationship that existed between the two young people and that he could speak freely in front of John. In fact, was pleased that he was here.

'My dear,' began the doctor, 'as you know your father

4

suffered badly after losing your mother and I prescribed something I thought would help him. I suppose it has done so, but not in the way I intended.'

Katherine gave a little gasp. 'It's true then?' She saw the doctor glance at John and then back to her. 'You can speak freely, Doctor. John knows what I found.'

'The empty bottle is not positive proof that your father took his own life, though in his depressed state after the loss he suffered six months ago it is possible.' He saw Katherine looked shocked, took her hands in his and looked her straight in the eye. 'Don't ever condemn your father for what he might have done.' He was careful to make no positive pronouncement on what could have happened in the bedroom. 'As far as I am concerned there is no proof. The constable and I have had a long talk about this. Your father was much respected and we want no scandal to surround his death. We are agreed that he died from natural causes. The constable's report will say that there is nothing suspicious and I will sign the certificate accordingly. You, my dear, should think of your father's death in that way.'

Katherine had listened, at first with concern at the stigma that might be attached to her father, and then with relief at the way two understanding men had co-operated to save his name. She bit her lip and with a catch in her voice said, 'I am so grateful to you both. Thank you.' She swallowed hard, held back tears of gratitude and continued, 'I am faced with a painful time ahead that would have been even more painful but for your kindness. I will ever be beholden to you both.'

'Think nothing of it, my dear.' The doctor gave her hand a kindly pat, rose from the sofa and started for the door. John hurried to open it for him. The constable, still standing stiffly, gave Katherine a weak, embarrassed smile, but she saw kindness in his eyes. He turned and followed the doctor.

John escorted them to the front door where the doctor hesitated and said to him, 'Take good care of her.'

5

'I will, sir.'

John hurried back to the drawing-room and sat on the sofa beside her. 'Thank goodness for understanding people,' he said.

She nodded then gave him a frightened look. 'What am I going to do?'

'We'll work something out, my love.' He was longing to tell her his own news but this was not the right time. Bewildered and distressed already, she would not grasp the full implications of what he had to tell her. Events had conspired against him. He needed time to think things over and reassess what he should do. His decision could affect the future for them both, but that lay ahead. Katherine's immediate predicament was of paramount importance.

She had no family to turn to. Her nearest relatives, an uncle and aunt, had emigrated to America two years ago after their daughter's marriage. Though her cousin Rachel was nearly two years older they had been close as children, but after Rachel's marriage had taken her to the tiny Northumberland fishing village of St Abbs they had seen nothing of each other.

John saw the fear of utter loneliness in the girl's eyes. He took hold of her hands with a pressure he hoped would reassure her as he said, 'We'll get over this together. I'm sure Mrs Nicholls will be of great help with what has to be done, and I know my parents will guide you in those matters if you wish. And don't forget I'm here to help in any way I can. I know there will be Mrs Nicholls and servants in the house but I think you should come home and stay with us until after the funeral. My parents would want that.'

He had no hesitation about making such an offer. When, a year ago, he had first taken Katherine to meet them, they had been captivated by her charm and vivacity. They had seen before them a beautiful young woman with a light in her pale blue eyes that reflected her every mood, whether it be curiosity, laughter, pleasure or a quiet reflection that bespoke a sharp and intelligent mind. She had a well-formed oval face with a tip-tilted nose; a bow-shaped mouth that was not too wide to distract from the smooth curve of the chin. Thin eyebrows arched above the line of her eyelids and matched for colour the swirling mass of the copper-tinted hair drawn up from the nape of her neck. Though her heart had been fluttering at this first meeting she'd betrayed no sign of anxiety. She had held herself proudly but graciously and had won the hearts of John's parents who were pleased that their son had found such a girl.

She for her part let her heart sing in the joy of having met a young man who was not only considerate and charming but had a rugged masculine attraction that did not detract from his good looks. His dark brown eyes were bold, restless and enquiring but could be gentle, sympathetic and understanding whenever the situation demanded it. At six foot tall he held himself erect, seeming to add to his height. Though he was slim there was a strength and easy grace about him. His slender hands had power in their fingers and wrists. At their first meeting Katherine had felt comfortable in his company. As the days and weeks moved into months and they came to know each other better, that feeling of comfort grew and she sensed his ambitious and determined nature.

When her mother had died six months ago he had been there, helping her to cope and adapt to life without the one she had loved dearly. As her father, shattered by the loss, had sunk into a depression, John had given her all the support he could. Now, an even greater tragedy demanded of him a role he might find difficult.

So it proved. The first few days after the tragedy were trying. The arrangements for the funeral, the service and the burial on a dull, rain-spattered day when a northeast wind blew cold across the bleak cemetery, the acceptance of commiserations, and the reading of the will, all took their toll on Katherine.

John's heart ached for her. He longed to see again the vibrant girl with glowing skin and bright eyes.

He battled hard in his own quiet way, aided by his parents who took kindly to her staying with them. But once the funeral was over and a week had passed they all sensed a restlessness in Katherine. It therefore came as no surprise when she informed them that she wanted to go home. They quickly saw that their protests would be to no avail and realised that to insist on her staying might have adverse results.

So John saw her safely home where Mrs Nicholls fussed over her without being too intrusive. When he left, he made Katherine promise to send for him if there was anything he could do.

'Thank you, John, you and your parents have been more than kind to me and I will ever be grateful to you all.' Katherine forced her voice to be strong. Though she wanted to reach out and hold him back, never let him go, she knew she could not. John had his own life and she must face her sorrow. When the door clicked shut and his presence was no longer there she felt so alone in the vastness of a house that less than a year ago had vibrated with family life and help a promise of comfort and security. The silence, the absence of two dear presences, was overpowering. She took one step towards the stairs then burst into a run. She raced up them, tears streaming down her face, to reach her bedroom where she hurled herself on to her bed and wept and wept.

As September moved into October and October into November, John searched for a slight improvement in Katherine's melancholia that he'd fought hard to counteract. Plans were forming in his mind for when she was stronger. But one November day when he made his usual call on Katherine, he was greeted by a worried Mrs Nicholls.

'Miss Katherine is particularly low today, it would have been Mr and Mrs Kemp's wedding anniversary. You know they always made a special occasion of it? Miss Katherine feels the loss very badly. She has sat in there all day.' Mrs Nicholls inclined her head towards the drawing-room. 'She has eaten nothing, does not speak. The person in there is not the Miss Katherine we know. The loss of her parents so close together was a terrible shock but she's young, has a whole life before her. They would not want her to mourn in the way she is. I fear that mentally she may slip away from us, if not worse. Please try and do something, Mr John.' By the time she had finished, tears were streaming down her face.

'I'll do my best, Mrs Nicholls.' He patted her arm reassuringly but was alarmed at the prospect she had raised and hurried to the drawing-room.

He found Katherine staring into a grate in which the embers burnt without any cheery glow or warmth. A leaden sky muted the November light, adding to the feeling of depression in the room he once remembered being filled with Katherine's gaiety and laughter.

He dropped to his knees beside her, reaching for her hands but feeling little warmth in their touch. He received only a wan smile of recognition.

'Katherine, you should not be sitting here like this,' he said forcefully.

'What else is there to do?' she replied listlessly.

'You've a life to live.'

'It's meaningless.'

'Not for me. I need you beside me. Need your support.'

'I'd be no good to you.'

'In your present state you wouldn't. But this isn't the real you, not the girl I remember and whom I know will return.'

'Will she?' There was doubt in the shaking of her head.

'Of course she will. I know she will. Katherine, I want you back. I'll do anything to achieve that but there must be some effort from you. I cannot do it alone. You must fight against the depression that has gripped you since your father's death.'

She looked at him with misty eyes. 'And we know how that came about.'

'I realise what you are implying but you must get it out of your mind. After all, the doctor and the constable said they were satisfied there was no real evidence to prove your father had taken his own life.'

She gave a wan smile. 'But we know otherwise, don't we?'

'We don't.' John tried to make his words strong enough to penetrate an oppressed mind. 'You have got to stop thinking like that. For your own good and our future, you must cast that idea from your mind. To dwell on it in such a way is actually being selfish. You are doing it because you want to crucify yourself. If you continue to do so you will sink even further. The choice is yours. In your position you can stay where you are or you can make the effort to rise from the abyss and seize the chance to begin living again, not just for yourself but for me and the people around you.'

She turned her eyes to his, lifted her fingers to his cheek and touched it gently as if to test that he was real. Her pale smile mocked his statements.

John's temper flared a little. 'I'm right, Katherine, I know it. I believe deep down you know it too, but you've got to make the effort to recognise it. If you can lift your present mood you will find life much easier. Try, Katherine, please try. I have some ideas that may help, but I need you to co-operate.'

Though her eyes were lifeless, her demeanour dejected, he drew some hope when she whispered weakly, 'What do you want me to do?'

'I want to see determination to succeed in you. But in a more practical way, I want you to come home with me.'

'But this is where I should be.'

'I think not.'

'But ...'

'You should not be on your own.'

10

'I have Mrs Nicholls and the servants.'

'Yes, but they are not companions for you. You need people constantly around you to amuse and divert you. I would like you to come home with me now. I know Mother and Father will welcome you but it is your decision. You must decide whether or not to take up my offer.'

She remained silent.

The passage of a few minutes seemed eternity to him. On what she said now her whole future, and his, would rest. She could either face up to the challenge or slip into oblivion.

'I'll come.' Her words were so quiet that under normal circumstances he would have missed them. But, hanging on her decision, he was listening intently.

Relief surged through him. Hopefully this was the first step on the road to recovery, though he knew there would be a long way to go.

Mrs Nicholls' fear for Katherine was alleviated when John called her and told her of the mistress's decision. She quickly organised some clothing for her to take and within the hour John was explaining to his parents what had happened while Katherine, with the help of a maid, was unpacking.

The tender care she was given and the love with which the Chamberses surrounded her had its effect, as did John's gentle persuasion and encouragement for her to rise above the depression that threatened her. The light of interest began to return to her eyes; she joined in conversations more readily, accompanied Mrs Chambers to take tea with friends, and John noticed that she was making more observations when they walked together in the nearby park. Signs of the girl he remembered and still loved were returning and soon the pace of recovery quickened. He began to think it a suitable time to break the news he had held secret from her since the fateful day of her father's death.

John observed her even more closely in the week before Christmas. He knew the Kemps had always made a lot of

11

this time, keeping the religious observances and making it a happy festive time. This would be the first Christmas without her parents and John hoped this would not threaten the progress that Katherine had made. He consulted his parents about the attitude they should adopt and they all agreed that, while making this a happy time, they should keep festivities low key. Having noted the progress Katherine had made, his parents agreed that this could be the right time for him to break his news to her. It could help to take her mind off past Christmases and focus it on the future.

The opportunity came on Christmas Eve. Katherine and John had returned from an invigorating walk in the frosty afternoon air. Katherine glowed. Laughter had returned to her lips and her eyes shone with the sparkle that had been missing from them for months.

'I loved that, John. We must do it again tomorrow if the weather stays like this.'

'We will. It's good to see you enjoying life again with your old zest.'

'I feel so well.' She smiled the smile that used to set his heart racing. It was racing now. 'I owe you so much for making me see my future, and your parents for letting me stay here through this trying time. I will never be able to repay you all.'

'You've repaid us by getting well again. But it's yourself you should thank. No matter what we have done, the real progress had to be made by you. I am proud of you, Katherine, and I think now is the time to give you some more news.' He took her hand and led her to the drawing-room. He knew they would have it to themselves. His parents were visiting neighbours for afternoon tea.

They sat down on the sofa, half turned towards each other.

'Don't look so serious, John.' She ran a finger over the corner of his lips as if to make him smile. He started to speak but she stopped him with the pressure of her fingers.

'Let me say something first.' She took his hand in hers. 'I know you feared what Christmas might do to me but I'll be all right. What I am going to say might sound strange, but the other night I was woken by a peculiar sensation. I'm sure my mother and father were close by. It was as if they were telling me to be happy, to remember the Christmases we had shared but not to look on them with sadness. I should regard them as a pattern for this Christmas and all those in the future. They also told me to live as they would have wanted me to and to seize happiness while I can. So you see, John, we should celebrate properly tomorrow and throughout the rest of the festive season.' She paused, seeing tension had left his face. 'Now, what did you want to say to me?'

'Oh, Katherine, I'm so pleased to see you fully recovered.' He pulled her to him and hugged her. 'Now I can tell you what I came to say on the day your father died.'

'And you've kept it to yourself all this time?'

'It was news of particular relevance to us both. Then was hardly the right time and ever since I have been wanting to tell you but needed to see you fully recovered.'

'Well, I am.' She looked at him intently, eager to hear what he had to say.

'The day before I came to visit you, Mr Allberry called me into his office. Mr Carson was with him. When the partners who own the firm you work for need to see you together, you know it is something serious.

'I tell you, when I saw them both there, my knees started quaking and I feared the worst. I think they must have sensed this for they glanced at each other and then as one turned to me with smiles on their faces. "Young man," said Mr Allberry, "we have been watching your progress in our firm. You have done well and we have had good reports of your work: efficient, competent, not afraid to make decisions and stand by them."' John paused to smile modestly then continued. 'They said that although I was junior to a number of members of staff, they saw in me an ability to shoulder responsibility that impressed them and therefore were offering me a new position, helping Mr Drew, their senior manager, to open offices in London and expand their trade through there. They told me to think about it and let them know my decision the following day. I talked it over with my parents, and although they did not like the prospect of losing me to London, they saw that it was a wonderful opportunity for me and gave me their blessing. I informed Mr Allberry the following day and came to tell you, but could not when I found out what had happened.'

'And now?'

'I have to go at the end of March.'

Katherine was silent. Her joyful demeanour slowly disappeared as she considered the implications of this news. Then she shook herself. She should not be melancholy, this was important to John.

She looked him steadily in the eye. 'I am so pleased for you. It is wonderful that you have gained promotion to such a responsible job so young. I am proud of you.' Her pleasure dimmed then. 'But it means I'll lose you, John.'

He smiled reassuringly. 'You needn't, my love. Marry me and come with me?'

Having accepted in her mind that his departure for London would mean their separation, his proposal took her by surprise. She stared at him, unable to grasp the idea and give him an answer.

'Say yes,' he prompted.

Her eyes widened. Excitement sparkled in them. This really was happening. The horrors and setbacks she had suffered recently were lost in the joy that flooded her mind.

'Oh, John! Yes, yes, yes!' She flung her arms round his neck.

He grasped her waist and their lips met in a kiss of betrothal that promised a future of love and passion.

'This is the most wonderful Christmas present,' he said, a statement that was emphasised by the love and adoration in his eyes.

'I will never have a better. You have made me so happy.'

'And I intend to keep you that way.'

Katherine's parents came to mind then. How she wished they were here to share her joy! She felt the past closing in on her. Tears came to her eyes but she stiffened her determination not to give way to sadness. Her parents had told her to be happy and to live for the future. Well, that future was bound to John now. She knew her mother and father would indeed have been happy for her.

'My parents would have been very glad. I know they approved of you, John. Do yours know you intend to propose?'

'No, but I think they suspect as much. They will be delighted.'

So they were. When Katherine and John heard them return from their afternoon visit, he hurried into the hall. A few moments later he was ushering them excitedly into the room, not even giving them a chance to take off their outdoor clothes.

'Mother, Father, I have told Katherine about my appointment to London and have asked her to marry me so that she can accompany me there as my wife.'

Mrs Chambers' face broadened into a delighted smile. She came straight to Katherine, arms wide, hugging her and kissing her on both cheeks. 'Oh, I am so pleased. Through all your setbacks I hoped and prayed you would make a full recovery so that this day would come.' She kissed Katherine again and then turned to heap congratulations and approval on her son who had been receiving vigorous approval from his father.

Mr Chambers came over to Katherine, his smile benevolent and admiring. He kissed her on the cheek, allowing his lips to linger a moment as his mind reverted to the moment he had proposed to his dear Louisa. 'Be happy,' he whispered.

She leaned back from him and looked into his eyes. 'I

am, and I will be with John. Thank you for all your kindness to me and for your son.'

'It is I who should be thanking you for accepting his proposal. Ever since I first met you, I hoped this day would come.'

'But I did not make it an easy passage, I'm sorry.'

'You have nothing to be sorry for. Circumstances were not in your favour, but you battled them and won and I think are all the stronger for it. But it's in the past, let's not dwell on that. It's the future that is important.' He turned to his wife. 'Louisa, this calls for a bottle of champagne. I'll get one from the cellar. And you can tell them all in the kitchen we shall have the full celebratory Christmas meal as usual tomorrow.' He hurried from the room, dragging his outdoor coat from his shoulders as he did so.

'You have more than pleased him, my dear,' said his wife, directing her gaze at Katherine as she removed the pin that held her hat to her hair. Katherine crossed the room and took the hat from her so that John could help her with her coat. Louisa took them in her arms and started for the door. She stopped to look back lovingly at the young couple. 'Be happy, you two,' she said.

When the door had closed behind her Katherine and John flung their arms round each other and whirled round the room in joyous dance, laughing when dizziness forced them to stop.

Katherine leaned back in John's arms, his hands firm upon her waist. 'I love you, John Chambers. I'll make you so happy, through all the thousand years we live and beyond.'

Chapter Two

As the *Cheviot* moved into the vast embrace of the sea after leaving the sheltered waters of the Tyne, Katherine watched the land retreat further and further from view. She drew her cloak a little more tightly round her and felt John's arm strengthen around her waist as if protecting her from the thoughts that had caused her involuntary shiver.

She saw these moments as marking a watershed in her world. The old was past if never to be forgotten; a new life lay ahead in London and the years she would have there with John.

Since her acceptance of his proposal life had been hectic. Christmas Day and Boxing Day had been full of excitement and festivity. Then had come the sobering consideration of all that had to be done before sailing day which Mr Allberry had allowed them to postpone for a month. Katherine's home and its contents, except for a few personal items she would have crated for London, had to be disposed of, her packing to be done, and though she was under no obligation to do so she felt she should try to find other employment for her staff. Then, of course, there was the wedding to arrange. John's mother and father had been a great help to her there without being intrusive. Their advice was kind and given in such a way that she made the ultimate decisions without any pressure. The question of accommodation in London gave them some concern until

17

Mr Drew, who was going to the capital six weeks ahead of John, offered to find something suitable for them, a base from which they could look for their own home.

The clean sea air was fresh and salty. Katherine breathed in deeply, enjoying the sharp sensation in her lungs. It was as if she was taking on a new mantle of life and she determined, there and then, that she would make a success of it. The natural, uncontrolled sounds – the cracking of the sails, the creaking of ropes, the moaning of timbers and the swish of the sea – did not mar the silence that settled between the young couple. It was the silence that only true lovers can share and it drew them closer. These moments were precious and Katherine tried to fix them into her mind so that in the future she could recall the happiness she was experiencing now.

'Let's walk a little, love.' John straightened up from the rail. She took his arm and they strolled around the deck, pausing now and then to pass a few words with fellow passengers who, like themselves, were taking advantage of the fine day and calm sea.

Neither had been to sea before and they were pleased that they had so quickly found their 'sea legs'. Katherine had expected the ocean to be so vast that they would be the only speck on it. Vast it was but she was surprised by the number of ships in sight.

'Most of them are colliers, love,' explained John. 'Taking coals from Newcastle and the Tyne to various ports along the east coast, and of course to London. With the rapid expansion of the capital it's a growing and lucrative trade. I expect we'll follow some of them into Whitby.'

'We're calling there?'

'Yes. Passengers to disembark and no doubt some new ones to pick up.'

'Will we be there long?'

'Captain said a day.'

'Time to go ashore?'

'Yes, if you want to. Let's see what it looks like before we decide.'

Katherine was resting in their cabin later when John bustled in. 'Whitby's in sight,' he informed her.

She pushed herself out of the chair, looked in the mirror and patted her hair into place. He slipped her cloak around her shoulders, she put on her bonnet and, glancing in the mirror again, tied its ribbon under her chin. He took her hand and they left the cabin.

'See, there,' he said when they reached the deck. He pointed to the starboard quarter and led her to the rail.

She took in the scene for a few moments without speaking, awestruck by the rugged coastline where towering cliffs swept down to a more accessible beach before soaring upward again to shut out their view of the land beyond.

'Good evening, young people.'

They turned to find a ruddy-faced gentleman with bushy sidewhiskers standing beside them. He raised his hat to Katherine. His friendly smile was reflected in warm brown eyes that held the sparkle of a man who got the most out of life in any way he desired and circumstances permitted, but lines upon his face showed that some of his days had not been so free from trouble and anxiety. For all that he emanated a kindly aura that made people take to him immediately.

'I noticed you when you came on board and you reminded me so much of my wife and myself when we were your age and faced life with eager anticipation. Reuben Simpson, at your service.' He held out his hand to John.

'John Chambers, sir, and my wife Katherine,' he returned, feeling warmth in the stranger's handshake.

'Newly married, I would guess?'

'You are very perceptive, sir.'

'Is it that obvious?' Katherine blushed along with her embarrassed smile.

Reuben smiled back. 'Experience of an elderly man. Are you on your way to Whitby?'

'No, sir,' replied John. 'I'm taking up an appointment in London.'

'Then may I wish you every success and a long life filled with happiness?'

'Thank you.' Katherine, charmed by his open friendliness, accepted his salutations. 'What is that ruin?' she asked, eyes fixed on the stark outline on the distant cliff.

'Whitby Abbey,' replied Reuben. 'It was built by Cistercian monks on the site of a previous abbey, sacked by the Danes. And this one was destroyed by Henry VIII.'

'What a marvellous position, and the coastline is very attractive.'

'I'm a Whitby man myself. I travel this route five or six times a year on business and the approach to my home town never fails to stir me.'

'I can see why,' replied Katherine. 'It is truly wonderful, but where is the harbour?'

Reuben gave a little chuckle. 'You can just see the piers at the foot of the cliffs. There's a huge cleft there that runs inland. The River Esk flows down from the moors beyond Whitby and joins the sea between those piers. We'll sail up the river on the morning tide to a berth at one of the quays.' He glanced at John. 'If I may ask, which firm will you be working for in London?'

'Allberry and Carson, a Newcastle concern who are opening offices in London. I will be there with our senior manager.'

'I've heard of them when I have been in Newcastle. Not my line of trade, however. I deal in jet.'

'Jet?' Katherine was curious.

Mr Simpson smiled. 'Have you never heard of it, young lady?'

'No.' She gave a slight shake of her head.

'To put it simply, it comes from the fossilisation of a particular tree and is found in seams of jet-bearing shale. We find it where the coast has eroded leaving these seams exposed. It can be carved into a variety of objects and is developing into a considerable trade as jewellery. I can see it expanding even more, and that is why I have gone in for

20

it. The first jet workshop opened in Whitby in 1808. Now there are dozens of them and there will be more.'

'Do you do this carving yourself?' asked John.

Reuben laughed. 'Alas, no. I'm no artist, I concentrate on its commercial possibilities. Whitby being the important port it is, I first developed what is now a lucrative ropery. Looking round for another investment, I decided jet was the thing to be in so, a couple of years ago I bought two workshops. I have two good foremen and some excellent carvers. My shops are in Church Street, on the east side of the river. The ship will be lying over before entering the river in the morning. If you are ashore tomorrow, pay me a visit.' He turned away from the rail. 'Enjoy the sail into the harbour, it is breathtaking.' He raised his hat to Katherine and strolled towards the stern.

'Evidently a lover of his home town and his work,' commented John. 'If we have time we'll certainly pay one of his workshops a visit.'

'It's a pity we have to lay up until the morning but I suppose it could be dangerous unless the tide is right.'

When Katherine and John came on deck the next morning they were surprised to see the number of ships that had joined them awaiting passage into Whitby. When they had gone below the previous evening there were only three colliers lined up to await their turn to enter the port, now there were seven.

'Seeing all those ships, it's a wonder Mr Simpson isn't in the coal trade,' remarked John, commenting on the Whitby man's commercial activities.

'Maybe he is,' observed Katherine. 'Maybe he just didn't mention it, or he might be satisfied with supplying ropes for those ships. I would think that is a lucrative enough trade.'

With the time and tide set right the *Cheviot* got underway, using the minimum amount of sail to take her towards the gap between the piers. It looked so narrow that there were moments when Katherine thought they would smash into them but the skill of the captain and his crew carried them safely into the smoother waters of the river. With each man knowing what was expected of him, progress was rapid. Ropes were thrown out to waiting boats so that the *Cheviot* could be taken under tow. Men climbed aloft to furl the sails that had been used for the final manoeuvre to reach the thriving Yorkshire port. As the *Cheviot* was towed further from the piers, colliers were lining up to follow her.

Katherine was fascinated by all the activity on shore. The quays were swarming with people going about their business or watching the arrival of the vessels on this tide. Housewives with baskets on their arms stood talking in groups, while others hurried to do their shopping; artisans strode quickly to reach their place of employment on time.

Houses climbed the cliff face on both sides of the river, seemingly perched one on top of another as if attempting to reach for the sky. Smoke curled from numerous chimneys to be caught by the breeze and whisked away to oblivion.

'We'll never get through there!' Katherine's exclamation was tinged with alarm when she saw the narrow opening where the drawbridge had been raised to allow the ship to pass into the upper reaches of the river and the quays that lined its banks.

John smiled. 'I think our ship will have been through there before. The captain will know what he's doing.'

Orders rang out, based on judgement and information shouted from the towing boats to the *Cheviot*. The ship edged through the gap while wary eyes were focussed on the rigging lest it foul the raised leaves and counterweights of the bridge. Safely through, the ship was manoeuvred to a quay on the east bank. Ropes were thrown out, gathered and wound round capstans. Shouts cut through the air, sailors bustled, curses were yelled and returned. People gathered in groups on the quay, there to greet friends or relations from the Tyne or else merely drawn by curiosity at the arrival of another vessel. Youngsters raced around in games of chase and were berated for getting in the way. Old sailors, features lined by the wind and sun of many years, watched and reminisced about the days when they would have been part of all the activity, and now regretted the passing of the years that had condemned them to a life of crippled inactivity.

Katherine and John watched in enthralled interest, feeling an urge to be ashore and to mingle with the crowds exploring the town that was new to them.

'Wonderful place.' A voice beside them caused them to straighten from the rail. They turned to see Mr Simpson, small valise in hand, smiling at them. 'Enjoy your short stay here. I'll be in one of my workshops in two hours' time if you care to see them.'

'Thank you, sir,' returned John. 'We might just do that.'

'You'll be welcome.' Reuben smiled, raised his hat and bowed to Katherine. 'I look forward to seeing you again.'

'It will be my pleasure too,' she replied graciously.

Reuben made his final goodbye and walked to the gangway that had been run out.

Once the people disembarking had become a trickle, John and Katherine joined them and left the ship.

They spent a pleasant two hours exploring. They were fascinated by the way the houses had been built up the cliff-side and seemed to be clinging to it as if their very existence depended on their tenacity. Narrow yards ran up the cliff or down to the river. They were amazed at the contrasts within a short distance, for some yards were ill-kept and shabby, bordering on degradation, as if the inhabitants did not care or were driven to this state by the poverty of their existence, while not far away other houses showed every sign of the love and care of owners who thrived on hard work, good fortune or capable management. There was bustle and noise everywhere with people going about their business.

John, solicitous for Katherine's well-being amongst the crowds, guided her through them, pausing whenever she

23

wanted to look in a shop window or exchange observations and opinions with him on this new experience.

John fished his watch from his waistcoat pocket. 'We've been ashore nearly two and a half hours, we're in Church Street, should we pay Mr Simpson a visit?'

'Why not?' returned Katherine, a note of enthusiasm in her voice.

They soon found one of the jet workshops. Not knowing what to expect, they tentatively opened the door and stepped inside. They found themselves in a rectangular room. The two longest sides were lined with workbenches at which several men were seated working on pieces of jet at various stages of its development into the final product that would be put on sale. A metal stove stood in a central position, its round chimneystack rising to a hole in the sloping roof into which windows had been positioned so that light fell into the workshop from above.

Some men looked up when the door opened then returned immediately to their work. One man rose and came to them. He was tall and thin. His outward demeanour spoke of contentment but behind the look in his eyes was restless determination, as if his ambitions had not been fulfilled.

'Good day, ma'am.' He inclined his head in a token of acknowledgement as he took his small peaked cap from his head. 'Sir.' He turned his gaze to John with an enquiring look.

'We are looking for Mr Simpson,' replied John. 'We met him on our voyage from Newcastle and he said we might find him in one of his shops.'

'You have chosen the right one, sir. He arrived about a quarter of an hour ago and warned me that we might have visitors. Please follow me.' He led them to a door at the far end of the workshop. He knocked, paused and then opened it. 'The lady and gentleman you said might call, sir,' he announced, and stood to one side to allow Katherine and John to enter a tiny room lit by one window.

Reuben, a broad smile of welcome on his face, rose from

behind a desk on which were two stacks of papers and an inkwell.

'I'm so pleased you have come. How are you enjoying Whitby?' He shook hands with them both and drew two chairs towards the desk for them. When they were seated he returned to his own.

'We are finding it a fascinating place,' said Katherine, 'and we thank you for inviting us here. From what I saw as we came through the workshop it looks to be delicate and intricate work.'

'How intricate and delicate depends on the skill of the carver and that is only achieved over years of practice and experience. Some have a natural gift for it and develop more quickly, turning out exquisite pieces. Here, I'll show you.'

He took them into the workshop where he explained the processes that went into producing the finished product, showing them the belt-driven wheels that milled, cleaned and polished the jet after the best pieces had been selected from the raw material. They watched the carvers ply their craft admiring their skill with simple, elementary tools.

When they returned to his office, John thanked him then added, 'You certainly have a thriving business. May I wish you continued success and that your firm goes from strength to strength?'

'Thank you, young man. I'm sure it will, though I will play no part in it.'

John frowned enquiringly. 'Oh?'

Mr Simpson smiled. 'Yes, I am retiring in two years' time. Alas, I have no family.' A touch of sadness came into his voice. 'My wife and I desired to have children but it was not to be. I hope the same misfortune does not befall you young people.' He sharpened his tone as he went on, 'But enough dwelling on the past, it is the future we are looking at. I threw myself into my business enterprises as a sop to my disappointment, and my dear wife Jane approved and took an interest in them as well as following her own good works of charity. I amassed considerable wealth. You might think, what was the point? Well, apart from providing ourselves with comfort and good living we have nephews and nieces of whom we are very fond. They will inherit everything except for my jet business. None of them is interested in that trade so I have decided to give both workshops and the accompanying trade to my foreman.'

'A very lucky man from what I saw,' said Katherine.

'And a very capable one. I am pleased that my business will go to someone who loves jet and is very able in every way. I'm sure it will thrive under him. Apart from being a reliable, honest man who has the respect of the workers, he is one of the best, if not the best, craftsman of jet in Whitby.'

'He knows what you are going to do?' asked John.

'No, not yet. I am having the necessary papers drawn up and will be telling him next week.'

'I would love to see his expression when you reveal your intentions.' Katherine laughed at the picture her remark conjured up.

'I know he has always hoped that one day he would have a workshop of his own so I'm more than delighted to give him the opportunity, knowing that in this way the business will carry on. He has a son, Peter, who is sixteen and learning the trade. I think he will become a good carver, though he does have a passion for the sea and in his spare time is always to be found around the quays and the ships.'

'No doubt he will prosper from the opportunity you will give his father,' commented Katherine.

'I think you are right, young lady. Now, I have a proposal to make. In fact, two. First of all, you are here until tomorrow so I should like you to dine with my wife and me this evening.'

'That is most kind of you, sir, but we couldn't impose on you,' protested John.

'Impose?' Mr Simpson threw up his hands in protest. 'Of

26

course you aren't. It will give Jane and me great pleasure to have the companionship of two charming young people for the evening. We will dine at the Angel. I shall pick you up at the *Cheviot* at seven.' As if to brook no protests he went straight on, 'Now, the other proposal: I would like to make a present to Katherine of a piece of jet in memory of her first visit to Whitby and the pleasure she – and of course you, John – has given to an old man.'

'Sir, I couldn't accept such generosity. And you are not an old man,' replied Katherine.

Mr Simpson smiled. 'You are kind. The years are there but maybe I am only as old as I feel. Now, I will not agree to your first statement. You can accept a piece of jet and you will. You shall have your choice of whatever is on display. I will not influence you. Come.'

He took them back into the workshop and shepherded them to a display cabinet. 'There. Whatever you choose is yours with my best regards.'

Katherine cast her eyes over the pieces: rings, necklaces, brooches, bangles. All looked exquisite. 'Oh, this is difficult! They all look so fine.'

'Take your time,' advised Mr Simpson.

She handled some of the items, feeling the smoothness of the jet, running her fingers across the etchings and carvings. She turned to John as if for help in her choice but before she could speak, he said, 'You must decide, my love.'

She turned back to the objects, cast her eyes across them once more, handled a brooch, put it back and picked up a silver chain. She raised it at arm's length to admire the jet cross that hung from it. This was no ordinary cross, for the simple design was held within a circle of intertwining strands in the Celtic style.

'Is that your choice?' Reuben was gauging her reaction.

She nodded. 'If you are sure it's all right to . . .'

He held up his hands. 'My dear, I said you can have any piece you choose.'

27

'Then this is it.' Her voice was firm, eyes bright at the beauty of the jet cross.

'You have a discerning eye, Katherine. You have chosen what in my opinion is the best piece we have at the moment. It was produced by my foreman, the man I believe to be the best carver in the business. I am so pleased you chose that piece. I really think I was willing you to do so.'

'Thank you, sir. I will always wear it with pride.'

Reuben was watching her intently. As she looked at the cross with appreciative eyes, he thought of the daughter he might have had.

'I would like to thank your foreman myself for carving such a wonderful piece.'

'Certainly.' He took her across the workshop. 'I'm presenting Mrs Chambers with a piece of jet and she has chosen a cross made by you, Stephen.'

He laid down the piece of jet on which he had been working and stood up, saying, 'Ma'am.' She held out the cross for him to see. 'Ah, the piece I finished just four days ago. I hope you will enjoy wearing it and that it will give you much pleasure.'

She smiled her appreciation. 'It certainly will. It is exquisite, so delicate and finely executed.'

'Thank you, ma'am. You must visit us again.'

'I would like to but I don't know when that will be, if ever. My husband is taking up a post with his firm in London.'

'Then may I wish you every success?'

'Thank you. I will always remember my first visit to a jet workshop.'

The next morning Katherine and John held hands as they watched Whitby's piers slip away from them and felt the ship meet the first undulations of a calm sea. They stood by the rail in silence, impressing on their minds the rugged beauty of the coast, the clean fresh air and wide open spaces of sea and sky, knowing that henceforth they faced the confines of streets, smoke and crowds.

'That was a wonderful visit.' Katherine broke the silence between them with a sincere observation.

'One I'm sure we will never forget,' commented John.

She fingered the jet cross hanging round her neck, her thoughts lingering on the workshop and the kindness she had been shown there.

Chapter Three

As they progressed steadily up the Thames Katherine was enthralled by the activity on the river. The water seemed to be full of ships, boats and barges toing and froing along the waterway. The flat countryside began to show signs of further habitation until she could see in the distance the solid appearance of the great city itself. Over it hung a hazy pall of smoke rising from the numerous coal fires heating homes and places of manufacture. Spires rose skywards as if trying to escape the soot and grime while the dome of St Paul's dominated them all. Katherine was thrilled by the prospect of seeing the great cathedral at close quarters. Then her attention was drawn back to the river where, as they approached the heart of the city, ships filled her view. Forests of masts rose everywhere. There seemed scarcely room to manoeuvre but somehow the branch pilot and those responsible for the final berthing brought their ship safely to its allotted quay.

River and shore were alive with bustle. Cry contested cry as commands rang out from ship and shore close to London Bridge. Greetings were yelled, curses were thrown amidst the creak of ropes, the rumble of carts and clop of hooves as carriers tried to curb restless horses impatient to be on their way.

'There!' cried John excitedly. 'There's Mr Drew!'

Katherine followed his pointing finger and relief at

seeing a familiar face among the hustling masses flooded through her.

A few minutes later John, carrying two valises, and Katherine, with a small case and handbag, were on the quay being welcomed heartily by Charles Drew. A warm handshake was exchanged between the two men and then Charles turned to Katherine. He doffed his hat and bowed as he took her hand and raised it towards his lips before making his welcome. 'I trust you had a pleasant voyage, Mrs Chambers, and that you were comfortable on board?'

'It was a most pleasurable experience, thank you. We are indeed grateful you are here to meet us. If you hadn't been, I think this mass of people and unending noise would have overwhelmed us.'

He smiled. 'It is rather overpowering at first but you'll get used to it, though I should explain London isn't all like this. Now, I have a carriage waiting. I suggest we leave right away, we can talk as we go.' He picked up one of the valises, took Katherine's case, and led them to a carriage that was standing on the other side of the quay. Once the coachman had seen them comfortably seated, he took his place and sent the horse on its way.

'I think it is fortunate for us that you came to London first, Mr Drew,' said John.

Charles sat upright against the back of the seat. He was a small stubby man of thirty-five, his diminutive size belying a strong determination and a sharp mind. John knew he was not a man to be easily fooled, nor one to let others in the trading world get the better of him. He had a keen perception of what was fair and beneficial to both parties without any detriment to his employers. John had always got on well with him in Newcastle and knew that Mr Allberry and Mr Carson had the utmost faith in him therefore deeming it an honour he had been chosen to be Charles Drew's second-in-command. John viewed his superior across the coach with contentment and satisfaction. He noted Charles's neat dress. Grey trousers, finely

31

creased, were topped by a light blue waistcoat. He wore a white shirt with a red tie carefully knotted. His three-quarter-length coat was of a dark red that verged almost on the side of black. His black shoes were highly polished and he wore a grey bowler hat. While his appearance would attract attention it was his eyes that would hold it. They were set in a roundish face with a small straight nose and neatly trimmed dark whiskers. The eyes themselves were sharp, never missing a thing, even at times when they appeared languid. Their deep blue seemed to lighten with amusement but darkened deeply when Charles was serious.

For now they were in between. For him, the arrival of newly-weds in London for the first time was a special occasion, serious yet full of joy, their future filled with untold possibilities.

'Before I explain a few things, I suggest that, as we will be seeing a lot of each other, we abandon formality and use Christian names – except, of course, John, when we are conducting our business dealings.' He looked questioningly at them for their agreement.

'That suits us,' said John, getting a nod of approval from Katherine.

'Good, good.' Charles beamed. He noted that John's demeanour relaxed. He had thought the young man rather prim and stiff in Newcastle, a bit too serious for his liking, but maybe Katherine's illness had made him see that there were enough troubles and trials in the world and it was good to grab the lighter side of life and instil it into every-day living whenever possible. 'Evelyn and I found a house in a quiet street near Hyde Park. I had strict instructions from Mr Allberry to find somewhere salubrious as the firm would be buying the property for which I would pay a nominal rent. I was told to do the same for you, on the same terms.'

Katherine gasped at this unexpected generosity and shot a sharp glance at John. 'Did you know this?'

He shook his head. 'No. I am as astonished as you.'

32

Charles looked a little surprised. 'Mr Allberry did not tell you?'

'No,' replied John.

Charles gave a little smile as he recollected his own interview with their employer. 'Mr Allberry surprised me too with his generosity. I thanked him so profusely that I think he was embarrassed. Maybe he didn't want to go through that again and therefore left it to me to tell you when you got here. I've taken another house three doors from us on a temporary basis. If you like it then I have the option to purchase on behalf of the company. If you want to find elsewhere then I will complete the negotiations when you decide where you would like to be.'

'This is marvellous,' replied John. 'It takes a great load off our minds.'

'Good.'

'What about the business?' asked John.

'Ah, there's lots to talk about but let it wait. We are, after all, travelling through London and I see Katherine is trying to take in the new sights as we talk.'

'There seem to be two different worlds out here. I know I've seen contrasts in Newcastle but not as marked as here,' she said.

'That's London for you,' replied Charles. 'The contrasts will become fewer when we move into more attractive parts.'

Katherine noted before they left the dock area that well-dressed men whom she took to be shopkeepers and merchants, ship owners and captains, mixed with the dockers and unskilled labourers so essential to this great thriving port. Clerks hurried past, needing to get the papers they carried to their destination on time. Boys in tattered clothes raced barefoot in chase or tried to solicit a penny from a passerby.

As they moved away from the docks the streets were still crowded but the pace of life seemed to have slowed a little. Their progress was hindered by the press of horse-drawn vehicles on the roadway. Katherine's attention was held by the fine-dressed ladies shopping at a variety of outlets where shopkeepers paraded their wares and tried persuasively to heighten a lady's interest. A young girl with a basket on her arm sold apples politely to a lady then hurled curses at an urchin who, racing past, snatched one from her basket with the dexterity of someone who had done so many times before. They turned into a quieter street where people were going about their everyday lives more sedately and groups of well-dressed men in three-quarter-length coats, hats on heads at jaunty angles, were deep in conversation.

'There'll be a few deals being made there,' commented Charles. 'We're close to the financial part of the city.'

Further on the pace of life had slowed even more and few people were about. They turned into a street of identical terraced houses, three stories high. A front door was reached by four steps, with another flight leading down to a basement. Large sash windows, their frames painted white, allowed in plenty of light. The street was quiet. Two people were walking on the opposite side of the road and no other carriage was to be seen. The coachman brought his horse to a halt.

'Here we are,' cried Charles heartily. 'Welcome to my home. Yours is a little further on. Evelyn has prepared some refreshment. Come and enjoy it, relax, and then we'll take you to see where you are to live – that is, if it is to your liking.'

The coachman opened the door of the carriage and helped Katherine to the ground. She waited, looking around her, wondering what they had done to deserve such a welcome and a home in an elegant street that bore the air of people who were very comfortably off. She had imagined she and John would be living in much less salubrious surroundings until they found their feet. She had not counted on the generosity of Mr Allberry and Mr Carson.

'Come, my dear.' Charles led her up the steps and rang the bell.

34

The door was opened by a young woman neatly dressed in a black frock, white cap and apron.

'Hello, sir,' she said with a bright smile.

'Hello, Betsy,' replied Charles. 'This is Mr and Mrs Chambers whom we told you about.'

'Good day, ma'am.' Betsy made a small curtsey. 'Good day, sir.'

Katherine and John returned her greeting. She waited to take their outdoor clothes. While they were disrobing, a door on the right of the hall that ran towards the back of the house opened and a small lady, her thinness in marked contrast to her rotund husband, emerged. Katherine, who would have described her as petite, was taken by her lively eyes and the feeling of warmth and caring she gave out without any apparent effort. It was part of her make-up, an endearing one that captured Katherine immediately. She knew they would get on well and that here was a friend.

'Hello, John,' she greeted him, holding out her hand to him.

He took it and bowed slightly as he replied with, 'I am pleased to see you again, Mrs Drew.'

'Surely Charles told you, no such formalities as that.' She was already turning to Katherine. 'You must be Katherine. I'm Evelyn.' She took Katherine's hand as she kissed her on the cheek. 'Welcome to London.'

'Thank you,' replied Katherine.

'I'm sorry I did not meet you before we left Newcastle, but alas your illness did not allow it. I trust all is well with you now? It must be, you look so radiant.'

'I'm very well,' replied Katherine. 'But you flatter me. Radiant? I doubt that.'

'My dear, if you look as you do after your journey, what must you be like at other times? But I'm sure you would like to freshen up.' She led the way to the stairs.

Ten minutes later the four friends were gathered in the drawing-room enjoying a cup of tea and some scones.

'Charles will have told you we have found a house for you?' said Evelyn.

'Indeed,' replied Katherine. 'We are most grateful for the trouble you have taken.'

'Think nothing of it,' Evelyn made a dismissive gesture with her hand. 'I enjoyed doing it. I must say, we were a little fortunate. Having found this house, we heard that some people were moving out of one further along the row and thought you might like it. If you don't, you will at least have a roof over your heads until you find another more to your liking. We arranged a tenancy for you for a month at the end of which there is the option to buy.'

'That, as I explained in the carriage, will be undertaken by Mr Allberry. He did not want the purchase to be completed until he was sure the property was something you liked,' Charles put in.

'I'm sure it will be most satisfactory if it is like yours.'

'You'll find that all the houses in this street are identical.'

'Then it should prove most acceptable,' John declared.

'Well, you've a few weeks to decide,' put in Evelyn. 'Now, we also had instructions from Mr Allberry to see that the house was furnished.'

Katherine and John exchanged astonished glances.

'This is far more than we expected,' explained Katherine. 'Mr Allberry is more than generous.'

'He did exactly the same for us. He said that unless there was something particularly personal that we wanted with us, he saw no point in our having all the bother of crating everything up and transporting it to London when we could make new purchases here for which he would pay.'

'John,' put in Charles, 'I must say at this point that Mr Allberry thinks very highly of you and sees you as a great asset to the firm. He said it would not be fair to do something for me and not for you when we would be working so closely together. Mr Carson was in complete agreement. They both said that comfortable circumstances in pleasant surroundings made for contented and satisfied employees. He puts great faith in us.'

36

'I'm sure we will not let him down.'

'We'll discuss the business tomorrow. In the meantime, Evelyn, you carry on.'

'As I was saying, I have furnished the house, not completely but sufficient to see you both settled in. Then you and I, Katherine, could complete the furnishing according to your requirements. I did not know your tastes, so do change anything you don't like.'

'What about servants? Where will I find them?'

'Mr Allberry said I was to engage servants as I saw fit and that as part of your salary the firm would regard them as their employees and pay their wages through you. I decided that we required a cook, a scullery maid and a housemaid. I thought the same for you.'

'All this overwhelms me,' gasped Katherine.

'And me,' added an astonished John.

Charles gave a little chuckle. 'We too were more than surprised by such generosity when Mr Allberry first put the idea of a London office to me. I think he believed we wouldn't want to move here and so made an offer that we would find difficult to refuse. Mr Allberry is a shrewd businessman. He has seen great possibilities here and is prepared to do all he can to secure them. He sees a well-satisfied staff as being to his advantage. Believe me, he won't lose by this generosity.'

'He certainly won't as far as I'm concerned.'

'We are lucky to have such an employer. Many would squeeze blood out of a stone,' Charles agreed.

'Oh, Evelyn,' exclaimed Katherine, 'you've no idea what a relief it is to have all this arranged for us. I was worried about finding somewhere to live. Thank you for all you have done, both of you. You are so kind.'

'It has given me something to do,' she said. 'You met Betsy when you came in. She is indeed a find. I learned that she had a sister, Pauline, a year younger who was wanting a place so I engaged her to be your maid. For your scullery maid, ours had a friend of the same age, fourteen, both of

37

them wanting to escape from rough homes. Ours is called Alice, yours Dorothy but goes by Dot. I had a word with both of them about what was expected, not only by way of work but in loyalty and standards of behaviour. They assured me they would give no trouble and would be hard workers. So far Alice has measured up to expectations. For our cook I found a widow, Mrs Sargeant, in her mid-forties. I asked her if she knew of anyone who was looking for a similar post. She did – these people always do, you have to be careful – but Mrs Sargeant was as good as her word. I conducted a thorough interview with her friend and hired her on the understanding that the final decision would rest with you. Mrs Dewsbury will be with you on a month's trial.'

'You have taken a lot of trouble for us,' said Katherine gratefully.

'I thought it would help you to settle in more easily and I know that Charles is anxious to integrate John as soon as possible into the business, so with fewer domestic problems to confront he'll be able to do that. Now, if you are ready, I'll show you your house and introduce you to your staff. I had intended to invite you to an evening meal with us but I know Mrs Dewsbury is wanting to show off her skills and make you feel at home straight away, so we'll dine together some other time.'

A few minutes later Evelyn was ringing the bell at a house three doors away.

'Mrs Drew.' There was no mistaking that the girl who opened the door was sister to Betsy. They could have been taken for twins. Realising these strangers must be her new employers, her smile was warm.

Evelyn ushered Katherine and John inside and waited for the maid to close the door before she said, 'Pauline, these are the people I told you about, Mr and Mrs Chambers.'

Pauline bobbed a curtsey. 'Ma'am, sir.'

'We are pleased to meet you, Pauline,' replied Katherine, 'and appreciate the help you have given Mrs

38

Drew in getting this house ready for us. I'm sure we will get on well.'

'Pauline,' put in Evelyn, 'ask Mrs Dewsbury and Dot to come to the drawing-room.'

'Yes, ma'am.' She hurried along the hall to the rear of the house.

Evelyn took Katherine into the drawing-room. The high ceiling added to the feeling of spaciousness. The room was not overcrowded with furniture. Two easy chairs stood to either side of the fireplace where flames leaped cheerily, while a small sofa faced the fire. A side table stood by each chair and an oak sideboard against one of the walls which were covered with a floral patterned paper.

'Very pleasant, Evelyn. This will suit us admirably, don't you think, John?' said Katherine.

'Indeed it will,' he agreed.

There was a knock on the door. It was opened by Pauline who said, 'Mrs Dewsbury and Dot, ma'am.'

The cook was not at all as Katherine had expected. She had anticipated a stout person, round and rosy-cheeked. Instead she faced a thin woman whose plain brown frock hung from her and fell unimpeded to ankle length. She wore a white apron over it, and a white cap covered her hair. Her looks had clearly been ravished by a hard life. Her eyes were lively but that could not hide the sadness that dwelt there. Her long-fingered hands rested on the shoulders of a girl whom she ushered in front of her. The girl's dress was too big for her. The print was faded and the belt of the same material slackly tied. The dress came just below her calves and revealed woollen socks in black shoes, the toes of which were badly scuffed.

'Good day, ma'am.' Mrs Dewsbury's greeting came with a respectful nod which extended her words to John and Mrs Drew. She leaned down to speak to Dot. 'Say what I told you to the lady and gentleman,' she said quietly, close to the girl's ear.

Dot glanced shyly at the three adults and then cast her

39

eyes down as she muttered in a tone that held only shyness, 'Good day, ma'am, sir.'

Katherine smiled. 'Hello, you must be Dot. I'm certain we'll like each other.' She looked to Mrs Dewsbury, sensing compassion and consideration in the way she was treating the young girl. 'Mrs Dewsbury, I am sure that applies to us too. I must say that when I came in and smelt your cooking, it made me feel at home straight away.'

'I hope it will be satisfactory,' replied Mrs Dewsbury.

'I'm sure it will. We'll talk later, but before you go, I hope you have sufficient of what you are cooking for us to share it with our staff?'

'Er ... well ...' Mrs Dewsbury was embarrassed by being caught off guard.

'I take it that means you will be doing something different for you three. Is that because you prefer it so?'

'No, ma'am.'

'In future then, cook for five. And divide this evening's meal that way even if it means a little less for us.' Katherine smiled to herself. She had seen Dot's eyes brighten as she looked up over her shoulder at Mrs Dewsbury. She knew there must be something scrumptious being prepared in the kitchen.

'Yes, ma'am.' There was gratitude in the cook's tone. Not only did it mean the staff would dine as well as the master and mistress but it would make preparations in the kitchen easier and, with the time saved, she could extend her talents to dishes she had always wanted to try. 'Come, Dot.' She turned the girl.

''Bye, ma'am,' called Dot brightly over her shoulder.

'Goodbye,' returned Katherine.

As the door closed they heard Dot comment, 'She's a nice lady.'

'You've certainly won a heart there,' said Evelyn. 'In fact, all of them I would think.'

Katherine chuckled. 'It's surprising what food can do.' She glanced at John. 'I hope you agreed with what I suggested?'

40

'Of course, I'm glad you did. You run the house, I'll not interfere.'

'Now should I show you round?' Evelyn suggested.

The next room opening off the hall was the dining-room furnished with a table in the centre and six matching chairs around it. A glass épergne held some grapes, apples and pears. Places were laid for two people with the necessary cutlery and glasses. Evelyn took them next to the kitchen and the scullery beyond. Mrs Dewsbury and Dot did not interrupt their work but Katherine was aware of the scullery maid casting admiring glances in her direction.

They went into the basement but did not linger there as the room was empty, not having received any attention from Evelyn when planning for John and Katherine's arrival. It was one large room, the use of which they could decide at their leisure. Upstairs there were two large bedrooms, one of which had been furnished for their arrival, the other left empty for them to resolve how to utilise it. The third floor contained the rooms for the staff. These were sparsely but comfortably furnished with bed, chest of drawers, wardrobe and table on which stood a bowl and ewer. Dot's seemed crowded as it was the smallest but Katherine guessed it was luxurious to what she had been used to.

When they returned downstairs Evelyn took her leave. 'Anything you want to know, or want help with, come and see me. I expect Charles will be whisking you away tomorrow, John, so Katherine, tell Mrs Dewsbury you'll be dining at midday with me.'

'Won't John be home for lunch?'

Evelyn smiled and gave a little shake of her head. 'No. Coming back and forth would waste too much time for the men. They will get something at one of the inns.'

Katherine hid her disappointment. John would be away most of the day. 'Thank you, Evelyn. I'll be with you at noon then.'

As Katherine returned to the drawing-room after they

41

had seen Evelyn out she felt a surge of euphoria run through her. She turned when she heard the door click behind her as John closed it. Her eyes sparkled with a delight which matched that in her smile. John felt his own excitement well up. He knew they were thinking alike. Without a word they flung themselves into each other's arms. Their lips met in a long passionate kiss that was filled, not only with the deep love they felt for each other but also with excitement at their good fortune.

When their lips parted there was laughter on them. With their arms still around each other, they leaned back to see the exhilaration in each other's eyes.

'Isn't it wonderful?' she cried.

'Marvellous!' His arms tightened round her waist and he whirled her round and round the room, her steps matching his, both heads thrown back with joyous laughter.

'We're the luckiest people alive!'

'What a glorious start for us!'

'Thank you, Mr Allberry!' she called.

'And you, Mr Carson!'

'We'll be so happy here!' Her tone was ecstatic.

'We won't want to move!'

'Never, ever!'

Secure in this vision of their life ahead, they danced until, breathless, they collapsed on the settee side by side, laughter on their lips and joy in their eyes.

Their mood of euphoria continued into the evening meal when they counted themselves lucky that Evelyn had found them such a skilful cook and obliging maid.

'We must show our appreciation to Mrs Dewsbury, John,' said Katherine when they finally left the dining-room.

They went to the kitchen where Katherine was pleased to see Dot sitting at a large oak table devouring some treacle tart. She looked up from her plate sheepishly but there was adoration in her eyes as she met Katherine's smile.

'Are you enjoying that, Dot?' she asked.

The girl nodded and turned her attention back to the treacle tart. She wasn't going to let even the lady of the house hold her up. Katherine and John smiled broadly as they turned to Mrs Dewsbury who was also smiling, though there was some embarrassment in it too at Dot's attitude.

Katherine saw that she was about to apologise for the girl so held up her hand to stop her. 'No need, Mrs Dewsbury,' she said, 'I'm delighted she's happy. Thank you for that wonderful meal.'

Mrs Dewsbury relaxed. She had been on tenterhooks, wondering if the food had been satisfactory for her new employers. 'Thank you, ma'am.'

'I hope they're all as wonderful,' put in John.

'I'll do my best, sir,' replied Mrs Dewsbury, delighted at the flattery. 'I hope you will tell me if there is anything you don't like?'

'I don't think there is,' said Katherine, but glanced enquiringly at John.

'I can eat anything,' he confirmed.

Mrs Dewsbury nodded appreciatively.

'If there is anything you need for the kitchen ... utensils, knives, whatever ... please let me know. I'll give you a note and you can open an account with a tradesman. I presume you know a good honest one, charging fair prices?'

'I do indeed, ma'am.'

'Do likewise with provisions.'

'Very good, ma'am.'

Katherine turned to the housemaid who had been standing quietly by. 'The same arrangement applies to you, Pauline. If there is anything you need for your household duties or that needs replacing, let me know.'

'Yes, ma'am.'

While they had been talking Dot had finished her treacle tart and was now sitting listening to the conversation, her eyes bright as her gaze flitted from speaker to speaker.

When they left the kitchen, Pauline followed them. In the

hall she made for the stairs as she said, 'I'll turn down the bed, ma'am. Would you like me to help you unpack?'

'No, thank you, Pauline,' returned Katherine. 'I'll deal with the things we brought with us shortly. Tomorrow you and I can see to the clothes we sent ahead. I saw the three crates had arrived.'

'Yes, ma'am.' She went nimbly up the stairs and Katherine and John went back to the drawing-room.

'We are lucky to have such staff,' observed Katherine. 'Evelyn is a shrewd judge of people.'

'I'm sure she is, but her opinion of you cannot come up to mine.' As he spoke John slipped his arms round his wife from behind and kissed her neck. She stretched under his touch, encouraging his lips to seek more. For a few moments she enjoyed the anticipation of things to come then twisted in his arms to meet his lips in reciprocation of the passion he sought.

Their mouths parted reluctantly. 'I love you so very much,' he whispered as he nuzzled her ear.

'And I you.'

An hour later clothes lay cast across the bedroom floor but the valises remained unopened. Among rumpled bedclothes they smiled the smile of love, kissed and made love again, this time gently, revelling in the sweetness of tender touch in contrast to the burning passion that had devoured their bodies in their first naked contact in their new home.

The following morning they were enjoying a final cup of coffee when Pauline came into the dining-room.

'Mr Drew is here, sir.'

'Show him in, please.'

'Yes, sir.' Pauline returned to the hall and a few moments later Charles stepped into the dining-room.

'Good day, good people,' he enthused. 'I trust all was well yesterday evening?'

'Very much to our liking,' replied John. From the little

twitch of his lips Katherine deduced he was implying a different interpretation of his words to her from that addressed to Charles.

'Excellent, excellent,' beamed his superior. 'I'm sure our day will be just as successful.'

'A cup of coffee, Charles?' enquired Katherine, indicating the pot.

'Thank you, but no.' He raised his hand in a gesture of refusal. 'We should be away.'

John drained his cup, kissed his wife on the cheek, winked as he drew away, and hurried into the hall.

Charles followed, calling over his shoulder, 'Expect him home about four today. Might be later other days.'

John was shrugging himself into a dark-brown calf-length redingote with astrakhan collar.

'Wise man,' commented Charles, indicating the apparel. 'It's a mite sharp outside. No rain, thank goodness, otherwise some of the streets can become very unpleasant underfoot.'

'We have far to go?'

'I sometimes take a carriage but thought this morning it would be best to walk so you can see something of London.'

'Very good,' said John, picking up his curved-sided beaver top hat. It was of pale grey and contrasted pleasingly with his darker coat but matched the colour of his trousers. He set it at a slight angle that gave him a jaunty look. 'Ready,' he said with a smile.

'A credit to the firm of Allberry and Carson,' Charles said with an admiring look.

They left the house and, as they progressed towards the city, Charles pointed out various landmarks and informed John of all he had done since coming to London.

'When Evelyn and I arrived I gave myself four days to help her settle in and then I looked for a property to rent as an office. I found a suitable place in Threadneedle Street, but you'll see that soon enough.' He gave a dismissive wave

45

of his hand. 'Mr Allberry told me to look for business in goods in which we do not already deal. I've made some initial contacts I think will be beneficial to us. The shipments of farm produce from Northumberland to London will continue. It is into goods for the return voyages that Mr Allberry wants to expand. As you know, up to now that trade has been in the hands of an agent, but acting for several firms throughout the country he hasn't had the real welfare of any particular company at heart. Mr Allberry thought it wisest to set up our own office staffed with people who have a real interest in the firm. We have a unique opportunity here with goods coming into London from all parts of the world – coffee, cocoa, sugar, rum, spices, cotton and so on. It will be a challenge but we have every encouragement to make a niche for ourselves and if we are successful I have no doubt it will be to our financial benefit.' He glanced at John and was pleased with the enthusiastic reaction he saw.

'Here we are.' Charles stopped at a door, newly painted dark green.

John pointed at the brass plaque fastened to the wall at eye-height beside the door. It announced that these were the premises of 'Allberry and Carson, Merchants'. He gave a nod of approval.

Charles smiled. 'I thought it best to let people know immediately who and what we are. I've had several enquiries: some just curious about newcomers, others more interested in trading possibilities. The chaff always has to be sorted from the wheat.' He opened the door and they stepped inside.

The wide passage that ran to the back to the building was newly decorated. Halfway along on the left a staircase gave access to the upper floor.

'I've designated an office for each of us up there. First I'll take you to meet Cornelius Whitaker, our factotum.' He paused with his hand on the knob of a door to their right. 'He was one of fifteen applicants, has worked previously for London merchants but was wanting a move which would bring him more responsibility. I was prepared to give him that because he brings with him valuable knowledge of the London trading scene.'

John nodded. Charles opened the door and they stepped inside a large square room. A desk was placed across one corner so as to capture light to the left from a tall sash window.

A man of about forty rose from his chair behind the desk. He was slim, his narrow-cut clothes emphasising his build. He held himself straight which lent him an air of confidence. A long face tapered to a pointed chin. His hair was dark, almost black, and well cared for. His eyes were alert and John guessed from the interest he was showing that this sharpness would always be there, no matter in whose company he found himself, for business or for pleasure.

'Good day, sir,' he greeted Charles as he came out from behind his desk.

'Good day to you, Cornelius. This is Mr Chambers of whom I spoke when I employed you.'

'I'm pleased to meet you, sir,' said Cornelius, holding out his hand.

John felt a firm, friendly grip that he returned in equal measure, knowing that this man would be making a judgement of him through all that passed between them in the next few moments.

'And I you,' he replied. 'Mr Drew has spoken highly of you and from what he says I am sure you will be a great asset to the firm. I can see no reason why you and I should not get on well.' John made sure his tone was reassuring and that he was not just uttering a platitude. 'As a stranger to London I will need to lean heavily on your advice and direction.'

'Thank you for that confidence, sir. I am here for whatever you need but am sure you will soon become familiar with the city. I trust you and your wife had a pleasant voyage from the Tyne?'

47

'We did indeed,' returned John, and gave a little smile. 'But I can tell you I was relieved to see Mr Drew at the dockside to meet us.'

'Did anything arise while I was away?' asked Charles.

'I checked on the *Mary Anne*. She's due in three days from now from the West Indies. I'm sending Jeremiah to check her cargo. If it is not all spoken for there might be something that could interest us.'

'Good. Let me know if there is and we'll all go and see what's what.' Charles turned to John 'Now, let me introduce you to our two rascals across the passage and then I'll show you your office.'

As they turned to the door, Cornelius spoke. 'Mr Chambers, I hope you and your wife will soon settle and be happy in London.'

'Thank you, Cornelius. I'm sure we shall.'

Charles led him into a square room of medium size. Two young men immediately slid off stools high enough to enable them to work at a tall sloping desk.

'Good morning, sir,' they chorused brightly.

'Good morning,' Charles returned. 'This is Mr Chambers whom I told you about.'

'Good morning to you too, sir,' they said with equal brightness.

'And to you,' returned John with a friendly smile. 'I'm sure we'll all work well together for the benefit of Allberry and Carson.'

'Jeremiah and his brother Emanuel,' Charles introduced them.

John liked the bright breezy demeanour that emanated from the two young men whom he estimated would be twenty or so with little more than a year between them.

'I have every confidence in those two,' said Charles as he led the way upstairs. 'I'll tell you more about them after you have seen your office.'

It was furnished with a desk and chair, a sideboard and shelves for storage, and two chairs for visitors. The high ceiling added to the air of spaciousness. The walls were painted in a neutral colour which did not detract from the pictures of sailing vessels that hung on three of the walls.

'This is very pleasant,' remarked John.

Charles gave a little shrug of his shoulders. 'Well, I didn't know how you would like it or if there was anything else you wanted. Alter it as you like. Now, come through to mine and I'll tell you something about Jeremiah and Emanuel.'

Charles's office, at the front of the building, was of similar size to John's but, having been in use, had Charles's touch on it. Some books and files were on the shelves. His desk was laid out with papers, pens and pencils with a glass inkwell beside them. A diary lay open, handily placed for reference. The carpet was similar to that in John's office but he had a wool rug in the well of the desk where he placed his feet for extra warmth.

'Sit down, John.' Charles indicated one of the chairs as he went to his own behind the desk. 'I interviewed over thirty applicants for the two clerks' jobs before I finally settled on the brothers. I was impressed by their smartness, but more so by how keen they were. They come from a respectable family. Their father works for a printing firm. As you will be aware from their accents they are London born and bred so know the capital like the back of their hands. That is an asset since you and I are not familiar with it. They will run errands with messages, documents – you know, the usual things in our line of business. They will do a certain amount of ledger work, and I have also instructed them to keep a daily record not only of transactions made but any happenings within the firm, visitors, meetings, etc.'

'You have done well,' commented John, 'and seem to have got things nicely organised and settled.'

'I hope I have. Now all we want is some trade. No good being organised and settled without that.'

'I guess not. Maybe the *Mary Anne* will give us a start.'

'Yes. We'll have Cornelius's report later today and can

49

then decide if there is anything of interest to us. Tomorrow I'll take you to meet some acquaintances within the trade that I have made.'

Chapter Four

Charles continued to impart information to John in a way that did not overwhelm him but helped to put him at ease with life within the firm and in London. At eleven o'clock he drew a deep contented breath that betrayed his satisfaction with the morning's proceedings.

'Now,' he said rising from his chair, 'I think it's time to introduce you to some of our fellow merchants and traders.'

Though curious, John followed him from the room without question.

Charles looked in on Cornelius. 'We are going to the club. We'll be back for Jeremiah's news this afternoon.'

The two men left the premises and walked further into the City.

'We're going to one of the old coffee houses of which there were once many. They have been going steadily out of favour since the price of coffee began to fall, putting it within most people's reach. Then some merchants got together and decided to found a club along the lines of the well-established gentlemen's haunts of the last century, in order to establish congenial surroundings in which to enjoy some leisure hours and provide accommodation at reasonable rates for any merchant visiting the city, or for bachelors in responsible positions within the trade requiring living accommodation. But mostly the club is a venue for the exchange of information, a place to strike deals and expand commerce.'

'Do we qualify for membership even though we are not owners?' queried John.

'Yes. The men who originally established the club realised that there were managers who were entrusted by their northern employers to run London offices on the same lines as they would themselves. They recognised that such people were vital to trade and that their knowledge of northern ports and conditions would be very useful. So it was agreed that such managers should be admitted provided they interviewed well with the Committee who like to see applicants before they approve their admission, no matter how strongly they are recommended.'

'You are already a member?'

'Yes. As soon as I heard of such establishments I made enquiries and chose this one as likely to be the most helpful to us in expanding Allberry and Carson. It was through a conversation I heard here that I was alerted to the possibilities offered by the *Mary Anne*'s cargo.'

'Will they accept me as a member as well as you?'

'I told them you were joining me in the same capacity and, like myself, had full authority of Mr Allberry and Mr Carson to act as you saw fit on their behalf. I said I felt sure you would like to become a member of the club. Your interview is arranged for this morning.'

'This morning?' John's panic was evident at this unexpected announcement.

'Yes. I didn't want you to dwell on it when you had just arrived.' Charles smiled reassuringly as he added, 'Don't worry. It will only be a formality. These men aren't ogres. Forget about it.'

They turned into Mincing Lane where Charles stopped in front of an imposing though not ostentatious building. The central doorway was flanked by three sets of tall sash windows that were matched on the next two storeys while the upward pattern was completed in the roof by small dormer windows.

He opened the door and led the way into a hall floored

with black and white marble. Two men in matching livery were standing behind a desk placed between two doors to the right. On seeing the new arrivals, the younger of the two men came to meet them.

'Good day, Mr Drew,' he said. 'May I take your coats?'

After they had shed their apparel, Charles went to the desk where he was greeted by the older man and handed a pen. He signed in and added John's name as his guest. 'Mr Chambers is hoping to become a member, Gilzean.'

'Ah, he'll be the 11.30 appointment,' replied the footman, and glanced at John. 'Best of luck, sir, but I'm sure as how any friend of Mr Drew will be elected. If you'll both take a seat in the club room, I'll call you when the Committee says so.'

Charles led the way to a door across the hall and John found himself in a large room admirably furnished with comfortable leather chairs of varying sizes. A number of small tables were placed conveniently about the room. The walls were half-panelled in light oak. Above that they were painted a plain off-white so that carefully hung paintings showed the artists' gifts to best advantage. Several of the chairs were occupied by men so engrossed in the newspapers of the day they did not even look up to see who had entered the room.

Charles indicated two chairs close to the door. He leaned forward and said quietly, 'Don't be nervous, and don't be put off by this.' He cast a gesture indicating the sombreness that pervaded the room. 'It isn't always so quiet, it's just that we've hit a lull. That is no doubt why the Committee have chosen to see you now. Less chance of being disturbed. You'll find it much livelier at other times. There is a small dining-room next to this. I sometimes eat here, but more often at one of the inns. There is another room similar to this on the next floor where there are also some bedrooms as there are on the floor above that. There are rooms in the roof space for any attendants who do not have homes or accommodation elsewhere.'

'It sounds as though the founders thought things out very carefully?'

'They made sure it was a success and attracted the right people from the start. Membership is strong. Men have been quick to see the advantage of being able to meet others in like trades in salubrious surroundings.'

The door opened quietly and Gilzean appeared. Spotting John, he stepped closer. 'The Committee will see you now, sir.'

John sprang nervously to his feet and cast Charles an anxious glance.

'You'll be all right,' said his friend with a reassuring smile. 'I'll be here when you are ready.'

John swallowed hard and followed Gilzean from the room.

Ten minutes later he was back accompanied by a man in his sixties who held himself erect with a natural air of authority. His distinguished bearing was enhanced by his white hair and sidewinders that stopped short of a small pointed beard. His pale blue eyes sparkled and there was laughter on his lips when he came into the room.

'Ah, my dear fellow,' he greeted Charles who rose from his chair. 'Wish you'd bring us more young men like this.' He tapped John on the shoulder and gave him a broad smile. 'Admirable. The club could do with more of his kind.'

'You've accepted him then, Lord Faulkner?'

'Accepted? I should damn' well think so. Talent like his? He certainly knows trading conditions. He'll be a fine asset to the club. Unanimous decision of the Committee.'

'Well done, John.' Charles extended his hand.

John could feel delight in his superior's congratulatory shake.

'Now, don't keep him hidden away in that office of yours, Charles. I want to see him around here, maybe pick his sharp mind.' Faulkner gave a brief nod and left the room.

The two men sank back into their chairs, thankful that the interview was over with the result they'd wanted.

'You've certainly impressed Lord Faulkner, and as you no doubt know he's one of the biggest traders in the country. Made a fortune in the Indian trade.'

John gave a little smile. 'Although I wish Katherine had not had to suffer her illness, the delay it caused in our coming to London served me well. I spent my time learning as much as I could about trading conditions here in London. The questions the Committee put to me presented no problems.'

'Well done,' returned Charles. 'Now let us get a bite to eat. We'll have it here today. I'll introduce you to some of the better inns as time goes by.'

After a simple meal of roast lamb followed by apple pie, they returned to the office feeling well satisfied with their day so far.

Charles looked in on Cornelius. 'Jeremiah back yet?'

'No, but I expect him within the hour.'

'Let us have his report immediately he arrives.'

The two men went upstairs where Charles familiarised John with some of the trading avenues he thought they might explore. Forty minutes later there was a knock on the door and Cornelius came in. 'Jeremiah's back, sir. He's found out what the expected cargo is but can't get full verification until the ship docks in three days time.' He handed Charles a piece of paper on which he had jotted the information brought by the clerk.

Charles's perusal of the list was quick. He passed the paper to John.

He read it carefully then looked up with a knowing eye. 'You will be aware that trading in some of these commodities is new to me, but I think that dealing in and shipping on to the Tyne would be advantageous in all those spices. No doubt the well-to-do ladies of Tyneside and Northumberland will be interested in the lace too. Of course, what we bid for will be dictated by the prices asked.'

'I agree,' replied Charles. 'There's one other item we might consider – sugar.'

'Sugar? But won't other merchants . . .'

'Ah, you are right, but there is a cross beside that consignment.' He glanced at Cornelius and inclined his head towards John.

Cornelius nodded. 'Mr Chambers, Jeremiah has instructions always to keep an ear open for a bargain or an especially advantageous purchase. He heard a rumour that two vessels carrying sugar had been wrecked shortly after leaving Barbados. If that is the case this consignment could be doubly valuable.'

Charles directed his gaze back to John. 'Cornelius always marks anything of importance with such a cross as a signal to me if I am conferring with anyone. You weren't to know that. Now you do, you can be on the look out for the sign yourself.'

'Very good,' John acknowledged, then added, 'but won't other merchants in the city have the same information?'

'Possibly. But I think there might be more behind that mark than the information we have just received. I can see a glint in Cornelius's eye.' He glanced at his manager. 'What is it?'

'Well, sir, the *Mary Anne* is owned by its captain. If he sailed before his rivals he won't have knowledge of their loss and therefore won't be aware that his sugar will be more valuable than he thinks.'

'And so we meet him down the river before he docks,' Charles took up knowingly, 'and make him an offer he'll snap up.' Charles gave a little chuckle and looked at John. 'Learning something?'

'Oh, yes,' he replied with a smile. 'Craftiness, swift thinking, and that we have a team with the best interests of Allberry and Carson at heart due in no small measure to the astuteness of our manager.'

Cornelius gave him a slight bow. 'Thank you Mr Chambers. You can always be sure of that.'

'Well done, Cornelius,' Charles added his praise. 'And thank Jeremiah, though I'll do so myself on my way out. Now, a few details. We need to know when the *Mary Anne* will reach the river and we will need a boat to convey us three to meet her. Brief Jeremiah and Emanuel that they will be in charge here that day.'

'Very good, sir. It will be seen to.' Cornelius left the office.

'I must say, Charles you have succeeded beyond expectations with this staff,' John said as the door closed.

'I'm most particular about the characters of our employees. These three seemed exemplary when I interviewed them. Stood out from the others. And of course it is surprising what paying a little above the average will do.' He let out a deep breath and said jocularly, 'And there endeth your first lesson.' He pushed himself from his chair. 'Let us away home.'

As they left the office he thanked Jeremiah which pleased the young man.

'Always let them know they are appreciated,' Charles advised as they stepped outside. 'Let's take a hackney carriage.' Around the corner he hailed a driver and in a matter of moments they were seated in the one-horse vehicle. Their progress was constricted by congested roads but once he was clear of any obstruction the driver urged his horse on, no doubt anxious to deliver his passengers, collect his hire and be away for further custom.

Reaching home, Charles paid the driver who made his thanks, touched his forehead and drove off, keeping his attention alert for anyone wishing to hire his services.

'Come along in,' said Charles. 'We'll see what the ladies have been up to today.'

John could do nothing but accept though in his mind he hoped Katherine was at home. He wanted her to himself, to tell her all about his first day in the employment of Allberry and Carson in London. He breathed a sigh of relief when Evelyn told him that, although they had spent a pleasant time together, Katherine had wanted to be at home when her husband returned. John made his goodbyes and left the house.

On hearing the front door being unlocked, Katherine hurried into the hall from the drawing-room where she had left the door open so she could hear his arrival.

'Welcome home, love.' She greeted him with open arms.

He shed his coat and hat, and with their arms round each other they walked into the drawing-room. He pushed the door shut and turned her to him.

'I love you.' His voice was low and sensual.

'I've thought of you all day,' she replied.

He brushed her lips teasingly with his.

'And I you.'

'Tell me about it?'

'In a few minutes.'

He kissed her gently but in it was a passion that kindled hers. Her arms tightened around his neck, his around her waist. The kiss lingered, gradually intensifying into desire and a promise of even greater delights.

When their lips parted Katherine leaned back temptingly against his arms and looked into his eyes with a playful twinkle in her own. 'We'll have to wait until later, darling. Pauline will have heard you arrive and be bringing some tea in a moment. Come sit down and tell me about your day.'

They had only just sat down on the sofa when the maid brought a tray set with tea and newly baked scones.

When Katherine started to pour the tea she told him that she had invited Evelyn and Charles to dine with them this evening. 'A way of saying thank you for all they have done to enable us to settle comfortably and quickly.'

Though disappointed that he would have Katherine to himself rather later than sooner, John agreed that it was a good idea. 'And Mrs Dewsbury is delighted to show off her skills, no doubt?'

'Revelling in it,' replied Katherine, handing him a cup of

tea. 'Now tell me all about your first day at work in London?'

She listened intently as he regaled her with all the details. She noted the excitement in his voice and was happy for him.

She was even happier for him three days later when he arrived home in an exuberant mood to announce that he had been instrumental in securing an even better deal from the captain of the *Mary Anne* by agreeing to take his cargo of rum as well as the sugar. The march they had stolen on other merchants by meeting the ship in the lower reaches of the Thames had not pleased them, but their enterprise in doing so had reluctantly elicited general admiration.

Life continued in a rich vein for Katherine and John, especially John who, determined to be a success, became engrossed in his work. She settled down to her new life and was kept busy adjusting the house to her liking, always seeking John's approval and opinion. She was not averse to consulting Evelyn also and was thankful for her guidance in the social aspects of London life. Evelyn introduced her to new friends and their circle widened through giving and receiving calls. But Katherine never became totally at ease in London. Apart from Evelyn, who of course had come from the North, she cultivated no particular friendships. These were pleasant acquaintances but no deeper than that.

After the euphoria of settling into her new life the monotony of daily repetition set in and with it came introspection and loneliness. These feelings she hid from John for she dismissed them whenever he was with her. She looked forward to their evenings together, whether in company or not, and in particular welcomed the weekends when they would enjoy walks, visits to the theatre, art galleries and museums. She leaned heavily on the deep love they shared and let it counteract any misgivings she had about life in the city.

John had settled into his work without any trouble and

continually enthused about the exceptional chance he had been given here and the prospects it held for them both. Katherine, in her love for him, determined to give him every support she could and keep from him her own doubts about life in the capital. To all outward appearances they had slipped into a comfortable life without anything to ripple the calm waters of their existence.

But eight months later the ripple became a reality.

John was in high spirits when he reached home. An afternoon meeting with a shipping firm to discuss a cargo of cotton had gone well for him. It had crowned a deal for an onward shipment of goods to Newcastle orchestrated by Charles earlier in the week. He had decided not to return to the office but to go straight home and inform Charles later when he too had returned. With his hat set at a jauntier angle than usual, John walked with a brisk step, whistling silently to himself. He was eager to tell Katherine his news and suggest that in celebration they should dine out tomorrow evening with Charles and Evelyn.

He opened the front door quickly, was across the hall in the minimum of strides and into the drawing-room with no hesitation. There he was pulled up sharp. Katherine was sitting in an armchair from which she could see the door. It was as if she was waiting there especially for his arrival. But the thing that struck him most was the sense of excitement and exhilaration that surrounded her. It was as if she was already caught up in his euphoria. When he entered the room a broad smile lit up her face, enhancing its beauty. She looked radiant. She jumped to her feet and came to him for an embrace.

'Oh, John, I'm so pleased you're home. I've been bursting to tell you what you've done.'

'How could you know?' Even in the midst of his excitement his expression became puzzled.

Katherine laughed delightedly. 'How could I know? Well, I can be the only one to know. Not even you know yet!'

'What are you talking about?'

'I'm going to have a baby!'

For a moment he stared at her in astonishment. 'Baby?' His eyes widened.

'Yes.' She laughed at his reaction. 'Don't look so bewildered. It's the most natural thing in the world.'

His expression softened. 'You're wonderful.' He smiled and kissed her, his soft touch expressing all the love and respect he had for her. 'You are the most marvellous thing that ever happened to me. I love you so much.' His expression altered to one of seriousness. Concern clouded his eyes. 'You should be sitting down. Come on, on to the sofa, feet up.'

She laughed loudly and resisted his attempts to lead her there. 'I'm all right. There's no need for fuss yet. Don't mollycoddle me.'

'But you should take care.'

'I will, don't worry. I'm feeling so well. You came in here with a very jaunty step. What was that about? You looked as if you'd had some news?'

'Nothing as momentous as yours.' He continued to impart the happenings of his day, his delight at the contract he had signed and its importance to the firm. 'I had thought we'd take the Drews to dine as a celebration tomorrow evening. But now you probably won't feel like it?'

'Of course I'll feel like it. And now we have two things to celebrate. We'll break my news to Evelyn and Charles then.'

'You're sure?'

'Of course. I'd like nothing better.'

Seven months after her announcement a healthy boy was born and christened James. Katherine came through the birth without giving cause for serious concern, and found new happiness with a son in her arms. John viewed him with the eyes of a proud father and a determination that his child would have the very best he could provide. The future

61

looked bright for the Chamberses as they settled down into the routine of family life.

Katherine found that love for her son had tempered her unease about life in London, while John now had an even greater incentive to work hard.

'John, it's James's second birthday today, you should be getting home early for the tea party,' said Charles at midday. 'Don't linger over that deal this afternoon. Get it over with and go straight home. Evelyn and I will look in later.'

'Thank you,' said a grateful John. 'That's a great help. I have a couple of presents I want to pick up after the meeting.'

He left the office mid-afternoon. A breeze from the southwest had cleared the smog that hung over the city and allowed the sun to add to his sense of well-being and contentment.

John cut through one of the many side streets to reach a shop where he had ordered a wooden fort and set of soldiers for his son. The shop was small and cramped for space but housed a craftsman who was proud of his work. The items were ready, and after he had inspected them the shopkeeper carefully laid them in a box and wrapped it up. When John pulled his wallet from his pocket he half turned to catch the light from the window overlooking the street. He fished out some money unaware that two pairs of eyes had noted the bulk of the wallet while ostensibly appearing to examine items in the window.

John paid for the goods, made his thanks and left the shop. The two men continued to look in the window for a few seconds then followed him. When John turned into a quiet street they closed the distance rapidly. They glanced at one another knowingly and nodded. A few yards on they were alongside him. Clutching his parcel, thinking with pleasure of surprising James with his gift, John hardly gave them a glance as they passed him.

They were only two paces beyond when they abruptly stopped and turned. He cannoned into them. Startled, he lost his grip on his parcel. As it fell he automatically grabbed at it but it was beyond his clutching fingers. He heard the splinter of wood and a vision of the broken pieces flashed across his mind. Despondency at his loss surged into anger at the unknown men. He would have fought but it was already too late. He felt himself being bundled into an alley close to which the men had chosen to stop. He was pushed face-first into a brick wall, gasping as the air was driven from his lungs. He grimaced when this was followed by a hard blow to the neck and a fist slammed into his kidneys. He fell to the ground. Two kicks to the head and darkness enveloped him.

'Quick!' The urgent command came from the man standing over his companion whose hands moved swiftly through John's pockets. He found the wallet and straightened up.

'Come on!' They ran to the far end of the alley, slowed down and walked casually away, soon to be lost in London's masses, knowing there was little chance of their being traced as the perpetrators of this robbery.

Katherine glanced at the clock. Five. John had said he hoped to be home early today for James's birthday. A party tea for just the three of them was laid. Mrs Dewsbury had done a special baking of bread, scones, and cakes. The rich fruit cake with its icing had pleased her especially. She had also used moulds to turn out jellies in the shape of rabbits, knowing it would surprise James.

The clock moved on, its ticking now more prominent in Katherine's mind. James played happily on the drawing-room floor. After another twenty minutes he began to say he was hungry and ask where Daddy was.

At half-past five Katherine began to feel the first pangs of anxiety. John was never as late as this. She began to wonder if Charles was home, and if so why wasn't her husband?

The monotonous sound of the clock, each tick seeming to drive more space between her and John, and the more regular queries of 'Where's Daddy?' began to fray her nerves. A quarter of an hour later Katherine could stand it no longer. She left her chair and jerked the bell-pull.

'Pauline, look after James for a few minutes, I want to slip to the Drews,' she said when the maid appeared.

'Yes, ma'am.'

Katherine was already on her way out of the room and a few minutes later was admitted to the house further along the street.

'Thank you, Lizzie. Mrs Drew?'

'They're in the drawing-room, ma'am.'

Katherine was across the hall quickly, the word 'they' thundering in her mind. It implied Charles was home. Oh, where was John? She knocked upon and opened the door without waiting.

'Katherine!' A hint of alarm tinged Evelyn's voice at the sight of her friend's agitation.

'John isn't home!' The statement came automatically at the sight of Charles calmly laying the paper he had been reading on his knee.

He raised an eyebrow in surprise. 'I thought he would have been by now, though something may have delayed him. He had a meeting this afternoon. I told him not to come back to the office.'

'Where can he be? What time was his meeting?'

'It was at two o'clock.'

'Surely it would be over before this?' Concern rose in Katherine's voice.

'I would have thought so, but there may have been some snag.'

Katherine's lips tightened in exasperation.

Evelyn came to her and put a comforting hand on her arm. 'I'm sure there's a perfectly good reason for this.'

'I would have thought less of it if Charles hadn't been home, but . . .'

64

'He did say he had a present to pick up for James,' said Charles. 'Maybe that has delayed him.'

'I didn't know about that,' said Katherine, who was beginning to feel more and more out of touch with what was happening. 'Do you know where he was getting this present? I could make enquiries there.'

Charles shook his head. 'I'm afraid not.'

Katherine frowned. She felt frustrated and worry was swamping her. She bit her lip. 'Oh what can I do, Evelyn?' she cried, turning to her friend.

'Calm down, Katherine. I'm sure there's a perfectly good explanation. Sit down. Stay a while, if we can be of any comfort or help?'

'Oh, I don't know. I should get back to James.'

'I'm sure you've left him in Pauline's capable hands, but maybe you'd rather get back. Would you like me to come with you?' Evelyn cast a glance at her husband who gave a nod of approval.

'Would you?' Katherine felt grateful for her friend's consideration. The time would not seem quite so long if she had Evelyn for company. But she hoped John would soon be home. 'Oh, I'm being such a nuisance!'

'No, you're not,' Charles replied. 'What are friends for? Now, don't worry. He'll be home soon enough. May be there now.'

But Katherine's hopes were dashed when she and Evelyn reached her home. John had not returned.

James jumped up and ran with laughter on his face to greet his Auntie Evelyn. She settled down to play with him, trying to draw Katherine into the game. Though she did participate there was no enthusiasm in her contribution. And Evelyn saw, as the minutes ticked by, that she was getting more and more anxious. Though she hid it, Evelyn admitted to herself that she too was beginning to become worried by John's non-appearance.

Half an hour went by and Katherine could stand the pretence no longer. 'I've got to do something. He wouldn't

65

be as late as this, Evelyn. Something's the matter. He must be lying ill somewhere. But what can I do?'

Evelyn's lips tightened into a thin line. She wished she could offer some constructive advice but she too was frustrated at not knowing which way to turn.

'Mummy, me hungry.'

'It might be an idea to get James something to eat,' suggested Evelyn.

'I suppose so. It's well past his time for tea.' Katherine stood up and held out her hand to James. He scrambled to his feet and put his tiny hand in hers. She drew some comfort from his touch. 'Oh, dear,' she said to Evelyn with a forlorn expression, 'this was to have been so special.'

'Never mind. You can celebrate together another time.'

They were crossing the hall to the dining-room when they heard the bell ring, announcing that there was someone at the front door.

Katherine glanced at Evelyn, her heart soaring with relief. 'He must have forgotten his key.'

Pauline appeared but Katherine was already at the front door. She pulled it open. Her smile of welcome disappeared into an expression of concern at the sight of a constable.

'Mrs Chambers?'

'Yes.'

'May I have a word, ma'am?'

'Er ... yes.' When the man hesitated, Katherine realised he wanted to say what he had to say inside. 'Oh, forgive me, do come in.' She moved to one side and the constable stepped past her and waited until she had closed the door.

'Hello, young man.' The constable smiled at James who looked up at him with wide eyes.

Sensing that the policeman did not want to speak in front of the boy, Katherine said, 'Pauline, take James and give him some tea.' She forced herself to appear calm but her heart was racing and an ominous premonition weighed heavily on her.

As Pauline took James by the hand and headed for the dining-room he looked back over his shoulder at his mother as if he sensed she needed help.

'Let us go into the drawing-room,' Katherine suggested.

The constable hesitated. 'It this lady a friend of yours, ma'am?'

'Yes. Mrs Drew, a neighbour. Our husbands work together.'

'I think it would be best if she accompanied us.'

Katherine nodded, unable to find her voice. She glanced at Evelyn who, sensing that the constable's news could be catastrophic, came to her side. The constable followed the two friends into the room.

He closed the door carefully. When he looked up he saw that Katherine and Evelyn were standing in front of the sofa facing him. He cleared his throat and looked steadily at Katherine. 'Mrs Chambers, I'm afraid I have some bad news.'

He hesitated and in that moment Katherine said, 'It's my husband, isn't it?'

He nodded. 'Yes, ma'am, I'm afraid it is.'

'What's happened? Where is he?' Alarm rose in her voice. Her eyes widened with anxiety.

'He was waylaid, robbed and beaten.'

'How badly? Where is he? I must see him.' The words poured out.

The constable licked his lips nervously. 'Ma'am, I'm afraid he's dead.'

Katherine's face drained of colour. She was filled with disbelief. She stared at him as if this couldn't be true. Strength left her and she sank on to the sofa. She was oblivious to Evelyn sitting down beside her and taking her hand in hers in an attempt to support her against the shock.

'He can't be.' The drawn out whisper came with an emphatic shake of Katherine's head as if that would dispel the horror behind the constable's words and negate the truth. 'It's James's birthday . . . he said he'd be home for that.'

'Ma'am, he was found an hour ago in an alley. A passer-by was drawn to a pile of paper and shattered wood. On examination he saw it was a child's fort and there were toy soldiers scattered around. Then his attention was caught by a figure lying in the alley.' The constable hesitated.

'John?' whispered Katherine.

'Yes, ma'am. We identified him by the purchase slip for the fort which was in his pocket. It had this address on it.'

Katherine's shoulders heaved as a huge sob shuddered through her. She became aware of Evelyn. At the sight of her friend's look of concern which spoke of a desire to do something to ease the pain but knew that there was nothing, Katherine broke down. Tears flowed. Sob after sob tore through her. She sank against Evelyn who put an arm round her shoulders. 'No! No!' Her cry rang around the room. Evelyn's grip tightened. Katherine shuddered. 'My God, what am I going to do?'

Chapter Five

The door closed on the last of the sympathisers, Mr Allberry, who, shocked by the tragic loss of a bright prospect, had come 'specially from Newcastle. He had brought the news that John's parents were devastated at the loss of their only child and too ill from shock to travel. He had also reassured Katherine that he would continue John's salary for six months and said that if he could be of further help in the future she was not to be afraid of contacting him. Now only Evelyn and Charles remained with her.

The funeral, ten days after the finding of John's body, had been small. Katherine and John had few close friends. Some acquaintances felt duty bound to attend as had some members of the commercial world. John had entered their circle. If he had lived he might have made a lasting impact on it, but now he was gone and in a short while would be forgotten as they became newly engrossed in deal and counter-deal in their pursuit of ambition and wealth.

Evelyn and Charles had been most supportive, as had Cornelius, Jeremiah and Emanuel as well as the household staff. Katherine dreaded to think what it would have been like without them. But what did the future hold now? She faced a grim desert of loneliness.

At least she would not be short of money. John had earned well, and there was her own inheritance from her parents and the proceeds of the house in Newcastle that she had sold. But that would not last forever. There was James's future to think of. She should find something that would bring her an income, but what? There were few opportunities for any woman of her class, let alone a widow with a young child.

'Charles and I will stay with you again tonight,' Evelyn offered, fearing that the depression that hung over Katherine might result in a repetition of the breakdown she had had in Newcastle. Alert to this possibility, she and Charles had stayed with her every night since the tragedy.

'That is very kind of you and I am most grateful but I must learn to manage, for myself and for James. I cannot go on imposing on you.'

'We are only too glad to help. You must not rush into any decisions,' Evelyn insisted.

'Consider all the possibilities carefully. If you need any advice or wish to talk about anything then don't hesitate to come to me,' added Charles. 'I will do what I can, and I know Evelyn feels the same way.'

'Of course I do.'

'You are most kind.'

'What are friends for?'

Three days later, knowing she must face life without their continual support, Katherine made her first decision.

'Please don't think me ungrateful but I would like you to return to your home. I must stand on my own two feet and putting this suggestion to you is the first step towards my doing that.' Katherine made her voice firm.

'I understand, my dear,' replied Evelyn. 'If you are sure that is what you want?'

'It is. I have the staff and you are only a few doors away.'

'Very well, but don't hesitate to send for us.' Evelyn was pleased at the new determination in Katherine's attitude. She felt sure that the young mother would cope now. The vibrant girl who had come to London had re-emerged these last few days. But there were still decisions to be made and Evelyn hoped that they would not weigh too heavily on Katherine's shoulders.

In the solitude of her bedroom Katherine prayed each night not only to God but to John, asking them both for guidance so as to make the right decisions for her future and that of James.

Twelve weeks later she invited Evelyn and Charles to dine with her in the evening.

Evelyn had seen Katherine every day during those weeks and had been pleased by the growing assurance that was evident in her. But this evening she and Charles were even more surprised by her air of self-confidence when she welcomed them. There was a new air of authority about her, not over anybody else but over herself. It was as if she knew her capabilities and was in charge. Her black dress was plain with only the slightest decoration around the neckline. She had draped a pale grey shawl around her shoulders, making sure that it did not obscure her beloved jet cross hanging from her neck. It held so many memories of John and the happy day they had spent in Whitby.

Evelyn thought Katherine looked as well as she had ever seen her, and from her effervescent manner suspected that decisions had been made that took a load off her mind. So it came as no great surprise to her when, over drinks in the drawing-room after a delicious meal, Katherine made her announcement.

'Apart from my desire to spend another pleasant evening with my dear friends, I had a further reason for inviting you this evening. I have come to a decision about my future.' She allowed herself a slight pause. She had rehearsed this moment over and over again, seeking the right approach, but had always come to the conclusion that the best way was to jump straight in and make her announcement without any preamble. 'I am going back to Newcastle.'

There was a moment when time seemed to stop for them.

71

Then Charles spoke up. 'Are you sure you are doing the right thing?'

Katherine nodded. 'I've thought it through very carefully. This is no impulsive decision. I waited until I could cope better with John's death, and I know he has helped me to reach this conclusion.'

'I am not surprised by your decision,' put in Evelyn. 'I know you never really liked London but tolerated it for John's sake and his ambitions.'

'Was it so obvious?' said Katherine.

'Not always, and I suspect that John never knew.'

A touch of relief came to Katherine's face. 'I hope he didn't. You are right, Evelyn, I have never liked London. I hoped with James's birth my attitude would alter, but it didn't. Oh, he helped to take my mind off things but I did not relish the idea of his growing up here. If John's work had kept us here then so be it, but without him . . . well, we can escape London. Apart from both of you, the staff here and at the office, I never had any real friends. Oh, yes, numerous acquaintances but nobody to whom I became really close. So I have decided to leave and return north where I really belong. John's mother and father are in Newcastle. They have never seen James. I think they should get to know their grandson.'

Evelyn nodded. 'I understand.'

'We will miss you and little James,' said Charles, and took a sip of his wine to try to control the lump that had come to his throat.

'And I will miss both of you too. You've been so kind. I can never repay you but you will be ever in my thoughts.'

'When will you go?' asked Evelyn.

'I haven't decided yet. There are lots of things to see to. I'll set about those and then fix a date.'

'You don't have to worry about the house. I've had a communication from Mr Allberry in which he instructed me to tell you to stay here as long as you like. If you decide to remain permanently you can do so at the same nominal rent. If you choose to do that he has instructed me to find somewhere else for the person he will appoint in John's place. His arrival, I believe, is imminent. Of course if you do leave then the new man can live here, but that should not influence your decision.'

'I am grateful to Mr Allberry and shall tell him so when I get to Newcastle. Charles, there is no need for you to look any further than this house. My mind is made up, and in view of what you have just told me, I will act as quickly as possible.'

'My dear, you are not to rush on my account. The appointment is not finalised. If it is before you leave, I can find the newcomer a room at the club or rent a house for him if he has a family.'

'Very well, but I won't waste any time. The bulk of the furniture was provided by Mr Allberry so it remains in the house. Only the pieces that John and I bought will need to be crated and sent north.'

'Jeremiah and Emanuel can see to that. Just say when you are ready for them to do it.'

'Thank you, that's very kind, but don't force them.'

Charles gave a little smile. 'They'll need no forcing. They liked you from the first time you visited the office. They are appreciative of your thoughtfulness, never forgetting them at Christmas or their birthdays among other kindnesses.'

'It was always a pleasure to see their smiling faces and experience their willingness to help. Cornelius's dependability and quiet assurance too. I will miss them all.'

'And they you.'

'It will be hard saying goodbye to them, but the hardest task I face, the one I'm not looking forward to, is telling my staff that I am leaving.'

'They'll take it hard,' said Evelyn, 'especially Dot.'

Katherine nodded. 'Especially her,' she whispered, saddened by the thought of leaving the little girl she had come to like so much, whose appearance had improved

73

beyond recognition with good food and guidance from Katherine and Mrs Dewsbury. At sixteen she had thrown off her early shyness and was now a bright-eyed youngster with an endearing cockiness and a strong loyalty to the family. 'Maybe Dot will be able to go with Mrs Dewsbury.'

Evelyn pursed her lips doubtfully. 'It's a nice idea, and from what you tell me they like each other. Mrs Dewsbury would certainly be a good influence on her, but it's not always possible to find someone wanting a cook and scullery maid at the same time.'

'I suppose not.' Katherine tightened her lips with regret. 'I hope Dot doesn't slip back to what she was before she came to us.'

'When will you tell them?'

'I'd rather do it later than sooner but I must be fair to them, give them time to find new positions before I leave. Maybe this weekend – on Sunday after I come back from church.'

The sun shone from a clear blue sky on Sunday morning, creating a feeling of well-being among most of the people leaving church, but Katherine was not one of them. In fact her mind was so occupied with the unpleasant task ahead that she was barely aware the day was pleasant. She had no thoughts about the sermon, for the words had made no impact on a mind grappling with the problem of how to break the news of her pending departure to her staff. Her usual bright 'Good morning' to the regular church-goers was missing and her normally brisk walk was today the desultory pace of someone wanting to delay a task as long as possible in spite of knowing that it could not be avoided.

When she entered the house, Pauline was coming down the stairs.

'Hello, ma'am,' she said, 'I hope you enjoyed your walk on such a pleasant morning?'

The brightness of her housemaid struck so hard that it

brought more confusion to Katherine. 'Oh, yes,' she replied unconvincingly. She took off her coat and hat and handed them Pauline.

'I'll bring your hot chocolate to the drawing-room, ma'am. Nurse has taken James for a walk.'

Katherine, lost in thought, merely nodded and went to the drawing-room. She sank into a chair with a weary sigh. Last night her sleep had been restless. Awake, her mind had been active. Had she made the right decision to leave London? Should she stay and make her home here? But she still felt, even after three years, that it was a foreign land. The north called. But if she went back, she would have to start rebuilding her life all over again. True, she would have the support of John's mother and father, but beyond that who was there unless she went to her cousin in St Abbs? But they had drifted apart. Could one really step back in time? Life continually changes. Was there a future for her if she went north? And yet what tied her to London? What would John want her to do? So the questions and the sought-for answers tumbled over and over in her mind. The small hours of the morning were long but eventually she had fallen asleep and when she woke the answer was there: stick by your decision to leave. Had John planted it? Now, with the moment of disclosure imminent, the doubts were back. She straightened her spine and chided herself for confusing her own mind.

There was a knock on the door and Pauline entered with a tray. She placed it on a small table beside Katherine. 'Shall I pour, ma'am?'

'I'll do it, Pauline, thank you.' She saw it as a chance to compose herself. 'But will you make sure Mrs Dewsbury and Dot, along with yourself, come to see me in ten minutes?'

'Certainly, ma'am.' Pauline left the room wondering what this summons was about. Madam had not been her usual perky self. Had something at church upset her? But that wouldn't merit wanting to see her staff. Well, in ten minutes she would know. When she broke the news to Mrs Dewsbury and Dot they were equally inquisitive but could reach no conclusion.

Ten minutes later, when they answered her call of 'Come in', Katherine invited them to sit down. 'I have something to tell you.' She indicated the sofa and a chair. Mrs Dewsbury and Dot took the sofa and Pauline the chair which Katherine had placed beside the sofa so that she would be facing all three.

'I have something I want to say to you.' She had to clear her throat and in that moment, with all eyes on her, she felt guilty. She could reverse her decision even at this last moment. It was so tempting to spare the people she had come to like so much, who had been so supportive when John had been murdered, but she must be firm. She had made a decision which she thought would be for her own good and that of her son. 'I have decided I am going to return north, to Newcastle where I came from.'

The words were out, the announcement made. Katherine felt a surge of relief. The moment was over, but she was still filled with anxiety about the reaction of her staff. The last thing she wanted was to hurt them and yet she knew they must be feeling that now, even though she faced expressions of incomprehension. They had heard words they'd never expected to hear. Each one of them faced upheaval and they were not prepared for it.

'Oh, ma'am.' Mrs Dewsbury's voice was low, shock mingled with disbelief.

Pauline, her face draining fast, could only stare in confusion, trying to make sense of the unexpected.

Dot's world was collapsing around her. She stared at Katherine for what seemed an eternity but in reality was only a few seconds. 'Ma'am, you can't.' The words came out sharply from shock, as if they could prevent what would be an overwhelming disaster.

'I'm sorry but I must,' said Katherine quietly. 'I have no relations in London. James's grandparents are in Newcastle

76

and should see their grandson and have some say in his life. They can't do that if I stay here. Please try and understand.' There was a catch in Katherine's voice as she looked from one to the other, willing them to do so.

Mrs Dewsbury bit her lip, holding back the tears that dampened her eyes. 'We are all sorry you are going. When will it be?'

Her words seemed to drive home to Dot that this was truly going to happen. The girl burst out crying and fell against Mrs Dewsbury who put a comforting arm round her shoulders.

'Now, now, Dot, don't upset Mrs Chambers. She can't stay here just because of us.' But there was a catch in the cook's voice and sadness in her eyes.

'Why not?' wailed Dot. 'I don't want her to go.'

'None of us does, but if it is best for Mrs Chambers we should not try to stop her. Rather we should help her.'

'But what am I going to do?'

'I'm not leaving immediately,' said Katherine, 'I'll try and find you another position. I'll do that for all of you.'

Pauline, who was only just beginning to get over the shock, said quietly, 'There'll be no one as good as you, ma'am.'

Katherine gave a small sympathetic smile. 'That is kind of you, Pauline. I'll do my best.'

'I know you will, ma'am, but ...' Her sentence was interrupted by the clanging of the front door bell.

Katherine looked exasperated. Who was calling at this inopportune moment? 'Pauline, please see who that is and tell them I'm not at home.'

She hurried from the room. A few moments later when she reappeared there was an apologetic expression on her face. 'I'm sorry, ma'am, it's Mrs Drew. I told her you were busy but she insists on seeing you. When I said you were talking to the staff she emphasised she must see you now and requested that you go into the hall.'

Puzzled, Katherine nodded. 'Very well. I'll only be a

moment. All of you, wait here.' She left the room with a brisk step. 'Evelyn, what is it? I'm just informing the staff of my departure.'

'Oh, dear. I was hoping to see you before you did.'

'Why?'

'Earlier this morning, Charles gave me a surprise. He took me to see a house, standing on its own small plot of land.' Evelyn, who had been talking quickly, paused to catch her breath.

'I'm excited for you, but what's this got to do with me?' Katherine's irritation at what appeared to be an interruption of no consequence showed, but Evelyn ignored it.

'It's a bigger house and I'll need more staff, especially as Mrs Sergeant has given notice. Her elderly mother is ill and she will have to look after her.'

'You mean, you want to employ all my staff?' Katherine asked, incredulous at this solution that had materialised from such an unlikely source.

'Yes.' Delight at what she able to do shone in Evelyn's eyes.

'Oh, Evelyn, this is a God-send.' Relief and gratitude were in Katherine's every word. 'I'd just told them and they are all so upset. Come on, let's give them the good news together.'

The two friends hurried into the drawing-room.

'Listen, everyone, Mrs Drew has something to say to you.'

Evelyn smiled, taking in everyone. 'Would you all like to come and work for me?'

There was a stunned silence. The sadness in the atmosphere changed to incredulity.

Mrs Dewsbury was the first to query Evelyn's question. 'Work for you, ma'am, but you already have a staff?'

Dot checked a sob, sniffed, and wiped a hand across her tear-streaked cheeks. Her mind was confused. What did Mrs Drew mean?

Pauline hung on her reply.

'Mr Drew and I are going to move to a bigger house and will require more staff. So, as I know Mrs Chambers is going to return north, it is convenient for me to offer you the new positions. I know how dependable you all are.'

'But do you require two cooks?' asked Mrs Dewsbury doubtfully.

'Mrs Sergeant's mother is ill and she is going to have to leave me, so if you will take her place I will be delighted to have you.'

'Of course I will,' replied Mrs Dewsbury, overcome by her good fortune. A world that a few moments ago was collapsing around her had suddenly been rebuilt.

Dot looked at her with an uncertain expression. 'Does this mean I can stay with you?'

'It does, love.' Mrs Dewsbury gave her a hug, expressing her pleasure that they would not be parted.

Dot grinned through tear-dimmed eyes. She swallowed hard, sniffed and wiped her fingers across her eyes again. Her gaze, directed at Evelyn, was filled with wonder and gratitude.

'And you, Pauline?' asked Evelyn.

The maid started. She had been lost in bewilderment at this sharp change of fortune.

'Oh, ma'am, if I can no longer work for Mrs Chambers there is no one I would rather work for.'

'Good, then it is all settled.' She turned to Katherine. 'When will you be leaving?'

'Well, now I can plan. Probably three weeks' time.'

'I think the purchase of the new house should be completed by then.'

In a relieved frame of mind Katherine's staff made their thanks and left to carry on with their daily tasks.

Katherine came to her friend and gave her a hug of thanks. 'What consolation you've brought me! And I'm so pleased for you, finding a new home. I hope you will be very happy there.'

'Charles wanted to surprise me so kept it a secret until

yesterday when he took me to see it. We did not make a
final decision there and then, decided to sleep on it, but
when we woke this morning we looked at each other and
both said at the same time "We'll have it." I realised that
we'd need more staff and immediately thought my problem
would be solved by taking yours. You said you would tell
them of your decision after church this morning. I hoped I
would see you before you broke your news.'

'It doesn't matter, everything turned out perfectly.'

When Evelyn had gone, Katherine sat down at her desk,
took out a sheet of paper and penned a letter to John's
parents telling them that she was returning to Newcastle
and would write again giving details of when she would be
leaving London. She had written every week since his death
and though she did not always receive a reply, she knew
they would be delighted by this decision. She re-read the
completed letter. Satisfied, she folded it, slipped it into an
envelope, sealed and addressed it. She laid it ready to be
despatched on the mail-coach for Newcastle then hesitated,
staring at it, wondering for a moment if she had made the
right decision. She started.

Unconsciously she had been fingering the jet cross
around her neck. Now its touch brought back memories of
a happy, though brief time in Whitby when the future had
held so much promise. This cross would always remind her
of that day and of the generosity and kindness of Mr
Simpson. She took up her pen again.

Reuben Simpson looked up from the newspaper he was
reading when the maid came into the front room of 4 New
Buildings, one of a row of houses situated close to the top
of the cliff on the west side of the River Esk, dividing the
two sections of Whitby. Here the 'new' town was developing as more and more of the merchants, shipowners,
captains and business people moved across the river.
Reuben Simpson and his wife had moved here on the back

of the wealth he had gained from his ropery and jet businesses. Now, with his two jet workshops passed to Stephen Harris two months ago, Reuben had a little more time to spend at home.

'A letter for you, sir,' said the maid as she crossed the room. 'Delivered by Peter Harris.'

Reuben took the letter and thanked the maid who left the room. He examined the envelope. 'I don't know this writing, Jane.'

His wife, who was sitting close to the window embroidering a tablecloth, asked with an amused lilt to her voice, 'Why do you always try to identify the sender before you open any correspondence? Open it, man.'

He slit the envelope and withdrew a sheet of paper. He unfolded it and cast his eyes immediately to the signature. 'Katherine Chambers' he read. He pursed his lips thoughtfully, trying to make an identification in his mind. His eyes moved quickly across the text. 'Oh, my goodness.' He looked at his wife. 'You remember the young couple we took to the Angel on their way to London about three years ago?'

'You gave her a jet cross?'

'Yes. Lovely person. Nice young couple. They had just been married. He was taking up a new job in London. He's been killed.'

'Oh, no!' Jane, shocked, held her needle in mid-stitch.

Reuben rose from his chair and took the letter to his wife.

She read it quickly but took in every detail. 'Murdered!' she muttered. 'For the sake of a few pounds. What a terrible shock for ...' she glanced again at the signature as she was speaking '... Katherine. And left with a two year old. It won't be easy for her.'

'I see she has decided to return north. She says she might find the opportunity to visit Whitby where she spent such a happy day. I hope she can.'

'She says she wears the jet cross every day, to remind her of that visit.'

'I'll go and tell Stephen. I'm sure he will remember her. It was his piece she chose.'

Stephen was supervising his son, who was polishing a piece of jet, when Reuben arrived at the workshop to impart the sad news.

'I remember her, Father,' said Peter who overheard. 'A nice lady.'

When he left the workshop in mid-afternoon he recalled Katherine again as he walked along Church Street towards the quays.

His father set no restrictions on his time as long as he did not neglect his work. One day the workshop would be his and he must hold the respect of the employees. Spending too much time away from the premises would undermine that, but Stephen knew his son was too conscientious to abuse his privileges. He was delighted with Peter's talent and application. He could become an outstanding craftsman. He also recognised Peter's love of the sea. Though there were times when he feared it, he did not want to curb that interest for he saw it would never snatch Peter from the jet industry, but instead provide relaxation away from work.

Peter had made many friends among Whitby's sailors, and listened to their stories of other climes with rapt attention. Along with most Whitby folk he never missed the departure or arrival of the whaleships that contributed so much to the economic life of the port. He was excited by the whalemen's tales of the icy wastes of the Arctic and of their contests with the huge creatures that gave them their livelihood. He willingly helped fishermen unload their catch or mend their nets, and as a reward they would sometimes let him accompany them on a short expedition.

Now he threaded his way through the crowds going about their business and came to the quays on the east side of the river. He darted about, watching the loading of two merchant ships and learning that they were both bound for Spain. Then he made his way to a boathouse near the West Pier. The arrival of two new lifeboats in 1822 to replace the original of 1802 had made such an impression on five-year-old Peter that the excitement had remained with him ever since. The stories his father had told him of the bravery of the men who manned them had fuelled an interest that had never left him. The West Side Lifeboat was his favourite. As he went along the Promenade towards the boathouse he saw that, across the river, the East Side Lifeboat was hanging on its davits on the side of Tate Hill Pier.

The boathouse was open, as he knew it would be, with the boat resting proudly on its carriage ready to be run out if needed.

'Good day, Mr Holmes,' he greeted the man sitting on a chair in the sun beside the open door.

David Holmes, in his shirt sleeves, looked up as he removed his pipe from his mouth. His gansey, hand knitted in the Whitby tradition of a rope pattern with the middle of the sleeves plain, hung over the back of the chair. He would need its protection against the wind and sea if there was an emergency. With his other hand he pushed the peaked cap further back on his head. 'Hello there, young Peter.' A smile of pleasure at seeing the youngster wrinkled the weather-beaten face, tanned by the sun, browned and roughened by the salt-laden wind. Eyes that had searched many a horizon sparkled to see the boy. He knew he was in for a pleasant hour's chat. Peter always had ready questions but he was a good listener too. 'Finished work for the day?' he queried.

'Aye. Got through my polishing.'

'How's the carving going?'

'That's what I like doing best. Father says I'll be better than him.'

'If he says that you've something to live up to 'cos he's good ... no, he's the best carver in Whitby.'

'I hope I don't disappoint him.'

'You'll not do that, lad, if you work hard enough and practise. From what I hear you're pretty good yourself.'

Peter turned to gaze at the boat, set ready to be run out at a moment's notice. 'Some day I'll be a member of her crew, Mr Holmes.'

David smiled to himself at the sheer determination in the youngster's voice. He had no doubt that Peter meant it and would fulfil his ambition. There was a light in his eyes that verified his love of boats and his desire to be part of the crew of this one in particular. But David felt it his duty to issue a warning. 'It's a tough, dangerous job, Peter. You want to think hard on it before volunteering. Them oars are heavy, thee needs strong muscles to use them.' He made a pretence of feeling Peter's muscles and grunted doubtfully.

'I've been lifting heavy things to strengthen them,' blurted the lad, anxious to erase any doubts Mr Holmes might have about his ability.

'Aye, maybe you have, lad,' returned the older man with a grin that showed there was teasing behind his previous words. He then became more serious. 'But consider this – it's dangerous, very dangerous at times. The sea can be unrelenting, demanding, unforgiving. It will take what it wants, when it wants it, and you won't stop it. Remember that, lad, before you express your desire to join the crew of that boat.'

'Did you Mr Holmes?'

'Aye, lad, I did.'

'But you still volunteered.'

'Aye. Show me your hands.'

Peter held them out.

David gazed at the long fingers. 'I hadn't hands like yours. Those aren't the fingers of a sailor. I know you like to be on a boat and have been fishing but I still say you should think on. You have a gift, you can create with those fingers and give pleasure to people through them. Damage them and think what is lost. And you could so easily damage them in a boat, especially doing what you might have to do during a hazardous rescue. I know your father

84

has ambitions for you in the jet trade. Don't disappoint him by hurting those hands that have a God-given gift.'

Peter was still. David could sense his disappointment at the discouragement he had just meted out. He had to break the silence between them.

'You can still be interested in boats and ships. It would be strange, living in Whitby, if you weren't. You can still sail, but nothing heavy to endanger those hands of yours. Now, there are some interesting ships leaving soon. How about we watch them together? I can tell you some good stories about them.'

Three weeks later Katherine tried to hold back the tears as she came downstairs but could not when she saw all the staff assembled in the hall to say their goodbyes. Evelyn and Charles were standing by the front door with James.

'Mrs Dewsbury.' Katherine swallowed hard as she embraced her. 'Thank you for all you have done.'

Tears streamed down the cook's face. 'It has been a pleasure to work for you, ma'am. Have a safe journey. May God be with you.'

'Dot, be a good girl. Serve Mrs Drew as you did me.' Katherine gave the girl a hug.

She nodded, too full to speak, unashamed about sobbing and holding on to Katherine as if she could stop her leaving. Katherine disentangled herself from the girl's arms with difficulty, gave her an extra hug, straightened up and turned to Pauline.

'I thank you for all you have done for me, especially over these last three weeks. Without you I would never have been ready for today.'

'Oh, ma'am, it was nothing. I will miss you.'

'And I will miss you too.' Katherine stepped into the centre of the hall and looked around. Her eyes dampened with the thought of what might have been if John had lived, of a life that had held so much promise, plans unfulfilled, a shared love cut short. She started for the door. Charles opened it. Katherine stopped, swung round and said, 'Goodbye to you all.' She stepped outside where a carriage was waiting. Evelyn followed with James. The coachman opened the door. Katherine got inside and leaned out to take the boy when Evelyn lifted him to her.

'You were so good,' praised Katherine, hugging him, finding comfort in his touch to ease her departure.

Evelyn sat down beside her and Charles sat opposite. The coachman closed the door, climbed on to his seat and set the horse in motion.

The weather had been fine early in the morning but now it was closing in, with dark clouds driven by a freshening wind from the north-west.

Reaching the quay from which the *Hope*, a three-masted barque, would sail, the coachman handed Katherine's two cases to Charles who took them on board where he was directed by the first mate to Mrs Chambers's cabin. When he returned to the quay he informed the two ladies that sailing would be in half an hour.

'Please don't wait,' said Katherine.

'We must,' returned Evelyn.

'Please, don't, it makes for an uncomfortable time for all of us. We will be trying to find things to say and the atmosphere will become embarrassing. I will be all right. James and I can get settled before we sail and then he will be ready to see all the activity on the river as we head downstream.'

Evelyn gave a little smile. 'I know what you mean. But we'll stay if you want us to?'

'I don't mean it unkindly but I think it would be better for all of us if we said our goodbyes now.' She held out her arms. Evelyn came to them. The two friends embraced in a gesture that said everything of the love and friendship that had grown between them in London. Words choked in their throats but there was no need for them.

Charles, who had crouched beside James, embraced him and said with a lump in his throat, 'I'll miss you, little fellow. Take care of your Mama.'

James flung his arms round Charles's neck. 'Goodbye, Uncle Charles.'

Charles straightened, lifted the boy and handed him to Evelyn who hugged him tight.

Charles opened his arms to Katherine who accepted his embrace with tears running down her cheeks. 'Dear, dear Charles, thank you for all you have done for me. I don't know what I would have done without you.' She kissed him on the cheek, gave him another and let it linger a little to express how deeply she valued his friendship.

She took James from Evelyn and looked at her friends but was too choked to utter another word. She turned. Holding James by the hand, she hurried up the gangplank. On deck she stopped, swung round, raised her hand then lifted James into her arms and spoke to him. They both waved. A moment later she was gone.

Chapter Six

Peter left the workshop in Church Street in mid-afternoon with the approval of his father who knew his son would head for the quays and possibly the West Pier. A strong sea, brought by a change of wind to the northeast, was crashing along the seaward side of the stone structure. At such times Peter loved to walk on the pier, feel the spray and be drawn by the tremendous power of the waves. Stephen did not discourage his son's interest. The sea was part of the fabric of Whitby life and no one born and brought up there could fail to be aware of it.

Peter quickened his step, crossed the bridge and felt the strength of the wind as it funnelled between the East and West Cliffs, sending eddies of ripples along the river. On the west side he turned along St Ann's Staith and through Haggersgate to the Promenade leading to the pier. His cheery greetings were returned by seamen at their various tasks: mending nets, repairing sails, coiling ropes, washing down. As he veered on to the pier he waved to David Holmes, sitting in the shelter of the lifeboat's hull, in the boathouse. It was returned by the brandishing of the pipe in the sailor's hand. No doubt Peter would stop for a chat on the way back.

Further along the pier he sensed the wind freshening. He ran his hand through his hair, filled his lungs with the salt air and lengthened his stride. It was like being on the deck of a ship without the motion. He felt good and life was kind. He had an understanding father and mother who gave him a freedom that many of his age did not enjoy. His parents knew that in return they received his love and respect. They also knew that though he had a great love of the sea he would never make it his career, for he recognised that he had a gift which gave him unbounded pleasure, creating exquisite jewellery from jet, and besides a deep interest in the business which one day would be his.

He reached the end of the pier and stood gazing out to sea. He had left the world of jet behind. Now only the vastness of the ocean dominated his thoughts. The sea, angry that its run had been denied by the two piers, pounded them with a ferocity that strengthened with every incoming wave. The air was filled with sweeping mist that he ignored in the invigorating feeling of being one with the water and the wind that whitened the wave crests as they rolled in to crash foaming on the beach stretching to Sandsend. He had an urge to sail again, to pit himself against the sea. He must try and arrange it with Mr Holmes.

On the way back he stopped to chat to him. Time melted away as they became intrigued by the weather pattern, watching it become more and more threatening as the wind strengthened.

'It'll have to get worse before it gets better,' commented David, eyeing the sky with misgiving. 'There'll be a few ships seeking shelter here before dark. I'm sorry for anyone who doesn't make a haven wherever it is. I'd not like to be out on the North Sea now, never mind tonight.'

Peter suddenly realised how time had fled and that he was late for tea. With a brief goodbye to David, he raced off.

'Sorry, Ma. I got talking to Mr Holmes.'

His mother and father, who had started their meal, smiled to themselves at their son's excuse and the enthusiastic way in which he tucked into his meat pie.

Half an hour later, when he had finished eating, he said,

'Mr Holmes says this weather will worsen and there'll be ships seeking shelter here. I'd like to see them.' While his words announced an intention, they also sought permission.

'All right, Peter, but wrap up well and don't go doing anything foolhardy.'

He pulled on a gansey, shrugged himself into a thick woollen jacket and stuffed a cap into a pocket. His father had settled himself with his pipe and his mother had busied herself at the sink when he shouted, 'I'm off,' and stepped out into the wind.

He realised how much it had strengthened when it tried to hinder his progress. He bent into it and pushed harder with his legs. It battered him and tried to spin him round but he defied all its attempts to stop him and ignored its screeching cries as it funnelled between houses, up alleyways and tore down narrow streets, rattling windowpanes and shaking doors.

When he reached the boathouse he saw that Fred Pallister and Tom Bond, two men who manned the rescue boat, together with David Holmes, were already manoeuvring the boat into the open. He ran to help.

'I see the East Boat's out,' he shouted above the wind.

'Aye, been gone over half an hour. Ship drifting off Staithes.'

He helped them steady the boat towards the slipway.

'Are you taking her round the pier?' he asked.

'Aye,' replied David.

Peter knew that they expected the storm to worsen which would make launching directly into the sea hazardous. Taking the boat into the river and the shelter of the piers made an approach to the sea easier if the boat was required.

By the time they had got her to the top of the slipway two more members of the crew had arrived.

They eased the boat towards the beach and in a matter of minutes, with the advantage of high tide, the vessel was afloat. The men scrambled into her, oars out steadying the craft against the waves that would have driven her ashore.

David took the tiller and eyed his men heaving on the oars. It was only then that he noticed young Peter had taken one of them. He experienced a moment's annoyance that the boy should have done this but it was swept away by his admiration of Peter's courage and desire to help. The waves were rolling in and all David's attention was devoted to guiding the boat through them. The bow dug deep into the walls of water, rose on the rolling sea, tipped over the crest and plunged into the trough ready to ride the next wave. Using all their skill and knowledge, the men rounded the end of the West Pier and were thankful when, protected by its stonework, they reached the calmer waters of the river. They brought the boat beside the pier, shipped oars, tied up and scrambled up the iron rungs let in the stonework. Reaching the top they felt the force of the rising wind and hurried to the shelter of the boathouse.

'You were right about the weather, Mr Holmes,' commented Peter as soon as they were out of the buffeting wind.

'Aye, lad, I was.' There was no pleasure in David's voice. It was an observation he never liked to make. Then he added, 'You shouldn't have been on board, Peter. It was dangerous.'

'I thought an extra oar would help.'

'Aye, it did and we are grateful, but you shouldn't have put yourself at risk.' In spite of the admonishment, he gave Peter a friendly tap of thanks on the shoulder. He pulled out his pipe and started to fill it. 'We've had three ships in already.'

'I saw them as I came along.'

'There's another three out there,' commented Fred.

Peter hunched his shoulders and stepped outside. He struggled to a point from which he had a better view of the changing conditions beyond the piers. The waves were high now with rolling crests that tipped over with a surge that turned the sea into a cauldron of foam. With it came a roaring sound that, combined with the howl of the wind, raised prickles on his scalp. The scene was hostile and no doubt the crews of the three ships heading for safety were gripped with a fear they would not make the shelter of Whitby. He stood transfixed by the pitiless force of the elements.

'Ma'am, the Captain's compliments. With the wind turning to the northeast the weather is worsening and it would be advisable for you to return to your cabin.' The mate touched the peak of his cap and moved on to speak to three more passengers. Katherine lifted James into her arms and went below deck.

Since leaving the Thames she had spent much of the time outside, enjoying the activity on board which helped to keep James amused, and exchanging words with some of the other passengers. The wind was strong but not alarming. She had dressed to be in the open rather than in the confines of the cabin. That would suffice after dark when she hoped she and James would sleep in spite of unfamiliar surroundings, sounds and the swaying of the ship. But now the Captain's advice had taken her below rather sooner than she'd wanted.

She had adapted her sea-legs to the roll of the ship but was not prepared for the extra lurch as she opened her cabin door. She was propelled into the cabin in a rush and only just managed to save herself from falling to the floor by collapsing on the bed. James let out a yell and started to cry when his head bumped the wall. Katherine pushed herself up and reached for him. She cuddled him, uttering soothing words as she sat down in the chair which was fastened to the floor.

'It's all right, James. The wind will soon drop.' She rubbed his head gently. His sobs and tears stopped but he still held on to his mother. 'Should we lie down, pet?'

He nodded. She eased herself from the chair and lay down on the bed, holding James close. He snuffled and a few moments later was asleep. The sea air had had its effect. There were no more sudden lurches. The ship seemed to have settled down again, though it was pitching and rolling more than it had previously done. She lay staring at the ceiling, wondering what life held for her. Maybe John's mother and father would have some suggestions about what she should do. Her thoughts drifted, became hazy and finally she slept.

How long afterwards she never knew, Katherine awoke with a start. A loud cracking noise had penetrated her sleep. Or had she been dreaming? But there was no mistaking the alarm in the voices that were coming from on deck. She could not make out the words but the raucous notes, rising thick and fast, heralded trouble. Unease gripped her. She scrambled from the bed. James was awake. He cried out for her.

'A minute, love.' She grabbed her coat and thrust her arms into the sleeves. She did not know why but something told her to get well-clad. She dressed James quickly with an extra woollen garment under his outer clothes.

'Everyone on deck!' The cry from the passageway was followed by a rap on the door. 'On deck! On deck!' The note of urgency in the voice required instant obedience.

Katherine snatched the door open but as she stepped out the ship heaved, sending her staggering back into the cabin. She heard what sounded like the tearing of timber and forced herself from the cabin. Other passengers, shouting in alarm, were already leaving, urged on by one of the crew. She followed, clutching James close, battling against the sway of the ship that seemed determined to stop her leaving. Then she was outside. She stopped on deck, overpowered by the dreadful sight and the chaos around her. Horror gripped her. She grasped at the nearest possible support as the ship lurched under the power of the waves that swept at her.

Thick dark clouds, driven by a ferocious wind, blanketed the sky, hastening the night. The darkness only served to emphasise the whiteness of the sea with its towering overhanging waves. Dense foam streaked the sea in the

93

maelstrom of the terror that stalked them. A huge wave hit the ship. The *Hope* shuddered. Spray rose high. A deluge of water swept across the deck and poured from the opposite side of the ship. Katherine was aware of someone swept past her by the force. Yells of alarm, cries for help and orders from the captain rang out, only to be torn away in the howling wind. Soaked by the spray from the pounding waves, hanging on grimly to the support she had found, Katherine looked around wildly for help. Men were fighting to launch boats only to see them smashed by the sea. Even if they had reached the water intact there was little hope of anyone getting on board.

Harold Mulgrave stared out of the window of his cottage in the tiny village of Robin Hood's Bay. Among the huddle of houses that clung to the cliffside, his gave him a view of the long sweep of the bay towards the towering cliffs of Ravenscar. It was a view he never tired of even when it was lashed by a storm, as it was now.

The sea was in his blood, had been ever since his birth thirty-nine years ago in this same village. From an early age he had accompanied his father in the coble from which he earned a fisherman's living. He'd inherited that boat and now saw his own two lusty sons, Mark and Crispin, sixteen and seventeen respectively, taking the same interest as he had at their age. He had fallen in love with Mary Palmer, along with her sister Elizabeth the 'bonniest lasses' in Baytown, as Robin Hood's Bay was known locally. He'd courted her, married her and was devoted to her.

He was a sensitive man, though few would have guessed it from his rugged appearance. Broad of shoulder, thick of hand, honed that way from long hours in his coble, hauling nets and gutting fish, his face was lined and marked by the sea-wind, the salt-spray and burning sun. He looked from his window now with the eyes of a man used to searching ocean distances.

A cloud-laden sky hastened the evening towards night.

Spray, whipped from the wave crests by the strengthening wind, was beginning to cast a veil across the bay. He was lost in his thoughts. At times like this, minutes drifted away without him being aware of their passage.

Mary called from the tiny kitchen at the back of the house. Her voice cut into his preoccupation. He started and then began to move away from the window only to freeze. His eyes narrowed, piercing the distance with greater intensity.

'Mary!' His yell rang to the far corners of the house.

She dropped the spoon with which she was mixing the ingredients for a cake. The urgency and alarm in her husband's voice demanded immediate attention. As she hurried to the front room she was aware of noises from overhead and knew that Mark and Crispin had detected their father's voice.

'What it is?' she cried. She came to her husband's side and followed the direction indicated by his pointing finger.

'Yon ship's going to founder!'

She saw the black shape of a vessel close to the Ravenscar cliffs. 'Oh, no!' Her gasp was charged with alarm and fear.

The boys were beside her, transfixed by the sight of impending disaster.

'Come on! We must do something.' Harold was already starting for the door. The boys went after him.

'A rocket!' called Mary and ran after them.

'Let's hope Ben has seen it,' said Harold, shrugging himself into his jacket in the passage that led to the front door. His sons were doing likewise.

Mary was casting a supervisory eye over them. She was fearful of the danger but knew better than to try to stop them. Such moments as this were part of a sailor's lot and that of his family. Knowing that lives were at stake brought an automatic unselfish reaction to do all they could to counteract the situation. 'Be careful!' was the only caution she could make. With that her menfolk were gone.

*

The gathering storm had brought Ben Carter to his front window from which he had a panoramic view of the whole bay. Five years ago, because of the position of his house and stables at the top of the cliff, he had volunteered his services as a lookout who could ride swiftly to Whitby and alert the rescue men if any ship was in distress off Robin Hood's Bay.

The clouds were dark and heavy. The strong wind was rising and piling the waves into ever-growing walls of water that crashed ferociously on the beach and pounded the cliffs at Ravenscar as if trying to beat them down.

He took a sip at his mug of tea and eased his stance. A ship! He stiffened and peered, cursing the spray that crossed his vision. He grabbed his telescope. He was right, there was a ship.

'My God!' The sight of the helpless vessel being driven towards the jagged coast galvanised him into action. He pushed his mug on to the table and turned for the door in one movement.

He was heaving himself into his coat as he strode out of the back door. He ran to the stables, cramming a cap on his head. The stable door crashed wide open as it was torn from his hand by the wind. He ignored it, thankful that he had taken the precaution of saddling a horse in case there was an emergency, a practice he always kept if the weather was threatening. He swung into the saddle and sent the animal into a gallop towards Whitby.

Harold and his sons ran along the narrow pathway to the main road that led down to the beach.

'Shipwreck! Shipwreck!' they called loudly, hoping they would be heard above the howling wind.

They reached the end of the roadway where their coble, among others, was drawn up from the beach. They took in the huge waves that were running in towards them, fearful for the success of a launch, but they did not hesitate. They were also aware that other men were at their own cobles.

Boats were speedily run on to the sand and pushed towards the high sea. Water ran around them. They bent their backs, ignoring the wind that would drive them back and the spray and rain that soaked them.

'Heave!' Harold yelled, judging a moment when the receding water could help them meet the oncoming wave. It lifted the boat. The three of them pulled themselves over the gunwale. Mark and Crispin grabbed an oar each and their father took the tiller. 'Pull!' he shouted, judging the moment when they would meet the wave running down upon them. It struck. The boat shuddered and swirled. The three men fought hard to keep it head on to the next wave. They succeeded and made a few yards' progress but lost it all under the mountain of water that struck them. As the wave broke it bore them back to the beach. The boat grounded, was lifted again to be stranded on the sand. They were swiftly out of it and heaving to catch the returning water.

How many times this was repeated no one ever knew but finally, with not one coble launched, they had to admit defeat. Succumbing to exhaustion, men lay in the bottom of their cobles where the sea had deposited them high on the beach in a final gesture of victory.

Katherine clutched James closer. Only then was she aware of his screams. A desperate craving for life seized her. The crew were too engrossed in trying to save the ship. Other passengers had their own safety foremost in their minds. She searched for help in vain. The frightening waves were never-ending and with each one the ship shuddered. Timbers creaked, cracked as they tried to withstand the onslaught of the sea.

Then she saw the dark, towering mass of jagged cliffs towards which the sea was driving them, as if the ship was a mere piece of flotsam it wanted to get rid of. She cried out, wanting someone to preserve her from the fate that reared ahead in the shape of a pounding battle between

97

raging sea and stubborn cliffs in between which the tiny *Hope* was caught. The sea lifted the vessel, heaved it forward and threw it against the rocks. The impact caused a loud crack. Timbers split, the main mast broke and crashed down across the deck. Fearful cries rang out and were swept away on the unrelenting wind. Screams pierced the howl of the storm. Wave after wave broke across the ship, helpless at the foot of the cliffs. She could offer no resistance. Her fate was certain. She could provide no further protection to the people on board. She surrendered.

The sea surged over her and swept everyone away. Katherine lost her grip and was flung across the deck when the ship lurched once more and broke in two, the sea sweeping over her with even greater power. James was torn from her grasp. She screamed. The waves showed no mercy. They closed over her.

'The sea's rising,' observed David.

'Aye, this is a bad 'un,' agreed Fred.

'Thank goodness those other three ships made it.'

Peter said nothing but wondered at the skill of the sailors who had brought their vessels to the safety of Whitby in a storm which was intensifying in ferocity by the minute. Huge waves were now driving in in endless lines, crashing onto the shore, pounding the stone piers and the cliffs below the abbey, casting a gossamer veil of spray over the whole town. The crests of the waves were frothing as they ran in with ever-more malevolent power.

'We're going to take a battering,' commented Fred.

'Better get off home, lad,' David advised Peter.

'He'll be better sheltered here,' countered Tom. 'That wind's mighty strong.'

'Maybe you're right,' agreed David.

The six of them stood in the doorway sheltered from the ferocious wind, hearing the crash of the sea as if it was bent on sweeping the town and its inhabitants off the map.

The sound of a galloping horse pierced the wailing of the

wind and the crashing of the waves. A figure burst from the gloom.

'Wreck! Wreck!' Ben called, hauling his horse to a halt in front of the boathouse. 'Ravenscar!'

Instantly there was action. Fred grabbed a bell and raced outside. He was almost swept off his feet by the buffeting wind, but steadied himself and ran. The men who crewed the lifeboat all lived on the west side of the river, not far from the boathouse. Nearing the first house he started ringing the bell and did not stop until he'd reached the last, then he turned, bent into the wind and made good time back to the lifeboat.

Men donned their protective clothing and raced for the West Pier and its lifeboat. Peter ran with them, eager to do anything to see the boat safely away.

Someone fell and cried out. Peter dropped to his knees beside him to help him to his feet.

'Leg's gone!' Peter saw the excruciating pain on Tom's face. 'Tell David! Someone will come!'

Peter jumped to his feet and raced for the boat. The crew were scrambling to their positions. He was down the rungs and into the boat with them.

'Tom's fallen, hurt his leg!' he yelled as he took the vacant position.

David had no time to argue. The boy shouldn't be here but there were lives at stake.

They pushed away from the pier and rowed strongly towards the roaring sea. They felt the full blast of the wind and saw the gigantic waves they had to face. There wasn't a man there who hadn't fear in his heart but it was something they suppressed and kept to themselves.

The boat reared. They held it on the crest, let it run into the trough and climb the next wave. Backs bent to steady the vessel and fight the sea that, given its will, would drive them back to the shore.

Peter was so determined to play his full part in whatever lay before them that all thought of danger had been driven from his mind. Within a few minutes his muscles were crying out for relief, his hands were sore and he was drenched to the skin. He had lost his cap and his hair streamed with water. A wave crashed over them but somehow they managed to keep afloat. David concentrated on his task of steering the boat. He recognised that the change of direction would have to be at the right time and in the right place. He set his whole mind to this, for he knew that every man in the boat realised what was expected of him. The only one he had any doubt about was young Peter, but from his first quick observations he saw the youngster was coping well, matching the man in front of him stroke for stroke and to the same rhythm.

They crested wave after wave that threatened to destroy them. Each man knew they had a battle on but people were in peril and they were determined to triumph. Backs and arms ached but with each dip of the oars they were a stroke nearer their objective. Each man concentrated on his own task, knowing that everyone else was doing the same so that they operated as a single unit.

David eyed the sea and the high waves rolling towards them, their crests streaming white. He started his man-oeuvre to bring them on to the direction he wanted. A quarter of the way into the turn they dipped into a trough, climbed the next wave, turned a little more, slipped down the slope streaked with white, climbed again, poised on the crest and looked down into a yawning abyss. They seemed suspended in time and then they were plunging down and down. It was only a matter of a few minutes but it seemed an eternity. Then they were climbing, swept up in the momentum of the sea. The boat reared as if reaching for survival. It succeeded under their skilful seamanship. They reached the top of the wave. For a moment they hung there. Time froze. David stared, his eyes widening in disbelief, his mind numb. He opened his mouth to shout but no sound came. His silent words 'My God' were more a prayer than anything else.

The next wave was big, but smaller than all they had encountered so far. As they slid down towards it he knew they would cope with it perfectly but it was the one following that had struck fear to his heart. It was huge, seemingly built on the water the previous one had discarded. He had never seen one like it. He had heard of freak waves. They were rare occurrences. Now he was faced with one. They reached the bottom of the trough, climbed the smaller wave, slid over the top and plunged down and down. It seemed they were heading for the bottom of the ocean. The wave towered over them, a gigantic wall of water foaming at its crest. It curled, threatened and then, without mercy, toppled, gathering speed as it plunged towards the boat. The force of the impact threw them over, swamped the boat and tossed it like a plaything, showing no mercy to the occupants. They were thrown into a seething cauldron of boiling water from which there was no escape.

People on shore who had defied the elements to watch the launch were transfixed with horror by the disaster. Prayers came to lips, hope hung in the air, but an ache came to their hearts with the realisation that no one could survive the enormous wave they had witnessed with disbelief.

In Robin Hood's Bay men instinctively tumbled from their shattered cobles, summoned energy from the depths of their bodies, ignored the elements lashing at them and started off along the bay towards Ravenscar. They had failed with their cobles, maybe they could do something from the shore.

They trusted Ben had seen the ship in distress and had reached Whitby but, having been absorbed in their own efforts, no one knew whether the lifeboat had reached the wreck.

Nearing the rising ground, they saw that any closer approach to the shattered ship was impossible with the sea running as it was. Bent against the wind, shielding their eyes from the rain and spray, they had to stand helpless and watch the *Hope* dashed to pieces.

As darkness settled over the scene they walked wearily back to their homes, wondering why they had seen no sign of the Whitby lifeboats. They were taken in by their wives and mothers and cosseted to counteract the extreme physical and mental demands they had been subjected to.

Stephen looked with misgiving at his wife when they heard a knock on the door. It couldn't be Peter, he would have come straight in. They had been wondering about him, hoping that he was sheltering somewhere. No doubt he would be, he was sensible.

The wind still howled, but some of the ferocity had left the storm. Now Whitby was lashed by heavy rain that bounced off the rooftops, filled the gutters and turned the streets into rivers.

Stephen went to the door. At that moment a flash of lightning brought stark shadows to a face gaunt with the grief of the unwelcome news he possessed. Stephen read the distress in it. 'Jake Fletcher! What brings you here?'

'Bad news.' His voice was low, sombre. 'Can I come in?'

Stephen started. Foreboding had numbed his mind. 'Yes, yes,' he stuttered. 'Sorry.' He stood to one side and when Jake had stepped past him, closed the door against the driving rain.

Jake removed his sodden cap and, as he followed Stephen into the room, mumbled his apologies about the wet that was dripping on to the floor. Stephen, sensing that there was much worse to come, ignored the words.

'It's Jake,' he said.

Elizabeth said nothing She saw that he was embarrassed at being there.

'Ma'am,' he said, hands clenching his cap as if trying to draw confidence from it. He shot a glance at Stephen. 'The lifeboats had to go out. The East Boat had been gone over

102

half an hour to a ship off Staithes when the West Boat was needed off Ravenscar. It met a freak wave as it left the river. It's lost. No sign of survivors.'

'Oh, those poor men.' A shadow crossed her face.

Stephen stiffened. There must be something else or why should Jake Fletcher call with news to which they had no direct connection?

'There's more.' Jake's voice lowered. 'Young Peter was on board.'

The atmosphere was charged with disbelief. Time stood still. Stephen felt his heart stop. This was not happening. It couldn't be. Peter had no right to be in that boat.

'Oh, my God.' The words driven from Elizabeth's lips pierced the air, driving away the disbelief, acknowledging the truth of Jake's statement. Her shoulders sagged. Her face drained of colour. She stared at him.

'I'm sorry,' he mumbled.

Stephen gathered his scattered thoughts. His son lost. The sea had taken him. His lips tightened in a silent curse that condemned the oceans to Hades. He felt paralysed. The future he had planned for his son, for himself and Elizabeth was gone, taken by the waves of a storm that had no mercy, that did not single out its victims.

'Why was he in the boat?' he asked in a whisper.

'He was at the boathouse when Ben Carter rode in from Baytown with the news that a ship was in distress. Tom Bond fell running for the boat. Broke his leg. Peter went in the boat instead.'

Aware that Elizabeth was reaching out aimlessly with one hand as if she wanted to know that there was someone else there, that she was not alone to take this burden that had come upon her, he stepped to her and dropped on one knee beside her. She turned her head to him. Her eyes brimmed with tears which overflowed. Her head sank against him. He enfolded her in his arms with all the love he could muster and let her weep. Though his body was drained of feeling, numbed by shock, he knew he had to find strength from somewhere. He had to overcome the vagaries of his mind which kept telling him this was not true, that at any moment his son would come through the door, yet at the same time insisted that the loss was a reality and there was nothing he could do to change it.

Elizabeth's sobbing gradually ceased, but still she clung to Stephen, needing the reassurance that he was there, that they would share this burden. Then came the realisation that the future for them would be bleak and cold. The thought of living without her beloved son was devastating. Time would be a vacuum for them. She could not comprehend it but there was nothing she could do to alter it.

Stephen looked up at Jake. He gave a small nod and moved his lips in a silent acknowledgement of a task that he he knew had ripped at Jake's heart.

He left quietly.

Stephen took Elizabeth's hands in his. Their eyes met, each seeking consolation from the other. No words were needed to express their utter desolation. Their world had collapsed. The future meant nothing to them now. They fell into each other's arms and cried.

Chapter Seven

By dawn the storm had blown itself out. The sea bore none of the fury that it had thrown at the Yorkshire coast the previous night. No tempest danced upon its waves. It lay tranquil under a quiet sky, but five bodies lay strewn on the beach among the wreckage of the lifeboat. Even as the eastern sky was showing the first signs of a new day boats were leaving the harbour to search for the rest of the lost crew. One by one they returned, successful in their objective. The bodies they found were brought to rest with those from the shore in a hall set aside to receive them, where they would remain until they were buried on the cliff top beside the parish church close to the ruined abbey.

A black pall of distress hung over the town. Life had to go on, but its tenor was muted. Folk knew that seafaring was always filled with danger but it formed an essential part of their living. Without it the port would wither, yet because of it Whitby's menfolk died. It was hard to connect the two and understand the meaning of it all.

Stephen and Elizabeth certainly couldn't as they walked to the hall to see their son. People cast them sympathetic glances. All paused in what they were doing, men removed their caps or hats, women dabbed their eyes, while Elizabeth and Stephen moved through a passage of silence. They clung to each other as they looked down on Peter, thankful he had not been marked.

They exchanged commiserations with the families of other victims but drew little comfort from that.

Word had come through from Robin Hood's Bay that the ship had been wrecked on the precipitous cliffs at Ravenscar on the south end of the bay. The Bay men had tried to launch their cobles but had been driven back by the ferocious sea that had pounded the beach. They knew those same men would already be engaged in the unenviable task of searching for bodies.

The shroud of tragedy hung over the small fishing village too. Though none of their own folk had been lost, the people of Baytown still felt a sense of deep loss, especially as their own attempts at rescue had been defeated.

Harry Mulgrave swung himself quietly out of bed so as not to disturb Mary who was still asleep. He went to the window. Dawn was sending its pale sheen across a tranquil sea. Thinking of the contrast with the storm that had hit the Yorkshire coast the previous evening, he gave a slight shake of his head. He dressed quickly. When he went on to the landing a door opened quietly.

'Pa, wait for us,' Crispin whispered.

'No, Crispin. It's no place for you. Stay with your mother.'

The boy knew better than to protest. His father had the welfare of them all in mind.

Harry went downstairs and left the house.

Throughout Robin Hood's Bay doors clunked shut, footsteps beat a rhythm on the narrow stone paths that passed for streets, or squelched through earth sodden from last night's rain. Shadowy figures hurried towards the mud-strewn roadway, Bay Bank, that plunged down the cliffside to the sands. They came together to form a stream of grim-faced men. Hardly a word passed between them, more often it was just a nod. Each knew the unwanted task that faced them. Many had done it before; others, new to it, only had the words of their neighbours to forewarn them of what lay ahead. Though many, in their heart of hearts, would have shirked the task, they accepted it as part of their life by the sea. A shipwreck could mean bodies strewn along the beach and no doubt the viciousness of last night's storm would have resulted in just that. There was little chance of survivors from the ship that had met its fate at the foot of the towering Ravenscar cliffs in the most vicious storm to lash this coast in living memory.

The men crossed the scaurs, avoiding the pools left by the retreating sea. Their steps became muted as they moved onto the sand and made their way around the bay towards the towering cliffs. Timber was scattered along the strand among torn sailcloth and personal belongings thrown ashore by the unforgiving sea.

Eyes searched ahead and when they saw solid forms each felt a pang of dismay for the stillness of these shapes went against their hopes that they would find someone alive. They started the grim task of bringing the bodies together ready for the horse and flat cart that was already making its way towards them. Each victim was handled and laid out with reverence. Tiny waves, so different from those that had cast their victims onto the beach like so many rag-dolls, now ran silently to swirl around the dead. The men of Bay Town lifted the bedraggled bodies from the rivulets of water and sodden sand and laid them higher up the beach. Never a word passed between them, each man respected the others' silence, knowing that they, like them, were almost overcome by their task.

'This one's alive!' The shout broke into an otherwise almost silent world in which only the plaintive cry of sea birds and the sigh of a regretful wind, sorry for the havoc it had caused, broke the hush. The words came as an intrusion, yet everyone on the beach welcomed them. They all hurried towards Harry who had made this unexpected announcement. He was on his knees.

'She moved an arm,' he informed them.

But now the lady was still. Her soaked clothes clung to

her. The hair strewn beside her was matted with sand. Her
face was pale, frozen in horror and dismay. Nevertheless
each man there could see that she was a bonny woman and
each hoped they were not about to witness her last moments
alive.

Her arm moved again. A low moan came from her throat.

'You're safe, ma'am,' said Harry. 'Thee's in good
hands.'

His words seemed to have penetrated a barrier for they
brought a flicker of her eyelids. Every man there held his
breath, willing her to open her eyes. Their desire was
granted a few moments later.

'You're safe, ma'am,' Harry repeated.

She turned her head and grimaced.

'Steady, ma'am. We'll soon have you to our women.
They'll help you.'

Her eyes widened. Puzzlement came to her expression as
she looked at the faces that peered down at her. Who were
these men? Why was she laid out like this? Fright gripped
her. She struggled to sit up but was held back. Alarm
surged through her as she tried to make sense of where she
was and what was happening.

'Easy, ma'am. We are here to help you.' The man's
voice was soothing. There could be no harm in that gentle
tone.

'Where am I?' Her enunciation was weak as if there was
no strength left in her.

'You're on the shore near Robin Hood's Bay, ma'am.
Do you know what happened?'

She looked bewildered, gave a feeble shake of her head.

'Best get her away,' Harry said, rising to his feet and
moving out of the group towards the two men with the
horse and cart. 'Alf, Reg, over here. This one's alive. Best
take her now.'

They were nearing the first body but turned in the direction of the group of men. The living must come before
the dead.

'Have you a name, ma'am?' asked Seth Rawlings who had taken Harold Mulgrave's place on his knees beside the victim.

'Name?' She cocked her head as if trying to drag some recollection from the depths of her mind and then shook it.

'What's that round her neck?' someone asked.

'A jet cross,' replied Seth.

'She has a bracelet too.'

Seth lifted her left wrist gently and fingered the silver bracelet. He looked at it more closely and read, 'Katherine and John.' He turned his gaze back to her. 'Are you Katherine, ma'am?'

She grunted as if she had not heard the name before and frowned in an effort to try and clear her mind.

'I think you must be Katherine, so we'll call you that.'

The subject was dropped when the cart arrived. Gentle hands lifted her on to it and then it started off in the direction of the village while the men resumed their grim task.

Alf wanted to hurry the horse but was concerned for the lady's comfort. The movement must be as gentle as possible. Reg walked beside the cart ready with words of reassurance should the stranger need them. He kept casting anxious glances at her but, after a flicker of her eyelids when she was first laid on the cart, her eyes remained closed. Reg was anxious. He did not want her to become another victim of the storm.

They reached the end of the beach and the horse clopped on to the harder ground. The cart rumbled after it. Reg hurried forward and hammered on the door of the Fisherman's Arms, standing with its back to the cliff, defying all the adverse weather that could be thrown at it.

The door was opened by Peg Harrison. She had the no-nonsense attitude developed by a woman who had lost her husband to the sea but was determined to continue running the inn in the way he had wanted. Many would call her hard but those who were close to her knew that beneath the veneer was a kind heart.

109

'Peg, we've found one alive!' The urgency in Reg's voice brought instant action.

'Bring him in.' She was already taking charge of the situation.

'It's a woman,' announced Reg.

'Well? Just the same, bring her in,' she snapped, then called over her shoulder, 'Maisie!'

A slip of a girl came running from the back of the inn. 'Yes, ma'am?' She had come to Peg as an orphan of twelve. Now seventeen, she knew Peg as a hard employer but one who was fair. Though Peg showed little outward affection for the girl, she in fact thought a lot of the youngster she had taken off the street. And Maisie knew it. She thought herself the luckiest girl in the world to have been given a home by Peg Harrison even though it meant long hours of work.

'Get Dr Bennett, quick!'

Maisie was through the door in an instant. Casting only a cursory glance at Alf and Reg, who were lifting Katherine gently from the cart, she was away up the hill as fast as she could go. Within three minutes she was gasping for breath as she hammered on the door of a house halfway up Bay Bank.

The door was opened by a girl of about her own age but before a word passed between them a middle-aged woman, long-faced and stern of features, appeared, drawn by the urgent, persistent knocking. 'What is it, girl?' she demanded haughtily.

'They've found someone alive from the wreck, ma'am. Aunt Peg wants the doctor urgently.'

'He's not here. He's with Mrs Croft,' she said, then added with a touch of disgust, 'she's having her seventh.'

Maisie waited to hear no more. She was away. A few minutes later her knocking on the door of an ill-kept house in Chapel Street brought a boy she recognised as Mrs Croft's second child to open the door.

A man's deep voice shouted impatiently, 'Who is it,

110

Midge?' amidst the wails and childish yells that assailed Maisie's ears.

'The doctor. I must see the doctor,' panted Maisie, staring at the boy.

He gawped at her. She was repeating the request when a big, burly man appeared. His stubbled face glared at her with annoyance.

'I said, who is it?' he barked, irritated that he had not received an instant answer. He pushed the boy out of the way, glowered at Maisie and said, 'Well?'

'The doctor's wanted, urgent like, Mr Croft,' she blurted.

'He can't come,' growled Seth Croft. 'Be off.'

Maisie recoiled before his dark piercing eyes. She was afraid of him. Always had been. He'd seemed so big and rough when she was little and that impression had stayed with her. But in these circumstances she knew she had to stand up to him even though she was shaking. 'He's got to!' she shouted in desperation.

'I tell you, he can't!' The fire in Seth's eyes burned more fiercely.

'He must!' yelled a defiant Maisie.

'Missus is having a baby. Now be off, I'll not tell you again.' He raised his hand menacingly.

At that moment the cry of a newborn pierced the air and resounded down the stairs. Seth spun round and thundered up the steps two at a time, leaving Maisie and his son staring at each other.

Maisie started. She had a mission to fulfil. A lady's life might depend on her. The way was clear. She took a deep breath to fortify her courage, pushed past the boy and started up the stairs.

'Hi, where's thee think thee's ganning?' Midge yelled after her, but she took no notice. He sprang but she eluded his outstretched hand.

She pushed the door through which she had seen Seth disappear. It crashed back and for a moment the organised

111

chaos that filled the room froze.

Mr Croft was by the bed holding his wife's hand. Maybe, Maisie thought, there was a tender side to him, maybe the bullying was a sham. Becky Cassidy, who readily attended all births in Baytown, was holding a crying baby, soothing it with a soft cooing voice. Maisie was surprised to see her normally severe features softened by a smile of satisfaction as if she drew pleasure from someone else's delivery, something she had never personally experienced. Dr Bennett, his face expressionless, was rolling down his shirtsleeves with a gesture that conveyed: 'Thank goodness that's all over without any complications. These two women could have managed without me. Why didn't they? Why bother me?'

Dr Bennett had come to Robin Hood's Bay from Manchester six years ago to escape the memories of the wife he had failed to save from pneumonia. A year after her death he could no longer face life there and had left for what he'd thought would be a more peaceful practice on the tranquil Yorkshire coast, only to find that its tranquillity could be fiercely disrupted as it had been by yesterday's storm.

The scene within a room cluttered with clothes, cloths bowls and towels impinged vividly on Maisie's mind for only a passing moment. The occupants stared at her in disbelief.

Before any of them could protest at her unwanted intrusion, she blurted out, 'Dr Bennett, you must come quick. There's someone alive from the wreck.'

The doctor went on fastening his cuffs. 'Someone survived?' He looked doubtful.

'Yes. The men found her on the beach. They've taken her to Aunt Peg's.'

The strength of her assertion convinced him. No one would make such a statement, nor have hunted him out, unless it was true.

The cameo unfroze. Seth turned back to his wife, Betsy tended to the child and the doctor threw some things into his bag then grabbed his coat.

'You can cope now, Miss Cassidy?' He made the query though he knew the answer.

'Yes, Doctor,' she replied, thankful that she could now organise things her own way.

'Come on, lass, let's away.'

Maisie needed no second bidding. She was down the stairs in a flash, putting her tongue out at Midge as she sped past him into the open.

Not a word passed between them as the doctor and Maisie hurried to the Fisherman's Arms. The scenario he might find was already going through his mind. A woman who had suffered the traumatic experience of a shipwreck, immersion in a raging sea, maybe a battering by rocks and exposure through a long night, was lucky to be alive, but what state must she be in?

Hearing footsteps entering the passage from the front door, Peg called, 'It that you, Maisie?'

'Yes, with the doctor.'

'Bring him straight up.'

Maisie led the way up the stairs and took him to the bedroom with its door left open.

He nodded to Peg but went straight to the bed where a young woman was lying with her eyes closed. At first glance he feared he was too late but then he detected her shallow breathing. He took her wrist in his fingers and an anxious silence filled the room.

In the few moments that passed he saw the woman had little colour but that did not disguise the fact that she was pretty with an attractive up-turn to her nose. Her oval face was framed by a mass of copper-coloured hair spread on the pillow. He pulled himself up sharp as his mind was swept back to the young wife who had once stood beside him in Manchester.

'Her pulse is very weak. She'll need careful attention if she is to survive, but I'd like to do a more thorough examination. You did well to get her out of her clothes quickly,

Peg.' He noted Maisie was gathering up a bundle from the floor where some clothes had been thrown in haste.

'Is there anything you need, doctor?' Peg asked.

'Some hot water, please.'

'I'll see to it, Aunt.' Maisie scurried away taking the clothes with her.

The doctor carried out his examination quickly but thoroughly. He was surprised to find only minor lacerations and no broken bones, but the young woman was obviously suffering from exposure and her beating by the sea.

'Do you know anything about her, Peg?' he asked as he washed his hands.

'Nothing except that her name is probably Katherine. This was round her wrist.' She showed him the bracelet. 'She has a plain gold ring on her third finger, left hand.'

'A married woman. Maybe travelling with her husband John – the name on the bracelet?'

'Possibly, but her dress was plain black, unusual for one so young. She could be a widow.'

He nodded. 'Nothing else? No bag fastened round her arm?'

'No. Only a jet necklace which is there on the table, but that tells us nothing.'

'Well, we'll have to see what she can tell us when she regains consciousness. Keep a close watch on her. I'll slip home and return shortly. It might be an idea to have some good broth ready.'

'Very well.'

Forty minutes later the doctor hurried into the Fisherman's Arms.

'Has she regained consciousness?' he asked anxiously when Peg let him in.

'Yes, about eight minutes ago.'

'Good.'

But Peg detected all was not well. There was an underlying shock to his voice. She looked at him curiously.

'Something wrong?' she asked.

'You haven't heard?'

'Heard what?'

'The Whitby lifeboat was lost with all hands last evening. The young woman upstairs is the only survivor of a double tragedy.'

'Oh, no!' Peg felt weak from shock.

'Carrier just in from Whitby brought the news. A freak wave at the entrance to the harbour overturned the boat. Not a chance for anyone.' He started up the stairs followed by Peg. 'I think I should go to Whitby to see if I can be of any help. Can you cope? I may not be back until tomorrow.'

'Of course I can, but have a look at her first.'

He entered the room. 'Now, young lady, how are you feeling?' he asked as he crossed to the bed.

The woman met his searching gaze as if she did not understand the question.

'Do you know where you are?'

She gave a little shake of her head without raising it from the pillow.

'You are in the Fisherman's Arms in Robin Hood's Bay.'

'I've told her that two or three times,' said Peg quietly. 'She didn't seem to grasp my words.'

The doctor nodded. 'Do you know your name?'

'Name?' The woman's voice had no strength.

'Yes.'

She made no response.

'We found a bracelet on your wrist. It has the name Katherine on it. Is that your name?'

She looked vacant.

'I think it must be,' said the doctor, 'so we'll call you Katherine.'

Again there was no response.

He took her wrist between his fingers. 'Do you know how you got here?'

There was a slight shake of the head.

'Were you on a ship?'

Another shake of the head.

'Were you travelling with anyone? Your husband perhaps?'

Katherine frowned. These questions were a puzzle to her.

The doctor exchanged glances with Peg and each deduced that they were thinking the same thing. He laid Katherine's arm gently on the sheet, patted her shoulder comfortingly. 'I have to go, but I will be back tomorrow. Peg will look after you. Do as she says.' He could not be certain whether Katherine had understood him. Peg followed him from the room. He did not speak until they were down the stairs.

'I believe we have a clear case of loss of memory. The trauma of the shipwreck that might have involved the loss of the person, John, named on that bracelet, has upset her mind. The experience would be catastrophic especially when coupled with that fearful sea and then exposure on the beach. She's lucky to be alive. Will you look after her until I get back tomorrow? We'll see how she is, and then decide what to do with her. Hopefully she'll recover her memory and we can get her back to her family, whoever and wherever they may be.'

'Very well, Doctor. She'll be all right with me. Anything special I should do?'

'See that she is kept warm. Try and get some food into her and jog her memory with little suggestions.'

The doctor took his leave and was soon riding in the direction of Whitby, hoping that by the time he returned the young woman would have regained her memory and that there'd be some colour back in the face that had impressed him with its beauty.

It was only when they were sure there were no more bodies to be found on the beach that the coble owners turned their attention to their own boats, righting those that had been tossed upside down by the waves and assessing the damage. No boat had escaped unscathed, but Harold Mulgrave considered himself fortunate.

His expert eye quickly assessed that there was no major damage to the boat itself, but two oars were beyond repair. He sighed and threw them to one side. He knew his sons would soon have them replaced and the boat repaired for they would want it ship-shape when their cousin Peter visited them. Whenever he came they always spent an enjoyable day sailing in the bay. Peter loved the water and was happy when he felt himself part of it. His lads knew they were destined to follow their father as fishermen, whereas Peter was marked out to use his gift for carving to keep his father's jet trade in the family. Though their destinies were established the cousins were certain that the rapport that existed between them would always be felt on the waters of the bay and sometimes beyond.

Early that evening Harry Mulgrave stood looking out of the window. His gaze ranged the distance, across the placid water, and he wondered if there were more things the men of Baytown could have done or should have done to save the lives of those people at the mercy of the storm last night.

Seeing him, and knowing his mind was troubled, Mary came to him and slipped her hand into his. He glanced sideways at her.

She gave him a sympathetic smile. 'You could not have done any more,' she said as if she had read his thoughts. Her voice was gentle as always, filled with her ability to soothe in troubled moments.

He put his arm round her shoulder in a gesture of love that told her of his appreciation of the life she had given him.

'Let's walk,' she said.

It was something they often did when the evenings held the light a little longer. They found relief and peace together at such times. Sometimes no word passed between them, but they were in full communion. This evening they strolled in the direction of the land rising towards the cliffs at Ravenscar. They reached a point where the waves of yesterday had climbed the lower reaches of the rising ground. Mary stopped mid-step. Her head was inclined as if she had heard something but was uncertain what. She half-turned, eyes reflecting her concentration. She relaxed a little but still looked puzzled.

'What is it, love?' asked Harry, curious as to what had caught his wife's attention.

His question made her doubt herself. She pursed her lips. 'I thought I heard a cry.' She shrugged her shoulders and started forward again. She had taken only three steps when she stopped abruptly. 'There, again!'

Harry shook his head. 'I didn't hear anything.'

She did not move. She listened intently. 'Harry, I'm sure I heard it again.'

They faced each other, watching for any reaction. A low sound came from the rising ground close to the sand. No word passed between them. Their expressions told each other that they had both heard it this time. As one they moved in the direction of the cry.

'Here!' Harry called as he dropped to his knees.

Mary was beside him in a couple of strides. He was already rising to his feet, lifting a boy in his arms as he did so.

'Oh, the poor mite!' she cried, holding out her arms to take the child who was shivering and sobbing.

He seemed to draw comfort from the touch of another human being, and from the movement of her gentle fingers as they brushed his forehead soothingly.

'He's soaked through and his arm is cut. He must have been on the ship ... Let's get him home, quick.' She started off, Harry falling into step beside her.

They met no one, and once in the house Mary soon had the boy out of his wet clothes and wrapped in blankets. She was thankful her sons were out visiting friends in another part of Baytown, and she able to concentrate on the foundling.

'What are we going to do?' asked Harry.

Mary looked a little wistful.

'No, we can't keep him,' he said, reading the motherly expression that had come into his wife's eyes. 'It wouldn't be fair on our boys.'

His words jolted her. 'No, of course it wouldn't. We don't want any fuss. We'll get him to Whitby right way. We have time before it's dark. Go and hire Ben Carter's trap. Say nothing to anyone. We'll let the authorities deal with this.'

Harry hurried from the house.

'Been expecting you,' said Ben when Harry put in his request.

'You have?' he said cautiously.

'Aye. I reckoned your Mary would want to be with her sister.'

Harry looked puzzled.

'Oh my God, you haven't heard?'

'Heard what?

'I've only just got the news of who was lost on the Whitby lifeboat. I assumed you'd know . . .'

'Ben, what are you talking about?'

'Your Peter was one of them.'

Harry was incredulous. He stared at Ben in disbelief. 'Peter wasn't a member of the crew. Are you sure?'

'Seems he was there when it was launched and someone was missing. He took their place.'

'My God! The trap, quick!'

Within ten minutes Harry had Mary and the child settled in it and was driving away from Robin Hood's Bay, having decided he would not delay their departure by breaking the terrible news to his wife until they were on their way.

'Mary,' he said eventually.

She turned her gaze from the child in her arms to her

husband. She knew from his tone something serious was about to be said. 'Yes?'

'Ben gave me some terrible news.'

She looked askance at him. 'Well?'

'He told me the Whitby lifeboat was lost with all hands and Peter was one of them.'

There was a moment when time hung between the unbelievable and believable, when the unexpected shock numbed both body and mind. Then the realisation of what he'd said pierced her mind. 'What?' She shook her head as if that would drive the truth away. 'It can't be true. Ben's made a mistake.'

'He assured me there's no mistake.'

'Oh, no!' Her whisper was drawn out with shock and an impotent desire to avert the truth. She felt sick. Her stomach tightened. She had gone cold.

'We'll go straight to Elizabeth's.'

'What about this little mite?' she asked automatically, her mind in a daze.

'We'll think about him after we've seen Elizabeth and Stephen. They must be grieving.'

Harry quickened the horse's pace. Not another word was spoken. Each was lost in their own thoughts of how Elizabeth and Stephen would cope with the loss of their only child, one in whom they had seen their own future reflected.

It was Stephen who opened the door to their knock. His face was drawn and gaunt. There was no life in his eyes.

'Stephen.' Mary kissed him on the cheek. Her tone expressed all the sorrow she was feeling. She stepped past him. He made no comment about the child she held by the hand. It was as if the little boy's presence had not registered on his grieving mind.

Harry, his face grave, nodded as he gripped Stephen's hand then followed Mary into the room. Elizabeth was standing with her head and hands resting on the wooden surround of the fireplace. Her shoulders shook with sobs.

Mary placed a hand on her arm. 'We've only just heard,' she whispered. 'We're so sorry.'

Elizabeth swung round. Looking directly at her sister through tear-filled eyes she desperately sought something she could never find, for nothing could replace the son she had lost. She collapsed against Mary who put her one free arm around her, hoping that she could bring some sort of consolation to her sister. It would be hard but there was nothing she would not do for her.

The two men stood silently by in the sorrow-charged atmosphere. At length Stephen stepped forward, put his hands gently on his wife's shoulders and said, 'Come, Liz, let's all sit down.' He eased her away from Mary. As she turned she stopped then looked down at the boy. Mystified, her gaze fixed on her sister. 'Who's this?'

'We found him on the shore.'

'What?'

'He was just lying there. We think he'd been washed up.'

'You mean, from the wreck?'

'Where else could he be from? He was soaked through.'

'But how could he survive?'

'It's a miracle.'

A charged silence filled the room.

Then it was broken. 'Why should he live and my Peter die?' The words came viciously from a wild-eyed Elizabeth. She stared at the child with hatred churning in her heart, then turned to her husband. 'Why?' she screamed. 'Why?'

He placed a comforting hand on her arm, looking at her with pity. Since the tragedy he had tried to see reason in it, tried to ease the pain for her though he was suffering as much. He needed her as much as she needed him. 'Liz, I don't know. I can't fathom God's ways.'

'God? There isn't a God. We've been good-living Christians yet He's done *this* to us. And He's left that child an orphan, left him to be brought up in degradation and poverty. What loving God would do that?'

'Liz, don't talk like that,' pleaded Mary. 'You don't mean it. God will give you the strength to cope.'

Her sister gave a grunt of derision.

'It's true,' said Stephen in support of his sister-in-law. 'But first we need to accept what has happened.'

'How can I accept the loss of my son? He should never have been there. Why, oh, why, was he?'

'He went because there was no one else,' said Harry comfortingly. 'He was a brave lad who did not hesitate to help.'

'And gave his life,' added Liz sarcastically, 'when there was no need. I'd rather have a live coward than a dead hero.'

'You don't mean that either,' said Mary.

'If it meant having Peter back, I would!'

Mary glanced down at the child who clung to her hand as if that would keep him safe from the hostility around him in which he played a part. She saw his troubled eyes and lips start to quiver and picked him up. He put his arms round her neck and snuggled closer, seeking sanctuary in this hostile adult world. He cast Elizabeth a suspicious glance. He was wary of her yet she saw a pleading to be liked. The gesture tugged at her heart. What had this little chap done to them? Nothing. She shouldn't hold anything against him. It wasn't his fault that Peter had died. A sympathetic expression came into her eyes. She shook her head sadly, came to him and stroked his forehead with her fingertips. He glanced at her, feeling safe in the comfort of the arms that held him. Was there safety in the touch that soothed his brow also? 'I'm sorry, little fellow, I meant you no harm.'

He looked directly into her eyes and smiled. She froze for a moment then swung round to face Stephen. There was excitement in her stance now. She was about to say something but stopped and turned back quickly to her sister. 'You're taking him to the authorities you said?'

'Yes.' Mary was puzzled. There was obviously something on her sister's mind.

'Does anyone know you have him?'

'No.'

'Then we can keep him?'

'A young woman also survived the wreck,' put in Harry.

'You think she's this little one's mother? Did she mention a child?'

'I don't know. I've heard she's suffering loss of memory.'

'Then she can't possibly look after him, even if he is hers. The authorities will put him into care. We can't let that happen. You said that we could not fathom God's ways. Well, we can't, but don't you see? He's sent this child as a replacement for Peter.'

'But, Liz . . .' Mary started.

'It's fate. You find the child, no one else knows. You call here before you go to the authorities. We are *meant* to have him.' She looked pleadingly at her husband.

Though he knew she would still suffer the loss of Peter just as he would, Stephen saw a way of easing that loss and maybe even banishing it completely as they watched this child grow up and guided him with love. Maybe he would even become a jet carver and eventually take over the business as they had planned Peter would do . . .

How old was he? Two maybe? By the time he reached Peter's age, eighteen, Elizabeth and Stephen would be in their mid-fifties. Too old? Not a bit of it. Stephen's pulse raced as he started to see the possibilities in his wife's suggestion. It would calm her, stop her dwelling on what had happened and what Peter's future might have held for them all. There would be heartaches in the immediate future but beyond that there could be much to gain. But he had to be cautious.

'How can we pass him off as ours?'

'No need. We say we've taken him to help a friend of mine from Staithes who got off with a fisherman from Northumberland when his ship put into Whitby. He's been lost at sea so she's landed on hard times and we've taken this little lad to help her out. And it suits us fine, having just lost Peter.'

Stephen gave a thoughtful nod. He saw that the advantages outweighed the problems. As far as he could see no one would question their explanation. He looked at Mary and Harry. 'What do you think?'

'We can't be certain that he belongs to this woman and he'd be better off with you than in care. From your expression I think you are hoping we'll approve. There is no doubt that Elizabeth hopes so,' replied Harry. 'What do you think, Mary?'

She met her sister's anxious gaze. Though she knew they should hand the child over to the authorities, she could not deny the pleading expression on Elizabeth's face. Her whole future depended on Mary's approval. Dare she risk destroying that? Dare she risk the mental anguish and the instability it might cause? If she said 'No', would she have that on her conscience for the rest of her life? Could she live with it, knowing she had two healthy boys and Elizabeth had none? She grimaced with doubt then nodded and said, 'Very well. But we tell no one the truth, not even brother Jack. As an attorney you know what a stickler he is for keeping to the law. If ever we learn that they are mother and son you will have to return him.'

'Very well,' agreed Elizabeth. Tension drained from the room. A tentative smile of gratitude and hope dawned through her tears of sorrow. She came to Mary. 'Oh, thank you. Let me take him.' The boy slipped into her arms naturally. He smiled at her. 'You're going to be happy with us.' She turned to Stephen, beaming. 'You'll not regret this.'

'I know I won't, love.' He came to her, kissed her on the cheek and let the child grip his thumb.

'We're a family again,' whispered Elizabeth, as much to reassure herself as anyone else. 'We'll call him Robert.'

Half an hour later the four of them had agreed on the fine details of the story about how Robert had come to live with them.

'Liz, are you sure about this?' said Stephen when Mary and Harry had gone.

'Of course I'm sure,' she replied in a tone that suggested he had asked a ridiculous question.

'All right, love. I only wanted to make certain. We shall treat him as our own.'

'Of course we will. He's ours. God sent him to us.'

She was sitting with Robert on her knee, eyes fixed on the boy. Stephen saw pleasure and love there but they were tinged with bewilderment too, as if she was trying to reconcile Robert with Peter. She glanced up at her husband, her expression secretive, as if she would close him out of her real feelings. It worried him as it was to worry him over the four days leading to the funeral. Was Peter's substitute to become so dominant in her mind he would shut out all recollection of the boy she had loved before?

'Mama. I want my mama.' The child's quiet plaintive cry cut into his thoughts.

'I'm your mama, love,' said Liz, giving the child a reassuring smile and an extra cuddle.

He looked questioningly at her, his lips trembling. It was something that was to happen regularly over the next three days, but his insistence became less and less. Both Elizabeth and Stephen drew hope from this, especially as Robert gradually began to accept them and his new impressions took over from those he had of his earlier life, locked deep in his subconscious mind.

The loss of Peter still hit them hard. His place in their hearts would never be totally eradicated. How could it be? They had devoted eighteen years to him. His clothes, his personal belongings were still there, reminders of a life taken just when it was blossoming. Could Robert ever replace Peter? What did the future hold for them all? It was something they both wondered when, before going to bed each night, they looked down on innocence asleep, lost in dreams, far from the horrors that had brought him into their lives.

Chapter Eight

Dr Roland Bennett halted his horse above Whitby. He looked back over the red roofs that tumbled towards the river. Even in the afternoon sunlight an atmosphere of gloom emanated from the town. The shock of the loss of so many lives in one tragic incident would not be eradicated easily. He'd realised that from the moment he had arrived in Whitby yesterday. His help had been appreciated though it could not go beyond words of comfort and some simple medical directions for the bereaved.

He turned his horse and sent it on its way to Robin Hood's Bay. His heart was heavy for it was at times like these he wished he had the support of his wife. Though he knew there was nothing else he could have done for Veronica, he still felt guilty that he had not saved her. His thoughts turned to the young woman he had left at the Fisherman's Arms. He must feel no guilt over her. She would survive and regain her memory. But recollections of the storm and the shipwreck might have a detrimental effect on her. If so, that would have to be faced in the future. His immediate problem was, what should he do with her?

He should take her to an institution in Whitby, but what trials and degradation might she have to face there? Something about her had told him she was from a class that would see such an institution as anathema to their standing. And there was the jet cross and the bracelet that seemed to

126

indicate she might come from a fairly well-to-do family. But to find out who they were, where she had come from or where she was going, required a return of her memory.

Reaching Robin Hood's Bay, he left his horse with Ben and then hurried down the hill to the Fisherman's Arms.

'How is she, Peg?' was his first question when he entered the inn.

'A little better. She has taken some nourishment this morning but she's still weak and at the moment wants to do nothing but sleep.'

The doctor nodded. 'Memory?' he queried.

Peg shook her head. 'No sign of it returning. She does not know where she is. She doesn't seem to have heard of Robin Hood's Bay.'

'That may not be loss of memory, merely ignorance.'

'True, but she does not remember her own surname, where she has come from, nor where she was going. She does not recall the shipwreck, and when I ask about her family she just looks vacant. We call her Katherine but that seems to mean nothing to her either.'

The doctor grimaced. 'All right, let me have a look at her.'

Peg led the way up the stairs and stood by the foot of the bed.

'Now, young lady, remember me?' He gave her a friendly smile and took her hand.

Her pale blue eyes gave no sign of recognition. Roland's memory was stirred. Those eyes were the same colour as his late wife's. He had seen hers go dull like these, but still remembered how they used to sparkle with life. Had these once done the same? They must have done. The person lying pale against the pillow was young with a beauty that must have shone from her.

'Do you know who you are?' he asked gently.

'I'm me.' The voice was weak.

'Have you a name?'

Katherine's gaze flitted to Peg then she said, 'They call

127

me Katherine.' She frowned, trying to make sense of it, and shook her head as if irritated by a contest in her mind that she had not won. She closed her eyes.

Roland looked at Peg who indicated they should leave the room. He followed her on to the landing.

'She soon tires,' said the landlady quietly.

He nodded. 'We have to decide what to do with her.'

They went downstairs where Peg took him into her parlour. 'Sit down and we'll talk about it. I'll be back in a minute.'

She returned with two glass of brandy, knowing it was the doctor's favourite.

'I expect you can do with that after your experiences in Whitby and the problem you face with yon one upstairs.'

'Thanks. You guess right, Peg.' He took a sip, appreciating the warmth it sent through him. While Peg had been absent from the room he'd recalled the thoughts he had had during his ride from Whitby. Then they had been only tentative but now he was prepared to pursue them, though he would have to wait until tomorrow before he could do anything about them.

'I'm not keen on taking her to an institution which could impair her recovery, especially as she's suffering from loss of memory. But we can't impose on you.'

'I'll do what I can as you see fit, but I do have an inn to run.'

'I appreciate that. It would help, though, if you could keep her for a few days more while I make arrangements. In that time I hope she'll gain strength so that we can move her. I wouldn't expect you to do more than that.'

'Very well. She's a bonny lass. There must be someone somewhere who is mourning her loss. Let's hope, not only for her sake but for theirs, that she soon regains her memory.'

'Thanks, Peg. I think with a rest and your good food I'll soon be able to move her.' He drained the last of his brandy and stood up. 'And thanks for that.'

*

Thoughts of Katherine kept drifting through his mind during the rest of the day and kept him awake that night until he finally fell into a shallow sleep. But even then he was not free from her nor of the other two women who competed with her and challenged her with their wraith-like hauntings.

His sister Amelia was a year older than him and throughout their childhood had always given her brother protection. It had continued during their teenage years, and even when Douglas Crane courted her and sought her hand in marriage. That marriage never took place for he was killed in a riding accident. The shock made Amelia resolve never to marry and she redoubled the attention she gave her brother, especially after the death of her mother to whom, as the devoted spinster daughter, she gave every care during her two years of her widowhood.

Sister and brother lived together, she contented with her lot, until one day he returned home and announced he was to marry Veronica Mowbray whose mother was one of his patients. Amelia was stunned by the implications of his marriage for her. Her ministrations would come second, if they were even still wanted, and she would be forever demoted to last place in Roland's affections. She gave the wedding neither her blessing nor her approval, though she did attend the splendid ceremony and reception. Neither Roland nor his bride was able to break down her dislike of Veronica nor the barrier of jealousy she threw up. She could not accept her brother's marital happiness, believing that only she knew what was best for him.

Though outwardly she mourned with Roland and followed all the conventions of the time when Veronica died of pneumonia, inwardly she rejoiced at the return of her position in his life. So overpowering were her ministrations now that he came to realise how he had been smothered by her for most of his life. So when he decided to leave Manchester and take up a practice in the remote fishing village of Robin Hood's Bay, to escape the memories the big city conjured of

129

Veronica, he'd kept the decision to himself until all the arrangements had been made.

Amelia was far from pleased but there was nothing she could do about it for as Roland pointed out, he could not renege on his move. When she said she would move with him, he shocked her even more by telling her he had already arranged for a housekeeper from among the women of Robin Hood's Bay. But if he had thought that he was putting the breadth of the country between them, he had another think coming.

Six weeks after he had settled on the Yorkshire coast, Amelia arrived on his doorstep to announce she had left Manchester and had settled in Scarborough. She would not be far away. While she had thought of taking a house in Robin Hood's Bay, her enquiries there had made her realise she could not settle in such a place. She needed the social life of a town and decided she would find it in Scarborough. Roland knew she would expect to see him often – her way of keeping an eye on him – though she did approve of his choice of housekeeper, a married woman in her sixties who came, with the approval of her fisherman husband, to run his house every day.

As Roland sat having his breakfast now he wondered what his sister's reaction would be to what he had in mind for the young woman who reminded him so much of his beloved Veronica.

Had fate played him another hand? It had brought him to Baytown. Had it caused the shipwreck, miraculously brought this stranger ashore and kept her alive – for him to find someone to take Veronica's place? Fanciful thoughts or not, he felt compelled to pursue the course of action he had in mind.

Accordingly, when he had finished his morning's rounds, thankfully only three short calls, he rode to Scarborough.

The sharp air of a bright day invigorated him, made him feel good and heightened his determination to persuade his sister to participate in his plan.

130

He stabled his horse at the hostelry he had used on other occasions and walked to the house in Castlegate. His use of the brass knocker on the front door was soon answered by a smartly dressed maid.

'Good day, Dr Bennett,' she said, showing a little surprise at his unexpected arrival.

'Good day, Miriam. Is my sister at home?'

'Yes, sir.' She stood to one side to allow him admittance. As she closed the door she added. 'The mistress is in the kitchen talking to Cook. I'll tell her you are here. Please go into the drawing-room.'

Roland crossed the hall and was standing looking out of the window when his sister came in.

'This is a surprise, Roland. A nice one I must say.' Amelia's voice was velvety smooth and he wondered if it would remain so when he disclosed his request? She came to him, her eyes bright and with a broad smile that lessened the severity of her thin long face. Ever one to keep up with fashion, she had already adopted the new style that was beginning to prevail. It edged towards genteel and delicate rather than flouncy. Her dress was exquisitely cut with the waist lower than had, until recently, been the usual custom. The bodice had a high neck and was trimmed with folds from the shoulders, creating an angle at the waist. The skirt was plain with an unobtrusive trimming down the front. She wore a lace fichu over her shoulders.

Amelia kissed her brother on the cheek. 'You'll stay for luncheon?'

'If it is no trouble?'

'Of course not, it will be a pleasure. I'll ring for Miriam.' She tugged the bell-pull beside the fireplace.

'Miriam, tell Cook the doctor will be taking luncheon with me,' she informed the girl.

'Very good, miss.'

'Now, I suspect that there is a purpose behind this visit. Sit down and tell me about it.'

It irritated Roland that his sister had always been able to

131

read his intentions but he kept his annoyance to himself. 'Well, I have a special request to make of you,' he said tentatively.

'Ah, relying on your sister as always. You know I'll do whatever you want if it is at all possible.' She smoothed her hands across her skirt but her eyes never left her brother. 'Well, what is it?' she added when Roland hesitated.

'After you settled in here you gave some of your time to charitable works . . .'

'Yes. I was fortunately situated after my inheritance from Mother and didn't want to be idle when I came here, especially when I no longer had you to look after.'

'There was a time when among those good works you devoted some time to girls in difficult positions who might otherwise have found themselves on the streets or incarcerated in undesirable institutions?'

'Yes. I must say I influenced the future of quite a few girls and was also instrumental in founding a hostel where they would be given a chance to better themselves. A number of them benefited from the fact that they found work from there.'

'You occasionally had a girl to stay here before she went to the hostel?'

'Yes, you know that. But only in certain cases where it was thought beneficial to the girl.' She knitted her brows in a puzzled frown. 'What is this leading to, Roland?'

'A ship was wrecked at Ravenscar in that storm. The following morning the men of Baytown found one survivor. It was a miracle she had lived though what must have been a terrible trauma. She is recovering at the Fisherman's Arms.'

'How does this concern me?'

'Physically she is little the worse for her ordeal. Nothing that care and attention won't take care of.'

'Then she'll soon be able to go home, wherever that may be.'

'That's just it, we don't know and she has not been able

132

to tell us. You see, she appears to have lost her memory. She does not know her name and has no knowledge of where she is or where she has come from, nor does she recall the shipwreck. We surmise she is called Katherine from the name on a bracelet that was on her wrist.'

Amelia nodded and pursed her lips. 'And you want me to take her in until she recovers or is fit to pass on to the hostel or some other suitable institution? If she does not recover her memory I cannot see any possibility of her going to the hostel, it may have to be the workhouse or even an asylum.'

'God forbid it should come to either of those two! If my judgement is correct she is of some breeding. That is why I have come to you.'

'Very well, I'll see what I can do. But I must tell my cook and maid that this woman has suffered a loss of memory.'

'All right, but be discreet.'

'You'll let me know when she is fit to travel?'

'Of course.'

'Are you sure you want to go, Liz?' Stephen, dressed in the sombre black suit that only saw the light of day for funerals, was concerned his wife might find the traumas of the day ahead too much.

'Of course I'll be all right, Stephen. Don't fuss.' Although she was putting on a brave face, Stephen knew that she was hurting deeply.

'Very well, my dear.' He took a watch from his waistcoat pocket. 'It's time we were going.'

She nodded, looked in the mirror and made a last-minute adjustment to the neck of her black dress. She picked up a bonnet, severe without any frills, and placed it carefully on her head before tying the black ribbon in a single bow under her chin.

They went downstairs and into the drawing-room.

'Mrs Johnson, we are going now,' said Elizabeth to the

middle-aged lady who was sitting with Robert on her knee, showing him a picture book. 'Thank you for looking after Robert.' She crossed to the boy and kissed him on the cheek. 'Mummy won't be long.'

Robert smiled at her and held out his hand which she pressed with affection.

Mrs Johnson smiled, pleased that this little boy had come into the lives of her neighbours at their time of great loss.

When Elizabeth and Stephen stepped outside they felt the oppressive atmosphere as if time had cast a pall over Whitby. The whole town was silent; even the usual cries of the seagulls seemed muted. No hammering came from the shipbuilding yards, there was no movement on any of the ships tied up at the quays, no boats plied the river. The only movement came from the people of Whitby as they walked to take their places in the cortège or went to line the streets it would follow.

The families of the victims had been unanimous in the decision not to follow the circuitous route of the hearse road but to go via Church Street to the one hundred and ninety-nine steps that led to the churchyard on top of the East Cliff. It was a hard climb carrying the coffins but there had been plenty of volunteers to be bearers for the eleven men who had given their lives for others.

The funeral procession left the boathouse near the end of the West Pier, where the bodies had been placed in their coffins. It moved along the Promenade into Haggersgate, St Ann's Staith, across the bridge and into Church Street. The streets were lined with silent sombre mourners for this tragic loss hit at the heart of every person in Whitby. The route was long for the coffin bearers but there were willing shoulders to take over. Sad though it was, each man deemed it a privilege to help carry brave souls to their final resting places. Throats were full, chests were tight, eyes were filled with tears. Slowly the bearers carried them up the one hundred and ninety-nine steps, only pausing at the levels especially made as resting places for coffins. People

134

already in the churchyard had left a channel between them to the site marked out by eleven graves dug side by side. The minister, knowing that the church was too small for such a gathering, had decided to hold the service outside.

His intonation of the prayers and his address carried to everyone. The air was strangely still on a cliff top that was never usually free from a breeze or tempestuous wind. He remarked upon it, linking it to the stillness that had come upon these men's lives in the midst of turmoil while giving their lives for others.

The coffins were lowered simultaneously. Tears streamed silently down Elizabeth's face as she watched Peter lowered to his last resting place. She gripped Stephen's hand tightly, drawing comfort and strength from it and hoping she was giving solace to him at a time when his heart too was being torn apart for the loved one he had lost and the dreams that had gone with him. In a last gesture of farewell they took the soil offered to them and let it fall from their unfeeling fingers into the grave. The dull thud numbed their brains even further. They paused, cast one last glance downwards, then Stephen exerted a little more pressure on his wife's hand and she automatically followed his lead as he turned away from the grave.

They were oblivious to the looks of silent sympathy and the tear-dimmed eyes that beamed consolation to them as they passed through the churchyard and down the steps. People still lined them all the way to the bottom. No one turned for home. They all wanted to make the climb and file quietly past the graves to pay their own final gesture of respect to the men who had taken to the sea without thought for their own safety.

Neither spoke as they walked with measured steps to their home. It was as if both had resolved that out of love and respect for their son, they would face life as he would have wanted and find comfort and joy in Robert who had come so unexpectedly into their life to take his place.

*

135

Dr Bennett was right. Peg's care and good food soon strengthened Katherine and brought colour back to her cheeks, but they did nothing to restore her memory. No matter what promptings or direct questions were made she could remember nothing of her past. That moment of recovering consciousness in the Fisherman's Arms seemed to be the start of life for her. The immediacy of the present was all she had. She could not understand what she was doing in this inn and no amount of explanation by Peg made any impression on her. After a couple of days the doctor took her outside, but the sight of the sand, the cliffs and the sea did nothing to aid the recovery of her memory. When the weather permitted he took her outside on each of the subsequent four days.

Roland did not recall the trauma for her in words, hoping instead that as they walked on the beach something might trigger off her recall. They strolled, talking idly, but he found his mind drifting to times he had shared with Veronica. To his mind they were very much alike. If only he knew more about her: where she had come from, where she was going on board that ship, who her family were? Maybe then his own future would be brighter and not lonely.

Even though Katherine lacked any memory of her past and expressed frustration about this, there was also a sense that she'd thrust it aside in order to come to terms with the present and draw what strength and well-being she could from it.

It was she who broached the subject of the future as they walked along the beach together one pleasant afternoon when a light breeze caressed the sea and the sand. 'Roland, I am grateful to you and to Peg for all you have done for me, but I cannot go on trading on the goodness of your hearts and I have no money, at least not that I know of. I have offered to help Peg in the inn but she refuses, saying, "That work isn't for the likes of you." I don't know what she means by that because I'm willing to do anything rather than remain idle.'

Roland kicked thoughtfully at some sand. 'She thinks you must come from a better background and so deserve more than serving in an inn.' He glanced out of the corner of his eye at her. 'Do you still remember nothing of your past?'

She frowned and tightened her lips in frustration, shaking her head. 'But I've got to do something.'

'I know Peg's situation and I did promise her that as soon as I thought you were well enough to go elsewhere, I would try and make arrangements.'

'And you think I am now?'

He nodded. 'Possibly.'

'What have you in mind?' She put the question with some excitement as well as wariness.

'I have been giving it some thought and think you need to go where you will be suitably looked after.'

'Roland,' she interrupted, 'I want to *do* something. I may not know who I really am, or where I came from, but I am still alive after all.'

'I know,' he said, his voice soothing, 'and have kept it in mind. I have a spinster sister living in Scarborough.'

'Scarborough? Where's that?'

'Not far. Just down the coast from here. She helped found a hostel for girls who were in trouble for various reasons. They were often found suitable work from there.'

'But I'm not in trouble,' replied Katherine indignantly. 'I don't want to go to a place like that.'

'I'm not suggesting you should. My sister sometimes took a girl into her own home for a while, depending on the circumstances and if it was thought that it would help. I am suggesting you should go to her. I have already mentioned the possibility to her and she is agreeable.'

'But what would I do for money? Your sister will have to be paid.'

'We don't need to worry about that now.'

'But it will be a worry.'

'You mustn't let it be. That will be taken of when you regain your memory. That is the most important thing and

137

I believe being with my sister will help. She and I were left reasonably well off. She occupies her time with charitable work, and you could help her with that.'

'But I would be living on her charity and yours!'

'You must not take that attitude,' replied Roland firmly. 'Regard it as all part of trying to regain your memory.'

She nodded thoughtfully. What he said made sense but it went against the grain to accept charity. Was that a call from the past? Had she always had that attitude? Did that feeling come from her parents? She dredged her mind but there was nothing there that helped.

'Katherine, may I ask you something?'

She started at the interruption to her thoughts. 'Yes.'

'I have noticed that when you become agitated or frustrated, you fiddle with the jet cross you wear round your neck. Does it mean anything to you?'

She looked down. Sure enough her fingers were toying with the cross. Mystifed, she stared at it for a moment, then looked up at Roland and shook her head. 'No.' She drew the word out as if trying to recall something.

He nodded. He had hoped that the cross might jog her memory. It must have been part of her past, otherwise she would not have been wearing it. But what part had it played?

'When will we go to see your sister?' Katherine asked quickly as if she wanted to get away from the subject of the cross.

'I will go tomorrow to make the final arrangements, and if she is agreeable we will both go the following day.'

'Peg, I don't know how I will ever repay you.' Katherine stood outside the Fisherman's Arms where Roland waited patiently for her to make her goodbyes.

'You'll repay me by making a full recovery,' replied Peg, taking Katherine in her arms and giving her an affectionate hug.

'I will,' she replied, her eyes damp. 'And I'll be back to

make my thanks proper and tell you all about myself.'

'You do that. Take care of yourself.'

'I will.' Katherine turned to Roland. 'I'm ready now.'

They walked up the hill to Ben's stables where he had the doctor's trap ready for him.

Within a few minutes they were on the road to Scarborough. Katherine looked about her, hoping that she might see something familiar in the landscape, but there was nothing to revive any memories. She enjoyed the ride, with the doctor pointing out interesting features on the way. He was pleased with her curiosity for it showed her mind was active, a good sign as there might be something here that would cause her to recall the past.

'I made all the arrangements with my sister yesterday. She will tell you what is what, but there was one thing. You will have to have a surname. We have only known you so far by the name on the bracelet you wear – Katherine. My sister and I thought that maybe Westland might be suitable. With your approval, of course?'

'Katherine Westland.' She savoured it. 'Yes.' She nodded her approval. 'Why not?'

Chapter Nine

'Good day, Miriam,' Dr Bennett said pleasantly when the girl opened the door to the house in Castlegate.

'Good day, Doctor.' She stepped to one side and bobbed a curtsey to Katherine as she walked into the hall. 'Miss Bennett is in the drawing-room.'

'Thank you.' Charles escorted Katherine to the room. He had noticed her cast a quick glance around the hall which was furnished with a small table and two straight-backed chairs, and attractively decorated with a simple floral-patterned paper. A highly polished banister rail flanked the staircase leading to the next floor. Katherine did not appear overawed by it. He got the same impression when they entered the drawing-room. It was as if she was familiar with such surroundings, a fact he noted with satisfaction.

'Amelia,' Dr Bennett greeted his sister, who placed her book carefully on the small table beside her chair and rose to her feet.

'Roland.' Her tone was dripping with sisterly affection as she came to kiss him on his cheek. She had only given the newcomer a casual glance as she concentrated her initial welcome on her brother. Whoever the girl was, Amelia was determined to make it clear from the outset that there was no place for anyone else in her brother's affections.

'This is Katherine, the young lady I was telling you about.'

Amelia turned and had to control her initial shock at seeing someone who so reminded her of Veronica, though she couldn't say that she was like her exactly. What was it? The way she held herself? Those high cheekbones? The set of her nose with a slight upturn at its tip? That sparkle in the eyes that had always appeared when something pleased Veronica or she wanted to capture someone's attention? That was it. This person wanted to make an impression, wanted to be liked. Why? Had she designs on Roland? The thoughts tumbled fast and in confusion through Amelia's mind. She pulled herself up sharp.

'I am pleased to meet you,' she managed to say. Then her mind was sharpened when she heard her brother speaking again.

'Katherine, this is my sister Amelia. I think she might be able to help you.'

'Miss Bennett, I am beholden to you.' She gave a little inclination of her head.

'My brother thinks you might benefit by spending a little time with me after your terrible ordeal.' Amelia purposely used the last two words to see if there was any reaction by Katherine. There was none that she could detect.

'I remember nothing about that though I am told I was lucky to survive a shipwreck in a ferocious storm.' Katherine did not flinch from making this statement.

Amelia gave a little smile of reassurance. 'Well, don't worry about that. We'll see if we can help restore your memory though with something more pleasant than that. Now let me take your things and I'll ring for some refreshment.' She went to the pull beside the fireplace and then came to Roland who was helping Katherine out of her coat.

Katherine smiled her thanks, undid her bonnet and handed it to Amelia. There was a tap on the door and it was opened by Miriam.

'Miriam, we'll have some tea, please.'

'Yes, miss.'

'Take these.' She held out Katherine's coat and bonnet.

141

'Put them in Mrs Westland's room.'

'Yes, miss.'

'Katherine,' Amelia started then hesitated only a fraction before adding, 'you don't mind me calling you by your Christian name? I think it will make for a more amiable relationship.'

'Of course I don't.' Katherine smiled sweetly.

'I'll show you your room and the rest of the house after we have had some tea. Now, do sit down.' She glanced at her brother. 'I took it that you would be staying the night so had your usual room prepared.'

'Thank you. I will have to be away early in the morning.'

'Just give me a time and I will be up to see you go.'

Protests sprang to Roland's lips but he knew it was useless to utter them. No matter what time of day or night he left Amelia's house she would always see him go and no doubt have the usual parcel of baking for him, as if she didn't trust his housekeeper to feed him well.

Over tea, Roland was observant of his sister's line of conversation designed to make Katherine feel comfortable and at the same time occasionally probe for information about her family and her past, but none was forthcoming. He also kept his attention on Katherine's reactions as she was familiarised with the house. As she showed appreciation of things of beauty and elegance he came to the conclusion that, in the past, she had moved in similar surroundings. She seemed at ease here.

'You are indeed fortunate with your cook,' Katherine commented during the evening meal.

It could have been a comment culled from the present, a reaction to the skill she'd seen demonstrated, but Roland had a feeling that it came from somewhere deeper than that. He felt sure that Katherine must have enjoyed a class of cooking above the ordinary. That she had come from a background of good living, yet when he said, 'Your family had a good cook?' it brought only a frown as if Katherine

142

was annoyed that she could not remember.

Amelia quickly changed the subject to divert her mind and occupy it with the present. 'Tomorrow, Katherine, you and I will go to buy you some clothes. You cannot exist permanently in those supplied by Peg Harrison, adequate though they are.'

'But I have no money, Amelia, and I cannot live on your generosity. I must find some work that will help me pay for these things.'

'Roland and I talked this over yesterday. You must not worry about such matters at the moment but concentrate on getting well again. After a full recovery of your memory we can discuss any repayment, but for now let's not talk about such things.'

The rest of the evening passed off pleasantly. The day's happenings, the excitement of the move to Scarborough, the overwhelming kindness she had been shown and her attempts to penetrate the fog that clouded her mind, eventually took their toll and Katherine had to excuse herself and retire to bed.

Amelia decided that she had Roland should take a night-cap together.

'She is a pleasant person,' commented Amelia.

'She is indeed,' agreed Roland, a little too enthusiastically for her liking. It confirmed what she had noticed throughout the evening. Her brother had seen similarities to his late wife and was smitten by Katherine. She knew he would be thinking, What does the difference in our age matter? It is how you feel that does. Amelia was infuriated by these thoughts. She would not lose him again.

'Pretty too.'

'Yes.'

'You know, I can see a similarity to Veronica.'

'Indeed, it is in her eyes. They sparkle and draw you in as Veronica's did.'

'Well, a word of warning, dear brother: don't *you* be drawn by them. Remember, if she recovers her memory you might learn things you'd rather not know.'

Roland made no comment on this. 'I thank you for your help,' he said instead. 'From the moment I saw her I thought that here was someone different who did not deserve to be cast into an institution just because she had lost her memory in such trying circumstances. That is why I came to you.'

'And I will do my best to help, you know that.'

'I know you will, thank you.' He finished his brandy. 'Now I must get some sleep. I have to be up early in the morning.'

'What time?'

'I must leave no later than half-past six.'

'Very well.'

'There is no need for you . . .'

Amelia's raised hand stopped him. 'Mrs Draper will not be up but I will prepare you some breakfast. You cannot make the ride to Robin Hood's Bay on an empty stomach.'

Roland made no further protest. He knew it would be useless. Besides, an early breakfast would be most acceptable and this was one aspect of his sister's smothering he could endure. He bade her good night.

After the door closed Amelia poured herself another brandy and settled in her chair, her thoughts turning to the young woman who had entered their lives and was now asleep upstairs. Her future as it touched on theirs would need to be handled carefully.

'Good morning, Katherine. I hope you slept well?' Amelia was coming from her own bedroom, opposite the head of the stairs, as Katherine was walking down the passage from her room.

'I did, thank you,' she replied.

'A strange bed did not bother you?'

'No, though I did wake once and wonder where I was, but then my confused thoughts straightened themselves and I remembered I shared a roof with you and drew comfort from that.'

144

Amelia smiled. 'Kind words,' she said smoothly.

They had moved down the stairs and crossed the hall to the dining-room.

'My brother and I did not disturb you when he left?'

'No. He left early?'

'Yes. Rather than have Cook up sooner than usual, I saw to Roland's breakfast before his journey.' As they entered the dining-room Amelia added, 'Help yourself to anything you want, I had mine with my brother, but I'll sit with you, maybe have another cup of tea, and we can talk.'

Katherine went to the sideboard and selected a slice of ham. She cut herself a piece of bread which she buttered sitting at the table where a place had been set for her.

When Amelia turned from the bell-pull with which she had summoned the maid, she asked Katherine, 'Would you like some oatmeal porridge?'

Katherine gave a slight shake of her head. 'No, thank you. This will be sufficient.'

When Miriam appeared Amelia ordered tea for two and sat down at the table opposite Katherine.

'As I said yesterday, the first thing we will do is to get you some new clothes.'

'These should be adequate until I earn some money,' Katherine demurred.

'Adequate they may be, but they are not what ladies wear in the Scarborough social circles in which I mix.' Amelia inclined her head with a knowing look. 'So, there is no more to be said. New and suitable clothes it will be.'

'But I don't want charity,' protested Katherine. She felt something dragging at her mind as if this bid for independence was rooted somewhere in the past.

'It won't be charity, my dear,' replied Amelia. 'We will keep a note of what we spend and you will repay me when you can.' She hesitated slightly and added, while watching carefully for Katherine's reaction, 'When we find your family.'

Katherine shook her head. 'If only I could remember them,' she sighed, annoyed with herself that she could not.

'You will one day.' Amelia took this opening to raise a point. 'Does that ring on your finger mean anything to you?' Katherine looked down at it but said nothing. A look of bewilderment came to her face. 'Have you a husband?'

Katherine looked up slowly and met Amelia's intent enquiring gaze. She bit her lip, then gave a slow shake of her head as she said in an exasperated whisper, 'I don't know.' Dampness dimmed her eyes as she gave her hostess a forlorn look. 'Oh, Amelia, what am I to do?'

'Be patient. I'm sure that in time you will make a full recovery.'

'But how long will that take?'

'I can't tell you that. No one can. All I can say is, live for the present. Make the most of today as you know and see it.'

'But the past influences the present. For instance, if I don't know whether I have a husband or not, what if someone somewhere is searching for me?'

'Take the days one at a time. Today we'll be getting you some new clothes. Fix your mind on that. Don't tax your brain trying to remember. I'm sure one day all will be clear, and it could well happen when you least expect it.'

'I hope so. The doctor said you had helped young women in the past, have you ever come across anyone else who had lost their memory?'

'Yes.'

'How bad was she?'

'Worse than you. When she was brought to me she could barely remember one day to the next. She had to go into the home for girls that I had helped found.'

'What happened to her there?'

'She became so bad that the authorities in the hostel started proceedings to put her into an asylum.'

'How awful!' A touch of alarm had come to Katherine's voice, as if she could see this happening to her.

'Three days before she was due to go there her memory came back.'

146

'What?' Katherine stared in disbelief as if she thought Amelia was making it up.

'I assure you, it's true.'

'How long had she been . . .' Katherine allowed the question to hang in the air.

'Nearly a year.'

'What happened to make her memory return?'

'No one knew. It just came back. Who understands the strange ways of the mind? Now, don't you go worrying, you're not as bad as she was.' Amelia decided it was time to change the subject. 'We shall pay Mrs Dawson at four The Cliff a visit. She is regarded as the dressmaker supreme in Scarborough. She has a great deal of experience and keeps up with all the latest fashions. Day dresses, evening wear, pelisses, bonnets . . . whatever you want, she will produce. You can tell she is in great demand for she has three apprentices and two experienced dressmakers, as well as having others whom she can call on for casual work when she has more orders than she and her permanent staff can cope with. Have you any preferences for materials, styles and colour?'

Katherine tightened her lips and shook her head. She found this talk of fashion tweaking something in her mind but her brain could not form it into something definite. Had she made such choices in the past? She must have, but what and where?

'Well, never mind. We'll sort something out when we see Mrs Dawson.'

They were having their final sip of tea when there was a knock on the door and Miriam came in.

'The carriage you told me to go and order, is here, miss.'

'Thank you, Miriam. Tell him we will be there in a minute or two.'

Katherine enjoyed the ride through the narrow streets, some of which bustled with activity. People going about their

147

everyday lives called to each other or paused to talk. Housewives shopped, artisans worked on buildings, boys bowled hoops, urchins raced in chase or pulled faces at prim little girls in clean frocks holding their mother's hand. Shopkeepers called out their wares, trying to entice buyers. Katherine caught glimpses of the sea as they progressed towards The Cliff from where she had an uninterrupted view of the bay curving south. She frowned, not understanding the strange feeling that came upon her, seeing the sea rolling towards the cliffs. It only bothered her for a moment, then it was gone in her sudden awareness of the carriage coming to a halt.

The coachman jumped to the ground, hitched his horse with a quick twist of the reins around a wooden stake erected for such a purpose two paces from the front door. He assisted both ladies to the ground.

'Wait for us,' Amelia instructed him. 'We may be a little while.'

The coachman nodded and touched his forehead.

The front door of the building was to the left of three graceful twelve-paned sash windows. The windows above were even bigger and most impressive. The dark green of the door was enhanced by its white surrounds and highly polished brass knob and knocker with a brass plaque alongside announcing, 'Mrs Dawson, Highclass Dressmaker'.

Amelia rapped hard with the knocker and a few moments later the door was opened by a girl of about sixteen neatly attired in a black dress with a white lace collar at the neck and matching lace around the cuffs. She wore a bob cap small enough to allow wisps of ginger hair to show around its edges.

'We wish to see Mrs Dawson, Polly,' said Amelia, a little imperiously.

'Yes, Miss Bennett,' replied Polly,' recognising the speaker from previous visits. 'Please step this way. I will inform Mrs Dawson that you are here.'

Amelia and Katherine entered the house, paused while

148

the maid closed the door then followed her to a room on the right of the small, neatly furnished hall.

Katherine found herself in a parlour that had been papered with a subdued floral pattern, its furniture arranged to create an atmosphere in which clients would feel comfortable and welcome. Mrs Dawson clearly recognised that such an ambience made them more inclined to place good orders with her. A number of small paintings were carefully hung on the walls so that a viewer could concentrate on a particular one without feeling that any of the others intruded.

'Are you interested in the paintings?' asked Amelia, hoping that they were triggering some recollection in Katherine's mind.

'It is the first time I have seen them.'

Amelia wondered if it was an evasive answer or was it a way of saying she did not know?

'Did you ever paint?'

'I don't recall doing so.' Katherine moved to scrutinise another painting and stared at it for a few moments.

Amelia watched her, wondering what this strange young lady was really seeing in the red roofs that climbed a cliffside towards the stark ruins of an abbey painted against blue sky where a few white clouds showed traces of gold from a sun that was out of the picture.

'Where is this?' asked Katherine, her voice scarcely carrying to Amelia who had seated herself in a comfortable armchair.

'Whitby,' she replied.

'Whitby.' Katherine repeated the name to herself as if she was trying to drag some connection from the depths of her mind.

'Do you know it?' queried Amelia.

Katherine hesitated and then shook her head.

'The look you gave ...' Amelia's comment, by which she hoped she might prompt more from Katherine, was interrupted when the door opened and a tall, slim woman

149

whose dress fitted her to perfection, indicating the establishment's skills, swept in.

'My dear Miss Bennett, how nice to see you again.' Mrs Dawson's greeting was warm and friendly.

'The pleasure is mine, Mrs Dawson.' Amelia's smile was as wide. She knew of people who would frown on this type of intimacy, regarding Mrs Dawson purely as a tradeswoman, but Amelia, on coming to Scarborough and looking for a dressmaker, had quickly recognised that Mrs Dawson was a cut above the middle-of-the-road practitioners of whom there were a goodly number in this fashionable coastal town. 'May I introduce you to a friend of mine, Mrs Katherine Westland?'

'I am pleased to meet you, Mrs Westland.' The dressmaker smiled and gave a little inclination of her head. 'Do you live in Scarborough?'

Amelia was quick to step in with an explanation. 'My friend is from Manchester. She has not been well and is staying with me for a little while in order to recuperate. I thought a complete new outfit of two day dresses and an evening dress would be a good way to cast off recent misfortunes and help her face the future.'

Mrs Dawson gave a nod of understanding. 'I am sure you are right, Miss Bennett. There is nothing like a change, especially new clothes, to help we ladies cope with the trials and tribulations of this life.' But she was curious about this stranger. She had detected an odd, uneasy look in her eyes as Katherine turned from the painting of Whitby. Mrs Dawson knew better than to probe, though. To express curiosity about a client, other than in any tastes that would influence their choice of material and pattern, could be detrimental to a continuing business relationship. If a client desired to use her as a discreet listener then so be it; she would not instigate a confession or seek an opinion on a controversial matter, especially if it was personal.

Katherine felt a little awkward. She was aware that Mrs

Dawson had scrutinised her apparel and was conscious of the fact that her dress did not match the quality of the clothes worn by the other two ladies. She knew that the dressmaker must be speculating about her. But what could Katherine do? How could she answer truthfully when she did not know the answers herself?

'I will have material and patterns brought for your perusal. Will you take a cup of chocolate or maybe a glass of Madeira while we discuss your preferences?' While she was speaking Mrs Dawson had moved to the bell-pull beside the fireplace.

'I think a glass of Madeira would be most enjoyable,' replied Amelia. 'What about you, Katherine?'

She hesitated, wondering what Madeira was, but could not be sure. She was not inclined to show her ignorance so agreed with Amelia.

Mrs Dawson gave the pull four sharp tugs, waited a moment and then tugged it twice.

'I see you have not changed your signals, Mrs Dawson,' commented Amelia with a little smile.

'No. Everyone is used to them now.'

Amelia glanced at Katherine. 'Four pulls means that Mrs Dawson has a client and would like patterns and sample material to be brought.'

'And two means that I would like Madeira to be served,' Mrs Dawson took up the explanation. 'One would have signified chocolate.'

Katherine nodded but made no comment. She sat still, her hands folded neatly on her lap. Mrs Dawson adjusted the small table between the seats occupied by her customers.

There was a knock on the door. It was opened to admit a slender young woman, exquisitely dressed in a plain dark blue dress that flared slightly from a dropped waist. Her hair was brushed straight and taken back into a graceful knot. She smiled pleasantly and went to the table in the centre of the room where she placed the patterns and material she had brought with her.

151

'This is Helen, my senior assistant. She has been with me since she was thirteen. A quick learner, she soon displayed an ability that has since been recognised and treasured by many of my customers. Helen, you know Miss Bennett.'

'Indeed I do,' she replied with an engaging smile. 'It is a pleasure to see you again, Miss Bennett.' She turned her smile on Katherine.

'This is Mrs Westland, a friend of Miss Bennett's,' Mrs Dawson explained.

'I am pleased to meet you.'

'Thank you.'

The door opened and two maids came in, one carrying a tray with four glasses and the other a decanter of Madeira. They placed them on the sideboard and left the room. Helen poured and served the wine.

During the next twenty minutes, while they enjoyed their drinks, Mrs Dawson and Helen tried to ascertain Katherine's tastes.

At first she was a little evasive and not readily forth-coming, but gradually she made decisions. Amelia watched her with curiosity, wondering if she had been used to going to dressmakers of the quality of Mrs Dawson?

For one of her day dresses Katherine chose a white embroidered muslin. A spur-of-the-moment fancy or had she known one of these fashionable materials before? It was a question Amelia pondered until her attention was drawn to Mrs Dawson's suggestion for the second day dress.

'I can see a change in fashion and materials beginning to take place and think we should anticipate them in your next choice.'

Amelia saw Katherine's blank expression, as if she did not know what Mrs Dawson was talking about. Was she not aware of trends in fashion? Had that awareness vanished with her loss of memory?

'Whatever you say, Mrs Dawson,' Katherine said meekly.

'Well, a wool and silk mixture is beginning to make its appearance, and very nice it is too. Helen, have you a sample there?'

She brought a piece over. Katherine handled it and then passed it to Amelia. 'What do you think, Miss Bennett?' Her tone indicated she wanted Amelia to make a decision for her.

'It is very nice indeed, and why not keep up with the fashion?'

'Yes,' agreed Katherine.

'We have a very striking design of red and yellow roses. As you will notice, the floral motifs are tending to become larger. I think it is a most attractive effect after the smaller patterns we have been used to.' She saw that Katherine was not going to make any comment and took that for approval, quickly adding, 'Now as to the design of the dresses. What do you think, Helen?'

The young woman pondered a moment, studying Katherine briefly, though she had made most of her assessment during the previous minutes. 'I think for Mrs Westland we should keep the lines plain, relying on the embroidery and the cut to draw attraction without overlaying it with fancy lapels. We'll let it fall a little more fully from the waist, thread two one-inch ribbons of red around the lower half of the skirt. A similar but much narrower ribbon threaded round the neck-line, which we'll make a little off the point where the shoulder falls away.'

'The sleeves?' queried Mrs Dawson.

'I think it would be very elegant to anticipate the change in style we see coming, and which we can anticipate more in the second dress. Let us make the sleeves less full, not tight except at the wrists.'

'An excellent idea,' agreed Mrs Dawson. 'I think you should have a broad belt of figured silk ribbon in yellow, red and green for the muslin dress. You won't need one for the second dress because of the way we will shape the waist to fit tight. Because of the bare neck area, I suggest we

153

provide a light blue silk scarf to match your eyes, woven with floral ends of red and yellow so that it can be worn with the second dress when you don't want to wear its matching pelerine.'

Katherine accepted these suggestions and Helen took her into another room to take measurements.

Before leaving Amelia advised her to have a cloak, and then on their way home took her to a shoemaker who produced a pair for outdoor wear, one for indoors, and a pair for evening wear.

When they reached Amelia's house again and had settled down, Katherine thanked her most profusely for her generosity and help. 'You insisted that I had a pair of light evening shoes but I cannot see myself wanting those.'

'You will, my dear. There are a number of social functions we can attend.'

'But I could be faced with some awkward situations if I mix with people. Questions may be asked which I could not answer. I don't know who I am or where I come from and that could ...'

'You must not think like that,' Amelia cut in. 'You managed today. Mixing with people could help to restore your memory. If you like, I'll ask my brother's advice on that.'

'Would you, Amelia? I would be so grateful.'

'Of course I will. And if he agrees it is a good thing then we will return to Mrs Dawson and order you an evening dress.'

Katherine frowned and for one moment Amelia thought she had gone too far, too rapidly. She did not want to cause a set-back and was relieved when Katherine merely said, 'I don't know when I will ever be able to repay you.'

'One day you will, I'm sure of it.'

'I hope you are right, Amelia. I don't like this semi-world where only the present is relevant. I need to know who I am and where I come from.'

Chapter Ten

It was four days before Dr Bennett was able to go back to Scarborough. He found Amelia alone in the drawing-room and showed concern that Katherine was not there.

'She was feeling a little depressed when she came down for breakfast and said that she had had a bad night so I sent her to sit quietly in her room.'

'You thought it wise to let her be on her own?'

'I thought it might be better for her.'

'What form is her depression taking?'

'Silent spells, inability to keep up a flow of conversation, morose, inward introspection, worry and impatience at herself.'

'Because she can't recall the past?'

'Possibly. Or maybe because of her nightmare.'

'Nightmare?'

'That is what she said woke her up, she could not sleep after it.'

'It troubled her?'

'It seems it did.'

'What was this dream about?'

'She wouldn't tell me.'

'You tried to find out?'

'I did, but she would not be drawn.'

'Do you think it concerned the shipwreck?'

'I don't know. It could have been, or else something

155

from her past had disturbed her.' Amelia looked anxiously at her brother. 'I think she has a very troubled mind that will have to be handled carefully. There is no telling what may be revealed.'

Roland looked thoughtful. He remembered his first sight of Katherine and how she had reminded him so strongly then of Veronica in spite of the furies that had haunted her stricken face, how she had stirred in him a desire to know more about her, a desire he had never felt for another woman since the day he had first seen his wife and fallen in love with her. 'Would you like to bring her down so that I can talk to her and see if there is anything I can do or suggest?' he prompted.

'Very well, but before I do I must tell you that we visited Mrs Dawson to get Katherine some dresses.'

'How did that go?'

'Very well, really. At first Katherine seemed indifferent but when her enthusiasm was roused I got the impression she had known similar encounters. Then her interest waned and she was only too willing to agree to any suggestion Mrs Dawson or her assistant made, as if she wanted to be led.'

The doctor nodded thoughtfully.

'I have indicated to her that we would be going to certain social functions.'

'How did she take to that idea?'

'She was wary, fearing that she might be asked awkward questions. I said I thought it might help her recovery, but I would seek your opinion first. She seemed pleased by that.'

'Let me talk to her.'

Amelia rose from her chair and left her thoughtful brother. She returned a few minutes later accompanied by Katherine.

Roland was standing with his back to the fireplace when they came in and immediately stepped forward to greet Katherine with a warm, friendly smile. At the same time his eyes searched her face. It was pale but otherwise she looked as beautiful as ever, though the eyes perhaps lacked the sparkle he had seen in them when they had walked together in Robin Hood's Bay.

'It is good to see you again, Katherine. How have you been?'

Amelia stiffened at the anxious tone of voice and the way his concern was expressed. She said nothing but bristled inwardly as she sat down in the chair she always occupied.

Roland waited until Katherine had taken her seat before he too sat down opposite her. He noted that she seemed to have shrunk, not physically but as if she had drawn into herself. She sat primly, hands together on her lap, eyes cast down.

When he did not receive an immediate answer, Roland rephrased his enquiry, 'How are you feeling?'

Katherine hesitated and then looked up slowly to meet his searching gaze. 'I have a headache,' she answered meekly, as if she was searching for further meaning behind her own simple statement.

Roland recognised this and asked, 'What brought that on? Have you any idea?'

Katherine, wondering what she should say, bit her lip nervously.

'Didn't you sleep well?' He saw the question bring alarm to her expression. 'Was something troubling you?' When an answer was not immediately forthcoming he added, 'I can give you something for your headache, but exactly what depends on what else you can tell me.'

Katherine glanced at Amelia but could not tell from her cool expression whether she had told the doctor about the nightmare. She turned her eyes back to him. 'I had an awful nightmare.'

'Do you want to tell me about it?' He saw the colour drain from her face. 'If it bothers you don't say anything, but it may help if you can tell me,' he said kindly. 'Try,' he encouraged.

'I ... I felt as if I was in a deep, deep dark cleft with huge walls rising on either side of me. They were threatening to fall down and bury me. Then the rocky sides slowly changed into leering, laughing faces, swimming above and around me as if they were pleased with something they had done and were deriving pleasure from having me at their mercy.' She broke off, horror in her eyes at the recollection. Her voice broke. She stifled a sob.

Roland sensed there was more. Though he did not want to cause her further misery he thought it essential for him to know everything. 'Did they just disappear?'

She nodded and said, 'But not before they had returned to towering cliff-like structures which collapsed on top of me. I fought against them, trying to breathe the air they were threatening to cut off. Then I found myself immersed in water which pushed me upwards and flung me aside.' She shuddered.

'Was that when you woke up?'

'Yes.'

'How did you feel at that moment?'

'Drained of all energy.' She was embarrassed as she added words she felt a lady should not mention, 'And wet through with perspiration.'

The doctor nodded and said soothingly, 'I'm not surprised you felt like that after a nightmare of such proportions.' He pursed his lips thoughtfully and then asked, 'What is the first thing you remember in this new life of yours?'

'A bed with Peg looking down at me.'

'You did not know where you were?'

'No.'

'Do you remember the beach we walked on at Robin Hood's Bay?'

'Yes.'

'But you don't recollect being there before we were there together?'

'No.'

'I can tell you that you were conscious on that beach for a few minutes before your first recollections of the bed in the Fisherman's Arms.'

'How do you know? What was I doing there?' Katherine looked puzzled.

'You were found on the shore after a shipwreck.'

'Shipwreck?'

'You don't remember it?'

She shook her head.

'Do you remember being on a ship?'

'No.'

'I think your mind has dragged real experiences into a nightmare. The towering walls of rock were the cliffs on which you were wrecked. The faces could have been those of the men who found you on the beach, but they would not have been laughing. Can you think of anyone who might have laughed at your predicament or maybe taken pleasure in something bad that happened to you before?'

Katherine shook her head again. 'I can't remember a thing.' Her face screwed up with frustration. Tears came to her eyes. 'Oh, what can I do? What can I do?' Desperation came to her voice. She shuddered and the tears flowed. 'I want to remember ... I want to know who I am!'

'You will one day, I'm sure of it.'

'But when? When?' Her cry was filled with desperation.

'I cannot tell. No one can. But I believe this nightmare reflects events in your former life, still locked in your mind. You may have this nightmare again and there may be others, but I believe they are all part of the process of moving towards a full recovery. It may be slow progress, and I'll be honest with you, it could last weeks, months, even years. All you can do is take everything as it comes and live your life in the present.' He turned to his sister. 'Have you any immediate plans?'

'We shall walk in the town – I'll show Katherine something of Scarborough. Maybe we'll take the carriage into the countryside.'

'Good, but don't overdo things. Our patient has been through a traumatic time.'

Amelia bristled but held back the retort that came

159

instantly to her lips. As if she didn't know it! She felt like a schoolgirl in front of her teacher.

Roland looked intently at Katherine. 'Now, don't get overtired. You will gradually feel stronger and then perhaps could go to social functions and meet people. It will be good for you to do so. You might see something, hear words or experience a situation that triggers off further recollection. That could happen at any time, any place. Be patient. Now, I must be going.' He got to his feet. 'I'll visit again in a few days.' He made his goodbyes.

'I'll see you out, Roland,' said Amelia, rising from her chair. She did not speak again until they were outside the front door. 'I think maybe you should hand this case over to a doctor here in Scarborough,' she said then, rather stiffly.

'There's no need for that,' he replied swiftly. 'Katherine has no evident illness. She is suffering from loss of memory, I know, but I have first-hand knowledge of her case, having been involved from the start.'

She sensed determination in his voice. Knowing her brother as she did, she realised it was best to agree for now, then he would be easier to manipulate. 'Very well, but let me issue a warning. Don't get too involved, will you? You know nothing of her past.'

'I realise that, but I have to try to help her recover her memory.'

'Very commendable, but you don't know exactly how long that may take. Besides, you said she must live in the present – you mean, as if her life had begun in Robin Hood's Bay?'

'Yes.'

'If she follows that advice you must be ready for her to move on if she wants to, even if she has not recovered her memory.'

'We shall see. Now must be off.' He gave his sister a token kiss on the cheek and hurried away.

She watched him for a few moments, her eyes narrowed.

You don't fool me, young Roland, she thought. You see something of Veronica in Katherine and think you can recapture the past through her. Well, I'm not having our relationship upset a second time. I've given up a lot for you.

She swung on her heel and strode into the house, freshly determined to make the future go her way. Whether that was achieved through the full recovery of Katherine's memory or by some other means she would have to see.

When Katherine said goodnight to Amelia she was fearful that the terrible nightmare of the previous night might return. She reluctantly closed the door of her bedroom and immediately crossed the room to the oil lamp that had been lit by one of the servants. She turned it up, hoping to drive away the shadows that lurked in the corners. She glanced around her hesitantly. The room was silent, its atmosphere oppressive. Hostility seemed to hover in the air. Was this from the previous occupant of the room, whoever that might have been, or was it the result of her own nightmare here? Katherine's mind began to toy with all sorts of scenarios. Uncertainty accompanied them and she tried desperately to obliterate them by probing for the past. That only brought back images of the shipwreck though not in detail; she still felt she only knew of it second-hand from Dr Bennett. She forced herself to occupy her mind with preparations for bed. Still wide awake, frightened to go to sleep in case the nightmare returned, she picked up a copy of *Rob Roy* and, enthralled by the story, her personal concerns became lost in the adventure until she fell asleep.

She awoke with a start and was surprised to find the first rays of daylight beginning to filter through the lace curtains. The book lay on the bed, the lamp still burned. When she had fallen asleep she did not know but she was overjoyed that she had slept soundly and that the bad dreams had not returned.

*

Concerned about Katherine's nightmare and wondering if she had had any recurrence, Dr Bennett paid another visit to Scarborough three days later. He was reassured by Katherine's demeanour and calm response to his enquiries.

As he was leaving he said to his sister, 'She is still looking pale. I think she wants more fresh air and sun. I will come again tomorrow and take her out.'

'Roland, do no such thing so soon.' Amelia's voice was sharp. 'You must not neglect your practice in Robin Hood's Bay. You will soon have complaints if you are so frequently absent.'

'Let me be the judge of that,' came his swift retort.

'Just a friendly warning, dear brother. But there is another thing: it would be more fitting if she was better dressed. After all, you and I must keep up appearances. Wait at least until Mrs Dawson has the new dresses ready.'

'When will that be?'

'Another week.'

'Not before then?' Roland's lips tightened in exasperation.

'Mrs Dawson is making a special effort for me. I had a private word with her explaining that ...'

'I hope you gave nothing away?' he interrupted quickly. 'It could interrupt Katherine's recovery if she became the object of scrutiny.'

'Of course I didn't,' Amelia replied indignantly. 'You know as well as I do that I have always dealt discreetly with the cases of any of the young women I have helped.' She tempered her own annoyance by putting on a hurt expression.

'Amelia, I meant no criticism of you. I am concerned only for Katherine's welfare. Meanwhile I will take your advice and call again in ten days' time. If you can get her some fresh air before then, please do so.'

'I will. I agree she needs to be getting out, and once she does so I will gradually introduce her to my friends here in Scarborough which should lead to some invitations.'

'Be careful not to do that too fast,' said Roland with marked concern.

'Brother,' Amelia snapped, 'I know what I'm doing.'

He made a brief goodbye and left with a brisk step. She watched him for a few moments, mentally adding, I only hope you do.

Life for Katherine settled into a routine decreed by Amelia. Though she would have liked it to be more active Katherine made no complaint, knowing that Amelia wanted her to be suitably clad for extensive excursions. So, after two visits to Mrs Dawson's for fittings, she welcomed the day when she and her hostess could collect the completed dresses.

'If I were you, I would wear the muslin now. Peg Harrison doesn't want hers back, does she?' asked Amelia.

'No.'

'Then I'm sure Mrs Dawson can dispose of it.'

'Certainly,' replied the dressmaker. 'I'll pass it on to the needy.'

Katherine was pleased with Amelia's suggestion. She had begun to feel dowdy, having to wear the same dress all the time. Now life could take on a different aspect for her.

Amelia noticed a change in her attitude and even traces of a personality she had not witnessed before. Could this be something of the real Katherine? Could she be unconsciously behaving as she had in her past? She also detected an attractive glow about her charge. And if it had made such an impression on her, what might it do to her brother who had already shown he was attracted to Katherine, deny it though he may?

The day was fine and pleasantly warm so on the way home from Mrs Dawson's Amelia ordered the driver to stop, informed him that they would walk the rest of the way and told him to deliver the remaining package to her house in Castlegate.

As the carriage moved away she looked apologetically at Katherine. 'I hope you don't mind walking? I thought it would be good for us both.'

163

'Not at all,' came the enthusiastic reply. 'I'm sure it will be most pleasant.'

Amelia led the way to St Nicholas Cliff where groups of people stood engaged in conversation while enjoying the sunshine and the views across the harbour and along the coast.

'This is the area in which to be seen. Local people of fashion know they are likely to meet friends here. Visitors soon attach importance to the area and enjoy it for its commanding position. Visiting gentlemen like to bring their telescopes with them as you can see,' Amelia indicated four men scanning the sea for ships. She pointed out the Spa. 'One day I'll take you there and you can try the chalybeate waters. The minerals in them are attracting those seeking remedies or merely pick-me-ups. I can't say I have taken to them myself, though you may. We shall see.'

Amelia started to stroll on but then, realising that Katherine had not followed her, stopped and looked back. She saw her companion staring at the rugged coastline that ran to the south, her gaze distant and vacant. Amelia wished at that moment she could probe Katherine's mind. What was that scene conjuring up for her? Vivid events or nothing at all? She caught a glimpse of fear in Katherine's eyes but it was only momentary, as if it had intruded on other thoughts with which she was battling.

Katherine started and shivered. She saw Amelia standing waiting a few yards away. 'Oh, I'm sorry.'

'Did something bother you?' Amelia asked quietly, her eyes trying to interpret Katherine's reaction to the question.

'No.'

'You seemed far away for a moment.'

'Did I?' Katherine's tone was evasive. 'Oh, look at those riders.' She was quick to change the course of the conversation as she indicated people on horseback below on the beach who splashed through the glistening pools left by the retreating sea. 'Do you ride, Amelia?'

'No. I never had the opportunity in Manchester. What

164

about you?' She tried to probe for information again.

'No.'

Was that a definite link with the past? Had she really remembered that she didn't ride or was she being evasive again because she could not remember?

Amelia made no further comment and they strolled on.

'That is a most pretty and becoming dress,' observed Dr Bennett the next day when he arrived at his sister's, 'and I am sure that the other one will equally enhance your charms.'

Katherine inclined her head in acknowledgment of his compliment. 'Thank you, Dr Bennett.'

He held up his hands in a gesture of protest. 'I say no more than anyone would say. You look most elegant.' He admired her a little longer then added, 'And another thing: you will probably be with my sister for some time and should be regarded as one of the family. Won't you please call me Roland?'

'Only if that is what you wish,' she replied.

'It is.'

Amelia inwardly seethed at these compliments paid by her brother, and at their smooth delivery.

'It's a nice day so I'll take Katherine for a stroll,' he said. 'That is, if she would like to accompany me?'

He saw Amelia's eyes flash with annoyance at her exclusion from the invitation.

'That would be most pleasant,' replied Katherine, rising from her chair. 'I will get my pelisse.'

When she had left the room Roland looked embarrassed by the withering look his sister gave him.

'I've warned you before, and I'll do so again. Don't make a fool of yourself over this one,' she snapped.

'I did not invite you to accompany us because I think it best if I observe Katherine with no one else around,' he maintained.

Amelia gave a little sneer. 'Excuses! I know you are

165

thinking you can have Veronica back, through her, but it can't be done.'

'I don't think anything of the sort!'

'You are trying to convince yourself with your denial, but you don't fool *me*.'

Their acrimonious conversation was interrupted by Katherine's return. She had donned her pelisse and bonnet.

Roland took her on to the headland near the ruins of the Norman castle, knowing it would be quieter in that direction and they were less likely to meet any acquaintances of his.

He did not press the conversation in any direction but let it drift through various topics. He gleaned nothing that might give him a lead as to her past, for she still could not go back in time beyond finding herself in bed in the Fisherman's Arms. Her knowledge of life was confined purely to what she had gathered since then.

'What a magnificent view,' commented Katherine when they reached a point that gave them a vista along the coast to both north and south. 'I did not know there were such rugged cliffs to the north. I only saw the coast to the south when we came from Mrs Dawson's yesterday.'

'But you remember the cliffs I showed you when we walked on the beach at Robin Hood's Bay?'

'Yes.'

'Well, these are an extension of them.'

He was about to add more but left the words unspoken when he saw the look on her face. Her eyes were fixed on the cliffs to the north. In her vacant gaze he saw a momentary flash of fear. Had she recollected the terrifying ordeal she had been through? He waited, watching her intently. He did not speak, for he did not want to mar any reaction that might help the restoration of her memory. After a few minutes when she seemed to be in another world, she shivered. It brought her back to the present. She looked startled and puzzled by his presence. For one moment he thought she was going to ask him who he was but then she spoke.

'I'm sorry, Dr Bennett. I don't know what I was doing just then. It was most rude of me.'

'Think nothing of it, my dear. It is perfectly all right. You were only taking in the view.' His tone was quiet and comforting. He started to stroll again before he put the question he hoped might elicit a helpful answer. 'Do these cliffs mean anything to you?'

She shook her head. 'No.'

'They don't remind you of anything?'

She frowned. 'No. Should they?'

He shrugged his shoulders. 'I just wondered.' He saw her nervous agitation so did not pursue the matter, thinking it might disturb her. But he speculated. Hadn't there been a clear indication then that she was remembering her involvement in the shipwreck?

Katherine tossed and turned in her sleep. The sea was swelling into towering white-flecked waves. They hovered over her before, with demonic ferocity, crashing down, pounding her deeper and deeper into the depths of the ocean. Then she was pushed upwards with ever-increasing speed until she burst from the surface in a powerful upward thrust only to be caught and twisted again and again as the sea seethed around her, carrying her ever onwards towards the huge, dark and towering walls of jagged rocks. She reached out for something that the sea had torn viciously from her grasp, cried out with a penetrating shout of horror only to have it stifled by the water pouring into her mouth. She gasped for breath. Fought the whirling sea for air. It was essential that she won and recovered what she had lost. The sea dragged her away from the object it held high on the crest of a huge wave. Desperate to retrieve it, she reached out once more but the object of her concern was lost. The air was rent with her agonising cry of despair.

She sprang up in bed, her cry still ringing round the room and beyond. She drew air deep into her lungs, seeking reassurance with every breath that she had beaten the sea that would have claimed her. She was sodden with sweat as if soaked by the waters of the ocean.

The door of the room opened and the light of an oil lamp revealed Amelia's expression of alarm and concern.

'What is it, Katherine?' she cried as she hurried straight to the bed, appalled at the look of horror on the young woman's face.

Katherine shook violently and became aware of the present, of Amelia setting the lamp down, sitting on the bed to enfold her in her arms and let her sob. Tears flowed freely down her cheeks. She drew comfort from Amelia's touch. It instilled peace and drove the horrors of her disturbed rest far into the night.

'What was it?' asked Amelia soothingly.

'The sea.' Katherine shuddered.

Amelia stroked her shoulders with soothing fingers. She made no comment or further query. Let Katherine tell her as and if she wanted.

After a few more minutes Katherine straightened and her red-rimmed eyes stared at Amelia as if she sought an explanation of what was in her mind. 'The sea took something from me.' There was a frightened tone in her voice as if she feared she was to blame for the loss.

'Took something from you?' Amelia was cautious in her query.

Katherine nodded. 'Yes.'

'You don't know what?'

'No.'

Amelia hesitated, wondering how far she should pursue this topic. 'You shouldn't think any more of it,' she advised. 'It was only a nightmare.'

'But it was so horrible!'

'You must try and put it from your mind. It probably meant nothing.'

'What could I have lost?' Katherine insisted.

'I don't think you have lost anything.' Amelia tried to sound reassuring. 'It was just something that crept into your dream, probably has no significance whatsoever.' She took Katherine's hands in hers. 'You mustn't let it worry you. That would be bad for your recovery.'

Katherine nodded and gave a deep, sobbing sigh.

'I'll light your lamp. Leave it on,' said Amelia, rising from the bed. When she was satisfied that the lamp was burning steadily she looked at Katherine with a small re-assuring smile. 'Call if you want me.'

After the door had closed Katherine lay staring at the ceiling, trying to make sense of the nightmare. Her mind whirled, steadied then tumbled again. There were moments when the horror of the sea pounding the cliffs returned, but her dominant thought was focused on the fact that she imagined she had lost something to the storm and the sea. It worried her that she could not identify what it was. Finally she concluded it was only a figment of an imagination made more prominent by ... There her battle to remember stopped.

Amelia lay awake, considering Katherine's nightmare and the course of action she should take the next morning. She decided to say nothing unless Katherine did, but of one thing she was certain: she would have to report it to her brother and insist that, if there was any recurrence, Katherine should come under the attention of Amelia's own doctor in Scarborough.

When they met over breakfast Katherine was embarrassed and in a weak, tentative voice apologised for disturbing Amelia, who brushed the apology away with a dismissive wave of the hand and the words, 'Think nothing of it. I am only too glad that I was there to help. Forget the whole thing, it may never recur.'

On her brother's arrival the following afternoon, Amelia expressed surprise that he should visit again so soon.

'Is Katherine about?' he asked quietly.

'She's in her room.'

'Good. I wanted a word with you before I see her. I've

come because of what happened when we were out yesterday.' He explained Katherine's reaction on seeing the cliffs and the sea. 'I will take her out again and see if there is a similar reaction today.'

'I saw the same response when she and I were returning from the dressmaker's. Now I know you saw it too it makes me think that it is linked to what happened last night.' She went on to relate Katherine's nightmare.

'Most interesting.' Her brother looked thoughtful as he rubbed his chin. 'You say she thought the sea had taken something from her?'

'Yes. I wondered if it might be her husband – the John engraved on the bracelet?'

'That is possible, and probably the most likely explanation. Did she recall anything about her nightmare this morning?'

'No. I told her to forget it, so I think it might be wisest for you not to mention it. If you do, it could trigger off another unsavoury reaction. Also she will know that I have told you which could prevent her from taking me into her confidence in the future. We may then miss something that would aid her recovery.'

Roland agreed with his sister and later, when they took Katherine on the same walk as she and the doctor had taken on his previous visit, they saw no reaction in her at the sight of the towering cliffs. The hope that it had been a passing phase in her recovery was confounded three nights later.

The atmosphere had been heavy all day. With no breeze, the air hung oppressively over Scarborough. The night fell sooner under the dark clouds holding the district to threatening ransom. When none was forthcoming they unleashed their fury on the town. Rain lashed down, preceding the lightning that split the sky above the inland moors and sent a forewarning that it would do the same over the cliffs, the sands, and the roofs that huddled together for protection

170

beneath the promontory on which stood the ruined castle, stark and ghost-like in the last fading remnants of light.

An aura of change permeated the house in Castlegate. A pervading mood of foreboding filled the building. Katherine sat uneasily in her chair. Amelia glanced at her but hid her anxiety with a reassuring remark. 'We might have a storm but they often pass us by and move out to sea.'

Katherine made no response but a few minutes later excused herself. The hall was gloomy. She lit one of the lamps left conveniently on a table at the foot of the stairs. Satisfied that it was burning steadily, she picked it up and started up the stairs. She took each step slowly as if she feared what the immediate future held for her, yet was compelled to go on. There could be no thought of turning back. She began to feel the enveloping power of some unseen and unknown force. Light from the lamp sent slow-moving shadows along the walls ahead of her, or sent them drifting downwards to be swallowed up by the darkness in the hall.

Katherine paused at the top of the stairs. The passage ahead looked unwelcoming. It brought a hazy recollection of a passageway in another life, one which held menace yet offered escape. She frowned, shook her head as if trying to make sense of the thoughts. Menacing with what? Escape from what? How did that link with the passage along which she now started with a slow step? With each advance a little more of the darkness retreated from her. She reached the door to her room, turned the knob and pushed the door open tentatively as if she expected to be confronted by an unknown being. She held the lamp high and entered the room.

The flame was sent flickering by the rush of air from the partially open window. Shadows were sent dancing around the walls. They seemed to mock her with their flowing movements. She hesitated then stepped towards a table and placed the lamp on it. She swung round, eyes roving as if she might see something unexpected, something menacing. She crossed to the door which she had left open and closed

171

it, leaning with her back to it. She must get a grip on herself, stop letting her imagination run away with her. The room was just as she had left it. Why should it be any different?

But as she pushed herself from the door she felt the atmosphere become more oppressive. Warmth from the outside seemed to be flowing into the room, borne on the wind that had strengthened, defying her to do anything about it. But do something she would. She crossed the room to the sash-window, reached up to pull it down. As her hand touched the woodwork there was a penetrating flash of lightning. The walls of the houses outside took on the shapes of jagged towering cliffs; the rain became huge waves threatening to engulf her. The wind grasped the trailing edges of the curtains and dragged them through the window. Katherine screamed and grabbed at them but missed and was sure she had lost them forever.

Her cry, filled with horror, distress and helplessness, pierced the house. It tore through walls and closed doors, and brought Amelia leaping from her chair. She rushed across the hall and straight up the stairs in spite of the gloom. She reached the landing with screams still coming from Katherine's room. She heard footsteps at the bottom of the stairs and knew Mrs Draper and Miriam had also heard the screams. She burst into her guest's room without ceremony. A vivid flash of lightning lit up the scene: Katherine, her hands pressed to the sides of her head, was standing at the window. Her screams crashed around the room like the cries of a demented animal. The wind pulled at the curtains, threatening to tear them from their hooks.

'Katherine!' Amelia was across the room, arms coming round the young woman's shoulders, turning her away from the window. Katherine resisted. There was desperation in her struggle to reach the opening. Amelia fought to keep control.

Shocked at the sight of their mistress grappling with her guest, the others sprang to her aid. Mrs Draper grabbed

Katherine's arms, pinning them to her sides.

Amelia called to Miriam to close the window.

She ran across the room, grasped the billowing curtains, dragged them back and pulled down the sash. With the tormenting wind no longer swirling round the room, the atmosphere changed to one of stillness charged with menace. Mrs Draper and Amelia sat Katherine down on the edge of the bed. She shook hysterically, her wide eyes staring at the curtains which now hung limply. Amelia, making soothing sounds, held her tight.

'Thank you, Mrs Draper. Would you like to make Mrs Westland a hot drink?'

'Certainly, miss.' The cook rose from the bed but, before she left, mouthed silently to Amelia, 'Will you be all right?'

She nodded and turned to Miriam. 'Pass me that shawl.' She indicated a grey garment that lay on a chair beside the wardrobe.

Miriam helped Amelia to drape it comfortingly round Katherine's shoulders. She continued to shake with frightened sobs. Outside the air still throbbed with thunder and the dark sky which glowered over the town was vanquished momentarily by slashes of lightning.

'It will soon be over, Katherine,' said Amelia soothingly to the young woman who had buried her head against her shoulder. She patted Katherine's back gently. She was curious, wanted to ask questions but knew she should hold them back until Katherine was calmer. She looked at the maid. 'It will be all right now. Something must have upset Mrs Westland.'

'Maybe it was the storm, miss. I don't like storms meself. I was thankful I was with Mrs Draper.' Miriam flinched at another clap of thunder.

'It's passing,' said Amelia. 'It will soon be gone.'

'Thank goodness. I'll see if Mrs Draper has that drink ready.'

Amelia was still sitting on the bed holding Katherine

when Miriam returned with a tray of tea. Miriam took it to the table, poured the tea and brought a cup to Amelia. She eased Katherine from her, saying, 'Try this drink.'

Katherine's sobbing had gradually stopped and the comforting feel of Amelia's presence had eased the trauma in her mind, but the experience had left her drained. She nodded and reached for the cup. She sipped the tea, shuddered and took another sip.

'Feeling better?' asked Amelia gently.

Katherine gave a little nod.

'That will be all, Miriam,' said Amelia. 'Thank you for your help.'

Amelia waited patiently while Katherine finished her tea before she put any query. 'What was the matter? Did the storm frighten you?' she asked at length.

Red-rimmed eyes stared at her with a forlorn look. 'I lost him again.'

'Him?' Amelia grasped at the word. Katherine had not mentioned anyone appearing in her nightmare. Had this come about because whatever had frightened her had occurred while she was awake?

Katherine nodded.

'Who?'

Katherine shook her head. 'I don't know!' She turned pleading eyes on Amelia. 'But I want to!'

'You will one day. I'm sure you will.'

'The waves took him out of the window.' She stared across the room.

'There are no waves here,' replied Amelia. 'And there was no one here, only you.'

'Yes, there was.'

Amelia shook her head. 'No. There is only you and me, Mrs Draper and Miriam here, and we aren't anywhere near the sea.'

'But ...' Katherine broke off her protest and then, with a cry that tore at the heart, added, 'Amelia, what is happening to me?'

174

Chapter Eleven

'Roland, there could be times when I cannot accept full responsibility for Katherine. I need someone with authority to turn to if such events occur again. I know you want to supervise her condition and recovery, but I cannot reach you quickly. The natural choice is Dr Crabtree, who lives only a few doors away.'

With Katherine in bed, still weak and disturbed by her experience, Amelia had taken the opportunity to tackle her brother after relating the incident to him.

'I did not like the nightmare and its effects, but this episode was in the evening and she was wide awake. If she has further incidents like these, I fear for her sanity. It won't just be loss of memory then. If that happens, I will need immediate assistance and you are too far away for that.'

Roland knew from past experience, going back as far as the first time he was aware he had an elder sister, that she was determined to make her view prevail. As much as he wanted to keep Katherine's welfare in his own hands, he realised he would be at the receiving end of his sister's wrath if he did not comply with her wishes.

Besides, his deepest instincts told him she was right. She had agreed to help Katherine, just as she had helped girls and young ladies at other times, but he could not expect her to be responsible for someone who, if these violent assaults on her mind continued, might be sent spiralling beyond his sister's control.

'Very well, but I want to be kept informed of any recurrence of the nightmares or any daylight aberration. In fact, anything that could lead to recovery or setback, and of course anything that may shed light on her past. Now please go through the latest events again, in detail? There might be something we have missed.'

Amelia hid her exasperation at this repetition, kept her counsel and started to relate the incident from the moment Katherine's screams had alerted the house. When she reached the point where she and Katherine had sat on the bed, Amelia said, 'I asked her if it was the storm that had frightened her. Her reply was evasive.'

'I think you said she thought she had lost something?' he put in.

'That's right, just as she did after the nightmare.' Her words stopped abruptly as if something had suddenly come to mind. 'No. This time she said, "I lost him again".'

'*Him*? Are you sure of that?'

Amelia thought again before verifying her statement.

'She wears a wedding ring,' Roland reminded her. 'She was dressed in black when found on the beach. A widow? Him could refer to her dead husband. It seems most likely. She was travelling as a widow.'

Amelia noted a touch of excitement in her brother's voice. She must administer a note of caution. 'She might not necessarily be referring to a husband, she could have been in mourning for any relative. Don't jump to conclusions to suit yourself, Roland, she could still have a husband somewhere.' Her voice was stern, her gaze penetrating. 'Now you've agreed to my consulting Dr Crabtree, you'd be well advised to forget that she reminds you of Veronica and concentrate on your patients in Robin Hood's Bay.'

Roland ignored the comment but reminded her that he wanted to be kept informed of Katherine's condition.

As she watched her brother walk away from the house she spoke silently to herself: You'll be told what I want you to know, dear brother.

Twenty minutes later Amelia was pleased to find that Dr Crabtree was at home and able to see her.

He was a man in his fifties, tall and thin, with an air of authority that instilled confidence in anyone seeking his advice. Amelia had done so ever since coming to Scarborough. He lent a sympathetic ear to anything she had to say and was a great supporter of the work she did for girls and young women in need, especially connected with the hostel she had helped to found.

He listened carefully to what she had to tell him about Katherine.

'I can understand your brother wanting to be kept in touch with Mrs Westland's progress. After all, he ministered to her in Robin Hood's Bay and brought her to your care. But you did right by insisting you should have someone in Scarborough to turn to if needed. Don't hesitate to call on me. I think it might be a good idea if I made the acquaintance of this young lady informally as soon as possible.'

'Then you are invited to tea tomorrow, say at four o'clock?'

'Capital. Her condition and what she has been through must not be mentioned then, mind?'

'Very well.'

When Amelia reached home she found Katherine sitting in the drawing-room reading *Rob Roy*.

'Ah, hello, Katherine. I'm pleased to see you downstairs. Are you feeling better?'

'Hello, Amelia. Yes, I feel much better, thank you.'

'Good.' Amelia noted that Katherine's eyes were bright and her whole demeanour more confident.

'I'm sorry for all the bother I caused.'

Amelia, who had sat down beside her on the sofa, gave a dismissive wave of her hand. 'Think nothing of it. Now, tomorrow, we will have a visitor for tea at four.'

'Would you like me to retire to my room while you entertain?' Katherine asked.

'Of course not. You must start meeting people, and I thought it might be a good idea to begin with a friend of mine, Dr Crabtree.' She saw alarm flicker in Katherine's eyes and added quickly, 'It is a social call, nothing to do with your problem.' Katherine still looked doubtful. 'I assure you it has not. You'll find him a charming man who will not intrude on your private life unless he is called in professionally. Relax, and don't worry.'

But Katherine did not find that easy and became fidgety the next day as four o'clock drew near. Her unease was swept away by the doctor's charm. Never once were her traumas or the past mentioned.

'Now that wasn't so bad, was it?' said Amelia when the doctor had left.

'No.'

'Then we will do as my brother suggested – have you meet more people, visit more places, attend more functions.'

During the next six months that was exactly what happened. Katherine met more of Amelia's friends, attended the theatre, visited the Spa, walked in the fashionable areas and helped Amelia to entertain whenever she invited friends home for the evening.

With Amelia's help she mastered the art of avoiding questions about her past, using the information that Amelia imparted: that she was a friend from Manchester who had come to Scarborough to recover her health after a tragic loss had undermined it. With that, people did not press to know more. Her confidence grew and, with her mind focused on the present, she became part of the small society of Scarborough. But in the privacy of her own room she reflected on her situation and felt there was no substance to her existence when she could not relate it to the past. Amelia, keeping a watchful eye on her, saw no evidence that the past was any clearer to Katherine than on the day that Roland had brought her to Scarborough. She saw Katherine developing into a vibrant person, readily able to hold conversations and become the centre of attention. It seemed to her that the loss of memory was going to be permanent and everything would have to be related to the present. As Katherine's vitality increased, Amelia realised her brother's visits were becoming more frequent and were less to make enquiries about her health than excuses to spend time with her.

'What? Here again?' Amelia's greeting was sharp when her brother walked in unexpectedly. 'You are becoming besotted with Katherine.'

'I'm not!' Roland put on a mask of indignation.

Amelia gave a little grunt of derision. 'I'm your sister, I know you. I can read the signs. Let me warn you once again – for all we know she's a married woman. And if her memory . . .'

'Don't lecture me, Amelia. You've run my life for too long. I won't have it, I should have made a stand before.'

Amelia sneered. 'Where would you have been without me? If I wasn't looking after your interests now you'd be making a fool of yourself over her. Besides, I see no reason for her to continue being here. She is quite well enough to take up employment as she said she wanted to.'

'Work? What sort of position could she take?' rapped Roland indignantly. 'Knowing nothing of her past, we can't ascertain her capabilities. Besides we cannot take responsibility for pushing her out into an unknown world unless we're absolutely certain it is best for her.'

'Governess? Teacher? I'm sure there is someone who would welcome her. I'll start making enquiries.'

'You won't!' There was a determination in Roland's voice that surprised Amelia, for she had not heard it before.

179

Her lips tightened, eyes narrowed. 'Just listen to yourself,' she hissed. 'It's plain for anyone to see that you are besotted with her. Is she encouraging you? Does she see you as a way to a secure future even if she can't remember her past? Or is she conveniently forgetting it so she can ensnare you without any qualms?'

'Don't talk rubbish, Amelia. She's not like that. I won't listen to such talk.'

'Only because you don't want to hear the truth about yourself.' Amelia's eyes were ablaze with fury.

Roland met her anger with equal hostility.

Then Amelia's stiffness gave way. She seemed to shrink. An expression of pain dispelled her wrath. She spread her hands in entreaty. 'Roland, can't you see what is happening? She's coming between us. Don't let that happen.'

He turned and strode out without a word, letting the door crash behind him.

Amelia glared at it then slammed her hand down hard on the table. Her lips were taut, her eyes blazing. 'It won't!' she snapped. 'I'll see to that one way or another!'

On the three occasions that Roland visited Scarborough during the next two weeks he devoted all his time to Katherine, with the excuse that he was concerned for her welfare, and avoided being alone with his sister. The manoeuvring was not lost on her and she determined to take action soon.

Amelia's suggestion to Katherine that she was now well enough to take employment and move on was met with the rebuff: 'Your brother does not think that is immediately desirable. He tells me that he is on the look out for something suitable for me and will let me know immediately he finds a position. He said I shouldn't mention this to you but I thought you should know as you have been so kind. Please don't say anything to him.'

'I won't,' Amelia promised politely, but inwardly fumed at her brother for acting on his own without even consulting her on this matter. Hadn't she complied with his wishes when he was first concerned for Katherine's welfare? Hadn't she taken care of her? And for what? For her to steal Amelia's place in Roland's heart? Oh, she could read his moves. He would try and find her a position near Robin Hood's Bay. Had purposely said nothing to his sister, knowing how vehemently she would oppose that. And oppose it she would! She would find a way to destroy this relationship.

One day after they had finished their afternoon cup of tea, Amelia and Katherine were relaxing in the drawing-room, Amelia reading *The Mysteries of Udolpho* by Mrs Radcliffe, and Katherine widening her knowledge of the town through *The History and Antiquities of Scarborough* by Thomas Hinderwell, when Amelia noticed her becoming fidgety. She made no comment but a few minutes later realised the cause: the air was becoming heavy and oppressive. While pretending to be engrossed in her own book, she studied Katherine for a few minutes then placed it on the small table that stood beside her chair. Amelia rose to her feet and walked with slow deliberate steps towards the window as if she had something under consideration. Reaching the window, she stood staring out at the darkening sky.

'It looks as though we are going to have a storm,' she said casually over her shoulder.

'Oh, no!' Amelia's words had reminded her of the last storm and the recollections it had engendered. Katherine did not want another encounter like that.

With thickening clouds spreading across the town the room became more gloomy. Amelia sensed that Katherine was tense even without turning round. She smiled to herself. Awareness of the shipwreck still lurked deep in Katherine's mind. Maybe this was the time to take advantage of that.

'I'm afraid so.' Amelia wanted to strengthen the possibility in Katherine's mind. She allowed the inference behind those words to seep into the atmosphere and then quietly raised the bottom panes of the sash window a few inches. A strong breeze flapped the curtains.

Lightning momentarily lit the room with an eerie white light, leaving it even more gloomy and forbidding. Amelia straightened and stretched her shoulders as if taking in some of the charge in the air. Thunder rolled. Its vibrations penetrated Katherine's mind, bringing terrifying memories of her nightmare. She wanted to escape its power but was frozen to her seat. Her mouth opened to scream when the next crash from the sky broke over the house but the sound was stifled in her throat. She needed to close her ears but her arms were like lead, she couldn't raise her hands. Lightning blazed over the sky again and again, driving the darkness from the room only for it to return with greater intensity.

'Katherine, come and watch.' Amelia did not turn from the window. Her voice was quietly persuasive, seeming to have power to penetrate the thunderous sounds from the sky. 'Come.'

Katherine started. Someone called her. The voice was soothing, outweighing the terror in her mind. It brought feeling back to her body. She no longer wanted to escape, no longer wanted to close her ears or scream. She rose slowly from her chair.

'Come. Come to me,' the voice called.

A vivid light poured into the room. A black shape stood at the window. Katherine was transfixed. Amelia! She would be safe with her.

'Come,' the voice enticed again.

Katherine walked towards safety and peace. She reached Amelia and stood beside her, looking out through the glass. Lightning fell from the sky, thunder split the heavens. Katherine did not recoil. She stood staring out at it, peacefully removed from the scene.

'What does it remind you of, Katherine?' Amelia's voice was smooth.

She did not immediately reply.

'What?' Amelia coaxed. 'What?'

'A storm.'

'A particular storm?'

'Nightmare.'

'Any other?'

Katherine frowned as if trying to remember.

'A few nights ago?'

Katherine did not speak.

'I'm sure you remember. It was a particulary bad storm, though not as fierce as this. This one is wonderful, don't you think? But maybe you have experienced worse.' Amelia leaned close to Katherine's ear and whispered in a penetrating tone, 'The one that caused your nightmare.' Katherine shivered as something from the past momentarily shadowed her mind only to be torn away and lost in another crash of thunder. Amelia saw confusion cloud her face. 'You lost something? Someone?'

Katherine gave a little irritated shake of her head.

'You did! You did!' The voice pierced Katherine's mind, leaving no possibility of escape. 'Who was it? Where did you lose him? Him! Him!'

The room was filled with the boom of thunder and it brought demons with it.

Katherine began shaking. 'No! No! Get them off me.'

'Who?'

'The sea demons!'

'Who are they?' Amelia's voice was pressing, demanding she reply.

Katherine's eyes widened unseeingly. Amelia knew that even though they were fixed on her, Katherine's mind was focusing on something else entirely.

'Who?' Amelia grasped her arm but Katherine seemed unaware of the contact.

'Those . . . driving us on the rocks!' Katherine saw huge dark cliffs, flying foam as the sea crashed against them. 'He's gone!' Her voice rose like a mounting wave. At the moment when it paused high above her there was a resounding crash of thunder and a flash of lightning that seared deep into her mind. With it came that demanding voice: 'Who? Who? Who?' But she had no answer. It was somewhere inside her but she could not find it. With every ear-splitting crash of thunder and every jagged finger of vivid lightning that pierced the dark rolling clouds, the question was repeated over and over again by an unknown voice close to her ear. 'Who? Who? Who?'

Katherine tried to twist away from it but was held by the arm. What was holding her? She must get free. Where was she? Why was there no one to help her? There had been no one then. Why didn't they help her now? She must fight to save herself.

She struck out with her free hand, feeling flesh and bone. The grip on her arm loosened. Talon-like, her fingers curled. They dug into flesh as she pulled them downwards. She heard a cry and felt a blow to her chest. As she staggered backwards, hands pushed her harder. She stumbled against a chair, spun and crashed to the floor. She lay dazed, unaware where she was until a moment later the rumble of thunder took over the room and cleared her mind. What was she doing on the floor? Why did her chest hurt as if someone had hit her? Her clouded eyes made out a figure standing over her but no detail. Then it was gone. She struggled to make sense of everything.

She became aware of the room she was in and it came to her then that she had been here before. She heard a shout, 'Mrs Draper! Miriam!' Those names were familiar and gave her a moment's comfort. A figure appeared.

'Katherine!'

The concerned voice sounded familiar. The person was on her knees beside her.

'Katherine, it's me, Amelia.'

Her mind rapidly cleared and her eyes focused on Amelia's face. The sight of four bloodied scratches down each cheek finally brought Katherine back to the present.

The boom of thunder, the flash of lightning, were still there but they meant little now. She struggled to sit up. 'Amelia, what happened?'

Amelia ignored the question, hearing footsteps entering the room. 'Mrs Draper, Miriam, help me get Mrs Westland into a chair.' In a few moments they had Katherine sitting down.

'Miss Bennett, what happened? Your face ...' There was alarm in Mrs Draper's query. 'Miriam, hot water, lint and ointment – quick!' The girl hurried from the room. 'I think you too had better sit down, miss.'

Amelia did so. She had found a handkerchief and was patting at the blood which still trickled down her cheek. She saw Katherine staring at her with an expression of bewilderment. She wondered how much exactly Katherine remembered, but it would be her word against Amelia's and whose story was anyone likely to believe?

'We were by the window watching the storm. It seemed to affect Mrs Westland and when I suggested we should come and sit down, she turned on me with the result you can see.'

'Oh, Amelia, I'm so sorry.' Katherine bit her lip and tears welled in her eyes. 'I wouldn't hurt you for the world. I don't know what came over me, I don't remember a thing.' Her eyes fixed on Amelia's dress. 'Oh, my goodness, I've been the cause of ruining your dress.' She burst into tears. 'I didn't mean ... Can you ever forgive me?'

Miriam returned, thankful that they always kept a kettle hanging on the reckon over the fire.

Mrs Draper quickly cleaned Amelia's scratches and applied some ointment. 'I think they will be all right, miss, but I'd better send Miriam for Doctor Crabtree. Just as a precaution.'

'Maybe you are right.' Amelia smiled to herself. This suggestion coming from someone else had played nicely into her hands,

'Miriam, take these things away and then run to Dr Crabtree's and ask him to come straight away,' instructed

185

Mrs Draper. 'Can I do anything for you, Mrs Westland?' Katherine, still sobbing, shook her head. 'A cup of tea maybe?'

'No, nothing.'

Mrs Draper looked at Amelia and raised her eyebrows. Amelia, with a slight inclination of her head, indicated that she thought it better to say no more.

Mrs Draper nodded. 'If there is anything else I can do, ring for me, miss. I'll listen for Dr Crabtree's arrival.'

'Thank you, Mrs Draper.' Amelia waited until the cook had closed the door before she spoke again. 'Katherine, please stop sobbing. That won't make things any better.'

'But I've done a terrible thing and I wasn't even aware of it. I must be losing my mind. Oh, Amelia, what is happening to me?'

'It must have been the storm. Thank goodness it seems almost to have gone.'

'But why should that affect me?'

'Only you can tell us that, Katherine.'

She gave a deep sob. 'I can't! I wish I could.' She jumped from her chair and rushed to Amelia. Dropping to her knees, she looked up with plaintive eyes. 'Please help me, Amelia, please.'

She reached out and stroked Katherine's hair. 'I'll try, but you must also try and help yourself.' Katherine laid her head on Amelia's lap.

She continued to stroke her hair, seeming to comfort her, already scheming what she would say to Dr Crabtree.

Judging from Miriam's agitation that something must be terribly wrong, Dr Crabtree grabbed his hat and medical bag and hurried to Miss Bennett's. Leaving Miriam trotting in his wake, he bustled into the house. Knowing from the maid's information that he would find Amelia in the drawing-room he was across the hall in four strides. He knocked on the door and flung it open. The peaceful scene with Amelia stroking Katherine's hair pulled him up sharp.

A little bewildered by the unexpected sight, he exclaimed, 'I thought Miriam said Mrs Westland had attacked you?' When Amelia turned her head to look over her shoulder and acknowledge him, he gasped, horrified by the scratches down her cheeks. 'Miss Bennett!' He strode over to them. 'Out of the way, young lady, let me examine Miss Bennett.'

Katherine shrank back from his glare, scrambled away from Amelia and struggled to her feet.

The doctor quickly examined the scratches. 'Thankfully they are not too deep. Mrs Draper has done a good job. They will mend quickly and there will be no permanent disfiguration.' The relief in his voice vanished as he turned on Katherine, standing close by, concerned and bewildered. 'This is diabolical! You might have disfigured Miss Bennett for life. A little higher and you could have damaged her eyesight. What on earth were you thinking about?'

Tears were welling in Katherine's eyes under the lash of his tongue and the condemnation in his eyes. 'I don't know.' Her voice was scarcely above a whisper. 'I didn't realise what I was doing . . .'

'Don't talk nonsense, young lady, you must have known. Unless you are losing your mind!'

Katherine's eyes widened. She stared at him for a moment then burst into floods of tears. She ran from the room shouting, 'No! No!'

Dr Crabtree shook his head and rubbed his hand across his eyes. 'Oh, dear, I shouldn't have spoken so harshly, but the sight of what she had done to you, Miss Bennett . . . it shocked me.'

'My dear Doctor Crabtree, don't worry about it.' Amelia's voice was smoothly persuasive. 'I will explain the reason for your severity.'

'I should be grateful if you would.'

'Of course I will. Anything for a friend.'

'In the light of what you have already told me about Mrs Westland, I think you should tell me what happened here tonight?'

'Very well, but before you sit down, pour us a glass of Madeira.' She indicated the decanter and glasses that stood on a side table.

'Thank you.' Before he went to pour the wine, he closed the door. He did not speak until he was comfortably seated. 'Now, if you please, I'd like to hear the story?'

'Yes, I think it is best you should know. For Katherine's sake.'

Amelia explained the incident, leaving out her own role in it: the careful prompting aimed at disturbing Katherine's mind, though she had never anticipated an attack on herself. Now, though, she saw how advantageous that could be even though she would have to stay indoors until the marks on her face were no longer visible.

Dr Crabtree sipped his wine while he listened without making any comment, occasionally nodding his understanding. He was silent for a few moments when she had finished, trying to draw conclusions from the facts he had been given and linking them with what he already knew of Katherine. 'Obviously there is a link in her mind between the recent storm and the shipwreck in which she was involved, but I am inclined to believe that for her the trauma runs deeper than that. I am worried by the fact that she appears to have lost something, or more possibly someone as you tell me she used the word "him". That could mean someone in the shipwreck or, because she was found in mourning dress, someone in her life before that. The mind is a strange thing, we know very little about it as yet. We don't know how much Mrs Westland is relating to the past. We don't know if this attack is an isolated incident when her mind was deeply troubled or if there have been others. I must emphasise that you should be vigilant and exercise the utmost caution. If violence occurs again the consequences could be much more serious, even tragic. I could, if you wish, have her confined to an institution?'

'Oh, no, I don't think we should do that,' Amelia was quick to object, and made sure that her protest sounded genuine. No one in the future would be able to point a finger at her.

'Well, it's something to bear in mind. We cannot have you living under threat. Let me add that when I say an institution, I am not thinking of some of the places that are a blot on our society. I have a friend in Hull who is making a study of the behaviour of the mind. He runs a respectable institution which is backed by some of the wealthy philanthropists of the town. I'm sure that he would be most interested in Mrs Westland's case and be willing to have her under his supervision. I shall be visiting Hull in two days' time. Allow me to inform him of this case, and then if he is interested things will be in place for him to receive her if she has any further relapses.'

'That is considerate of you, Doctor.' Amelia smiled her thanks, inwardly rejoicing.

'Now, I must insist that you keep me informed of any unusual occurrences in Mrs Westland's life, and also if she refers to anything in her past, no matter how small. The merest detail could be important.'

'I will be sure to do that. Ah, your glass is empty, please help yourself to another.'

'Thank you.' While he was pouring the wine, he said, 'I think your brother ought to be told everything about tonight's events.'

'I intend to do so. I would not be able to give any other explanation for these scratches,' said Amelia. But she would tell Roland no more than she had told Doctor Crabtree. No one would ever know the part she herself had played in precipitating events.

'Good. If he would like to have a word with me, tell him to call. When do you expect him?'

'He could come any day. Though he agreed to my consulting you because you were close in an emergency, he still comes frequently to see how Mrs Westland is progressing.'

'It is natural for him to take an interest.'

189

'I suppose so, but I don't want him to take such an interest that his work in Robin Hood's Bay suffers! I think it might be advisable to keep the possibility of a move to Hull to ourselves. No sense in worrying Roland about something that might not be needed.'

'As you wish, Miss Bennett. Don't worry, I'm sure his work won't suffer. He'll be sensible about it, especially as he has such a loving and considerate sister.'

Amelia smiled graciously, but all the time her thoughts were on that bitch upstairs. She would see that Katherine did not take Roland away from her as Veronica had done. She could not expect an untimely death to come to her rescue again, but there were other ways for her to prevail. Especially when dear Katherine's mind was clearly not all it should be.

Chapter Twelve

Amelia sat in a pensive mood for twenty minutes after Dr Crabtree had gone, then rose slowly from her chair and went to the window. She stared unseeingly through the glass, the forefinger of her right hand idly stroking the scratches on her face. The action brought anger and hatred welling up inside her. It took all her will-power then to stop herself from casting Katherine on to the streets. No, it was not the way. Would only bring Roland's wrath down on her. There were other ways to make him see that Katherine had no place in their lives.

Calming herself, she turned from the window and walked slowly out of the room. Her steps were measured as she walked up the stairs and along the passage. She gave a light tap on the door to Katherine's room, opened it and stepped inside.

Katherine lay on the bed, her head buried in a pillow. Lost in the enormity of what she had done, she was unaware of Amelia's presence until she felt her sit on the bed and place a hand on her shoulder. She twisted over and stared at Amelia through red-rimmed eyes.

Amelia's expression gave nothing away. She wanted Katherine to speak first.

Katherine gulped, trying to control the sobs that had racked her body since she had fled the drawing-room. 'Oh, Amelia!' It was a cry from the heart. 'I am so ashamed.

Can you ever forgive me?'

'Hush now, don't think about it.' Her fingers stroked Katherine's brow.

'But I can't help it. Dr Crabtree was shocked and blamed me!'

'An instinctive reaction, before he had time to make a proper assessment of the facts. He asked me to apologise for his sudden condemnation. He meant nothing by it.'

'I can't think why I attacked you. I can't remember a thing about it.'

'The storm. Can't you remember that?'

Katherine stared vacantly at her. If she had ever been aware of it, it had vanished from her mind now and been buried along with the life she could not recall.

'There was a violent storm,' Amelia explained. 'Maybe that upset you as the others have done. Maybe they are linked for you to the storm in which you were shipwrecked. That experience could easily have upset your mind.' Her tone was low and insinuating, carefully calculated to un-balance Katherine further.

She recoiled. Horror and alarm crowded her face. 'Am I losing my mind? Oh, Amelia, what will become of me?'

'Only time will tell.'

'If only your brother could help me.'

'Leave Roland to me.'

It was three days before he appeared again in Scarborough.

During that time Katherine repeatedly expressed her worry that she could be the perpetrator of another violent act without realising what she was doing. Amelia outwardly always refused to consider the possibility – but made sure it had registered on her witnesses, Miriam and Mrs Draper.

'What on earth happened to you?' Roland asked with concern when he saw the marks on his sister's face.

He had come straight to the drawing-room on his arrival. Amelia was thankful that Katherine was in her room so she

192

was able to offer her brother an explanation without anyone else present.

'Katherine attacked me.'

'What?' He stared at her in disbelief.

'It's true,' she replied. 'Mrs Draper and Miriam can bear witness.'

He frowned. 'I'm astounded. What provoked her?'

'It was so sudden. We were standing at the window. The next thing I knew she was attacking me, with the results that you see.'

'You must have said something?'

'No.'

'Then what caused it?'

'I don't know. She doesn't know. In fact, she remembers nothing about it until she saw what she had done. The only thing I can think of is that, for some unknown reason, it was brought on by the storm that raged over Scarborough at the time.'

Roland frowned. 'Storms always seem to upset her. Did she mention anything new?'

'No. But why attack me?'

'That puzzles me. You are sure you did or said nothing to provoke her?'

'Roland!' Amelia assumed a hurt expression. 'Would I do anything like that?'

'No, no. I did not mean to condemn you.' He was quick to placate her. 'I thought perhaps an innocent remark might have upset her?'

Amelia shook her head. There had been nothing innocent about her remarks.

'You got Dr Crabtree to attend to you?' Roland enquired.

'Sent for him immediately.'

'Good. The scratches appear to be healing quite well. Did he make any comment on Katherine's behaviour?'

'In the heat of the moment he was sharp with her and she fled the room, but I assured her later he meant nothing by it.'

193

'I would not want them to be enemies, nor for her to lose confidence in him.' Roland paused thoughtfully. 'I'm worried this might happen again.'

'It may not, but we must be alert for anything untoward.'

'Are you perfectly happy for her to continue living here?'

Amelia knew that if she said she wanted Katherine to leave then he would find somewhere else for her to stay. Katherine would pass out of Amelia's supervision and directly into that of Roland. There was no telling where that would lead, especially if Katherine's memory returned and the past was clear. Amelia was not going to allow another marriage to mar her future. She would deal with Katherine in her own way and in her own time.

'Of course,' she replied.

'Good. Knowing she has you is a comfort.'

'Thank you, dear brother,' replied Amelia, and mentally added: Not if you knew my real intentions.

Any further conversation was halted when the door opened and Katherine came in. She stopped on seeing him. 'Oh, I'm sorry. I did not know you were here.' She turned to leave them.

'Wait, Katherine,' called Roland. 'There is no need for you to go. In fact, I came to suggest a walk. The air is brisk but it would refresh you.'

A troubled expression came over Katherine's face. 'You still invite me after what I did to your sister?'

'Of course. She has just explained what happened,' replied Roland gently. 'Neither of us holds it against you. I believe you did not realise what you were doing?'

Katherine shook her head. 'I didn't. It was terrible to recover and see what I had done.' Her voice tightened at the recollection.

Roland seized on the moment. 'It is best you do not dwell on it. Forget it completely.' He gave a slight pause to allow his advice to sink in. 'Now get your things and we'll go for a walk.'

Katherine nodded, thankful that the matter had not provoked anger in him nor any suggestion that she should leave, something that had worried her greatly since the incident. She looked at Amelia with a plaintive expression. 'You'll come too, Amelia? Please?'

'Of course I will.' She smiled to herself, for she could sense her brother bristle at Katherine's suggestion. 'I'll get a veil to cover my face.'

Ten minutes later as they left the house Roland suggested they should walk to the harbour.

At the end of Castlegate they took the steep steps to the end of Quay Street and made their way down towards the harbour and the shipyards. Carts laden with timber pulled by draught horses rumbled towards the shipyards from which came the sounds of mallets and saws in use. The smells of tar and newly sawn wood hung on the breeze, permeating the air along the roadway overlooking the sands. Cobles fresh from their inshore fishing were drawn up on the beach where they acted as fish stalls. Fishermen bartered with housewives or their servants over the price of cod, haddock, ling, whiting, halibut and skate, voices mingling with the cries of the seagulls that hovered overhead, hoping to sweep down and grab a tasty morsel.

Roland, observing Katherine's interest in the bustling scene, stopped and pointed to two ships under construction. 'Those two nearing completion are two-masted brigs and will probably be used in the merchant trade beyond the coasts of this country. Three of those smaller constructions are cobles and will be used by local fishermen while those two slightly larger ones will go further out to sea in search of cod for the London market.'

'A busy and thriving port,' commented Katherine.

'Indeed.'

'The best port between the Humber and the Tyne,' said Amelia. 'So I'm informed by Captain Drummond. He's sailed out of Scarborough for many years and knows not only all the ports along the Yorkshire coast but many on the Continent and Scandinavia too. By the way, he and his wife Phoebe are dining with us this evening. You'll stay, Roland?'

'I would like that, thank you.'

'Isn't Whitby more important?' The query came automatically to Katherine's lips.

Amelia and her brother exchanged quick glances.

'Do you know Whitby?' Roland enquired casually.

Katherine's puzzled frown, as if she was questioning herself, was not lost on him. He wondered if Whitby figured in her past.

She gave a slight shake of her head. 'No.' Her reply was tentative but then she added, as if pleased to find an explanation: 'Amelia, you remember that painting in Mrs Dawson's? That was of Whitby, wasn't it?'

'Yes.'

'It must have stuck in my mind. That's why I thought Whitby might be important.'

'It is, but its harbour is the river whereas here it is formed by those two piers.' Roland indicated the man-made construction built to form a safe anchorage. 'It makes for an exceptionally secure harbour that is frequently used by ocean-going vessels. Look at that three-masted barque, the *Neptune*, you can see against the East Pier. She could be bound for the Continent, or maybe homeward bound to Newcastle, but no doubt she will have made or be making a call at London. She's a fine vessel and is ...'

His voice trailed away when he saw that the colour had drained from Katherine's face. She stared with wide frightened eyes at the ship as if seeing something terrible. He looked sharply at Amelia and saw that she too had noted the change in Katherine.

Brother and sister were tense. Should they break the aura of horror that had settled around Katherine? Then her lips moved but no sound came. They watched. They waited. The few seconds seemed a lifetime. They heard a low moan followed by the faintly whispered words, 'You let him go. You lost him.' Her eyes closed as if she was trying to drive out a picture of horrific disaster. She shuddered violently, stiffened and then relaxed with a sigh. Her colour flowed back, driving away the expression of shock. Her eyes opened. They held their usual brightness. She looked steadily at her two companions. 'It is a beautiful ship.'

Queries sprang to Amelia's lips but she stifled them on receiving a signal to say nothing from her brother. He had recognised that Katherine was not aware that for a few moments she had visited a different world, one of trauma and horror. He was sure it was associated with the ship-wreck but felt it went beyond that too.

The incident was not mentioned as they continued their walk, during which Katherine was eager to learn more about Scarborough and what was happening around her.

When they reached the house in Castlegate Katherine immediately went to her room and Roland took the opportunity to tell Amelia to say nothing about the incident they had witnessed near the harbour.

'Most peculiar,' he commented. 'She went into another world and was not aware she had done so.' He shook his head sadly. 'I wish I could do something for her. It must be awful living in such uncertainty, not knowing your past, whether you have any family or relations. It must be terrible, wondering if at any moment the past might suddenly be cleared and your whole life be laid bare.'

'So be warned by your own words and don't get involved with her any more than as a medical adviser. And don't usurp Dr Crabtree's authority. He can deal with any problems immediately.'

'Let's hope there are none.'

That evening, during the visit of Captain Drummond and his wife, Roland made his observation of Katherine's behaviour discreet. She acted entirely normally, never straying beyond the bounds of convention, pleasant in both demeanour and conversation. Her only reserve came when the past was mentioned but she handled herself with skill and care. She showed no sign of the ordeal of the shipwreck, nor of the traumas it had left in its wake.

Life settled down to a comfortable pattern in the house in Castlegate. Amelia's friends visited to made invitations. Katherine was included in these and in public her personality became more vivacious. Both Amelia and Roland, whose visits were frequent, wondered how much this persona reflected the real Katherine, the person she had been before that terrible night when a ship had been pounded to oblivion on the Yorkshire coast.

As the weeks passed into months Katherine's main concern, the one she reflected on with shame in private moments, was that she was unable to contribute to the expenses she incurred. She depended on the charity of the Bennetts, but because of their insistence that the existing state of their relationship should remain, accepted their generosity. She was aware that this stemmed more strongly from Roland than Amelia, though she could not fault her hostess's outward friendship.

'Amelia, you remember Aunt Lena?'

'Father's sister?'

'Yes. I have received word she died a month ago.'

'Oh, goodness.' Amelia showed surprise rather than shock. 'We never saw much of her after she moved to Lancaster.'

'I did not understand why she went there in the first place.'

'We were young at the time but I did learn there was marriage in the offing, only her fiancé died. She was close to his parents and moved to be near them. That's why we didn't see much of her,' Amelia explained.

'Well, it seems she has not forgotten us. The solicitor in charge of her affairs has written to me saying he would like us to go to Lancaster as we are beneficiaries under her will.'

'My goodness! I haven't given her a thought in years.'

'Nor I. We must make arrangements to go.'

'What about Katherine?'

'It's over a year since her last upset. Except for the loss of memory she's quite restored. It should be perfectly all right to leave her on her own. Besides there'll be Mrs Draper and Miriam here. You can give them special instructions.'

'Very well. When do you propose to go?'

'A week today. I'll come here the day before and we'll leave from the Bell. Jack Rudston will know the time of coaches.'

'No, Roland, we'll not travel by coach. We'll be independent. Hire a post-chaise and driver. It will be more comfortable and we won't be beholden to the vagaries of coach timetables. It isn't as though we can't afford it.' Amelia's attitude signified that she was in charge and would not entertain any other suggestion.

'As you wish,' replied Roland. As usual his sister was the organiser.

'But consult Jack about the best inns en route. I'm sure as private travellers we'll receive far better attention than if we travelled by coach. I'll inform Katherine that we will be going and instruct Mrs Draper. I am sure everything will proceed as normal in our absence.'

Amelia waited until after breakfast the following morning before she told her guest of the visit to Lancaster.

Katherine, who had never been left alone since coming to the Bennetts, was apprehensive but, knowing it would be ill-mannered to voice any doubt, kept her feelings to herself.

'I'm sorry your relative has died and that your journey will therefore be a sad one.'

'An aunt we barely knew, with whom we have had no contact for goodness knows how many years, hardly merits mourning,' replied Amelia unfeelingly. 'Apparently she died some weeks ago and the funeral has already taken place. Some dunderhead of a solicitor has only just found out where we, her only relatives, are living. He needs to see us about the will. I can't imagine she would leave very much but I suppose she might have made some stipulation for us to see to the disposal of her belongings. So, tedious as it is, we'll have to go.'

'Don't give me another thought, Amelia. I will be perfectly comfortable. You make the most of your visit. It is most kind of you to allow me to stay here while you are away.'

'Where would you go? Where else could you go?' Amelia gave a dismissive wave of her hand as if the subject was not worth considering.

Katherine said, a trifle uncomfortably, 'I thank you and your brother for all your kindnesses. I lead an interesting life due to your including me in what you do. It is almost complete for me.'

'Almost?' Amelia inclined her head in query.

'It would only be that if I knew about my past. But I am beginning to think it has gone forever.' She frowned, annoyed that she still could not recall it. In her agitation she began fingering the jet cross round her neck.

Amelia noted her action and wondered if the cross held a clue to Katherine's past. 'You were wearing that when you were found on the sands at Robin Hood's Bay. You always wear it. Do you know anything about it?'

Katherine looked down at the cross, her brow puckered. She concentrated her gaze. '*It is beautiful. I am grateful for your generosity.*' The words were not spoken aloud but she was conscious of them in her mind, as if she had voiced them at some time. But when? To whom? Who had she thanked? Who had given her the jet cross? She paled. Had she imagined those words? No, that had been her voice as plain as if she had spoken aloud yet she had not uttered a word. Was the cross trying to tell her something? This had never happened before. Why should it now? Was it because

Amelia had drawn attention to it and had posed the question?

Getting no immediate reply and seeing Katherine's face lose colour, Amelia put the question again. 'Do you?'

Katherine shook her head slowly. 'No.' She bit her lip. 'I wish I did.' Her eyes clouded with a look that begged for help.

But Amelia knew she couldn't give it. She returned quickly to the subject of leaving for Lancaster to divert Katherine's mind. 'We are not going until next week. Mrs Draper will of course look after the household. There is no need for you to be bothered with anything. You must not feel tied to the house. Get out and take some sea air. I will instruct Mrs Draper to accompany you, and if she can't manage it she will tell Miriam to go with you.'

'You are most thoughtful.'

'I will also inform Dr Crabtree that I am going away so he will be aware of that if you should need him.'

'I hope I won't be any trouble?'

'Of course you won't.'

As the days drew nearer to Amelia's departure, Katherine became more and more anxious. She kept her anxiety to herself, however. This was the first time since she had been found on the beach over a year ago that she had been left alone. She was aware that Mrs Draper and Miriam would be in the house, but that was not the same as being in daily contact with Amelia.

When her brother arrived the day before their departure Amelia expressed to him her opinion that Katherine was taking the prospect of being left alone very well.

He frowned. 'I hope nothing happens to upset her. I did consider taking her with us.' He noticed his sister's hostile expression. 'But I realised that would mean leaving her in unfamiliar surroundings while we were seeing to Aunt Lena's affairs.'

'Just as well. I don't know why you ever entertained such an idea.'

'You've left everything in order for her here?'

'Of course,' replied Amelia testily, bristling at the note of concern. 'Do you doubt my efficiency?'

'Of course not,' he hastened to placate her. 'It was just that . . .'

'You are besotted with her,' she snapped. 'The sooner things are settled one way or another the better, then we will all know where we stand and can settle down to the life we knew before you brought her here.'

Roland was taken aback by the bitterness that had crept into her voice. 'Are you regretting helping her?'

'No.' She gave a sharp irritated shake of her head. 'But the situation has dragged on. I had expected things to be resolved by now. The attention you pay her has become more and more marked. Your visits have increased in spite of my continual warning that you know nothing about her. Think of your position if you take a step too far and then the return of her memory reveals an unsavoury past.'

'I don't believe there is anything unsavoury about Katherine.'

'There you go – besotted! You don't know what secrets lurk behind that pretty face. We can't go on like this indefinitely. Something will have to be done. I hope this break in Lancaster might give you time to consider the future in sensible terms.'

Or something might happen while we are away that will solve the problem for good, she added in her own mind.

When Katherine closed the door of her bedroom at the end of the day Amelia and Roland had departed for Lancaster, she felt loneliness seep into her. There had been no friend to wish her 'Good night'. Only a void, an emptiness about the house. As much as she tried to tell herself that this was silly, she could not escape the feeling that she was utterly alone. She shuddered, feeling goose pimples creep down her spine. This was ridiculous. The house was no different because Amelia was not here. She had known it for over a year. It was familiar and nothing had changed. Or had it?

She glanced anxiously around her. Everything was the same as usual, but the feeling of loneliness penetrated from outside this room and with it came hostility. Where from? Created by whom? Mrs Draper? Miriam? No, it couldn't be either of them, Katherine had little contact with them and besides they had no reason to resent her. Dr Bennett ... Roland? Surely not. It was he who had brought her here instead of putting her in an institution. For that she would be ever grateful to him. And he had shown her continued kindness ever since, his visits becoming ever more frequent. There had been occasions, though, when Katherine had feared Amelia might feel resentment at the attention Roland was devoting to the young castaway he had brought here from Robin Hood's Bay.

Katherine stiffened and frowned. Amelia then? No, surely the hostility couldn't stem from her? Even as she posed the question she felt the tension in the air heighten. Could her hostess be at the root of what she was feeling? But Amelia had shown her such kindness. Katherine shook her head in irritation. Something was nagging at her mind. From the past that could not be remembered? No, it couldn't be. If Amelia had figured in that unknown world Katherine would surely have remembered. Besides, Amelia would have been able to remind her of it. It was something from not so long ago. Was it here in this room? She glanced round nervously. Dark shadows lurked in the corners. She turned the lamp up to drive them away but only partially succeeded. Katherine told herself her only memory of Amelia in this room was as a comforter after that horrible nightmare of the sea and a storm which almost devoured her.

A storm! Katherine stiffened. Slowly out of the fog that clouded her mind came recognition. She and Amelia were

203

sitting in the drawing-room, both reading. But that was all. They were enveloped in calm. There was nothing hostile in the scene yet she had a feeling there was more to it to be discovered.

Thoughtfully she picked up the lamp and left the room. She walked slowly along the corridor towards the stairs, the light driving away the darkness from the walls. Reaching the top she stopped. A draught caught the light and the dancing flame sent flickering shadows ahead of her. The movement startled her. She hesitated to go further but strengthened herself with the resolve that she must know more. Slowly, step by step, she went down the stairs, driving light into the hall below and leaving darkness filling in the space behind her. She crossed the hall and, certain that she would find something beyond the drawing-room door, pushed it open apprehensively.

She stepped into the room, hoping the light would reveal its secrets. There were none. The room was as she had left it but a short while ago. And yet the atmosphere here was different. Or was it merely a figment of her imagination? She closed the door gently behind her, crossed the room and placed the lamp on a table, frowning and rubbing her forehead as if she was not fully aware why she was here. In the centre of the room, she looked around. Her gaze became fixed on the curtains drawn across the window. Memories flickered. They were vague but the curtains and that window gradually dominated them. Transfixed, she felt compelled to go to it. She felt fearful as she reached out to the curtains and drew them apart. She looked out of the window, her eyes drawn over the rooftops to the sky. It was clear, bathed in the soft glow of a silvery moon. Her mind contradicted the scene. This was different. It was not as it had been. Her mind whirled, searching for an answer to what it had been like.

'Katherine, come and watch.'

She jumped. Who had spoken? She looked over her shoulder. There was no one. The voice was in her head.

'Come.' The voice again. Persuasive.

Someone was beside her, whispering close to her ear. 'Come to me . . . storm . . . nightmare . . . you lost something . . . someone . . . who was it? Where did you lose him?'

Katherine clamped her hands over her ears. But the voice was still there, insidious, menacing. She had to free herself from it. Her fingers became claws. She raked them down again and again until she sank exhausted to the floor.

Ten minutes later she stirred. She shook her head and rubbed her hands across her eyes. Where was she? On a floor somewhere. Why? Her mind cleared slowly and she realised she was in the drawing-room. Her gaze travelled upwards and she saw the curtains were ripped and torn. Shock hit hard. She must have done it. No one else could have. But that voice? She fixed her mind on the moments since she had entered the room and a woman's voice became clear to her: Amelia's. But she was miles away. Katherine struggled to her feet and sagged into the nearest chair. She must make sense of what had happened. She recalled the storm and looking out of this window. Linking that with the voice she had just heard, she knew those persuasive insidious tones must date from the night of the storm. What had Amelia been trying to do?

She shuddered at the thought of what it might have been. But she had retaliated: those scratches on Amelia's cheeks had been her defence against the demons Amelia was trying to force into her mind. She had fought then just as she had done now. And she had won. Amelia had made no further move against her since that day unless it was in some underhand way. But why had she moved against Katherine at all? She always appeared so considerate and generous. Katherine wondered if she should confront her when she returned from Lancaster. Dare she? Would it jeopardise her own future? Antagonise Amelia and she could be turned out onto the streets. Would the doctor defend her against his formidable sister? She daren't risk that.

An hour later Katherine was shivering with cold. She rose from the chair, picked up the lamp and climbed the stairs to her room, still unsure how she should proceed in the light of this revelation.

Chapter Thirteen

Katherine's mind was in a turmoil and she was barely aware of her preparations for bed. She lay down, staring at the ceiling. The lamp on a table beside her bed tried to cast its light to the depths of every corner of the room but was only partially successful. Haunting shadows remained.

'Follow him. Go!' The voice came from the room's recesses.

Katherine stiffened. That voice again. Amelia! She sat up and cast frightened eyes around the room. There was no one here unless . . . was that a form in the farthest corner? Light brightened the area momentarily. There was no one. How could there be? Amelia was in Lancaster. Yet the whispered voice came again. 'Follow him. Go!' It was Amelia's voice. But was it in her own mind? Katherine pressed her head with her hands as if she could drive reason into it. Had she been dreaming all of this? No, what had happened downstairs this very night had been an echo of a previous occasion which had etched itself vividly on her mind, incriminating Amelia.

Katherine eventually fell into a fitful sleep, knowing that there was only one way to keep her sanity and that was to tackle her benefactress about what had really happened the night Katherine had attacked her. But before that she would have to face Mrs Draper about the torn curtains.

It was an apprehensive Katherine who entered the dining-room the next morning. She had only just closed the door when Mrs Draper came bustling in, her face wreathed with concern.

'Ma'am, I'm sorry to disturb you before you have your breakfast but there is something I must show you.'

'Yes, Mrs Draper?'

'I would like you to come with me, ma'am.' Mrs Draper started for the door and Katherine followed.

As they crossed the hall the housekeeper said, 'Miriam went into the drawing-room this morning to do her usual tidying up and came rushing to the kitchen for me. You will see for yourself what concerned her for I told her to do nothing until I had spoken with you.'

They reached the drawing-room and Mrs Draper opened the door for Katherine to enter. She did so and waited for the housekeeper to follow. Her heart beat faster. She had toyed with several explanations to try to fend off the servants' enquiries but none had really satisfied her.

'Here, ma'am.' Mrs Draper strode across the room towards the window. 'When Miriam came into the room the curtains were not covering the window as they normally are. They were drawn back as you see them and this one has several tears down it.' Her brow creased into a puzzled frown. 'I can't understand it. What could have caused it?'

There was a long silence as Katherine stared at the rent curtain before giving the only explanation she could. 'You remember the night of the storm?'

'When you attacked Miss Bennett and scratched her face?'

'Yes. Well, I had a nightmare last night in which similar events were very real in my mind. I must have come downstairs then and for some reason caused that damage.'

There was shock in Mrs Draper's expression now. 'You mean, you came back to the same scene and in your nightmare thought the curtains were Miss Bennett?'

Katherine bit her lip. 'Mrs Draper, I don't know what I

thought.' There was distress in her voice and a cry for help. 'It was terrible. There were voices ...'

'Voices?'

'Yes.' She did not want to name Amelia to Mrs Draper. That would sound very strange, and first she wanted to confront her hostess and seek an explanation from her.

'Whose voices?' queried Mrs Draper, frowning.

'I don't know. Maybe they were from the time I don't remember.'

The housekeeper nodded. 'Oh, Mrs Westland, I'm so sorry for the distress this is causing you. I only wish there was something I could do to help.'

'Thank you. I too wish the past would become clear to me. In the meantime, what can we do about the curtains before Miss Bennett returns?'

'I know where she had them made. Would you like me to see if they still have the same material and replace that one?'

'It would be wonderful if you could,' replied Katherine, relieved at the suggestion.

'I'll do that, ma'am, so don't worry any more.'

'Thank you.'

'Now come and have some breakfast and try to forget your nightmares.'

It was not as easy as that for Katherine. Her mind kept dwelling on the fact that in the overwhelming horror of the storm, strong enough to haunt her even on a tranquil night, Amelia had voiced a clear desire for her to go. Was the one she had relied on so much not quite the kind and generous person she appeared to be?

It was a thought that troubled Katherine over the next three days until Mrs Draper announced that the new curtain had arrived and the men who had delivered it were now hanging it.

'I didn't expect delivery so soon. I am pleased they have been quick. Thank you for seeing to it, Mrs Draper.'

'I thought it best to have it in place before Miss Bennett returned.'

'Quite right,' agreed Katherine. Thinking that Mrs Draper had arranged this so that Amelia need never know what had happened, Katherine saw no reason to mention this aspect to her.

But the new curtain did not alleviate the doubts in her own mind about Amelia and the voice she had heard. In fact they only heightened the tension for they helped her to recall memories that haunted her more strongly now she had doubts about Amelia. 'Who is he? Follow him. Find him. Go! Go!' That voice kept returning, becoming more persistent each time. Katherine grappled with the memories, turning them over and over, trying to force a meaning out of them. Him? Who was he? Someone she had lost? But who? Where?

Two days after the delivery of the curtain the words thundered in her recollection even louder and were joined by another as her mind dwelt on them. 'Beach. Beach.' That word became more and more prominent. Why? She puzzled over that. Amelia had not used it, so why had it come to her now? Was it connected with her forgotten past? Had she lost someone on a beach? Could that beach be near to where she was now? *He* might be there now. She might be able to find him!

Katherine stopped her pacing, grabbed her pelisse and bonnet and rushed from the room. She ran down the stairs.

The sound of urgent footsteps brought Miriam hurrying from the kitchen. When she saw Katherine shrugging herself into her outdoor coat she was thankful she had left the door from the kitchen open.

'Wait, Mrs Westland! I'll come with you.' Alarm entered her voice as Katherine started towards the front door.

'There's no need, Miriam,' she snapped, annoyed at what could be a delay.

'Ma'am, I must come with you. I'll lose my job if I

210

don't. Miss Bennett left strict instructions that either Mrs Draper or I should accompany you if you went out. Mrs Draper has gone to the shops so I must come.'

'Well, hurry up then.' The sharpness in Katherine's voice startled Miriam who had never heard her speak like this before. As she turned back towards the kitchen to get her cloak she saw wildness in Katherine's eyes. She had no time to consider it for Katherine snapped again: 'Hurry, girl, hurry! I might lose him again.'

Miriam stopped. 'Who, ma'am?'

'Oh, never you mind. Just be quick if come you must.'

Miriam ran into the kitchen, her mind troubled. To whom was Mrs Westland referring? As far as she knew Mrs Westland knew nobody she could be meeting like this. Was it another manifestation of her strange behaviour? Should Miriam try to keep her in the house until Mrs Draper returned? Oh, why wasn't she here? She shouldn't have gone out leaving Miriam with this responsibility. She was becoming so agitated she was nearly on the verge of tears but forced herself to be calm. She must stay with Mrs Westland. She ran into the hall.

'Girl, I thought you were never coming.'

The impatience in Katherine's voice was something Miriam had never seen in her before. In fact, she considered it alien to the calm, considerate woman she knew. What had happened to change her? But Miriam had no time for further consideration. Katherine was out of the door.

'Which way to the beach?' she rapped. 'Take me to the beach. Quick, come on.'

'Yes, ma'am,' Miriam scuttled down Castlegate with Katherine close behind her.

They were soon taking the steep path to the sands. Katherine ignored the busy harbour scene and the passersby strolling in the seaside gardens. She did not hesitate. She was across the roadway and on to the beach. Turning away from the harbour, she headed towards the Spa. Her gaze roved from side to side, constantly searching though she

211

knew not who or what she was looking for. Miriam saw doubt and frustration in her eyes and in her small gestures of irritation.

After about half an hour Katherine stopped. She looked around her, frowned, and when her eyes settled on Miriam, said, 'Where are we?'

The maid was taken aback by the question and also by the fact that Katherine's expression was more serene now and her voice gentle, without the hostility and impatience there had been earlier.

'Ma'am, we're on the beach.'

'Why? Why have you brought me here?'

'I did as you told me.'

'*I* told you to bring me to the beach?'

'Yes. You said you had to find someone.'

Katherine looked mystified but there was a little dawning of enlightenment in her mind and it was linked to that voice – Amelia's voice. She shrugged her shoulders. 'Oh, well, I must have been mistaken. Let's go home.'

'Very well, ma'am.'

Katherine made no mention of the matter as they walked home but chattered pleasantly about things they saw on their way back.

Mrs Draper had already returned and greeted them warmly. 'I'm so glad you went for a walk. The fresh air will have done you good.'

'Indeed. We enjoyed it, didn't we, Miriam?'

'We did, ma'am.'

'Thank you for coming with me.' Katherine went up the stairs to her room and Mrs Draper, followed by Miriam, went to the kitchen.

Once the door was closed the maid spoke. 'Mrs Draper, that woman's funny.'

'Miriam, you shouldn't talk about people like that,' she remonstrated.

'But she is! She came racing down the stairs and acted queer when I said I would accompany her. Said she wanted

212

to go to the beach to look for someone.'

'Who?'

Miriam snorted. 'I don't know, and I don't think she did either.'

'She didn't find whoever she was looking for then?'

'Naw. As I said, I don't think there was anyone.'

'But . . .'

'She suddenly stopped and asked what we were doing there. Asked *me* why *I* had brought her there when it was she who told me to! We came home then and she was quite chatty on the way, none of the snap she had given me earlier.'

Mrs Draper nodded. 'Thank you for telling me, Miriam. I will have to report it to Miss Bennett when she returns. Please keep this strictly to yourself unless Miss Bennett asks you anything about it.' Mrs Draper looked sternly at her. 'Remember, don't tell a soul.'

'I won't say a word, Mrs Draper. You know me. I can keep a secret.'

'I hope so. Miss Bennett won't be back for a few days yet so if anything like this happens again, or Mrs Westland seems out of sorts, let me know immediately.'

Three nights later, while going the rounds to see that all windows were closed and all doors locked, Mrs Draper was in the dining-room when she heard footsteps cross the hall towards the front door. She rushed to the dining-room door just in time to see Katherine leaving the house.

'Mrs Westland!' she called, but she was too late. The door closed, blocking off her cry. Her heart beat faster. Where on earth was her charge going? The housekeeper ran to the kitchen, grabbed her cloak and ran from the house. She must not lose sight of Mrs Westland. She was responsible for her, must bring her back. A shadowy figure headed for the beach. Mrs Draper's pace quickened but she made little impression on the distance between them. The darkness intensified as buildings crowded closer together.

They stopped any flow of air to alleviate the oppressive atmosphere. It was noisy here too. Raucous voices in profane exchanges, drunken singing, threats, all filled the air, with the crash of waves on the beach below forming a menacing background.

A door was thrown open, allowing a pool of light to spill across the street, silhouetting three figures reeling out of an inn. The door banged behind them.

Mrs Draper gasped to herself, 'Oh no!' She dare not think what might happen now. Panting, she tried to quicken her pace. She must get to Mrs Westland before these drunks became aware of her, but her effort was to no avail.

'What have we here?' The man's words were slurred but full of expectancy. The three of them blocked Katherine's path.

She ran on oblivious.

Strong arms grasped her. Though the man reeled under the impact he steadied himself and clung on. 'Ah, come on now, little lady. What's the rush?' He leered close to her face. The smell of drink on his breath brought Katherine to awareness.

The present overwhelmed her. Where was she? Who was holding her, pulling roughly at her? She felt other hands grasp her shoulders, forcing her to the ground. She cried out but broad fingers were clamped across her mouth, stifling any noise.

'Hold her, Sam!'

Panting hard, gripped by alarm, shouting at the top of her voice, Mrs Draper launched herself at the men attacking Katherine. Her momentum sent the one man still on his feet reeling. In his drunken state he staggered and fell over the man who had clamped his hands over Katherine's mouth. He rolled away from her. Mrs Draper spun round and kicked out at the man on top of Katherine. She caught him on the side of the head. He let out a howl of pain. Free from his weight, Katherine struck out and sent him rolling onto the cobbles. Mrs Draper's shouts and the yells of pain from Katherine's attackers brought customers running from the inn. Alarmed, the three men scrambled to their feet and ran off.

The onlookers helped Katherine to her feet. She started sobbing from the shock of the attack. Two others were concerned for Mrs Draper who, quick to reassure them that she was unharmed, turned her attention to Katherine.

'Mrs Westland, are you all right?' The housekeeper made no attempt to hide her anxiety.

Katherine looked up, thankful to hear a familiar voice. She nodded, then as a great sob racked her body, cried out, 'Oh, Mrs Draper, what happened to me? Where am I?'

'She's confused, ma'am,' said one of the men. 'Bring her inside.'

'Thank you, but I think it best I get her home as soon as possible,' Mrs Draper replied, taking Katherine's arm.

'Would you like us to escort you?'

'That is considerate but we will be all right, thank you.' She didn't want anyone to know where they were from.

'I don't think those drunks will molest you again, ma'am, not after the way you tackled them and sent them off with a flea in their ear,' chuckled one of the onlookers.

Mrs Draper thanked them all again and started off up the street, knowing that the men from the inn would remain on watch until they were out of sight.

'What happened, Mrs Draper?' asked a worried Katherine, still trying to grapple with the circumstances in which she had just found herself when all she could previously remember of that night was being in her room getting ready to go to bed. Now she was on a street with Mrs Draper after finding herself being molested by three men. What had happened in between?

'I don't really know, Mrs Westland. I saw you leaving the house. I called but you can't have heard me, so knowing you should not be out alone at that time of night I followed you. I tried to catch up with you but you were

215

going so quickly. Why did you leave the house, Mrs Westland?'

Katherine frowned and shook her head as if trying to clear her mind. She screwed up her face in frustration. 'I don't know, Mrs Draper. I don't know.' There was a cry for help in her tone.

'Don't worry about it now, ma'am. Let us get you home and then maybe you will recall.'

No further words were exchanged as they climbed the hill back to Castlegate. Once inside Mrs Draper felt relief. 'Let's get you out of your dress.' She ushered Katherine up the stairs and once she had shed her clothes, dirty from the unpleasant encounter, and was settled in a chair, Mrs Draper drew up another and sat facing her. 'Now, ma'am, maybe you can recall why you went out?'

Katherine's expression tightened. 'I'm not sure. I heard a call that had to be answered.'

'You heard someone call?' Mrs Draper was puzzled. 'I heard no one. There was only you and me and Miriam in the house.'

Katherine shook her head. 'It came from outside.'

'Outside?' Mrs Draper could make no sense of this. She had been going from room to room making sure that everything was secure for the night, and was sure if there had been someone calling from outside she would have heard them.

Katherine nodded. 'Yes. I had to go.'

'Weren't you aware it could be dangerous to go out alone?'

'I was compelled to.'

'What do you mean?'

'I knew something was wrong when he didn't come home.'

Mrs Draper was startled by this remark. 'Who?'

'I don't know.' Katherine rubbed her hands against her forehead as if trying to force recollection to it.

'Were you aware of any destination? What did you expect to find?'

Katherine tightened her lips in despair then said, 'I remember nothing after leaving my room until I felt hands grab me and smelt that awful drink-sodden breath.' She shuddered at the thought.

'You weren't aware of the men until they attacked you?'

'No.' A faraway look came into Katherine's eyes. 'Maybe that's what happened to him,' she whispered as if to herself.

But Mrs Draper caught the words. 'Who?' she asked, keeping her voice quiet so that no harshness would intrude and shatter Katherine's recollection.

Katherine continued to stare into the distance, then she started and her eyes focused on Mrs Draper. 'What did you say?'

'I asked who you were talking about?'

'What did I say?'

'You said, "Maybe that's what happened to him", and I asked who?'

'I don't recollect saying that. To what could I have been referring?'

'I don't know, ma'am. Would it have anything to do with the attack by those men?'

Katherine gave an irritated shake of her head. 'I don't know. Everything is so confusing.'

Mrs Draper realised that it would be better for Katherine to regain her calm. Any further pursuit of the matter would bear no fruit tonight. It would be better dropped. 'Will you be all right preparing yourself for bed while I get you a hot drink? It will help you settle for the night.'

'Of course I will, Mrs Draper.' The cook rose from her chair. 'And thank you for what you did. I am so glad you were there. There's no telling what might have happened to me otherwise.'

When Mrs Draper returned a few minutes later she found Katherine sitting up in bed. She placed a cup of hot milk on the bedside table. 'I hope that helps you settle down and that you have no bad dreams of your ordeal.'

'I'm sure I will be all right. Thank you once again, Mrs Draper.'

As the cook closed the bedroom door and went to her room she knew she would have to keep a careful eye on Katherine's behaviour and be sure that all doors were locked earlier than usual and the keys to outside removed so that there was no likelihood of a recurrence of tonight's episode.

Over the next few days Katherine showed no inclination to leave the house at night. During the day, if the weather was suitable, she always sought Miriam to accompany her on excursions. Mrs Draper began to wonder if there was any need to report what had happened to Miss Bennett when she and her brother returned, but decided that she should do so otherwise she could be in trouble if Katherine left the house at night again and it became known she had done it before.

'Amelia!' A smiling Katherine hurried across the hall to greet her.

Miriam had answered the door and from the drawing-room Katherine had recognised Amelia's voice.

'Katherine!' She held out her arms. 'How have you been?'

They hugged and then Amelia started to discard her outdoor clothes and pass them to Miriam.

'Very well, thank you. The doctor isn't with you?'

'No. I persuaded him to come back via Robin Hood's Bay. He's been away from his practice long enough and I thought he should get back as soon as possible. I'm sure he has a lot of things to see to, but he'll be here to visit us before too long.' She turned to Miriam. 'Tell Mrs Draper I'm home and then bring us some tea.'

'Yes, ma'am.' Miriam hurried away to dispose of Amelia's clothes and then go to the kitchen.

'I'll be with you in a few minutes, Katherine. I'd like to restore myself. The journey has been tedious.'

'Of course.' Katherine returned to the drawing-room.

She did not pick up the book she had been reading but sat looking round the room. Gradually her thoughts focused on the night of the storm and whispers began to penetrate her mind. 'Katherine, come and watch.' Persuasive tones. 'Come.' 'Him.' 'You lost something – someone'. 'Go to him. Go!' She remembered this voice haunting her before. It had been Amelia's and she had resolved to tackle her about it. Was now the time? Her thoughts were interrupted by Amelia's return.

She sat down. The tea arrived. Throughout it all Amelia seemed to be in a most friendly frame of mind, solicitous for Katherine's welfare while she had been away. Katherine wondered if she had been wrong in her assumption that Amelia had been trying to turn her mind and encouraging her to go. To accuse her now would seem horribly ungrateful after all her kindness and help. And Katherine could be wrong, it could all have been in her imagination. Accusations, especially unfounded ones, could lead to a rift, unsettle her future and drive the past even further away. She would say nothing, she decided. Unless some recollection arose to enable her to put her questions with more authority.

Amelia was interested in what Katherine had been doing while she had been in Lancaster. She kept to the mundane facts, mentioning nothing of the disturbing events and hoping Mrs Draper would not reveal them either. But she could not expect a person so devoted to her employee as Mrs Draper to keep such things from her, especially as she had been given overall responsibility while Miss Bennett was away and been told to report anything unusual.

That evening, after Katherine had retired for the night, Amelia went to the kitchen. She sent Miriam off to bed, and when the maid was out of the way turned to the cook. 'Now, Mrs Draper, make us a cup of tea and tell me if anything untoward happened while I was away?'

The kettle was already boiling on the reckon and while she mashed the tea Mrs Draper gathered her thoughts. Amelia, sensing that her cook had something momentous to report and was searching for a way to begin, did not speak but placidly watched her actions until Mrs Draper sat down opposite her across the oak table that held centre place in the kitchen. Their eyes met and Mrs Draper started to relate events. Amelia listened intently so that nothing escaped her attention and would be clearly remembered.

'I am sorry that you had so much trouble while I was away, Mrs Draper, but grateful for the way you handled matters.'

'Thank you, ma'am. I told Miriam she must say nothing to anyone about what happened when she was with Mrs Westland, unless you questioned her about it.'

'I don't think I need to. You have made a comprehensive report. Does she know anything about the night of the attack on Mrs Westland?'

'No. She was in bed and heard nothing.'

'Good.'

'Ma'am, may I express an opinion?'

'Yes.'

'I'm worried by these fits of Mrs Westland's. Last time you were endangered – this time it was Mrs Westland herself. Who's to say where it will all end?'

Amelia looked thoughtful. 'I wonder who and what she was referring to when she mentioned losing someone?' She paused then stiffened and rose from her chair. 'Thank you, Mrs Draper, for the frank and comprehensive report. It will be a help in determining Mrs Westland's welfare. But please, keep all this to yourself.'

'My lips are sealed, Miss Bennett.'

220

Chapter Fourteen

Amelia lay awake for a considerable time when she went to bed, digesting the new information from Mrs Draper. By the time she fell asleep her mind was made up on the course of action she would take to turn it to her advantage.

After a quiet breakfast together Amelia said she would like a word with Katherine in the privacy of the drawing-room. The sudden coldness in her voice struck apprehension into Katherine's mind.

'Sit down,' said Amelia to her when the door had closed. She herself remained standing in front of the fireplace. It gave her an appearance of authority, commanding all Katherine's attention, and made her words all the more effective.

'I am sorry to hear of the three upsetting incidents while I was away.' She raised her hand quickly to halt the words that were springing to Katherine's lips. 'Don't blame Mrs Draper for telling me. I gave her strict instructions to report to me any untoward events while I was away. As her employer I expect loyalty, so there is no blame attached to her for telling me what happened. Besides it is to your benefit that I should know. You should be helped. It disturbs me very much that you should have relapsed again, especially as you have been free from any disturbance of your mind for a considerable time. I was hoping you were getting better but now ...' She left her insinuation hanging in air, knowing it would have more impact that way.

Katherine had gone pale. She shook her head with annoyance. 'I don't know what happened.'

Amelia snorted. 'Well, I do. Mrs Draper told me, so don't play the innocent with me.' There was hostility in her voice and eyes.

'I meant, I don't know what caused these events to happen,' replied Katherine.

'Your mind,' snapped Amelia. 'You must be losing it.'

'Amelia! Please don't say that.'

The shocked look on Katherine's face spurred Amelia on. 'It is the only likely explanation. We have to face the fact that three times within a short space you behaved oddly. This indicates that your strange fits are becoming frequent again and we will have to do something about them.'

'You want me to go, as you tried to get me to do before.' Katherine knew she had to fight back.

'What do you mean?' demanded Amelia.

'That day we were in this room, looking out at the storm, you coaxed me over to the window, knowing how it would affect me.'

'Katherine, what are you insinuating?'

'That you used the storm to upset me when I was most susceptible. Tried to get me to leave.'

'Nonsense! Why would I do that?'

'I don't know, but you did.' Katherine sprang to her feet and glared defiantly at Amelia. 'You played on the fact that I can't remember anything of my past. Why?'

'I did no such thing. It's all another figment of your imagination. You see, there it is again – your mind is unstable. I've been kind to you and now you are turning against me. Link that with your unstable behaviour while I was away and I think we must make a serious assessment of your condition. I think I should act immediately. I'll send for Dr Crabtree.' She went to the bell-pull beside the fireplace.

222

Katherine was quick to react and grabbed Amelia's arm before she could reach the embroidered bell-pull. 'Don't!' she demanded wildly.

Amelia glared at her. 'Don't tell me what to do! It is for your own good. Your loss of memory leads you to attack people, destroy things, search for someone who does not exist, and place yourself at considerable risk. Now you are making wild and unfounded accusations. I think something will have to be done about it.' She saw alarm in Katherine's eyes and pressed home her insinuations. 'An unsound mind is something we cannot allow to go untreated.' She leaned closer to Katherine, her voice dropping to a whisper. 'You are insane.' The coldness of her tone made the words even more penetrating. They speared Katherine's mind, inflicting hurt and turmoil.

She clamped her hands to her head as if that would shut out Amelia's devastating statement. 'No! No!' she shouted. 'I'm not! I'm not!' Her eyes were wild and filled with tears.

'You are!' The words were delivered venomously.

As hard as Katherine fought them, Amelia's deliberate emphasis seemed to imbue them with truth. Insane! Insane! It rang in her head, making her doubt her own sanity. Her mind reeled. 'No!' she screamed. 'I'm not insane!'

She sprang at Amelia but she had already tugged at the bell-pull and was ready for Katherine's reaction. She swayed back out of reach of the clawing fingers and at the same time clamped her hands round Katherine's wrists. She struggled to control the frenzied attack and was relieved when she heard the door open and Miriam's voice cry out in alarm: 'Miss Bennett!'

The girl rushed across the room and grabbed Katherine from behind, using all her strength to pull her away from Amelia. She stumbled backwards, taking Katherine with her. They crashed to the floor. Amelia was quickly at the door and shouted at the top of her voice, 'Mrs Draper! Quick!'

Her urgency brought the cook rushing from the kitchen

to the drawing-room. Startled by the alarm on Amelia's face and by the sight of Miriam struggling with Katherine on the floor, she asked no questions but heard Amelia call out, 'Help Miriam.' The girl had twisted from under Katherine but still held on to one arm. Mrs Draper grasped at the other and made sure she held on. Briefly Katherine tried to free herself, then realising it was useless she gave up. Her body sagged. Tension drained away.

'All right, get her in a chair,' Amelia ordered.

Wary of allowing her too much freedom, Mrs Draper and Miriam pulled Katherine to her feet and sat her in a chair, her shoulders slumped, the picture of dejection. Her world, one in which she'd thought she was safe, had crashed down around her.

'Miriam, fetch Dr Crabtree as quickly as possible.'

She scurried away to do Amelia's bidding.

Alarmed, Katherine stood up. She reached out as if she would stop the maid. Protests sprang to her lips but remained unspoken under Amelia's withering look. A hopeless feeling pervaded her.

'What happened, ma'am?' Mrs Draper put the query tentatively, eyeing Katherine who looked utterly dejected with tears streaming down her face.

'She attacked me again.'

'Oh, ma'am! The poor woman to be disturbed so.'

'Something will have to be done. We cannot go on like this. We could all be in danger. We'll see what Dr Crabtree has to say.'

'I'd rather hear Dr Bennett's opinion.' The words came quietly from Katherine though she looked at no one, her gaze focused on the hands held together on her lap.

'He is not here, my dear,' replied Amelia smoothly, 'but Dr Crabtree will look after you.'

'Miss Bennett, are you all right?' Dr Crabtree's concern was directed at her immediately he bustled into the drawing-room.

'Yes, thank you. And my thanks for coming so quickly,' replied Amelia with a brave smile.

'Miriam says Mrs Westland attacked you again?'

'Yes.'

'Well, let us see if we can get to the bottom of this.' He turned to Katherine. 'Now, young lady, what is this all about? Why did you attack Miss Bennett again?'

Katherine did not reply, did not even look up but continued to stare at her hands.

'That will be all, Mrs Draper, and thank you for your help. You too Miriam. I'll ring if I need you again.' When the door closed behind the servants, Amelia said, 'Doctor, maybe I had better explain what happened and put it in the context of events while I was away.'

Dr Crabtree raised a surprised eyebrow. 'There have been other incidents?'

'Yes.' Amelia went on to relate what had happened when she had been in Lancaster. The doctor listened intently, not speaking, merely nodding his understanding of the facts. He puzzled over Katherine's reaction while Amelia spoke, but made no comment. It seemed she went into another world.

'Was today's event the result of what you have just recounted?' queried Dr Crabtree.

'Undoubtedly,' replied Amelia. 'Naturally I had to speak to Mrs Westland about what happened while I was away.'

The doctor nodded his agreement. 'How did she take it?'

'She turned nasty, accused me of wanting her to leave.'

Dr Crabtree raised an eyebrow. 'I'm sorry, Miss Bennett, I have to ask this. Do you want Mrs Westland to leave?'

'Of course not,' she replied indignantly.

'You do,' Katherine accused her quietly without looking up.

'Mrs Westland, what did you say?' Though he had heard the words distinctly, Crabtree wanted to hear them again.

Katherine looked up and met his gaze without flinching.

'She wants me out of this house.'

'Nonsense!' Amelia's retort was sharp.

'You do. You told me to go on the night of the last storm.'

'I did not!'

'Why would Miss Bennett want you to leave?' asked Dr Crabtree.

'I don't know. Unless it is because her brother shows me kindness, maybe too much attention in her eyes, and she's afraid I'll take him from her.'

'Rubbish,' snapped Amelia. 'Only a diseased mind would dream up such a thing, Doctor.'

'Insane was the term you used this morning, Amelia,' put in Katherine quietly.

'I never said such a thing!'

'You did. You said I was insane.'

She turned to the doctor. 'After all these wild claims and speculations, coupled with her obsession about losing someone, I am beginning to wonder if she *is* insane. If you think that there is any imbalance of the mind, I am afraid I can no longer take responsibility for her.'

Dr Crabtree nodded thoughtfully. 'What you say is perfectly understandable. But I'd like to ask Mrs Westland a few more questions.' Though he wanted to make sure that Miss Bennett was in no further danger by committing Mrs Westland to an institution, he did not wish to appear to be over-reacting to what had been said. He looked at Katherine intently. 'Mrs Westland, I would like to go back to the person you were looking for when you went to the beach with Miriam. Who were you looking for and why did you expect him – I think you have referred to the person as him – to be on the beach?'

'Because that's where I lost him.'

'On Scarborough beach?'

'I don't know.'

'Miss Bennett tells me you mentioned sea demons. Were they what you were looking for?'

226

'Don't be stupid! They took him.' Katherine's eyes had become glazed.

'On the night you were attacked, you referred to the incident afterwards, saying, "This must have happened to him." Was that the same person you were looking for on the beach?'

Katherine frowned. Her mind was becoming a jumble but there was something in the back of it trying to make sense. She hesitated.

'Well?' prompted the doctor. She stared unseeingly at him. 'Don't be silly, how could it be? The sea demons took one, the other I lost somewhere else.' She jumped to her feet, casting neither of them a glance. 'I must find them.' She rushed towards the door, but even though he was startled by her sudden reaction Dr Crabtree reached it before her.

'No, Mrs Westland, I'm afraid you can't go searching now. Besides, there is no one to find, I'm convinced of that. These figures are figments of your imagination, and that is supported by the fact that you imagine all these things of which you accuse Miss Bennett. She is not a vindictive kind of person. Indeed, she is extremely generous and forbearing. You need treatment, Mrs Westland, and for your own good and that of everyone else, the sooner you receive it the better. I will arrange to have you taken care of immediately.'

Katherine stared at him bleakly. Her need to leave and begin her search was threatened by all he seemed to imply.

Hands rested gently on her shoulders from behind. 'It is for your own good, Katherine.' The voice she heard was smooth, comforting. 'Come and sit down.' The pressure on her shoulders brought her round to face Amelia. She nodded and quietly went back to the chair she had just occupied.

Amelia glanced at the doctor. He met her gaze and inclined his head, indicating that he wished to speak to her alone. Amelia went to the bell-pull and a few moments later Miriam appeared.

'Tell Mrs Draper that I would like to see her.'

Miriam hurried away.

When Mrs Draper appeared Amelia instructed her to sit with Katherine while she had a word in private with the doctor.

'I am sorry about this, Miss Bennett, but it is the best thing,' he began.

'I have every faith in your judgement, Doctor. I presume you are thinking of your friend in Hull? He was mentioned some time ago, will that place still be available?'

'Most certainly. Dr Egan has kept the possibility in mind. In fact he asked me to continue supplying him with information about Mrs Westland's condition. That of course has remained stable for some time, but recent developments ... Hopefully Matthew will know how to deal with her case. He has much experience.'

'When will Mrs Westland have to go?'

'Tomorrow. The sooner the better. It is no use dallying in such cases. I am going to send one of my servants to Hull immediately with a letter for Dr Egan. Will you be able to manage her tonight?'

'Of course.'

'I'll bring her a sedative which should help.'

'Thank you for that and for what you are doing for her.'

'I'll return shortly.' As he left the house he was already preparing in his mind the letter he would write to his friend.

Amelia smiled to herself as she returned to the drawing-room. Things could not have gone better. Katherine would soon be out of the way, out of their lives.

She found her still sitting as if in another world. 'The doctor is making arrangements for Mrs Westland to be looked after. She will be leaving us tomorrow,' she informed Mrs Draper.

If Katherine had comprehended that information she gave no sign.

The housekeeper glanced at her then back to Amelia.

'I'm sorry about that, miss. I hope the treatment she will receive helps her recovery.'

'When my brother comes he will want to know what has happened. You can tell him what you told me yesterday.'

Half an hour later the doctor returned. 'My man is on the way to Hull. Mrs Westland, you have had a trying time, I suggest you get some rest. As much sleep as possible. We'll make an early start tomorrow.'

Katherine, who was still in a daze, said nothing but rose quietly from her chair and glanced at Amelia.

'Miriam will pack your belongings.'

'Give Mrs Westland a few drops of this now and some more tonight.' He handed Amelia a bottle containing some laudanum.

'Shall we go, Katherine?' She offered Katherine her hand but it was ignored.

In the last few minutes in the drawing-room Katherine's mind had cleared a little and pieces of what had happened that morning were coming together. As they did she realised it was no good reopening the battle. No one would believe accusations directed at Amelia. So she'd resolved she would go along with what Dr Crabtree had arranged in the hope that before long her memory would return and she could resume the life that at the moment meant nothing to her.

When she awoke the next morning it was to find that Amelia and Miriam were standing at her bedside.

'It is time you were getting up, Katherine,' said Amelia gently. 'Dr Crabtree will be here before long. Miriam has packed your belongings and will take your valise to the hall.' She nodded to the maid who picked up the baggage and left the room. 'Do you want any help?' Amelia asked.

Katherine shook her head. 'No, thank you. I can manage,' she said resignedly.

'Very well. Come down as soon as you can. You must have a good breakfast to face the journey to Hull.'

229

As she dressed Katherine tried to come to terms with what was happening to her, and realised that all she could do was to make the best of things.

'I am sorry it has come to this,' said Amelia over breakfast.

Words of contradiction sprang to Katherine's lips but she held them back, knowing it would be useless to utter them. It would still be as it had been, Amelia's word against hers, and who would they believe? Amelia, of course, after the strange things that Katherine had done.

'It is for your own good, Katherine. But you will have to make some effort for yourself to counteract the trying times you have been through and regain your memory. And remember, Dr Crabtree has used his influence to get you placed with his friend in Hull instead of just casting you into one of the awful places that exist for someone who is insane.'

'I am not insane, Amelia.' Katherine's voice was cold. If Amelia was expecting a similar reaction as the last time she had used that word, she was not going to have the satisfaction.

'Then how do you account for your actions?' replied Amelia, equally coldly.

'Some of them were reaction to provocation. Others I do not know. But what I do know is that if Dr Crabtree's friend can help me to recover my memory and discover who I really am and what my past held, no matter what, then I will be always grateful to him. And also to you, because if it hadn't been for your determination to get me out of your life under any pretext, I would not be going into his care.'

Amelia fumed inside. She could have dealt with this much better if Katherine had ranted and raved at her. But seeing good in what was happening ... that was a calculated insult. She rose from the table and left the room.

In full control of herself, Katherine smiled. She had turned the tables and Amelia didn't like it. Katherine felt something like triumph. Some of her apprehension about the institution in which she was being placed had been dispelled by Amelia's revelation that the doctor to whom she was going was a friend of Dr Crabtree's and his establishment was not like the usual places for the insane. She started. How did she know about them? She had never heard them mentioned since coming to Scarborough. Had that been in her previous life? Such places existed in towns and cities usually. Was that where she had once lived? Katherine went extremely still. Streets full of houses came into her mind. Carriages, crowds, people ever on the move. Then they too faded. Streets again, but more elegant, quieter, with fashionable ladies visible in them.

The dining-room door opened and Amelia looked in. 'Dr Crabtree is here,' she said unfeelingly.

Katherine's thoughts were banished. She closed her eyes for a moment. How close was she to knowing something about her past? Would she ever know? She rose from her chair.

In the hall Dr Crabtree greeted her with a smile. 'Good day, Mrs Westland. I trust you had a comfortable night?'

'I did, Doctor, thanks to the sedative you prescribed.'

'Good. Then there is no reason why you shouldn't enjoy the ride. It is a beautiful morning.'

Miriam helped Katherine into her coat and handed her a bonnet which Katherine quickly adjusted on her head. The doctor picked up her valise and went to the front door. He called to the coachman who collected it and put it in the carriage.

'Goodbye, Miriam, and thank you for all you have done for me.'

'Goodbye, ma'am.' There were tears in the girl's eyes.

'Goodbye, Mrs Draper, you have been very kind.'

'I hope you will soon be fully recovered, ma'am.'

'Goodbye, Katherine,' said Amelia smoothly. 'I am sure this is for the best and will speed your recovery.' She embraced her and gave her a peck on each cheek.

231

Katherine responded without any emotion. 'Goodbye, Amelia,' she said, and walked out of the door.

'I will return and report to you, Miss Bennett,' said Dr Crabtree, hurrying after Katherine to help her into the carriage.

'Thank you,' Amelia called after him. Feeling a warm degree of self-satisfaction, she did not mind that Katherine did not wave or even look back.

During the first half-hour of the journey Katherine purposefully showed an interest in the countryside they were passing through after leaving Scarborough. She posed intelligent questions that Dr Crabtree did his best to answer. He was rather taken by her flow of words and the different directions in which she led their conversation. Suddenly she stopped and looked straight at him. 'You see, Dr Crabtree, I am far from being insane.'

Startled by the firmness of this statement, so out of context in the flow of their exchanges, he hesitated for a moment.

'Well, Dr Crabtree?'

'I don't think I ever implied that you were, Mrs Westland. From the conversation we have been having, I certainly don't think it. But there are times when your behaviour is . . . irrational.'

'Irrational does not necessarily mean insane.'

'You are right, of course, but those events were sparked off by something. Dr Egan will do his best to find out what that is and why it occurs. If there were signs of madness then you would not be going to Dr Egan's special home. Oh, he treats madness but does so in another institution exclusively for such unfortunates.'

'I am grateful to you for seeing that such is not my case.'

'Far from it in my opinion, Mrs Westland. I believe you are a highly intelligent young woman who has had a good upbringing, and that you have had the love of a close family.' He watched her carefully for any reaction that

232

would prove he was close to the truth in this assumption, but there was none.

She gave a half smile. 'I only wish I could say you are right, but I can't even remember if I have one.'

Dr Crabtree smiled back and patted her hand sympathetically. 'Well, we'll see if Dr Egan can jog your memory.'

When the carriage pulled up in front of a row of elegant houses, Katherine expressed her surprise. 'Is this where I will be living?'

'Yes. This is Dr Egan's establishment.'

'But I had imagined something less ostentatious than this, something more institutional.'

Dr Crabtree smiled. 'I'm sorry, I should have enlightened you. As I indicated, Dr Egan, apart from his other work undertakes some special cases. About ten of them. These patients are treated here.'

'In this single house?'

'No. Dr Egan has the properties to either side. He has made connecting doorways so it is all one property though it looks like three from outside. Now, let us go and make our arrival known.' He helped her from the carriage and, followed by the driver carrying Katherine's valise, escorted her up the four steps to the front door.

'Good day, Dr Crabtree,' said the maid.

'Good day, Sally. I'm here with Mrs Westland.'

'Welcome, ma'am.' Sally bobbed her a curtsey. 'You are both expected. Please come in and I will tell Dr Egan you are here.' She held the door open while they stepped into a hall where the marble floor was spotless and an elegant staircase curved upwards to the next floor. The carriage driver placed the valise on the floor.

Dr Crabtree thanked him and added, 'Your accommodation is booked at the White Harte. I will want to leave at eleven in the morning.'

'Very good, sir.' The man touched his forehead and was gone.

Sally closed the door and escorted Katherine and the doctor to a room on the right. It was comfortably furnished with a sofa, two armchairs, two upright chairs and a console table against one wall. There were only four ornaments in the room but they were advantageously placed.

The door opened and Katherine received a surprise. She had expected someone of about Dr Crabtree's age. Instead she faced a young man maybe only three or four years older than herself. He was tall and his well-fitting clothes showed off an athletic figure. There was a clean-cut look to his features, as if they had been honed by a sculptor's chisel. An unruly lock of mid-brown hair fell over the right side of his forehead. His blue eyes were bright and sparkling, full of humour to match the broad smile with which he greeted them.

'Doctor, welcome.' He held out his hand.

Dr Crabtree took it and returned his smile. 'Matthew, this is Mrs Westland, the lady I told you about some time ago, in whose case you expressed interest.'

'Ma'am.' He took her hand gently and bowed. When he looked up Katherine was aware that he was making an appraisal of her. 'Welcome to my home. I hope that you will be comfortable here and that you will find your true self restored.'

She returned his smile. 'It is a pleasure to meet you, Dr Egan, and thank you for taking an interest in my case. I hope I'll be a good patient.'

'I am sure you will.'

There was a knock on the door and two maids entered carrying tea things.

'You will take some?' Dr Egan asked.

'I would love a cup,' replied Katherine.

'Take off your coats and do sit down, both of you.'

The maids took the outdoor clothes away with them and Dr Egan poured the tea.

Katherine, a little bewildered by the tack her life had now taken, gradually found her reticence eroded by Dr Egan's easy manner and charm. She realised that she was

234

being put at her ease while at the same time being shrewdly observed by the doctor without his parading any overt medical and psychological interest in her. She knew the more formal approach would come later.

With the tea finished he said, 'Now, Mrs Westland, I think we should get you settled. I currently have eight patients living here until I think it wise for them to return to their families. You will meet some of them later. As you will see, they are not mentally disturbed in any serious way but their minds are in such a state that help is needed to direct them away from the course upon which they have embarked. They are harmless but lost in a different world, though now and again they emerge into the present. I have two similar cases to yours, loss of memory with no recollection of an earlier life while remaining quite lucid and active in the present. Each of you has your own room and I have one helper to every three cases. I am assigning you to Miss Everet who is already responsible for the two cases similar to yours. I will ring for her and she will show you to your room.' As he was speaking he had risen from his chair and tugged at the bell-pull.

A few moments later a maid reappeared and Dr Egan instructed her to ask Miss Everet to come to meet Mrs Westland.

The next time the door opened it brought another surprise for Katherine. The matronly figure she had expected turned out to be a woman of no more than forty. She was thin, her close-fitting ankle-length dress of silk and wool flaring only slightly from the waist. The bodice with its U-shaped neck-line was also closely fitting as were the wrist-length sleeves. The shaded blue and pink stripes dotted with a small rose motif gave the impression that Miss Everet was a little taller than she really was. Her rounded cheeks and curving jawline gave the impression of a cheerful disposition. This was enhanced by the brightness of her blue eyes and the broad smile on her full lips. There was an effervescence about her personality which defied

235

anyone to dislike her. Her light brown hair held a natural wave that was allowed to express itself even though the hair was drawn neatly back.

The two doctors rose to their feet.

'Miss Everet, you know Dr Crabtree, he has brought Mrs Westland to us.'

Miss Everet and Dr Crabtree exchanged a brief greeting and then she turned to Katherine.

'I am very pleased to meet you, Mrs Westland. I hope you will be happy with us.' Miss Everet gave a warm smile of welcome.

'And I am pleased to meet you too, Miss Everet.' Katherine returned the smile and immediately both women knew that a bond had been formed. 'I am sure we will get on well.'

'I endorse that,' replied Miss Everet, and glanced at Dr Egan.

'I think you should show Mrs Westland her room and the rest of our establishment. Bring her back to me in about half an hour.'

'Very well, Doctor.' She turned to Katherine and smiled.

Katherine rose from her chair. 'Thank you for the tea, Doctor.'

'My pleasure, Mrs Westland. Feel free to consult me or Miss Everet at any time. I'll see you later.'

Katherine followed Miss Everet out.

'I'll take you to your room first.'

At the bottom of the stairs Katherine laid a hand on Miss Everet's arm, causing her to halt even as her foot touched the bottom step. She looked enquiringly at Katherine.

'Miss Everet, from what I have gleaned so far I am to be in your charge while I am here?'

'That is so, and I hope it is going to be a pleasant relationship.'

'I am sure it will be. As I expect we will be spending a lot of time together, I suggest we should be on Christian name terms.'

Miss Everet's face became wreathed in radiant smiles.

'I was hoping you would say that. It makes for an easier and more pleasant relationship. All stuffy formality goes, makes things a lot easier for us both. But I always like the suggestion to come from the patient. I don't like it to appear as if I am pressing for an informality that might not be wanted.' She held out her hand. 'I'm Barbara.'

'Katherine.' She took Barbara's hand in friendship.

When they reached the landing Barbara stopped. 'Your room is along there to the left. The corridor to the right leads to some consulting rooms and storage areas. It is a long passage because Dr Egan purchased the properties to either side of the house. There is another floor above this. Miss Hardy, who also has charge of three patients, is up there as is Miss Gabriel who has charge of the two worst patients. Now, your room.' She led the way along the passage to the left, stopping at the first door. 'This is it. I am in the one opposite you. The next two rooms to you are occupied by the other ladies in my charge. The room next to me is a large one, equivalent in size to two bedrooms. It is for the exclusive use of our group as a drawing-room.'

She opened the door to the room. Katherine gave a little gasp of surprise. She had expected it to be rather spartan. Instead she saw it was warm and comfortable with a red Turkey carpet. The light-oak bedstead had a pink chintz valance that was complemented by a patchwork bedspread of symmetrical design. Small tables were placed to either side of the bed-head on each of which stood a lamp. Light streamed in from a tall sash window and illuminated the pale blue wallpaper with its motif of twisting leaves. A dressing table was positioned so that light from the window would fall across it. An armchair occupied one corner of the room. As well as landscape paintings on the walls, a three-shelved book rack was fixed near the armchair.

'Books!' cried Katherine and went to inspect them.

'You are a reader then?' asked Barbara.

237

'I love books. Always have.'

'Since before you came to Scarborough?' Barbara asked casually.

'I expect so,' replied Katherine, a little uncertainty in her voice. If she noticed it, as had Barbara, she did not show it. 'Oh, you've *Rob Roy*. One of my favourites.' She ran her eyes across the other titles, saying them half to herself. '*Rookwood, The Talisman, The Last of the Mohicans, History of the Peninsular War, Pompeii*, and volumes of poetry. Oh, I'm going to love this.'

Barbara smiled at her enthusiasm. 'I'm so pleased. I love books too so we can have discussions about what we read and exchange notes. And of course there are plenty more around the house to keep us well supplied. Now, would you like to be left on your own to unpack or would you rather see the rest of the house before we return to Dr Egan?'

'I'd love to see the rest of the house now. I can unpack later.'

'Right then, off we go,' said Barbara breezily.

Before the half-hour was up Katherine had seen the spacious communal room on the ground floor, the kitchen where she met the cook and her four kitchen maids, and the oak-panelled dining-room with its long table big enough to sit sixteen people together. She also met again the two maids who were on duty when she arrived as well as three others each of whom was responsible for a particular floor.

Barbara told her that Dr Egan had started this enterprise with the backing of wealthy Hull citizens interested in bettering the health of the town. They had seen that the benefits of such private enterprise could spill over into public institutions taking care of similar cases.

'Mental disorders are not confined to the poor,' Barbara explained. 'Dr Egan recognised that putting the better off, more genteel ladies with the poorer and worse off cases was detrimental to their recovery and actually hindered his work among the mentally disturbed. What he gains in knowledge here could have been lost in a different environment. As it

238

is, that knowledge can now be spread to a wider field.'

'And yourself?' asked Katherine. 'How did you come to be here?' She frowned sharply. 'Oh, dear, forgive me. I shouldn't be so inquisitive.'

Barbara laughed. 'Not at all, Katherine. It is only natural you should wonder about me. After all, if we are going to spend time together it is better to know something about each other.' She lowered her voice as if she was being secretive. 'Not like Mrs Witherspoon whom you will meet. She's in the next room to you, but is a bit aloof and doesn't want to be on friendly terms. I'm an employee in her eyes even though her family is no better than mine.' Barbara shrugged her shoulders. 'But that doesn't worry me. Apart from that we get on well and she appreciates what I do for her, but friendliness doesn't come into it. Well now, my background. My father is a merchant in Hull.'

'Ah,' said Katherine in a knowing tone, 'and I'd guess he is one of the people who helps Dr Egan?'

Barbara smiled. 'Correct. My father is keen to see the health of Hull's citizens improved. He heard of Dr Egan's proposal and decided, along with other patrons, to support him. I'd always been interested in health matters so Dr Egan recruited me and trained me in the way he wanted.'

'But Barbara, you remain unmarried?'

She tightened her lips in an expression of regret. 'I was engaged to a wonderful young man but he was killed in an accident.'

'Oh, I'm so sorry. I shouldn't have asked.'

'That's perfectly all right. It happened a few years ago. Oh, I've been courted since by a number of others but Sam was so dear to me no one could fill his place. I choose to remain a spinster and be the maiden aunt that nephews and nieces adore.'

'And you have plenty of those?'

'Oh, yes. With four brothers and a sister what else would you expect? What about you? No children?' She dropped the question in casually as a follow-up to what had just been said, hoping that it might release something in Katherine's mind.

She grimaced. 'None that I know of.'

Barbara did not want to upset her before her interview so did not pursue the matter.

'I think it is time we saw Dr Egan.' She led the way to his consulting room.

Dr Egan was sitting behind his large oak desk. Two comfortable armchairs were drawn up on the opposite side. The doctor rose to his feet as the ladies entered the room.

'Welcome again, Mrs Westland.' He greeted with a warm smile. 'Do sit down.' He indicated the armchairs and waited until they were both seated before he sat down himself. 'I hope Miss Everet has given you an interesting tour and that you like what you see, especially your room?'

'My accommodation is very comfortable and Miss Everet has been most helpful,' replied Katherine. 'We are already on Christian name terms and she has explained I will be under her supervision.'

'I think you two will get along famously. I have been reading the comprehensive notes Dr Crabtree wrote for me. He has gone into great detail but I am sure that there is much more you can tell me.' He held up his hand when he saw that Katherine was about to respond. 'Before you say anything, Mrs Westland, I would like to observe that from my study of his notes, I don't see anything seriously wrong with you and there's no reason why your memory should not be restored. It may take a considerable time, however. I am telling you this because I do not want you to think you are here to find a miracle cure. If you think that way it could impede your recovery because disappointment and frustration will get in the way. You may not think you are making progress but you will be, even if you don't recognise the signs. I see you had a long period when you suffered no setbacks or strange occurrences, then more recently there were three incidents within a very short time. Can you account for this?'

240

'I thank you for being so frank with me.'

Dr Egan spread his hands. 'It is the only way in your case. Apart from these setbacks and the fact that you cannot remember your earlier days, you lead a normal life and that is a good sign. Now, can you account for these recent occurrences?'

'I wondered if it was because I was alone when Miss Bennett had to go to Lancaster with her brother?'

'That may be so. You had probably in your mind come to rely on Miss Bennett's presence and when she went away felt that a support had been taken away from you. Here you will have Barbara as your support, and if there are times when she is away there will be someone else for you. Would you like to tell me in your own words about what happened or would you rather postpone it until tomorrow?'

'I would rather tell you now,' Katherine replied. 'I do not know what Dr Crabtree has told you but the sooner you hear my version, the sooner you can link the two.'

'Splendid. Just relax and take your time. Begin where you think best and don't be put off if you see me or Barbara making a note now and again.'

'My first recollection is of finding myself in a bed in the Fisherman's Arms in Robin Hood's Bay ...' Katherine began her story, holding nothing back, not even her suspicions about Amelia. Dr Egan and Barbara could draw their own conclusions. She realised that throughout the process she was under close scrutiny from both of them, though that scrutiny was not intrusive or off-putting.

When she had finished Dr Egan sat back in his chair, his gaze directed at her. 'Thank you for your frankness. It will be most helpful. There are a lot of questions to ask you but those can wait until tomorrow by which time I will have digested what you have told me along with Dr Crabtree's notes.'

Barbara, recognising that this was the end of the interview, rose from her chair. Katherine did likewise and followed her from the room.

Chapter Fifteen

'Hello, Roland,' Amelia greeted her brother as she neared the bottom of the stairs.

He looked round from handing his coat to Miriam who had just admitted him to the house. 'Thank you,' he said to the girl who hurried away to deposit his coat and hat in the closet. He crossed the hall to his sister. 'I'm sorry I haven't been able to get over before now. A number of special cases that had arisen while we were away needed my constant attention.'

'It doesn't seem a week since we returned,' she commented, and called to Miriam who was heading for the kitchen, 'Some tea, please.'

'Yes, ma'am. Will Dr Bennett be staying this evening?'

Amelia cast an enquiring look at her brother.

'Yes, if that doesn't cause any trouble?'

'You know it doesn't,' returned Amelia. 'Yes, Miriam, the doctor will stay the night.'

'Yes, miss. I'll tell Mrs Draper there will be two for the evening meal and I'll prepare the doctor's room.'

'Two?' Roland gave his sister a curious look.

'Yes,' she replied, moving towards the drawing-room.

'Well?' he asked as the door closed behind them.

'I'm afraid there were some dramatic events while we were in Lancaster. I had to send Katherine away.'

'What?' Concern and astonishment clouded his face.

'Sit down, Roland. It's quite a story.'

He listened without a word as his sister related events. She made sure she emphasised each separate occurrence. 'So you see, Roland, I could do nothing else but call Dr Crabtree. He talked to Katherine and his conclusion was that she should be put under care.'

'Under care?' A vision of all the degradation that might imply alarmed him.

'Now, now, Roland.' Amelia gave a gesture as if dismissing from his mind the picture she knew he had conjured up. 'She is in very good hands, being looked after privately.'

'Where?'

'Hull.'

'Why so far away? Why couldn't you have looked after her until I was able to get here?'

'Roland, I could not tolerate the accusations she made against me.'

'Accusations?'

'Yes. I was not going to tell you this if you had accepted it was in Katherine's best interest to be put under care, but she accused me of trying to drive her away from here. Said that I was jealous of her closeness to you. When Dr Crabtree heard that and linked it with the other instances of instability, he deemed it wisest to have her committed to care. He feared she might make another attack on me.'

'I must see him.' Roland jumped to his feet and headed for the door.

'Be careful what you say and do,' his sister called after him. He stopped and looked round but before he could say anything she continued, 'Don't interfere with what the good doctor has done for the best.'

He left the house and hurried to Dr Crabtree's.

'Dr Bennett. May I see Dr Crabtree immediately?' His tone was curt, filled with impatience when the maid opened the door.

'Please step inside, sir. I'll see if Dr Crabtree is available.'

After she had closed the door the maid hurried away to return almost immediately.

'Dr Crabtree will be with you in a moment, sir. Please step this way.' She opened a door to a room on the right of the hall. Roland had a feeling it was rarely used. He stood looking out of the window. Thoughts of what Amelia had told him drove all consciousness of his surroundings from his mind. They were brought back to the present when the door opened and Dr Crabtree walked in.

'Good day, Dr Bennett. I thought you would pay me a visit when you came to Scarborough.' Dr Crabtree had been determined to get in first. 'You are no doubt here because of Mrs Westland. Let me assure you that she is in good hands and being well cared for. I am sure that your sister will have made you aware of the circumstances that brought me to the decision that this was in Mrs Westland's best interests?'

'She has, but I would like to hear from you what led you to reach that conclusion?'

'I am sure I have no need to go into the details of each incident. They clearly illustrate that the condition of Mrs Westland's mind had declined rapidly while you were away. Why that should be remains a mystery, for she had been quite well for some time beforehand. But the rapid change, coupled with the previous attack she made on your sister and the accusations she recently made against Miss Bennett, made me feel that your sister could be in danger and that the best course was to remove Mrs Westland.'

'You heard those accusations yourself?'

'I did.'

Roland's lips tightened. This was hard to take. Katherine had never appeared to be that kind of person. He had hoped her attack on his sister had been an isolated incident due to an aberration of her mind, but hearing of these accusations alarmed him. He saw them as a clear indication of derangement. 'Where is she?'

'I assure you she is in good hands in a very comfortable

244

environment. I realised that if I put her in the usual type of institution generally used for such cases she might suffer a setback that could be permanently damaging. I determined that better surroundings might be more conducive to her recovering her memory. I knew of such a place run by Dr Egan in Hull and supported by philanthropic men so there are no fees to pay.'

'Thank you. I will go and see her.'

'That would not be wise,' cautioned Dr Crabtree. 'Dr Egan and I have discussed Mrs Westland's case and think it best you don't make further contact with her. Meeting you again may trigger off memories of Amelia whom she now appears to regard as an enemy. That could upset her treatment and be injurious to her.'

'But I object to . . .'

Dr Crabtree halted Dr Bennett's protest vigorously. 'I'm sorry. Dr Egan thought this might happen and strongly objects to any visit by you or your sister. I think it best you forget this lady.'

Dr Bennett's lips tightened as he fought to control his temper. 'You assure me she is well cared for?' he snapped.

'Most certainly.'

'It is a case that greatly interests me. I would therefore be obliged if you would keep me informed from time to time of Mrs Westland's progress. I am right in supposing you will still be monitoring her condition?'

'As long as is thought necessary by Dr Egan. I am entirely in his hands.'

Dr Bennett nodded. He realised that this could easily mean that after a while Dr Crabtree would no longer be concerned and Mrs Westland would have passed out of his hands entirely. He rose from his chair and glared at Crabtree. 'If I learn of anything detrimental to Mrs Westland's welfare, you and Dr Egan will hear from me in no uncertain manner.'

He took a circuitous route back to his sister's, wanting time to think. He needed to come to terms with the fact that

Katherine, in whom he had seen much of Veronica, had made such accusations against his sister. Hadn't Amelia warned him from the start to be wary of her? Had his sister seen more behind her outward appearance than he had? And if she recovered her memory, might the world in which she had lived bar him from any closer association? He could easily make a fool of himself and risk his future.

Amelia greeted him civilly.

'You have been some time, Roland. I hope Dr Crabtree was able to convince you that what he did was in Katherine's best interests?'

'I went for a walk to digest what he had told me. That, together with what you had said, made me see that you were right all along.'

Amelia felt overwhelming relief. Her brother was hers again.

'Dr Crabtree will keep me informed of Katherine's condition and progress from time to time.'

'And rightly so. After all, you were the first to tend her,' she acquiesced quietly.

'I am sorry that I brought you this trouble,' he apologised.

'Forget it, Roland. Concentrate on your practice. I am sure Katherine will recover her memory one day and you will have played your part in that.'

'It is kind of you to say so after all you have suffered with her.'

'Let us take a glass of Madeira.' Amelia went to the table and picked up the decanter. She smiled to herself with satisfaction. As far as she was concerned Katherine was out of their lives for good.

'Mrs Westland, I have studied the notes from Dr Crabtree. They are fairly comprehensive. Obviously they contain a lot of information from Miss Bennett.' As he made this last statement Dr Egan was watching Katherine closely and was certain he detected flashes of anxiety and hostility in her eyes. 'I have linked these in my mind with what I observed yesterday.' He left a thoughtful pause. 'Do you remember attacking Miss Bennett?'

'I don't remember the actual event but I must have attacked her, the evidence was there in the scratches on her face.'

'Very well. Do you recall any reason why you attacked her?'

'Not specifically related to that particular moment but I do recall hearing a voice.'

'Miss Bennett's?'

'I'm not sure. Though she was the only other person in the room.'

'Could what have happened have been prompted by some similar event earlier in your life?'

'You mean that I might have attacked someone else in the time I cannot recall?' Katherine looked shocked at the inference.

'It is a possibility, but one to which I would not set a lot of credence because I have concluded you are inherently a gentle person. However, I do have to put such questions in order to explore every possibility and try to understand your mind. Now, this voice, did you hear it again?'

'Yes. This time I'm certain it was Miss Bennett's.'

'Was she there with you this time?'

'No. She was away in Lancaster with her brother.'

Dr Egan raised an eyebrow. 'You are sure it was Miss Bennett's voice?'

'Yes.'

'So, there is a possibility that on the second occasion your mind was echoing what you had heard the first time but on that occasion had been unable to relate it to anyone or anything specific?'

'I suppose so.'

'Did you feel threatened on both occasions?'

'Yes, but more so when I identified the voice as Miss Bennett's.'

247

Dr Egan nodded. He lapsed into thoughtful silence for a few moments and then directed his questioning along a different line. 'You wear a wedding ring. Do you remember your husband?'

Katherine frowned. 'Husband?' she whispered, trying to recall.

From the intensity that had come into her face Dr Egan thought he might be on the point of learning more. 'You were wearing mourning clothes when you were found on the beach at Robin Hood's Bay. Were you in mourning for your husband?' Katherine hesitated so he prompted, 'You have referred to losing someone, could that be your husband?'

When Katherine did not reply, Barbara put a question. 'I believe after you were attacked you were heard to comment that that must have been what happened to him, though you did not say who. Could it have happened to your husband? Was he killed in a similar attack?'

'How did you know?' The words were delivered automatically by Katherine as she faced Barbara.

Dr Egan and Barbara exchanged hopeful glances.

'You do remember something about it?' queried the doctor.

Katherine rubbed her temples. Her face was twisted with the effort of remembering.

'Mrs Westland, you said, "How did you know?" which implies there is some truth in what Barbara said. Was there truth in her theory? Try to recall anything that might be connected.' Dr Egan pressed her but saw that each word was causing Katherine anxiety.

'Oh, I don't know! I can't remember.' Her cry of frustration was also filled with a plea for help.

Dr Egan saw that his questioning was causing her strain that could work against the little he had achieved. He presented a relaxed appearance as he leaned back in his chair. 'Don't worry, Mrs Westland. You have done very well and have been most co-operative and helpful. I suggest we call an end to this session and let you have some peace with Barbara. Relax and enjoy some time with her. It is a pleasant day, why not take a walk?'

His voice was soothing. Katherine felt it wash around her, clearing her mind. At the same time it gave her the feeling that here were two people she could trust, who would do all they could to help her, provided she too played her part. Insanity had never been mentioned and she got the feeling it never would be. From that she drew further hope that one day she would know who she was and if she had a family she could return to.

The weather had settled into a fine spell and Barbara took every opportunity to get Katherine out into the fresh air. Today she had driven one of the traps that Dr Egan kept for such excursions into the country west of Hull. From the rising ground they had a good view across the Humber to Lincolnshire. Downriver they could see several ships, the sun catching their sails, heading for the sea. Leaving the horse safely tethered, they strolled along the pathway on the ridge.

Barbara had been in attendance at all the interviews Dr Egan had conducted with Katherine. She knew the line of enquiry he was taking, hoping that something would stir her memory. So far there had been little. Only the odd occasion had arisen when there seemed a glimmer of hope that he was pursuing something that would bear results, only to see it fade and become enveloped in the mist of clouded memory.

'That is a very nice jet cross,' commented Barbara, glancing at the piece.

Katherine smiled in appreciation of the observation. 'It is.' She fingered it.

'You wear it every day. Has it special memories for you?'

'I think so.' There was hesitation and doubt in Katherine's voice.

249

'Did someone give it to you?'

'I suppose so.'

'Maybe a present from your mother and father?'

Katherine's brow puckered. She gave a slight shake of her head.

Barbara's heart raced. Had Katherine made a connection with the past? 'Are you sure it wasn't a present from them?'

'Yes.'

Though there was still some uncertainty in Katherine's voice, Barbara felt that her memory had been stirred sufficiently for there to be truth in her statement. She needed to verify this so put it again. 'Are you sure?'

'Yes. I told you before that they are dead so they couldn't have given it to me.'

Barbara was almost taken by surprise by the baldness of this answer, and the clear implication that the cross had been given to her after they had died. 'If they didn't give it to you, do you know who did?'

Even as Katherine shook her head she said quietly, as if in an effort to remember, 'A stranger.'

'Surely a stranger wouldn't have given you such an exquisite article?' Barbara pointed out. 'It must have been someone closer. Your husband maybe?'

Barbara did not receive a reply but noted Katherine's shudder of irritation. She knew she would have to be careful or she might undo the progress she had made. Maybe it would be better to get away from personalities. 'Do you remember where you were given it?' Katherine gave a little shake of her head.

'Jet is made in Whitby.' Barbara dropped in the information casually, hoping that it might have some effect.

'Whitby? There was a picture of Whitby at Mrs Dawson's.'

'Mrs Dawson? Who was she?'

'Miss Bennett took me there to have some dresses made when I was with her in Scarborough.'

Barbara's heart sank a little. They had left the past that Katherine could not remember. She would make one more try. 'Did that picture mean anything to you?'

'No.' But before she answered Katherine had hesitated and that made Barbara wonder if the picture had drawn some recollection into Katherine's mind. She realised that this was the moment to stop questioning. She would report events to Dr Egan and let him proceed as he thought fit.

'You did well, Barbara,' he praised after she had presented her report to him. 'This is the second time she has said her parents are dead. We can take that as fact, and it is an important step because the loss of memory has been pierced. That information is out of the way and will no longer clutter her mind which will give scope for other memories to be restored. Your angle on the jet cross is a good one. If we can find out more about it we might learn more about her relationship with the person who made the gift, be it her husband or a stranger, and following on from that about where she has lived.'

But the progress he was hoping for did not materialise. It would take time and patience to break down the barrier that shut Katherine off from her former life.

Thunder rumbled in the distance. Anxiety crossed Elizabeth Harris's face as it had done every time there had been a storm since Robert had come into their lives. She had been thankful he had never shown a reaction to bad weather. It appeared that the trauma of the terrible night of the shipwreck had not affected him. Nevertheless she still felt anxious whenever storm clouds gathered.

They not only directed her thoughts to the boy she regarded as her son, who had quite naturally accepted her and Stephen as his parents, but also gave her pangs of conscience about whether she had done the right thing in taking him as her own. No one had ever questioned her story of how he came to be living with them, but when she had heard that a woman had survived the shipwreck she had

251

entertained the idea that she and Robert might be mother and son. She always pushed that assumption to the back of her mind, telling herself that the chances of it being so were almost impossible. She kept the possibility to herself, sublimating it to the stronger thought that Robert had been sent to replace Peter. If her husband and her sister and brother-in-law had entertained similar thoughts they had kept them to themselves for they feared that if Elizabeth were to lose this child she would be so devastated her mind might be turned.

The thunder came closer. The sky darkened. Elizabeth looked out of the window. This could develop into the worst storm since Robert had come to them. Lightning tore the heavens open. It struck earthwards. Torrential rain swept over Whitby, bouncing off the roofs, turning the streets in the old port to rivers. Thunder crashed overhead.

Elizabeth started. Where was Robert? She ran to the stairs and was soon on the landing. She flung open the door of his room. He was standing at the window but turned on hearing the door open.

'Mama, Mama, isn't it exciting!' His eyes were sparkling.

She crossed the room and crouched beside him, taking him into her arms. 'You like it?'

'Yes! Yes!'

Elizabeth closed her eyes in relief. He had taken little notice of previous storms but this one, so violent, had clearly roused interest and excitement in him. 'You're not afraid?'

'No, Mama, no!' His eyes were bright, and he cried out with glee at each flash and thunder roll.

Elizabeth held him, thankful that the ferocity of the storm which had led to the shipwreck and its consequences had not affected his mind in the way she had once feared.

When Stephen came home from his jet workshop, Robert ran to meet him. 'Papa, wasn't it exciting?'

'What?' he asked. Laughing at the boy's enthusiasm, he scooped him up into his arms.

252

'The storm! The storm!'

Though he did not show it, Stephen was surprised by Robert's reaction to what had been an outbreak verging on the terrifying. He kept his thoughts to himself until Robert was tucked up in bed for the night. When he and Elizabeth were seated in front of the fire, she with her knitting and he with his pipe, he commented on Robert's attitude.

'I was as surprised as you, Stephen. I found him in his room watching from the window. He was so drawn to it that he would not come away and we stayed there until it had passed. He was not in the least frightened.'

'For that I'm grateful. I thought when we experienced a really bad one it might recall the trauma he went through.'

'So did I. I hope it doesn't make him oblivious to danger. I couldn't face another tragedy like losing Peter. We must discourage him from being attracted to the sea.'

'Elizabeth, we must not stifle the boy's natural instinct. We'll give him our love and guide him as we did Peter.'

'And look what happened!'

'We must not let that cloud our judgement nor our advice to him.'

'Concentrate his attention on the jet trade when the time is right.'

'I have a mind to do that, but if he has no interest in it we can do nothing about that.'

'Encourage him, please?'

'Of course I will. You know that it was my intention that Peter should take over from me. Well, I hope that it can be the same for Robert.'

'I hope and pray it will be so.'

Patience was Dr Egan and Barbara's stock in trade. It was part and parcel of their profession. And in Katherine they had a charge who was a likeable person, in her present life as normal as anyone. She could take her place in the world outside at any time but Dr Egan was reluctant to let her do

253

that. He felt she still needed their help, and that if she became attached to anyone outside who was unsympathetic, all the progress he and Barbara had made could be destroyed. She might even revert to making attacks of which there had been no recurrence since she had come under their care.

So the weeks rolled into months with no marked progress, but there were small moments of recollection that he regarded as steps in the right direction.

One day she mentioned Newcastle but couldn't recall being there. The name John came to her lips when, some months later, Dr Egan resurrected her reference to Newcastle but he could elicit no further information that would connect the two. So his probing went on.

'Are you happy here, Katherine?' he asked on another occasion.

'Oh, yes. Most certainly.'

'What did you think when you heard you were coming here?'

'I expected it to be a grim place like those I had heard about.'

'You had heard about them? Where? In Scarborough?'

'Oh, no.' Her mind carried her back to the moment she had been alone in Amelia's drawing-room awaiting Dr Crabtree's arrival and had wondered where she was being taken. 'But I had heard about them and seen them from the outside – grim-looking places.'

'Where had you seen them?'

Katherine's face creased with annoyance. 'I'm not sure, but there were houses and other buildings all around.' She hesitated but Dr Egan sensed she had more to say.

'Go on? Say what comes into your mind.'

'There were rows and rows of houses.' The words came slowly as if they were being dragged from the depths of remembrance. 'There were crowds, people everywhere. We moved on. There were fewer people. Streets again but more elegant. Fine houses. Carriages. Fashionable ladies.'

She stopped. Her mind was still dragging at the past.

'Do you know where this was?'

She thought for a moment then shook her head slowly. 'No.'

'It must have been a town or a city. Maybe a big one. You once mentioned Newcastle, could it have been there?'

Katherine looked thoughtful. 'I don't think so. It seemed bigger.'

'Bigger? Are you sure?'

Katherine gave a little nod. 'Yes.'

'How did you get there?'

Katherine's gaze had become vacant. 'Water. I can see water.'

'You got there by sea?'

She nodded.

'Did you leave the same way?'

Again she nodded.

Dr Egan had made notes and was beginning to draw some conclusions but rather than pursue this line he switched it because Katherine had made a remark he wanted to seize on before it was fogged by the recollections she had just made. 'Mrs Westland, when you were describing the place you mentioned crowds and lots of people and then you said, "We moved on." Who was with you?'

'With me?' She looked puzzled.

'Yes. From what you said, I took it someone was with you.'

'I don't remember.'

'Where were you going?'

'Home.'

'To a house in the more elegant area you mentioned?'

'Yes.'

'But you don't remember where it was?'

'No.'

'You said it was bigger than Newcastle. Could it have been London?'

'I suppose so.'

255

Dr Egan looked hard at her. 'I am going to make some speculations from what you have told me just now and in the past. It is possible that you made a sea journey from Newcastle to London. I think you were married – you wear a ring. Maybe to John, a name you mentioned some time ago. I think that you lived in an elegant area of the city. Why you went there I have no notion except to guess that maybe your husband's work took him there. Then for some reason you left. You were found on the beach at Robin Hood's Bay dressed in mourning clothes. You do not remember for whom you were mourning. It could have been a family member, a close friend or even your husband. I mention the latter possibility because I was told, although you could not remember it, that after you were attacked in Scarborough you remarked that this must be what happened to him. It could have been your husband to whom you were referring. I surmise that because he was killed you decided to leave London and were heading north, possibly for Newcastle, when the ship was wrecked.'

Katherine had listened intently to his theory. She could see how he had reasoned it out from the information he had. 'You could be right, Doctor, but I can't say with certainty that you are. You would think if I was married to this John I would remember. The closeness of marriage would surely stick in the memory?'

'The mind is a strange thing, Mrs Westland. It has acted strangely in your case and could equally act as strangely in the way it brings some things back to you, and not others. Through my theory I have implanted thoughts in your mind. Let them germinate. As they do and you allow them to play one with the other, certain aspects may become more prominent and spark off the truth of your earlier life. I cannot guarantee that it will occur like a flash of lightning. It might do but it could also be a long process. You must be patient and not expect too much too soon. You have much to think about but don't overtax your mind. That could have a damaging effect. You have been a model

256

patient so far, please continue in that vein. I am sure Barbara will give you all the support and help she can.'

Later that day Dr Egan discussed this interview with Barbara and explained his theory so that she would be in full possession of all that had taken place and be able to use it when talking with Katherine.

She took in every word. She and Katherine had become very close friends and Barbara wanted to do all she could to restore Katherine's memory. She saw that every particle of information could be important to that end. When the doctor had finished she said, 'If your theory that Katherine sailed from Newcastle to London is true, it is possible that the ship put into Whitby and that her husband bought her the jet cross there.'

Dr Egan's eyes brightened. 'A strong possibility. It is something you could work on. Such a thing could be sufficient to put everything into perspective for her.'

'There is something missing from your theory however.'

Dr Egan raised his eyebrows. 'What might that be?'

'Katherine twice went to the beach in Scarborough supposedly looking for someone. Who could that be if your theory that her husband was murdered in London is right?'

'It could still be him ... though why the beach? Unless she is associating it with the shipwreck and she herself being found on the beach and thinks that is where he lost his life.'

Barbara nodded but wasn't convinced. 'Could there have been someone else?'

'I suppose so.' Dr Egan spread his hands. 'But who? She has only mentioned a John, who I think must be her husband.'

'But just as equally it could be the person lost in the shipwreck for whom she searched the beach. A child?'

'My initial examination showed that she had had a child but she does not remember that she had one. Maternal instincts are so strong that I think she would have remembered if a child was with her on the ship even though everything else was lost to her.' He paused then added, 'See what you can do. I think we are making good progress, slow but steady. Be careful not to press the matter of a child. If there was indeed a child with her on the ship then the sudden realisation that she had lost an infant in the shipwreck might damage her mind further.'

Chapter Sixteen

During the next few weeks Katherine pondered Dr Egan's theory. It was plausible but was it what had really happened to her? Barbara helped her with her recollections but put her under no pressure. She used the gentle approach, suggesting this and that without forcing Katherine's inclinations. The casual mention of a possible child brought no response but all the while Barbara sensed that there were certain things becoming clearer in Katherine's mind. Maybe something needed prompting so she suggested one day, when they were going for their daily walk, that a visit to the docks might prove interesting to Katherine who would see a side of Hull life she had still to witness.

Though the day was not cold they wrapped up well, for Barbara knew that the breeze blowing from the Humber would bring a bite to the air. They kept to a leisurely pace enjoying the bustle of the town which increased when they entered Mytongate; fashionably dressed ladies were looking in shop windows or emerging into the thoroughfare after making a purchase; a horse pulling a cart laden with sacks caused a girl skipping across the road to change direction; a mother with a babe in arms kept to the pavement, while a governess remonstrated with a little boy who insisted on running in the gutter; three men came out of the Victoria Inn and headed for the dock where their ship was berthed, having tasted their last ale for a few days or even weeks.

When Katherine and Barbara turned into Humber Dock Street the activity drew them to a halt. Carts rumbled across the cobblestones taking the latest cargoes to warehouses to await distribution. Others were arriving to be unloaded by the gangs of men hired to get the goods on board before sailing time. There was hustle and bustle everywhere. The dock was crowded with shipping. Masts soared high like a forest of trees with the rigging forming a mesmerising latticework; barrels of wine and molasses lay beside bales of cotton on the quayside; a cart stacked with milk churns trundled by, its driver shouting a greeting to someone he had recognised; orders were barked, exchanges were shouted, all aimed at making every operation more efficient and profitable.

Katherine was fascinated, eager to learn more. She stopped at the foot of a gangplank leading on to a vessel that appeared to be almost ready for sailing. A sturdy young man with a bag slung over his shoulder, cap set at a jaunty angle, moved past her to reach the gangplank. Katherine smiled and nodded. 'Excuse me,' she said, stopping the man in his tracks, 'where is your ship bound?'

'Spain, ma'am, with that timber you see stacked on deck, and there's woollen goods in the hold. We sail on the next tide.'

'A Hull vessel?'

'No, ma'am. We came in from Newcastle three days ago to collect this cargo.'

'Newcastle. I used to live there.' Katherine looked thoughtful then added brightly, 'I hope you have a good voyage.'

'Thank you, ma'am.' The young man touched his cap and strode up the gangplank.

Barbara had heard nothing of the final exchange. Her mind was racing with the implications of Katherine's statement, 'Newcastle, I used to live there'. Questions mounted in her mind but she held them in check. Katherine had made her statement casually in the course of conversation with a stranger. To rush in now with question after question might destroy any recollection that had dawned unexpectedly. Newcastle had been mentioned before but this time her statement held greater recall.

They strolled on, commenting on all the activity around them, fascinated by the sight of a working port which in spite of all its roughness carried a glamour through its connection with lands beyond the sea.

'I wonder if any more of these vessels are from Newcastle,' Barbara dropped in casually. 'You told that young man that you used to live there.'

'Yes, with Father and Mother.'

Now Barbara had verification of what Katherine had said before.

'Why did you leave?'

'My parents were dead.'

'Where did you go then?'

Katherine had stopped. She was gazing at one of the ships. 'London.' The word came as a whisper, almost as if she was doubting the truth of her own statement.

'London?'

Katherine nodded. 'Yes, on a ship like that.' She swung round with a swiftness that took Barbara by surprise. 'London, yes, I went to London.' Her eyes were bright with excitement. 'Barbara, my memory is returning. Newcastle, my mother and father, London ... I remember them now with certainty.'

Barbara gripped her by the shoulders. 'Steady, Katherine, there are lots of gaps to fill in, but this is a good start.' She let her enthusiasm for what she felt was an important step spill over and hugged Katherine to her. 'I'm so pleased!' She stepped back, still holding Katherine's hands. 'We must take this calmly and not try to rush things. Come, let us walk.'

261

They strolled on, now oblivious to all the activity around them as their minds were filled with hope that Katherine's recollections of the past would advance even further. Barbara knew she would have to be careful, though. If she rushed things she might confuse a mind still trying to escape from its dark shadow.

'Did you go to London on your own?'

Katherine stopped and looked at the ship that had brought back the memory of London. She tried to visualise the moments she had spent on a similar ship but they were hazy. She shook her head. 'I don't think so.' Frustrated that one recollection did not follow another, she stamped her foot. 'I thought my memory was returning.'

'Katherine, it is. What has occurred today is a significant step forward. Don't be upset that everything doesn't come back at once. We have established some facts and they will remain in your memory now as part of your life. The rest will come, I'm convinced of it. I'm sure your "I don't think so" is really a no. So, do you know who accompanied you?'

'Maybe it was the John Dr Egan theorised about. Maybe it was my husband. Maybe they are one and the same. But, Barbara, I can't remember.' She shook her head, screwed up her face and allowed the tears to flow.

Barbara placed a comforting hand on her arm. 'Don't be upset, Katherine, that won't help. Take heart from the progress we have just made.'

Katherine gave a wan smile. 'I'm sorry for making an exhibition of myself and embarrassing you,' she said, aware that passersby were casting them curious glances. She took a handkerchief from her sleeve and dabbed her eyes.

Barbara gave her a reassuring smile. 'You did no such thing.' She linked arms, and as they walked tried to divert Katherine's mind by commenting on objects on their way.

Dr Egan was pleased with Barbara's report of their visit

to the docks. He regarded it as progress but, though he tried to build on it, hoping for some fresh momentous recollection, only minor things stirred Katherine's mind. He was thankful, however, that the frustration she experienced upon not making the further headway she'd expected did not seriously upset the even tenor of her present life.

She enjoyed shopping and walking in the nearby countryside, especially along the banks of the Humber. She loved the vantage points from which she could see the ships heading for the sea and their unknown destinations, or watch them plying their way upriver to unload their cargoes from mysterious ports around the world. Her interest in ships and her insistence that they should make other visits to the docks surprised Barbara after the traumas of the shipwreck she had experienced. That, amazingly, seemed to have left no scars except for the loss of her memory.

Books continued to be a delight to her and she and Barbara had many an interesting discussion about those they were reading.

'I think I'll read *Rob Roy* again,' Katherine remarked one day.

'You've read it before?' Barbara queried.

'Oh, yes. It's a favourite of mine. I admire Rob Roy so much. He was not the villain some historians would have us believe.'

'When did you read it?'

'At home in Newcastle. My mother first gave it to me.'

'Was she a reader?' Barbara saw this line of the conversation as a possible way of establishing more of Katherine's past.

'Oh, yes, she loved books and I inherited her enthusiasm.'

'Was your father a reader too?'

'Yes, but he was not as passionate about it as my mother. I read *Rob Roy* again in London.'

'You must have liked it. Why did you go to London?'

Katherine frowned and gave a slightly irritated shake of her head, muttering, 'I don't know.'

'You went after your mother and father died. Did you go to a relation?'

'No ... at least, I don't think so. Now that I am remembering more about Mother and Father I think I would have recalled any other relations, but why I went to London and what I was doing there are still blank to me.'

'Never mind. I'm sure that just as aspects of your life in Newcastle have returned to you and are now a valid part of your memory, London will become the same.'

But although Barbara and Dr Egan frequently tried to implant ideas that might stir Katherine's memory, she made no further progress in her memories of life in London. One aspect of these endeavours that pleased them nevertheless was that she lost the despairing expression that used to creep into her face whenever she battled to recover her memory completely. She became resigned to the fact that she might never fill in the blanks that had once haunted her to the point of utter despair. Now she accepted them as part of her present life.

One day Dr Egan called her and Barbara into his office.

'Katherine, you have been with us eight years and over that time we have been delighted with your progress. Though, sadly, gaps remain in your memory we believe they are now no impediment to your leading a normal life in the outside world.'

The shock of the implication behind these words startled Katherine.

'There's nothing to be alarmed about,' went on Dr Egan quickly to reassure her. 'This does not mean you are going to be turned out and left to God and Providence. I will only allow your return to the outside world when I think the circumstances suitable. I am telling you this now so you can get used to the idea. I have discussed your case fully with Barbara over the past three days and she agrees with me.'

Katherine cast her a plaintive look.

'It is for your good, Katherine,' she said gently. 'I believe you can cope very well on your own. Please don't get the idea we are casting you aside. We will always be here if you need us, and the friendship that you and I have forged need never be broken.'

Katherine bit her lips to hold back tears. 'I hope not.' There was a catch in her throat. 'I will miss you both and all the other people here.'

'I have seen signs lately that you are coming to rely on us too much. It is better, at this stage, for you to rely more on yourself and make your own judgements. That could aid a full recovery of your memory for it may help you recall decisions you had to make in the past.'

Katherine nodded. She could see the reasoning but it was going to be difficult to move away from here.

'As I say, Katherine, there need be nothing immediate and you will not have to move until we all decide the time is right.'

'Dr Egan will not let you go to an unsuitable place, Katherine,' said Barbara comfortingly as they walked up the stairs to the first floor.

'I know,' she replied, 'but I will miss you.'

'And I you, but we will always be friends and need not lose touch. And of course I will always be interested in your progress.'

'If I make any more progress.' There was a touch of hopelessness in Katherine's voice. 'I don't think I will ever recover my memory fully.'

'You mustn't think like that. You must believe that you will.' They had reached Katherine's room and paused before the door. 'Let's go for a walk, I think we could both do with some fresh air. See you in the hall in five minutes.' Barbara did not wait for Katherine's agreement but hurried away to look in on her other two patients.

For a moment she wished that Barbara had not made the suggestion. She felt she wanted to be left alone to wallow in her own misery, but knew that her friend was only suggesting it from concern for her.

A few minutes later the two women were striding away from the house. By the time they returned Katherine felt that the impact of Dr Egan's suggestion had been lifted. There had been subtle aspects of Barbara's conversation that had eased her mind and made her realise that the future could be bright. She saw that she had come to rely too much on the security of Dr Egan's establishment and that she had now reached a stage where self-reliance could be better for her. Now she must await his advice about when to plunge back into the outside world.

Twelve-year-old Robert kept having to quicken his pace to keep up with his father as they made their way home from the jet workshop. He didn't mind, he was eager to get there. In his hand he clutched a round piece of jet on which he had scratched a geometric pattern of his own design, the first that had been completely his.

His father had encouraged him over the past two years to take an interest in jet. The boy had not been slow to respond and his father was pleased. He was also delighted that his employees encouraged the boy, liked having him around and were pleased to pass on their own skills, whatever aspect of the trade they followed. Most of all Robert loved to watch the men carving the jet into all sorts of pieces, lockets, brooches, bracelets, hair combs, or scratching intricate designs on it. Sometimes they would allow him to put his own touch on their designs, but today he had finally completed one that was all his own work and was eager to give it to his mother.

'Ma! Ma!' he yelled as he flung open the front door and raced along the passage.

'Here, love, in the kitchen.' There was laughter in her voice when she detected her son's excitement.

He burst into the kitchen. Elizabeth, bowl in hand, was standing at the oak table in the centre of the room. Since moving to the West Side of Whitby, into a bigger and more elegant house in Well Close Square, and employing a cook and three maids, there was no need for her to be in the kitchen, but she had always loved baking and was not about to relinquish the enjoyment completely. She put the bowl and mixing spoon on the table and stepped to one side to meet Robert's onrush. She laughed as he flung himself into her arms. The cook and the kitchen maid smiled broadly at the excitement that lit up his face. They liked the boy, loved his enthusiasm which at times flowed into mischief, knowing that he would never step beyond the bounds laid down by his parents.

'This is for you, Mother.' He wriggled out of her arms and held out the package.

'Thank you, Robert. What is it?' She looked up at her husband who heard this exchange as he came into the kitchen. His broad smile told her he would give nothing away.

'Open it,' pressed Robert. He could hardly contain himself as she unwrapped the item carefully.

'Oh, Robert, thank you. It is beautiful.'

'I did it all by myself,' he revealed with pride.

'You didn't?'

'I did, I did. Didn't I, Father?'

'You certainly did.' Stephen looked at his wife. 'His first piece and he did it especially for you.'

'It's beautiful. You did the design yourself?'

'Yes, look.' He came to her and ran his finger along some of the lines. 'The prow of a boat. A net hanging over the side. The edge of a cloud.'

Elizabeth nodded. Now that he had pointed them out she could see what an intricate design he had made and yet there was a simplicity about it that made it an attractive piece. 'Look, Mrs Reed.' She held the piece out to the cook who came to look at it and express her astonishment. The kitchen maid's eyes widened when Elizabeth showed it to her. 'By gum!' was all she could say. Robert laughed, pleased with the reception his piece had received from them all.

'Cup of tea, Mrs Reed?' Elizabeth gave the cook a conspiratorial glance, knowing that earlier in the day they had made Robert's favourite chocolate cake. 'Come, Robert, tell me all about it.' She took his hand and walked him to the drawing-room, proud of her son's achievement. She would treasure forever his first piece of jet work. As they reached the room, she said, 'Run and wash your hands, Robert, and then come down for some tea.'

Full of life, he raced up the stairs to his room.

Elizabeth turned to her husband. 'Oh, Stephen, this is such a wonderful day. I can see real talent there. Am I right?' The tone of her voice implied she did not want to be wrong. But she knew her husband would tell her the truth. If there was talent he would not diminish it. If he saw no future in the jet trade for Robert, he would not disguise the fact just because she wanted to hear otherwise.

'You are right, Elizabeth, he has real talent. At the moment it is in design. I have watched him drawing patterns for some time now and only advised when asked because I wanted the ideas to be entirely his own, particularly when he moved on from simple designs. The men have helped but I told them only to advise on using the tools, never to influence his designs. The next stage is carving. If he develops there in the way he has in etching then he will be a real craftsman.'

'As good as Peter would have been?' she asked with a touch of sadness in her voice. Even after all this time she had not forgotten the son in whom she had had so much hope.

'Yes,' replied Stephen, 'and his interest in all aspects of the trade is wonderful to see in one so young. We have indeed been blessed.'

The maid arrived with the tea, and a few moments after she had gone Robert burst into the room.

'Steady, Robert, steady,' called Stephen cautiously as the boy flung himself on to the sofa.

He twisted round, saw the chocolate cake standing enticingly on a glass cake stand. His eyes widened. 'Hurrah! Chocolate cake.' He watched his mother cut a substantial slice for him but his mind was racing on. 'Are we going to Aunt Mary's tomorrow?' His eyes were bright with anticipation.

Stephen laughed. 'Of course. It's the day for our monthly visit.'

'Good! Good! Good!' Robert bounced up and down on the sofa. He loved visiting his aunt, uncle and cousins in Robin Hood's Bay. It was such an exciting place, with its narrow streets twisting and climbing and dropping down the cliffside to meet at the slipway that let on to the beach where the scaurs held entrancing pools left behind by the retreating sea. A long strand of sand led to the towering cliffs at Ravenscar with much for a young boy to explore. He would hear tales or smugglers, Preventive Men and troops, of cutters and cobles and shipwrecks. And best of all there was often the opportunity to go out in his uncle's coble with his two cousins.

That was one aspect of the visits that Elizabeth did not relish. She loved to see her sister, brother-in-law and nephews, Mark and Crispin, both of whom were now married to local girls and still lived within a stone's throw of their parents. They enjoyed the enthusiasm of their young cousin, especially when they whispered in his ear, 'Like to go out on the bay?'

Elizabeth wished they wouldn't encourage him, though. She voiced this to Stephen out of Robert's earshot every time they went to Robin Hood's Bay, but knew her husband would do nothing about it except utter a caution to the boy.

'The horse and trap will be ready?' Robert asked eagerly.

'Has Mr Plunket ever let us down?'

'No. Hurrah for Mr Plunket!'

'Robert, just sit still and have your chocolate cake.'

Though this came out as a rebuke there was no mistaking the love behind it.

Robert was awake early the following morning. Eager to see what the weather was like he tumbled out of bed and ran to the window. He scanned the sky in a way that was knowledgeable beyond his years. He had learned to read the signs from the friendly sailors and fishermen he liked to talk to along the harbour side. They responded to his thirst for nautical knowledge but, because of the tragedy of Peter Harris, whom many of them remembered, they turned down his pleas to sail with them. Stephen knew they would stick to the request he had privately made. But he could not impose such a prohibition on his nephews at Robin Hood's Bay without Robert's knowledge and did not want the boy resenting him. He knew Elizabeth feared what might happen, and recognised the tension that came over her with every visit and the efforts she made to curb her anxiety.

Robert turned from the window with a broad smile on his face and excitement coursing through his veins. He had read good signs in the sky. This was proved right for the ride to Baytown passed in pleasant sunshine with a slight breeze to keep the odd cloud moving. Stephen eventually pulled the trap to a halt at Ben Carter's stable.

'Hello, folks, ye'll have had a grand ride,' he greeted them, rising from his chair where he had been enjoying a pipe in the sunshine.

'We have, Ben,' agreed Elizabeth, handing him a basket the contents of which were covered by a white cloth.

'Thanks, ma'am,' he said, taking it gratefully. He knew it would contain some scrumptious items of Elizabeth's latest baking. Ben winked at Robert. 'Now, young man, a likely day to search the rocks.'

'For sailing, Mr Carter,' replied Robert, with quick enthusiasm.

'Well now, if thee does, thee be careful.' He gave his

270

advice in the friendliest of ways, glancing at Elizabeth and seeing a shadow of concern on her face. 'You heed my words now, Robert.'

'I will, sir.' He turned to his father. 'Can I go, Pa?'

'Off you go. We'll see you at Aunt Mary's.'

With a whoop, Robert raced off down the hill towards the cluster of houses toppling down towards the sea.

Ben chuckled. 'You've a fine boy there, ma'am.' He inclined his head with a gesture of approval. He was delighted that this likeable couple had been able to take on a friend's child as a replacement for Peter, and that the boy was turning out to be a joy to them. He hoped that nothing ever happened to ruin their happiness again.

Elizabeth and Stephen started off down the incline and were soon being given a warm welcome by Mary and Harry.

'Can I go and see Crispin and Mark?' asked Robert, eager to be free from the adults whom he knew would spend the day gossiping. He would rather be with his cousins even though they were considerably older and had their own family responsibilities, but they liked the young lad who had come unexpectedly into their lives and had always been ready to befriend him.

'All right,' agreed Elizabeth, 'but don't make a nuisance of yourself.'

Mary gave a little chuckle. 'They'll never say he does that. They spoil him but it doesn't seem to do him any harm. You brought him up and taught him well, Liz.'

Elizabeth gave her a smile of appreciation. 'We do our best as we did with Peter. We can never repay you for what you did all those years ago. Did anyone ever suspect?'

'No. Nobody here ever questioned that you were helping a friend. After all, there was nothing to associate the child you took in in Whitby with the shipwreck here.' Mary put a livelier note into her voice as she changed the subject. 'The dinner is doing nicely in the oven. I'll only have the Yorkshire puddings to put in when we're about ready to

271

eat. So what would you like to do? The men have no doubt gone to have a smoke and a yarn with their cronies.'

'A stroll on the beach?'

'Very well.' Mary knew this was a bit of a ritual with her sister who used it to see if Robert was going out in a coble with his cousins.

They donned their coats and draped warm shawls over their heads. Taking a short cut through the narrow streets that were little more than paths along the frontages of cottages vying for space on the steep cliff, they came out near the slipway where a number of cobles were drawn up. The tide was high. Waves broke gently on the sand or scurried over the scaurs through which it was awkward to manoeuvre a boat. But Baytown men knew their bay, knew the tricky approach and had placed markers as guides to the gap between the rocks. But the approach was still fraught with danger, especially if there was a high sea running or a storm blowing up.

Mary was thankful that there was neither today, for she had recognised one of the cobles in the bay as that of her brother-in-law and his two sons. No doubt Robert had persuaded Crispin and Mark to take him out.

Mary read the expression of concern on her sister's face. 'Don't worry, Liz. He'll be all right. Mark and Crispin will look after him.'

'But what if the weather changes?'

'The boys will keep an eye on it.' Mary glanced skywards. 'I don't think you need worry today. The weather is set fair.' She glanced at her sister whose brow was creased with worry. 'Relax, Liz. You do yourself no good worrying as you do.'

'You haven't lost a son to the sea as I have.'

'I know. But I do know what a worry it is when your menfolk go to sea, as mine do almost every day. You haven't that to live with, Liz. But what do you think my life would be like if I let such a worry dominate it? Don't try and dissuade the boy from any natural instinct or ability.

272

That way he'll know you aren't placing any restrictions on him, other than those that are necessary, and he will love you all the more for it. You have been very lucky to have found such a fine lad who is a credit to the way you and Stephen have brought him up.'

'And I think we owe a debt of gratitude to his parents and what he must have inherited from them. I wonder who they were?'

Chapter Seventeen

Katherine responded to the knock on her door. When it opened, one of Dr Egan's maids slipped into the room.

'Sorry to interrupt your reading, ma'am, but Dr Egan says will you come to his reception room?'

'Certainly, Grace. I'll be right down.' Katherine laid her book on the table beside her chair and rose to her feet, wondering why Dr Egan had sent for her. Nearly two months had passed since he had suggested she should leave his care when he'd found a suitable place for her. Had he done so? Was this what the summons was about? She went to the long mirror that was fixed to the wall next to her wardrobe and looked critically at herself. She adjusted her dress, smoothed it with her hands, patted her hair and put some unruly strands into place before leaving her room and tripping quickly down the stairs to knock on the reception-room door.

When she entered, Dr Egan rose from the comfort of an armchair. Another gentleman got to his feet as well. He was well-dressed in a grey swallow-tail coat with short rounded tails. His trousers of matching grey were patterned in small checks of a darker tone. His waistcoat was also grey but had a touch of gaiety about its blue and pink spots. A matching cravat was tied at his neck over a white frilled shirt. His hair was greying at the temples, otherwise almost jet black.

Katherine sensed she had come under his close scrutiny from the moment she entered the room but judged it was something he felt obliged to do, for when she met his gaze he looked away and glanced nervously at the lady beside him who was also watching her closely.

Katherine was startled. The lady was very pale and, with her skin drawn tight across her cheek bones, the length of her face was exaggerated but not unpleasantly so. In fact, it gave her an extraordinary fragile beauty. Her eyes were a startling blue and shone with a radiance that came from the inner person. She smiled at Katherine with an expression that was not only warm but held hope that the two of them would be friends. Her clothes were of the best quality and immaculately cut, Katherine saw.

'Katherine, I want you to meet Mr and Mrs Bradshaw.' After greetings were exchanged Dr Egan invited her to sit down. 'There is something we would like to discuss with you.'

She took the chair he indicated. It had been placed so that she was half facing Mr and Mrs Bradshaw. The two men waited until she was seated before taking their own chairs again.

'I will come straight to the point, Katherine. Mr and Mrs Bradshaw are seeking a companion for Mrs Bradshaw and I thought this the ideal position for you. It has a great deal to recommend it, and I think the added responsibility could aid you to a full recovery.' He read in Katherine's startled look her concern that these strangers should know of her predicament. 'It is all right, Katherine. Naturally I have made Mr and Mrs Bradshaw fully conversant with your case. It was only fair that they knew all the facts before deciding to employ you.'

She had regained her composure. 'Quite right, Doctor. I would not wish to go into any employment under the shadow of deception.' She turned to Mr and Mrs Bradshaw with a question but it was never asked because Mrs Bradshaw spoke first.

'My dear Mrs Westland, let me assure you that we do not hold any reservations against you because there are certain aspects of your life that you cannot remember. I understand you have not let it affect the fine person Dr Egan assures us you are, and his assessment is backed up by Miss Everet whom we understand has been close to you. If you decide to become my companion there will be no pressure put on you to recall the missing past. If, however, your memory should return, as Dr Egan has indicated that it might, we will not influence any decision you might make to take up your former life again rather than stay with us.'

'Those are kind words, Mrs Bradshaw.' Katherine had been drawn not only by the thoughtfulness and consideration behind them but also by her smooth, gentle tone of voice that was very reassuring. 'I do appreciate your attitude. May I ask what my work will entail?'

'Of course.' She gave a little smile. 'You cannot be expected to accept without knowing that.' Mrs Bradshaw looked at her husband who, catching her eye, cleared his throat and took up the explanation.

'Mrs Bradshaw has not been well for some time now. At one stage her illness was serious but she had great determination and recovered. Not as fully as we had all hoped but sufficient for us to take heart and accept the doctors' reassurances that she could live as normal a life as she saw fit, without overdoing things.'

There was sympathy in the glance Katherine gave Mrs Bradshaw who smiled in return.

'Our two children are married and have moved away from our locality.'

'Which is?' prompted Katherine as he paused.

'We have an estate on the Wolds where we live at Ribton Hall. It is a little isolated. We have someone who manages the estate as I am frequently in Hull, sometimes staying there, depending on the demands of my shipping business. It is because my absences have become more frequent that we seek a companion for my wife.'

'Your duties will not be onerous, Mrs Westland,' said Mrs Bradshaw. 'It is more a matter of being there. I would not want to be a burden. I am sure we can find much of mutual interest to prevent your life from becoming boring.'

'I don't think it would become that, Mrs Bradshaw. I would not let it.'

She smiled. 'Nor would I. Now, is there anything else you would like to know?'

'No, ma'am.'

'The salary, Mrs Westland?' Mr Bradshaw raised an eyebrow.

'I trust you, sir. No doubt I will have accommodation and my keep. They, I am sure, will be most acceptable. Over and above that I trust you to be fair and expect you will be guided by your wife.'

'Very well.' Mr Bradshaw, caught off guard by Katherine's attitude, let his voice trail away.

Mrs Bradshaw smiled to herself. This was a shrewd lady. She had summed up certain aspects of their situation and relationship very quickly. 'You will want time to consider?'

'I don't think so, Mrs Bradshaw. I will come to Ribton Hall. In fact, if you have no objection to waiting, I could return there with you now?' She glanced at Dr Egan for his approval. He smiled and nodded. 'I have very few belongings so it won't take me long to pack.'

'That is admirable,' said Mrs Bradshaw, delighted that Katherine had accepted and that the matter had been settled quickly. 'Is it not, Daniel?'

'Indeed it is. Most satisfactory.'

Katherine hurried up the stairs, excitement in her brisk step. She had no sooner reached her room than there was a knock on the door and Barbara came in.

'Well?' she asked. She obviously knew that the interview had been taking place. There was eagerness and anxiety in her query.

'You knew about Mr and Mrs Bradshaw?'

'Yes. Dr Egan told me they were coming but said not to

say anything to you. Well, what are you doing?'

'I'm going,' Katherine said, laughing. Then reality struck. 'Oh, Barbara, I'll be leaving you.' Her face instantly clouded with sorrow.

Half laughing, half crying, Barbara flung her arms round her and they stood locked together, tears of sadness and of joy streaming down their faces.

'I'll miss you,' sobbed Barbara.

'No more than I you.'

'When do you go?'

'Now.'

Barbara broke their embrace. 'Then we must pack quickly.' She wiped the tears from her cheeks. 'What do you want me to do?'

'Clear those drawers.'

Within ten minutes, in spite of their tears, laughter and reminiscences, Katherine was ready to leave. They stood silently, looking at each other. Katherine stepped forward and took Barbara's hands in hers. Her friend's eyes were full of love and understanding.

'Thank you for all you have done for me,' said Katherine. 'I will ever be grateful to you.'

'Knowing you and sharing so much with you was payment enough,' replied Barbara. 'Be happy. If ever you need me, you know where to find me. Take care of yourself.'

Katherine was too overcome to reply. She took Barbara in her arms and hugged her tight, then broke away, grabbed her two cases and hurried from the room. She dare not look back. She put her luggage near the front door and crossed the hall to the reception room.

'I'm sorry I kept you waiting,' she apologised.

Everyone rose from their chairs.

'Not at all,' replied Mrs Bradshaw.

'You have seen Barbara?' queried Dr Egan.

Katherine swallowed hard and nodded.

Dr Egan gave her an understanding smile and took her

278

hands. 'You have been a delightful patient, Mrs Westland. I am sorry we did not achieve our ultimate aim but feel sure that you will achieve it one day. Don't forget, we are here if you ever need us. Take life as it comes. I am sure you will be happy with Mr and Mrs Bradshaw.'

'Thank you for all your help and patience with me. I am sure I was a trial at times.'

'Never. Take care of yourself.' He escorted her to the door.

Mr Bradshaw had called his coachman who had taken the two cases to the coach.

'Dr Egan, thank you.' Mr Bradshaw held out his hand which was taken in a firm grip.

The doctor turned to Mrs Bradshaw. 'I am certain everything will turn out for the best.'

'I am sure it will, Doctor, and thank you again for recommending Mrs Westland.' She turned to Katherine. 'Come along, my dear, we are going to enjoy each other's company.'

As the coach drove away, Katherine raised a hand to Dr Egan who was standing on the steps at the front door. Instinctively she glanced up at the windows of Barbara's room. She was there. Their eyes met across the distance. Barbara waved. With tears streaming down her cheeks, Katherine returned the wave. She quickly fished a handkerchief from her sleeve and wiped her eyes as she settled for the ride.

'You were happy there?' commented Mrs Bradshaw sympathetically.

'Yes, ma'am.'

'I hope you will be as happy with us.' She adjusted the rug that her husband had carefully placed around her legs. 'Now, there is to be no more of this formality, no more "ma'am". You are to live as one of us, not as an employee. You and I can share so much more on that footing. There will be no barriers between us.'

Mr Bradshaw gave a little cough. Katherine couldn't be

certain but thought it held a note of disapproval.

'So,' Mrs Bradshaw continued, impervious to his hint, 'we will be on first-name terms. I know you are Katherine. Is that what you like to be called or have you another given name?'

'I have always been Katherine.' As soon as she said it she wondered how she knew that? Maybe in the blank recesses of her mind there was another name?

'Then Katherine it shall be. And you must call me Agnes.'

Katherine nodded. 'As you wish.'

Mr Bradshaw offered no comment and Katherine knew she would always be 'Mrs Westland' to him, no matter that she was Katherine to his wife.

The coach rumbled northwards. Hull was left behind. After about seven miles they turned off on to a minor track-way running in a north-westerly direction. They climbed steadily until they reached the top of a long hill. Before them the countryside rolled away endlessly. Large fields filled the lonely landscape. They dipped into a valley and followed it for a mile before the coachman set the horses up the opposite slope. At the top Mr Bradshaw raised his cane and tapped on the roof of the coach. The coachman answered by drawing the two panting horses to a halt.

'There you are, Mrs Westland, your new home.' There was pride in his voice.

When Katherine looked out of the window she saw the reason why. The trackway they were on slid gradually down the hillside and passed between two ornamental gateposts. A driveway was centred between two wide swathes of grass lined with an oak avenue which led to a mansion with a frontage that had clearly been designed by someone with an artist's eye. It was big if not huge. Its proportions gave it a feeling of homeliness even from the outside, but Katherine knew that that really had to come from inside, from the people who lived there, and that it did not necessarily always exude the atmosphere she felt now.

'It is beautiful,' she commented. 'I'm sure I will like it and be happy here.'

Mr Bradshaw tapped on the roof again and the coach moved forward to pull up before the house. Two sets of steps with ornamental stone balustrades curved upwards to meet a terrace that stretched the full width of the house. Six large sash windows stretched to either side of a front door which was protected by a portico with four simple columns supporting a triangular pediment.

The coachman was quickly to the ground and opening the door. Mr Bradshaw descended from the coach and turned to help his wife but left the coachman to steady Katherine, who smiled her thanks.

Without a word Mr Bradshaw led the way up the right-hand flight of steps. Reaching the terrace, he paused to look back along the drive. Katherine again saw pride in his eyes and followed his gaze. From the terrace the majesty of the oaks and the way they fitted into the surrounding landscape was most impressive.

'A wonderful view,' she said, half to herself, but Mr Bradshaw caught the words.

'Indeed it is.' He turned and walked into the house.

Agnes took Katherine's arm. 'You said the right thing.' She gave a reassuring smile.

'I'm glad. It really *is* a wonderful view. Whoever built this house here and had the estate landscaped as we see it had a magical eye.'

When they strolled into the hall Mr Bradshaw was already handing his coat to a footman. The coachman appeared with Katherine's luggage and handed it to another footman who glanced at Mrs Bradshaw.

'The room we allocated, Medwin.'

'Yes, ma'am.' He hurried up the oak staircase.

'You'll find your things in your room, Katherine.' She turned to two maids who were standing by to take their coats. 'Laura, Elvie, this is Mrs Westland who will be living with us.'

281

They bobbed a curtsey and said in unison, 'Ma'am', then helped with the coats.

'Please take them to our rooms,' Agnes instructed with a gentleness that Katherine detected the girls appreciated.

A door at the back of the hall opened and a middle-aged lady appeared. She was slightly made but conveyed her authority in the way she held herself as she walked briskly towards them.

'Ah, Mrs Willoughby,' said Agnes, 'meet Mrs Westland. Katherine, this is my dear housekeeper who runs Ribton Hall with the utmost efficiency.'

'You flatter me, ma'am.'

Though she suppressed any outward show Katherine sensed that the housekeeper was pleased by her mistress's comment. She also detected admiration for her employer in the expressive eyes which now turned to her. Katherine felt herself under immediate scrutiny but in a flash the assessment had been made and she was thankful that those eyes, which for a moment had held suspicion, now held relief and warmth. She guessed Mrs Willoughby had held reservations about a companion for her mistress but now any doubts had been assuaged.

'I am pleased to meet you, Mrs Westland.' She gave a slight inclination of her head.

'And I you, Mrs Willoughby. I am sure we both have Mrs Bradshaw's interests at heart.'

'Indeed, if that is so, Mrs Westland, we will have a pleasant and fruitful relationship. I have appointed Martha to look after you personally. Obviously she has other duties to perform within the household, but primarily she is your personal maid.'

'That is most generous of you, Agnes. And thank you too, Mrs Willoughby. This is more than I expected.'

Mrs Willoughby made no reply but she had noted the use of Mrs Bradshaw's Christian name and was pleased, for it indicated that her mistress had taken to Mrs Westland immediately and that the newcomer must have unusual qualities. Mrs Willoughby half turned and gave a sharp clap of her hands. Immediately a girl of about seventeen appeared and hurried towards them. She was dressed like all the other maids.

'Ma'am.' She made a small curtsey to Mrs Bradshaw and then to Katherine.

'Martha, this is Mrs Westland. You will be her personal maid among your other duties.'

'Yes, ma'am.' Martha looked nervously from one to the other.

'I am glad to meet you, Martha,' said Katherine pleasantly, with a reassuring smile. She saw a thin, pale-faced girl, but there was about Martha a lively air that at the moment was held in check by the doubt reflected in her eyes. It was natural for her to be wondering what her new charge would be like. Katherine was determined to put her at ease. 'I am sure we will get on well.'

Agnes turned to her housekeeper. 'Mrs Willoughby, we'll take tea in the drawing-room in a few minutes.'

'Yes, ma'am. I'll have it sent through.'

'Martha,' Agnes continued, 'you and I will show Mrs Westland her room.' She and Katherine climbed the wide oak staircase. 'You are along here,' she said, guiding Katherine to the left at the top of the stairs.

Martha hurried past them to open the end door on the left and then stood to one side to allow them to enter.

Katherine found herself in a square spacious room which occupied a corner of the building. Sash windows gave a view to the south and the west. The walls were papered in a floral pattern of twisted vines lush with fruit. A large oval mirror hung above the fireplace which faced the bed, attractive in its pink covers. A dressing table stood across one corner, positioned so that it caught the light from both windows. Two armchairs were placed so that occupants could take in the view to the south. A large wardrobe stood against the north wall but did not intrude on the rest of the room.

Katherine's cases had been laid on a long stool at the foot of the bed.

'Would you like Martha to unpack for you now?' Agnes asked.

'I have very little but if we were to do it together we would perhaps get to know each other better. Could Martha be spared after we have had tea?'

'That is a good idea. She is at your call whenever you wish.' Agnes turned to the maid. 'I will ring when Mrs Westland is ready.'

'Yes, ma'am.' Martha nodded and left them.

'This is a beautiful room, Agnes,' said Katherine appreciatively. 'You are so kind to allow me to have it.'

'Nonsense. If you are to be my companion then you should have accommodation befitting that position.'

Katherine had wandered to the south-facing window. 'Such a magnificent view, I don't think I will ever tire of it.' Her gaze ran across the immaculate gardens. The lawns had been recently trimmed and the roses bed-hoed. The purple of the lavender beneath complemented the colourful blooms. Beyond the formal gardens stretched the driveway along which they had approached the house. From this window Katherine could fully appreciate the magnificent oaks that lined it. Fields rolled away into the far distance and sheep grazed the lush grass.

'How much of the land is yours?' she asked.

'Almost all of it. Do you ride, Katherine?'

'No.'

'I used to but no longer have the energy though I do enjoy seeing the countryside from the carriage. I hope you will too.'

'I am sure I shall. Though I have never been used to it, having lived in towns all my life.'

'Where was that?'

'Newcastle, London, Scarborough and Hull. I did see something of the country from Hull.'

'Let us go and have some tea.' As they walked to the

stairs, Agnes said, 'I have never been to Newcastle, nor to London. What are they like?'

Katherine hesitated, trying to form impressions of the past. 'Newcastle I remember as the place I grew up,' she said slowly.

'And London?'

'That was after I was married.'

'You lost your husband?'

'He was found dead in an alley.'

'I'm sorry. It must have been devastating for you.'

'I had good friends, who were a great help and were sorry when I decided to return north.'

They had reached the bottom of the stairs and this line of conversation ceased when they crossed the hall to the drawing-room, but Katherine's mind was racing with what had been said. After an initial hesitation she had come out with these facts without thinking. She had recalled having a husband though still had no recollection of what he looked like nor even where they had been married, though now she supposed it was Newcastle. But what had taken them to London?

Mr Bradshaw had risen from his chair when they entered the room. He folded his newspaper and laid it on the table beside his chair by the ornate fireplace.

'I trust you are satisfied with your room,' he asked politely, though without a great deal of interest.

'Yes, thank you,' replied Katherine. 'It is most generous of you to allow me the use of such a beautiful room with magnificent views.'

'I had nothing to do with the choice. It was my wife's decision.'

'Then I am beholden to her.'

'Sit here with me, Katherine.' Agnes indicated the sofa that was drawn at an angle to the fireplace opposite Mr Bradshaw's chair.

As they made themselves comfortable, two maids appeared carrying trays and quickly set the low table in front of the sofa so that their mistress could serve the tea.

The puzzling queries that had come to Katherine's mind a few minutes ago were pushed to the back of her mind in the pleasant conversation that ensued over tea. Though Mr Bradshaw tended to be aloof, with little obvious desire to enter the general conversation, he was pleasant enough. Katherine thought he did not pay enough attention to his wife. It was a feeling that strengthened through the succeeding weeks, though she could not put a finger on why she thought this. Maybe she imagined it, or perhaps he was shy of showing more attention in front of a stranger?

Katherine had settled in quickly to life at Ribton Hall. Her duties of companionship to Agnes were pleasant. She would see that her charge had everything she needed from the moment she awoke in the morning, accompanied her wherever she went: walking in the garden, riding in the countryside or visiting the local market town of Driffield. They became firm friends, fostering the feeling experienced on the day of their first meeting that they had known each other all their lives. Katherine sensed that their relationship brought enjoyment to Agnes and saw laughter come more frequently to her eyes and lips, though it tended to be held back whenever her husband was present.

Katherine felt she was getting no nearer to knowing him than she had on the day they first met. He kept very much to himself whenever he was at Ribton Hall, though she gleaned that this had become less frequent since she had arrived to be a companion to his wife. His business in Hull now kept him there most of the week and sometimes at weekends too. As far as Katherine knew this brought no protest or criticism from Agnes.

It took her a few weeks to get used to having a personal maid, but when she did she liked the attention Martha gave her, especially when she brushed her hair. Katherine found the sensation of the brush stroked smoothly through it relaxing. It also gave her the opportunity to get to know the girl better and eventually, with a growing bond between them, to hear the latest gossip and opinions from the servants' quarters and news from outside that filtered through that domain.

She learned that Martha, who came from a nearby village, had lost her mother when she was fifteen and had been the mainstay of her family until her father had died in a farming accident. Her younger brothers and sisters were taken into homes for such cases in Hull but she had managed to secure employment at Ribton Hall.

'Are you happy here?' Katherine asked.

'Yes, ma'am. Mrs Bradshaw is a kindly person though I don't much care for Mr Bradshaw. He keeps too much to himself. He's a strange man, leaves everything to his wife except his business in Hull which he visits frequently, as you will have noticed?'

Katherine agreed with Martha's sharp observations. She was aware that Daniel was attentive to Agnes in a superficial sort of way and never interfered in the running of the household. He never questioned her spending and always saw that there were adequate funds to run the house, to meet her every need and indulge her. It was as if he was playing to the gallery, seeking public approval of his behaviour. No doubt he thought such consideration adequate and was blind to the fact, as Katherine saw it, that Agnes needed warmth and a rekindling of the love that, she had no doubt, had once been between them.

'Did he always stay away as he does now?' asked Katherine.

'Oh, no, ma'am. That only started after the children left home, and it became more frequent when Mrs Bradshaw fell ill.'

'But she recovered?'

'Yes, ma'am, but she was never the same lively person she used to be.'

Katherine nodded but made no comment.

'I'm glad you came, ma'am,' went on the irrepressible Martha. 'Mrs Bradshaw is much brighter.'

Katherine was pleased that she had brought laughter and companionship to Agnes, and in her turn appreciated the new life Agnes had given her. Though satisfied with it, however, she still desired to fill the blank spaces in her memory. There were times when Agnes recognised this and subtly tried to jog her friend's recollections.

'You always wear that jet cross,' she observed on one occasion. 'Do you do so in memory of someone dear to you?'

Katherine did not answer immediately. She looked thoughtful as she pinched the bridge of her nose between forefinger and thumb, trying to force her memory. She finally shook her head and said slowly, 'I don't think so.'

'I think someone must have given it to you as a token of their affection, maybe even their love?'

'No.' Katherine shook her head vigorously. 'It was given me by a stranger.'

'A stranger?' Agnes raised her eyebrows in surprise. 'Surely not?'

'Yes ... I met him on a ship.'

'When you were going from Newcastle to London?'

'It must have been.'

'A young man?'

'No. He was more like a father figure. We got into conversation with him and he seemed to like us.'

'Us? Who?'

'I was with my husband.'

'Your husband? Yet it was a stranger who bought you the necklace?'

Katherine nodded slowly as facts tried to clarify themselves in her mind.

'If you met him on board ship, then he must have bought the necklace in London?'

'Oh, no, that was in Whitby.' The statement came out with such conviction it startled Katherine. Before her was a workshop with men carving, polishing and working with jet. Their faces were indistinguishable except for one man who was smartly dressed in contrast to the others in their working clothes. He had a kindly expression and made her a gift of the necklace. Excitedly she described the scene to Agnes who listened carefully even though she too was charged with excitement.

'Have you ever remembered this detail before?' she asked.

'No. But it's so real to me it must have taken place.' Katherine's eyes were wide. 'That's another piece of my memory that has returned.'

'Important, I would imagine. It shows you were in Whitby, possibly on your way to London.' Agnes thought it an opportune moment to press a little more but realised she would have to be careful. Too much pressure on Katherine might have adverse results.

'You said you were on ship with your husband. Now that you have linked jet and Whitby and a stranger with that voyage, can you recall any more about him or what he was doing?'

Katherine frowned. The euphoria of what she had remembered battled with the effort to recall more. She shook her head in annoyance and in frustration pounded her thighs with her clenched fists. 'No! I cannot even picture him.' She looked desperately at Agnes. 'Will I ever?'

'Of course you will. You have made significant progress today. I think it would be a good idea for you to go and report this latest development to Dr Egan. I'll arrange for Langton to drive you to Hull tomorrow.'

'There is no need for that. I could go with Mr Bradshaw when he journeys to Hull next week. I expect he will be doing so?'

'No!' Agnes was a little too quick to oppose Katherine's proposal. 'It would better for you to go as soon as possible. Silly for you to wait. Besides, Daniel will more than likely be staying in Hull.'

Katherine could tell from Agnes's demeanour that there would be no arguing with her. She would not change her mind.

'Very well,' she agreed.

The maid who opened the door of Dr Egan's establishment instantly recognised Katherine and gave her a warm welcome as she stepped into the hall. She showed Katherine into the waiting room. 'I'll inform Dr Egan that you are here.'

A few minutes later he hurried into the room. He held out his hands to Katherine who took them in hers. 'This is indeed a great pleasure, Mrs Westland. How are you?'

'I am well and happy at Ribton Hall. Mrs Bradshaw is such a kind person. We get on so well. I will ever be grateful to you for securing me that position.'

Dr Egan indicated a seat and as they sat down said, 'It came at an opportune time. I am so glad you've settled there and pleased that you have called on us. Is it a social visit?'

'Well, yes and no. I'm pleased to see you and hope I will be able to have a word with Barbara?'

'Of course you will.' He inclined his head. 'But do I detect another purpose to your visit?'

'I have had some further recollections and would like your opinion on them.'

'Certainly. By the sound of your voice they are important. Before you tell me, let me call Miss Everet. As you were her special patient, I think she should hear what you have to say.' He rose from his chair, rang a bell, and when the maid appeared told her to ask Miss Everet to come to join them.

When she came into the room Barbara pulled up short on seeing the visitor. 'Katherine!' Her face was suffused with a broad smile. She hurried to embrace Katherine who had risen from her chair. 'You are looking well,' she said admiringly. 'Life at Ribton Hall must suit you.'

290

'It does,' laughed Katherine. 'But you and Dr Egan had a lot to do with helping me settle there. If it hadn't been for you, I doubt I could have led an ordinary life again.'

'Mrs Westland has something to tell us,' said Dr Egan, indicating to them to sit down.

'Something good, I hope?' said Barbara.

'Well, I have had some further memories and thought you should know about them.' She went on to relate what had happened in her conversation with Agnes and how she thought it linked with her earlier recollections. 'What do you think?' she asked when she had concluded her story.

Dr Egan did not reply immediately but glanced at Barbara with a look which asked for her opinion.

'Whitby has assumed a greater significance than it did when you were here. I think that is an important step forward. It gives you a stronger focus for your recollections,' she said.

'But if that is so, why can't I remember more about what happened there?'

Barbara spread her hands. 'I can't answer that.' She looked to Dr Egan. Did he have an answer?

He nodded. 'There are several conclusions to be drawn from what you have told us. You now know that you had a husband but unfortunately cannot recall what he looked like nor anything about him except that he was killed, but the knowledge that you were married is a strong base for your memory to build on.'

He glanced at Barbara. 'You are right to point out that Whitby has assumed a greater significance in Mrs Westland's mind. That has brought an association with a jet workshop and a stranger met on board ship. While these facts are important, I am inclined to believe your husband bought you the jet cross and that the stranger is a figment of your imagination because you cannot see your husband more clearly. I also believe Whitby is only an interlude in a greater and more important memory which I believe is based in London. Concentrating on Whitby may block your recollection of later events that took place elsewhere.'

'But shouldn't Mrs Westland take the opportunity to use anything that comes to mind?' queried Barbara.

'Of course. But she should be careful not to become obsessed with one aspect. She must keep an open mind.' He looked at Katherine. 'I am so glad you came to see us and will repeat what I said when you left us for Ribton Hall. If you need to talk to someone, come to us.'

'That is very kind of you. And thank you not only for listening to me today but for what you both did for me when I was living here.'

'I hope you continue to be happy at Ribton Hall. Now, are you going straight back there?'

'No, I have some shopping to do.'

'Would you like Barbara to accompany you?' Dr Egan smiled to himself at the reaction his query brought from the two friends. 'I am sure you two would like a good gossip?'

'I would be delighted, and she can help me choose a present for Mrs Bradshaw. It was she who suggested I should come to see you today.'

'Then away you go, Miss Everet. I will get someone else to look in on your patients.'

They left the room with a light step and, after Barbara had got her outdoor cloak and Katherine had had a brief word with Langton to explain the reason for their delay in returning to Ribton Hall, set off for town.

'I'm so pleased to see you again,' said Barbara. 'I missed you when you left.' She gave a short laugh. 'That sounds as though I don't miss you now. I still do.'

'And I miss you too.'

'Do you get on well with Mrs Bradshaw?'

'Yes. She is a very kind person, easy to get along with. I'm treated as one of the family.'

'How does that suit Mr Bradshaw?'

'He accepts it. I think because his wife desires it that way and he does not want to upset her by protesting. Not that he does. He keeps very much to himself when he is at home but frequently stays in Hull. I think that is why he wanted, or agreed to have, a companion for his wife.'

'How is her health? He indicated to Dr Egan that that was the main reason he wanted someone to be with her.'

'She has been quite well since I have been there, though I must say that there are days when she seems very frail. We walk in the gardens but no further afield. If we do venture further it is by trap. Mrs Bradshaw drives and handles the horse well. I have noticed that the gloves she uses for that are getting worn so I would like to buy her a very good pair for allowing me to come here today. And maybe I'll get her some perfume as well.'

'The shops you want are in Mytongate.'

Their chatter never stopped as they made their way there. Katherine soon found the things she wanted and they started on their way back. As they passed the end of Vicar Lane laughter drew her attention. She glanced in its direction and saw a group of four people crossing the road, one of whom was no stranger. Mr Bradshaw and an elegantly dressed lady were arm in arm and sharing a joke with another couple. For one moment Katherine thought they might be coming to Mytongate but breathed a sigh of relief when they turned in the other direction. She had sensed an intimacy between them and automatically quickened her step to be out of sight in case Mr Bradshaw should look round and see her.

A trembling sensation ran through her. Flustered by it, she tried to bring her feelings under control. Barbara must not suspect that anything was wrong or that she had been upset. The temptation was to hurry, to get away from Hull and, in the seclusion of her own thoughts, try to reason out what she had seen and make some sense of it.

By the time she had reached Ribton Hall the only conclusion she could come to was that Mr Bradshaw was being unfaithful to his wife. Whether she should mention what

293

she had witnessed to Agnes remained unresolved until the trap was taking her down the long drive between the sentinel oaks with the house in sight.

Agnes loved it here. For Katherine to reveal what she had seen would shatter her peaceful life. The upheaval would be devastating. At present Mr Bradshaw was considerate to his wife; though he did not fuss over her, he brought her no trouble, indulged her every need and saw that she had every comfort. Katherine could not fault him in this respect, so, because she did not want to bring hurt and pain to Agnes, decided it would be best to keep quiet about what she had seen, unless circumstances changed and demanded she should reveal her knowledge.

As time passed this problem gradually faded to the back of Katherine's mind. There appeared to be no good reason to inform Agnes what might lie behind her husband's frequent absences in Hull. They shared so much time together and Agnes never once showed a sign of being unhappy. On the contrary, she was full of life in spite of the fact that the shadow of her illness still hung over her. Even that seemed to be fading, though, as she became more active and took to walking much more.

Katherine found life at Ribton Hall most pleasing and counted herself very fortunate to have found a position that brought with it the friendship of such a delightful person as Agnes. Though there were times when in the privacy of her room she despaired that there was no further progress in the recovery of her memory, she began to accept that there were parts of her life that maybe she would never recall, though she bore in mind what Dr Egan and Barbara had said. Something, no matter how trivial, might spark further remembrance into life at any moment.

It was during Katherine's second year at Ribton Hall that Agnes announced she was thinking of changing the curtains in the dining-room. 'What would you choose?' she asked.

Katherine's reply came out quickly, as if it had appeared

without conscious thought. 'I will have to think about it. Unlike you, I've had no experience of such matters.'

'But you had a house in Newcastle, and if you went to London you must have had one there?'

'I lived with Mother and Father in Newcastle. When John and I went to London everything was provided for us.'

'So was he your husband?'

Katherine stiffened. Her eyes appeared to be focused on the window but she saw nothing. Instead a face swam before her, indistinctly. Mist swirled. In her mind she reached out to part it, desperate to clear a way so that she could see the person whom she felt meant so much to her. The name 'John' was repeated over and over again in her mind. The face faded. She made a plea for him to return. For one moment the mist vanished, leaving every feature sharp. 'John!' she whispered. The incredulity in her tone was filled with love. She saw him smile. The smile faded and she saw him lying on the ground. 'John!' Her voice was more forceful, full of hurt at the loss of someone so precious to her.

Something snapped. The picture vanished and she was in a familiar room in Ribton Hall. Her hands came up to her face and she wept in the realisation that a vital part of her past had returned and would in the future be ever there for her to recall. John had been her husband who had died in a London alley.

Agnes had remained quiet throughout for she recognised that these were private moments and that if she spoke any retrieval of memory could be lost.

When Katherine stopped crying and glanced up she saw Agnes looking at her with sympathy and understanding. There was also joy. Katherine took a handkerchief from her sleeve and dabbed her eyes.

'I'm so sorry, Agnes.'

'Don't be sorry for crying. It was a natural thing to do, and under the circumstances, probably for the best.'

'I saw him, Agnes, I saw him!'

'Your husband?'

Katherine nodded. 'Yes, John.'

'And?' Agnes prompted when Katherine hesitated.

'He was there, then vanished. Oh, I wish I could remember more.'

'I understood from Dr Egan when we first went to see him that when you were found on the beach at Robin Hood's Bay, you were dressed in mourning clothes. Was that for your husband, do you think?'

'It must have been. My mother and father had died before we left Newcastle.'

'Did you have any family of your own?'

'No.'

'Again I understood from Dr Egan that you thought you had lost someone in the shipwreck?'

Katherine puckered her brow and grimaced. 'I must have got that mixed up with the loss of John.'

'Did the fact that you had lost your husband have anything to do with your returning north?'

'I don't remember.' Katherine tightened her lips with irritation. She had remembered new and vital aspects of her life but now there was that mental block again. 'I suppose it must have done.'

'Where were you going?'

Katherine shook her head.

'You had no family to go to?'

'No.'

'There must have been some reason for your leaving London?'

'I suppose so but I can't recall what it was.' Katherine looked worried.

Agnes recognised that the questions had gone far enough. They had elicited much for Katherine to deal with. To push too far now might undo the good that had been done. 'Don't concern yourself about that now. You have made good progress and I am sure you will do so again.'

Katherine had a great deal to think about when she lay

296

down that night. As Dr Egan had said, a chance remark had stimulated her memory again. Maybe something else in the future might do the same.

Chapter Eighteen

The following afternoon when Agnes complained of feeling a little off-colour, Katherine suggested she should send for Mr Bradshaw who was staying the week in Hull. But Agnes would have none of it.

'I will be all right if I have a rest,' she insisted. 'Daniel has plenty to do in Hull. He should not be disturbed or worried about an ailment that will only be short-lived.'

Katherine complied with her wishes but her own mind had immediately turned to that moment she had witnessed in Hull. Would Agnes be so considerate of her husband if she was aware of Katherine's suspicions? They troubled her as she left the house and walked along the terrace. She pulled her shawl a little tighter around her shoulders against the sharpness in the air. It brought her attention to the trees and made her aware that the first colours of autumn were beginning to show. She hoped that the coming winter would be as mild as the last one. True, snow had laid across the Wolds for four weeks but it had not hindered daily life.

Looking back to that time, Katherine could not fault Mr Bradshaw's behaviour. He was as attentive as ever to his wife, buying her the most exquisite diamond necklace as a Christmas present. They'd had ten guests on Boxing Day, five of whom stayed for New Year's Day. There had been lots of fun: skating on a field especially flooded for the purpose, and sleigh rides organised for Agnes who could not share any activities where physical exertion was required. Mouthwatering meals had been prepared and were all taken in a leisurely fashion, games were played and stimulating conversation only quietened when Agnes played the piano. Katherine wondered if it would be the same this year. If it was she must see that her friend did not overexert herself as she had done last year, becoming exhausted by the end of the festive season. She'd made a marked effort to downplay it and when, on the day after New Year's Day, her husband had said he should go to Hull for a few days, Agnes had insisted he should not remain at Ribton on her account.

By the time Katherine had done a leisurely circuit of the garden these thoughts had been superseded by a memory of the recent conversation she had had with Agnes and her own hazy recollection of John. She wandered aimlessly around as she battled with her thoughts. She was almost unaware of what she was doing when, in spite of the sharp air, she sat down on a wooden seat with its back close to a tall sheltering yew hedge. She drifted into another world. She seemed to be sitting on a similar seat but knew there were buildings beyond this oasis of parkland. She inclined her head, deep in thought, as present and past mingled in her mind. She had sat on a similar seat in a London park, but she had not been alone there as she was now.

'Kath.'

She started. Only John had ever called her 'Kath', and it had only ever been in the intimacy of their bedroom.

'John?' she whispered. 'Is it you?'

'Yes, I'm here.' There was no sound but the words were distinct in her mind just as if they had been spoken aloud, close to her.

She turned. No one sat beside her but she was overwhelmed with joy. The mist that had clouded John's face the day before had cleared completely. His smile stayed, reassuring, giving her confidence. Her mind flooded with every aspect of him: his slender hands that caressed with the gentlest of touches; his lips from which she had felt the passion that flowed from his slim, strong body; his dark brown eyes – at times bold, restless and challenging, and at others gentle and understanding.

Everything was coming back to her. The wonderful times they had spent together and the love they had shared. She recalled his consideration when her mother and father had died. How he had delayed going to London. The great city was foremost in her mind then. She shuddered. She had never really liked it, but had tolerated it for his sake. Because she didn't like it, it did not come completely to mind. There were gaps but she was not worried about filling them. That would come later, and if they were never filled would it really matter now she was so much more certain of her life with John? Besides hadn't London snatched him away from her? She would ever hate the place for what it had done to them.

'John,' she whispered, 'be with me always now that I have found you again.'

'I will, my love.'

She gave a sigh of contentment.

She smiled and saw it returned. But then his face began to fade.

'John, don't go!' she cried out.

'I must, my love.' His face became wreathed in mist, his voice was faint. But he was speaking again. She inclined her head to catch the words. 'Don't mourn . . .' What was he saying? The words were even fainter. '. . . our son.'

Katherine started. Puzzled, she looked around her. She was in one of the secluded gardens at Ribton Hall. There was no one else present. But she had seen John. Had heard his voice. She shivered and was aware that the afternoon had taken on a distinct chill. She should get back. She tugged at her shawl and rose from the seat. Her mind dwelt on what she had heard. She fought to recall his parting words. 'Don't mourn our son.' Was that right? His voice had been almost indistinct on the final two words, yet she felt sure that was what he had said. Or was that what she wished he would say? Had she put words into her own mind and imagined he had uttered them? She felt an overwhelming desire to talk to Agnes and quickened her pace.

As she entered the house she had misgivings about approaching her friend now. She had not been well when Katherine had gone for her walk. If she was not feeling better she would not want to be pestered by Katherine's experience in the garden. She breathed a sigh of relief when she saw Agnes coming down the stairs.

'Are you all right? Should you be up yet?' Katherine showed her concern as she hurried to the foot of the stairs.

Agnes smiled. 'Yes. The rest has done me good. I thought a couple of hours in bed would help and it has.'

Two hours? Katherine was startled. She had not realised she had been out so long. In another world, she had been unaware of time.

'Should we sit in the drawing-room and have some tea?' Agnes suggested.

'Yes, that would be nice.' Katherine shivered. She had not noticed that the sharp air had bitten into her. A cup of tea would warm her up.

Agnes rang for the maid and ordered tea. It was not until it had been served that Katherine embarked on her account of what had happened when she was sitting on the bench.

When she had finished she added, 'You may think me fanciful, Agnes, but I assure you, I was fully aware of John.'

'I don't think that of you. Though some would doubtless say your mind had been fed by a strong desire to make contact with your husband and therefore you imagined him.'

'I didn't. He was real to me,' replied Katherine, a little indignantly.

Agnes's smile was sympathetic. 'I was not suggesting otherwise but I had to make sure you were certain before we pursued the matter.'

301

'It was only John's final words that I was uncertain of.'

'You are not sure of his exact words, or not sure if you ever had a son?'

'Both. But why would he say that to me if it were not true?'

'Don't you remember a child?'

Katherine shook her head. 'No.' There was a catch in her voice and a pleading expression in her eyes that tore at Agnes's heart. She felt that Katherine was so near a full recovery of her memory, that if only this and a few minor gaps could be filled then her friend's life would be complete again. She wished she could help more than just by uttering words of comfort and hope.

'When we first approached Dr Egan he discussed your case fully with us. He mentioned that you might have had a child.'

'I wonder if he is right? I should hate to think that I had a son and can't remember him.' Distress sharpened Katherine's voice and filled her eyes with tears. 'I might pass him in the street and never know him.'

'Katherine,' Agnes brought all her compassion to her voice, 'you will have to face the strong possibility that if there even was a son he may no longer be alive.'

'Oh, no!' Tears welled in her eyes.

'I believe you mentioned losing something in the shipwreck. Could that have been some*one*?'

'I took it that I was mixing that up with my loss of John.'

'But now you have realised how John died, could the loss you think happened in the shipwreck be that of your son whom you were bringing north?'

'I suppose so,' said Katherine miserably, and then made a cry from the heart. 'Oh, if only I could remember! If only my mind would clear.'

'Patience, Katherine. Patience as Dr Egan prescribed.'

Agnes tried to occupy Katherine's waking hours as much as possible during the coming months as autumn moved into winter and the pattern established last year was followed once more. There were times when Katherine drifted into a world of her own and Agnes knew that her thoughts dwelt on John and the possibility that they had had a child. Agnes, convinced that remembrance would come gradually, did not broach the matter and allowed the preparations for Christmas and New Year to occupy both their minds for she too had a problem which she kept to herself lest it spoil the festive season. The nagging pains in her chest were becoming more frequent, though not bad enough to attract the attention of anyone else.

A week before Christmas Mr Bradshaw announced that his business in Hull had been taken care of and would allow him to remain at Ribton until the day after New Year's Day. Katherine was pleased. Agnes deserved more attention from her husband.

The day before the guests were due to arrive Katherine stood in her bedroom, gazing out of the window at an early-afternoon sprinkling of snow. It carpeted the lawns and tipped the trees with white. The sky was clear, frost was in the air. The scene glazed before her eyes and was transformed into a park with distant buildings on every side. Groups of people in twos and threes criss-crossed the park, leaving imprints in the snow as signs of their passing. Children ran and chased each other in glee, snowballs in their hands, or kicked the snow up into little clouds of white.

'Mama, Mama, can we go out in the park?' The query was high with excitement.

'Yes. Wrap up well, James.'

The boy ran off, eager to be outside as soon as possible.

Katherine started. The scene in the park had vanished. Only the lawns of Ribton Hall remained before her and no one moved there. The scene below was silent and still. But she had heard a voice and answered it using the name James. Her son? It could be no one else.

'James,' she whispered to herself. She loved the sound on her lips. 'James.'

Elation surged through her. Another gap had been filled. She had had a son and his name was James! Questions started to form in her mind but before she had time to consider them there was a knock on her door and Martha informed her that tea was being served.

She hurried down the stairs eager to tell Agnes of the latest development but did not get the opportunity then or later in the evening, for she was never able to get her friend to herself.

Telling Agnes would have acted as a catharsis. As it was, earlier events were still very much on her mind when she retired for the night.

Her toilette completed, Katherine swung a shawl around her shoulders, drew back the curtains and gazed across the silvery sheen of lawns sparkling in the moonlight. Nothing stirred, even the trees were still. A fox barked in the distance and was answered by an owl that took off on its night flight. She watched its silhouette cross the moon and followed the smooth motion of its wings until it was lost to her. These sights stirred no recollection of the past as she had hoped they might. She sighed, turned from the window and climbed into bed.

She snuggled down and was soon cocooned in the warmth of the feather bed. Her hand slid across the sheet, fingers reaching out in a voyage of discovery, but there was no one there. 'John,' she whispered but no answer came. If only she could ask him about their son. He had said not to mourn for him. What exactly did he mean? Mourning was associated with death, so was James dead? But John had said 'don't mourn'. How could she mourn for someone she could not visualise? And why not mourn? Did John mean it was no good stirring up misery from the past, that now was for the living? Slowly the questions faded in her mind and she fell asleep.

An hour later Katherine stirred. In her dreams a young boy held her hand as they walked up a gangplank on to a ship. Reaching the deck, she turned and waved to someone

304

– two figures, a man and a woman, but they were not clear, she could not identify them. Mist swirled. They vanished. She wanted to bring them back but couldn't. She felt distress tighten her stomach but that disappeared when she realised the ship was nearing open sea. She had to curb James's excitement but did it gently. The picture disappeared momentarily. She tossed in her sleep, anxiety gripping her. She called out. James clung to her as the ship, battered by a wave, shuddered. Someone was shouting. She hugged him tightly to her and staggered from the cabin. Katherine twisted in agony as she tried to escape from the doom that faced her in the nightmare that had returned after all this time. But now her son figured in it and with his coming a darker and more frightful development. Katherine tried to force it away but could not. She was compelled to let it carry her to its bitter end.

She found herself on a deck overflowing with water as waves crashed continually over the ship and drove her towards dark, towering cliffs. Katherine stared at them in horror. Was there no escape? She gripped James more tightly as if that would ward off the inevitable outcome. The ship lurched. She staggered and reached out for support. At that very moment, when her hold on James had slackened, a huge wave broke across the ship. The power of the water as it swept over the vessel tore him from her arms. Horror twisted her face as she reached out for him. But he had gone. She shouted in anguish but the sound was drowned by the howl of the mocking wind.

Katherine cried out and sprang up in bed. She gasped for breath as if she had just broken the surface of the raging sea. Her body, soaked in sweat, seemed to have been dragged from the ocean's depths. Her eyes were wide with the horror of losing her son. She sank back on her pillow, shuddering with the realisation that she had lost him because she had slackened her hold on him. She wept until, exhausted, she fell asleep.

Daylight woke her and with it came a recollection of the

horror of her dream and what it meant. Feeling an urgent need to talk to Agnes, she dressed quickly and hurried down the stairs. As she crossed the hall she hoped Mr Bradshaw would not be in the dining-room with his wife. If he was she must restrain herself from speaking until later. Her step faltered. She stopped and ran her hands across her dress, an action more to try to calm herself than to smooth the garment. She took a deep breath and stiffened her shoulders.

When she stepped into the dining-room she visibly relaxed. Agnes was alone except for a maid who was clearing away the crockery used by Mr Bradshaw. Katherine would have her to herself.

'Hello, Katherine, I hope you had a good night?'

'I'll tell you about that in a moment,' she said as she sat down.

Agnes hesitated to say more until the maid had left the room. 'What is it? You're a little pale and you were tense when you first entered the room.'

Katherine gave a small smile. 'You are a shrewd observer.'

'I have become so since my life was less active. Now tell me.'

Katherine told Agnes what had happened in the garden yesterday and said that because she was unable to tell Agnes about it the previous evening, she believed it had led to her nightmare.

Agnes listened carefully to the story. When Katherine choked upon reaching the point where she lost James, Agnes came to her. She crouched down and put her arm around Katherine's shoulders.

'I lost him, Agnes. I lost him.' Katherine's eyes filled with tears.

'Hush now,' she said, trying to comfort her friend. 'This was all so long ago.'

'I know, but to learn I had a son and that I lost him through my own fault ...'

'If this nightmare holds the truth it was . . .'

'I'm sure it's the truth,' interrupted Katherine vehemently.

'All right, but what happened was hardly your fault. You could never have combated such a vicious storm. You did everything you could. You must not let this destroy the life you have made for yourself. You must look at it positively – it has helped to bring back the past. You know more about yourself: you were married and you had a son.'

'And I've lost them both,' wailed Katherine.

'And they would want you to live your life now. You said that when John spoke to you he told you not to mourn for your son. I'm sure he would include not mourning for him in that advice too. Continue your life as you were before this realisation. That does not mean you'll forget the past. Why don't you write to Dr Egan and tell him all you have remembered now?'

Katherine gave a wan smile. 'You're right, Agnes. You are a good friend.'

'And I hope I shall remain so.'

As the months passed Katherine found that life had added meaning for her now that she could recall her husband and son. There were still a few gaps in her memory though these seemed trivial compared to the joy of recalling John and James.

Agnes realised what Katherine was going through and saw her through the difficult first weeks until life settled down again and the two friends became ever closer in their support for each other.

One day Katherine was concerned when she saw that the breakfast table was still set for two even though she was late down. She had slept in and had expected to find Agnes already there. Fear for her friend was uppermost in her mind as she hurried up the stairs. Agnes had been off colour for a few days but had refused Katherine's suggestion that

307

Mr Bradshaw, who was in Hull, should be informed and a doctor called.

Reaching Agnes's room she knocked, hesitated, and then opened the door. 'Agnes, are you unwell?' Katherine asked with concern as she crossed the room to the bed.

'Not feeling too good,' she replied.

'What is it?'

'The pain here,' she touched her chest, 'has worsened.'

'I'll send for the doctor.' Katherine turned towards the door.

'No!' The sharpness in Agnes's voice brought her to a stop.

'But . . .' Katherine started to protest.

'Later,' said Agnes. Her voice was calmer and she went on persuasively, 'What I would like you to do first is send for my solicitor, Mr Penny in Whitefriarsgate, Hull. Go and tell Langton to leave immediately then Mr Penny will have time to come today.'

This talk of a solicitor, and wanting him immediately, alarmed Katherine. 'Agnes, are you all right?'

She forced a smile. 'Yes. There is something I want to get settled.'

'Should I tell Langton to call on Mr Bradshaw when he is in Hull?'

'No!' There was alarm in her tone. 'My husband must not know of this meeting with Mr Penny. He will do, but all in good time. Now just go and do as I ask, and then will you come back and read to me?'

'Of course I will.' Katherine was delighted to do so. They had often read to one another, enjoying their mutual love of books by sharing them this way.

Without another word Katherine hurried from the room, and, after despatching Langton with an urgent request for Mr Penny, she returned with a copy of *Windsor Castle* by Harrison Ainsworth which they had been reading together.

'You've done that, my dear?' Agnes asked.

'Yes.'

'Mr Penny should be here this afternoon. So after I have had a little soup and bread at lunch-time, I want you to help me get dressed so that I can receive him in the study.'

'I don't know what all this is about, Agnes, but if you are not feeling well, do you really think you should come down?'

'It is essential I should get this interview with my solicitor over and done with. As for you, you will learn what this is all about in good time. Now, please read to me.'

Katherine quickly found the place they had reached two days ago. She chose a chair close to the window so that she obtained the best light and started to read. After a while she let her voice fade away for she realised that Agnes had fallen asleep. Katherine sat perfectly still for a while, looking out of the window but hardly aware what she was looking at for her mind was occupied with thoughts of her friend and how lucky she had been that Agnes had come to Dr Egan's looking for someone who might make a suitable companion. After a while she rose slowly from her chair and walked quietly to the bedside. She stood gazing down at her friend. Katherine's throat tightened. Agnes looked so pale, even against the snow-white pillows. Katherine could only pray there was nothing seriously wrong with her. She walked slowly from the room and closed the door behind her.

'Excuse me, ma'am, Mrs Bradshaw is calling for you. You asked me to let you know when she did so.'

'Thank you.' Katherine rose from her chair and hurried from the drawing-room. She paused at the foot of the stairs and turned to the maid who was crossing the hall. 'Will you see if Mrs Bradshaw's soup is ready?'

'Yes, ma'am.'

When Katherine reached Agnes's room she found her sitting up in bed and was relieved to see her cheeks had more colour.

'I'm sorry I fell asleep when you were reading,' she said with an embarrassed grin. 'But the sleep has done me good.

I feel much more perky and ready for Mr Penny. Now, help me dress.'

'You stay there a little longer. I have ordered your soup. You can have that in bed while I am here and then we will see about you getting up.'

Agnes read determination in Katherine's voice and in her eyes. She knew better than to protest.

A few moments later there was a knock on the door and a maid appeared with a tray set with soup and a slice of bread.

'Cook says she has a nice milk pudding if you would like some after this, ma'am.'

'Thank you. I may have that when I come down.'

Twenty minutes later Katherine was holding out Agnes's choice of dress. She thought her friend was a little unsteady on her feet but made no comment. Instead she was more solicitous to her than usual and stood close beside her as they walked down the stairs.

Reaching the hall, Agnes paused. 'I think I will have a little of that pudding. Please ask them in the kitchen to bring a tray to the study.'

'Let me see you there first.'

'I'll be all right,' replied Agnes, slightly irritated by the fuss.

Katherine hurried to the kitchen. When she returned to the study she found Agnes sitting behind the desk.

Agnes smiled. 'Do sit down and then we can talk before Mr Penny arrives. I have something important to say to you.'

Katherine did as she was bidden, wondering what lay behind the serious tone of her voice.

Agnes dampened her lips and met Katherine's enquiring gaze. 'I don't think I will be with you much longer,' she announced quietly.

The blunt statement shocked Katherine and it was a moment before she reacted. 'Agnes, I ...'

'I am far from well.'

'I didn't know it was as bad as that,' gasped Katherine. 'You haven't had the doctor.'

'No, but we shall send word to him after Mr Penny has left.'

'And he may have a different opinion,' Katherine pointed out hopefully.

Agnes gave a wan smile. 'We can always hope but I think I know my own body. This is a return of the illness I had before you came to me. That left me weak for a considerable time. I recovered much of my strength though not all. That is why I decided on engaging a companion and the rest you know, except that I have felt intense pain more frequently lately. It verifies the doctor's diagnosis on first treating me.'

'Oh, Agnes, what can I say?' Katherine felt tears fill her eyes.

'Don't try to speak. Just be with me. Your presence has brought me much happiness already.'

'But I don't want to be in the way. Won't Mr Bradshaw want to spend more time at home?'

Agnes did not answer that question directly. Instead she said, 'It is out of concern for what will happen to you that I have called Mr Penny. There are things that must be settled. I want to make provision for you.'

'I don't want you to worry about me.'

'I do, and so I have made certain decisions that will necessitate Mr Penny altering my will. You will not know that this house and all its land belongs to me. The estate came to me through my family. I, not Daniel, engaged a manager to run it. Daniel is interested not in the practicalities of running such an estate but in the profit it makes. Only natural, seeing he is not a man of the land but rather one of industry and enterprise. That is why he spends so much time in Hull. I have made proper provision for our children and the estate will pass to him.' Agnes faltered and a tear came to her eye but she controlled it. She took a deep breath and continued. 'I don't want you to feel that you must leave here immediately anything happens to me so I am going to make provision in my will for you to stay here until such time as you decide to leave.'

'It will not be the same without you, Agnes.'

'I know. But I don't want you to rush into anything, thinking that you must get away.'

'I could go to Dr Egan.'

'I don't think that would be wise. You would be returning to an institution, excellent though it may be. You are quite capable of remaining in the world, I'm sure of that. Therefore I would like you to take your time before you make any decision to leave, and that is why I am going to add a clause saying that you can do that.'

'This is more than generous of you. I don't deserve such consideration.'

'What? After all the joy you have brought me through your friendship? I only wish I had known you earlier. Now you know what I am going to get Mr Penny to do. If there is any attempt to breach my wishes, you must go to him.'

'You mean, Mr Bradshaw might contest your will?'

'No, my dear, I don't for one moment think he will do that but someone else might try to persuade him to do so.'

'Surely not your children?'

'No. They do not want any part of the estate and will be quite satisfied with the money I have left them.'

'Then of whom should I be wary?'

'The woman Daniel will marry.'

'What?' Katherine was stunned though immediately remembered seeing Mr Bradshaw and the lady in Hull.

Agnes smiled at her astonishment. 'It's true. As soon as the period of mourning is over Daniel will marry a Mrs Fairburn, a young, vivacious widow who has captured his affections. Why else do you think he spends so much time in Hull?'

'I thought . . . his business interests?'

'They take him there, true, but there is also Esther Fairburn.'

'But how do you know all this?'

Agnes smiled. 'I may not go to Hull but I do have my sources of information. Oh, and I met the lady at the same time Daniel first did. We were at a party given by a friend in Cliffe before my illness. Daniel was devoted to me then, we were deeply in love, but once my illness was diagnosed and I could not participate in all aspects of life as Daniel and I would have wished, his interest began to wane. I knew he would not desert me, there was the estate to hold him after all, and I must say he has never once been unkind to me ... except that his love was directed elsewhere. Rumours drifted, you know how it happens, and certain words were whispered in my ear. It doesn't matter how I continued to learn about the relationship, but I do know they will eventually marry. Now that will make the said Esther Fairburn mistress of Ribton Hall. I should warn you that, as far as the servants are concerned, she is not an easy person to get on with. And, being something of a snob, I think she will regard you as a servant.'

'I will not be here when she comes.'

'Katherine, you must not do anything hasty. You will be provided for in my will and can remain here until you deem it in your own best interest to leave. Don't overlook that point even when Daniel brings his new wife to this house. Promise me that? Hasty decisions may set you back and I don't want that to happen. Promise?'

'I do.' Katherine left her chair, took Agnes in her arms and hugged her while she wept and blurted out her thanks and sorrow.

Chapter Nineteen

Katherine lingered a moment longer at the graveside. She wanted to pay special respects to the lady who had been her very dear friend and with whom she had shared so much joy in the short space of three years. She also respected the privacy of the family as they walked from the churchyard in the tiny village two miles from Ribton Hall.

Household staff, estate workers and villagers stood silently by while Katherine stared down at the coffin and said her goodbyes. As she turned away from the grave a tear ran down her cheek beneath her veil.

When she passed through the lychgate the family were grouped beside the two carriages waiting to take them back to Ribton Hall. Three farm wagons awaiting the employees stood at a respectful distance. Other carriages held position ready to transfer friends to the Hall.

Mr Bradshaw nodded to Katherine and climbed into his carriage, followed by his son and daughter-in-law. Katherine rode with his daughter and son-in-law.

When they had arrived two days ago from the south of England both children had expressed their sincere thanks to Katherine for the happiness she had brought their mother. It therefore came as no surprise to them that their mother had made provision for Katherine in her will. In fact, they were pleased for her.

The following day, after his children had left, Mr

Bradshaw called Katherine to his study.

'Mrs Westland, I want to thank you personally for all you did for my wife. I know she thought a great deal of you and it must have been trying for you during the last weeks of her illness. I am grateful for the comfort you brought her during that time. I want to assure you that, no matter how my circumstances change, I will see that all the wishes in her will are honoured.'

'Thank you, Mr Bradshaw. I will do my best to find somewhere to go as soon as possible.'

'The way my wife worded her wishes in the will, there is no necessity for you to rush. You must be absolutely certain that where you go next is right for you.'

'Thank you. I feel that, as I am staying on here for the foreseeable future, I should make myself useful in some way, maybe in some household duty or by helping with the sewing?'

'Mrs Westland, there is no need. I will be away much of the time so you do what you think is best.'

Life settled down for Katherine though the house seemed very empty without Agnes. Yet as time passed she began to feel her friend's presence more and more. Katherine was not surprised when she found herself talking to her, and receiving replies and guidance in return. There was nothing to disturb her way of life and unless another prospect appeared she found she was content to remain here near Agnes, even though she had no proper companionship and fell into that disturbing limbo of being unable to mix readily with Mr Bradshaw's class or be accepted whole-heartedly by servants and workers. She missed Agnes and her friendship, becoming uneasy as the end of the official period of mourning drew near and she remembered her friend's prediction of what Daniel would do.

One day in the middle of the week he arrived at Ribton Hall unexpectedly and immediately called all the household staff and Katherine together in the hall. He took up a position on the second stair from the bottom as if it lent more authority to what he had to say.

'I have asked you all to gather here because I have an announcement to make.' He made a short pause, cleared his throat a little nervously and then continued: 'I will be getting married on Saturday.' Again he paused, allowing the mutterings of surprise to die down. 'It will be a quiet wedding in Hull, then Mrs Bradshaw and I will spend a few days in the Lake District, returning here two weeks on Saturday. I trust you will all see that the house is in the very best condition to greet my new wife Esther.' He let his words sink in and then said, 'That will be all.'

Murmurs passed between the staff amidst the dutiful congratulations given to their employer. He thanked them with a smile then turned and walked upstairs. When he came down ten minutes later he was carrying a valise. He looked in at the drawing-room where he found Katherine sitting looking thoughtfully out of the window.

'I expect this has come as a surprise to you, Mrs Westland?' It was on the tip of Katherine's tongue to say that it had not but she held it back as he went on, 'I want you to understand that this makes no difference to your position here as laid down by Agnes in her will. I will stand by her wishes.'

'Thank you, Mr Bradshaw, and may I add my congratulations? I hope you will be very happy. I look forward to meeting your new wife.'

'Thank you.' He turned and hurried from the room.

From the window she saw him climb into his carriage and drive away. As it disappeared from view Katherine wondered what the future held as Agnes's warning about Daniel's new wife dominated her thoughts.

Seventeen days later she watched from the same window as a carriage approached the front entrance of Ribton Hall. Word had preceded it that Mr Bradshaw and his new bride would be arriving at eleven o'clock that morning. She glanced at the clock on the mantelpiece, sure that the carriage would come to a halt at precisely that hour. She was tempted to stay and observe, make her first impressions of the new Mrs Bradshaw from the window, but deemed it to be more polite to do so in the hall.

The servants were drawn up in a line extending back from the doorway with the most senior, Mrs Willoughby, heading the line. Medwin the butler hovered near the glass door from which he would judge the carriage's approach and give the signal to two footmen to move to the vehicle.

The carriage rumbled to a stop. Medwin opened the glass door and stepped outside. The footmen who hurried past him and down the steps were on hand when the second coachman opened the carriage door. Mr Bradshaw stepped out of the coach and turned to help his wife to the ground.

Katherine, who had moved close to the door, saw the new Mrs Bradshaw step gracefully from the carriage, smile at her husband, straighten her dress, have a word with the coachman and then look up at the front of the house. Daniel offered her his arm and they walked up the steps. Katherine took a few paces back and waited. She could sense nervous anticipation in the servants and had to admit she shared it. She felt distinct apprehension about meeting the woman who had taken Agnes's place as mistress of Ribton Hall.

Words passed between the new arrivals and Medwin who then escorted them into the hall. Seeing Katherine standing to one side, the butler exchanged a look with Mr Bradshaw who gave a slight nod. With a slight pressure on his new wife's arm he turned her towards Katherine.

'Esther, my dear, I would like you to meet Mrs Westland.'

'Ah, the lady of whom I have heard so much, who exists here thanks to your generosity and tolerance.' There was mockery in Esther's voice to accompany the flash of disdain in her eyes.

Katherine ignored the sarcastic remarks and said, 'Welcome to Ribton Hall.' She was not going to offer the

317

salutation of 'ma'am' for she considered herself equal to the newcomer and certainly wasn't going to offer her the respect of 'Mrs Bradshaw'. Agnes would always be the only one deserving of that title.

She saw before her a woman in her late-twenties whom no one could deny had beauty. Her high-cheek-boned features matched the way she held herself and spoke of a proud self-possessed woman whose attraction also emanated from a personality that sparkled. It would captivate anyone around her but it could also create hostility in anyone who did not fall under its spell. Her eyes sparkled with a keen enjoyment of life, but Katherine judged that would only be evident when she was getting her own way. Now they cooled as they made their judgement of Katherine.

Esther Bradshaw was exquisitely dressed in the finest clothes of the latest fashion and Katherine had no doubt that they had cost Mrs Bradshaw a 'bonny penny'. But would this lady have given that any consideration? She thought not. She judged Esther had got exactly what she wanted. She had become mistress of a large estate which would open many social opportunities to her. She also had a man with money in his own right from his business dealings in Hull. There was no doubt she could twist her husband round her little finger.

'That is rather an exquisite jet cross you wear as a necklace, Mrs Westland.'

Katherine was so taken aback by the unexpected remark at this moment that she was unable to speak before Mrs Bradshaw continued.

'You and I will have a talk a little later.' Esther turned quickly to the butler. 'The staff, Medwin.'

He escorted her, with Daniel a step behind, to meet Mrs Willoughby. As they moved along the line of servants Katherine slipped quietly out of the hall and used the back stairs to reach her bedroom.

She closed the door and leaned back against it. Her lips tightened as the hostility that Esther Bradshaw had generated in her rose to the surface again. 'Oh, Agnes! Agnes! What do I do? Life will be intolerable here with that bitch, I know it.'

Katherine found out just what it would be like during the next few days.

She had managed so far to avoid having breakfast with the newly weds and was in her room a few days later when there was a knock on her door and a maid appeared to tell her that Mrs Bradshaw would like to see her in the study.

From the location she had set, Katherine judged that Mr Bradshaw must have left for Hull. She found Esther sitting imperiously behind the desk. The atmosphere was distinctly chilly and Katherine was sure this was intentional. She took no notice of a situation clearly designed to make her feel ill at ease but crossed the room and sat down in the chair opposite the desk. She knew from the way Esther's eyes gleamed and then narrowed that she had not expected her to do this and was annoyed.

'You wanted to see me?' asked Katherine casually.

'Indeed I do,' came the reply, sharpness in every word. 'I have been here long enough to assess the situation and the running of the household. Yours is an unusual situation, I find. My husband has explained to me the provision made for you in his late wife's will but that is not entirely satisfactory to me so we must have your status in this household cleared up.'

'Agnes was very kind to me and considerate for my future.'

'Indeed she was. More than I would have expected her to be for a mere companion.'

'We were more than that. We became very good friends.'

Esther gave a cold, meaningful smile. 'No doubt engineered by you with an eye to the future and what you could make of it?'

Katherine stiffened. 'I resent your implication.'

Esther gave a dismissive wave of her hand as if Katherine's protest was of no consequence. 'No matter. I am in no need of a companion. I understand that since the first Mrs Bradshaw's death, you have helped out with sewing?'

'I thought I must do something, little as it was.'

'Quite right. Now I think you should do more. I will have a word with Mrs Willoughby and tell her to allocate more duties to you. And before you make any protests, let me point out that according to the will, and I have seen it, you are to be given a roof over your head here until as such time as you "leave of your own accord". As Mr Bradshaw rightly pointed out, that has to be honoured. Though I think this a ridiculous situation, there is nothing I can do about it. But the will does not state what your position in this household should be. So, you will become one of the staff. Out of the kindness of my heart I will allow you to keep your room, but you will no longer use the rooms Mr Bradshaw and I use.'

Katherine bristled with indignation. She knew this was not what Agnes had meant but as the person before her said there was nothing in the will to oppose the restrictions she was imposing. 'That means I don't use the dining-room?'

'Exactly.' Esther's smile glowed with triumph. 'You will have to make separate arrangements with Mrs Willoughby.'

'Very well.' Katherine's eyes smouldered but she kept her temper under control. She would not give Esther the satisfaction of having riled her. She rose from her chair, met Esther Bradshaw's smile with a look of disdain, and turned for the door, only to be stopped again.

'There is one other thing that you must understand now that you are a member of staff. I have noticed a number of them wear brooches, earrings or necklaces. I am forbidding this and will take any such pieces into my own care.'

At the mention of necklaces Katherine's hand had automatically come up to her jet cross.

Esther saw the movement. 'Yes, Mrs Westland, I suggest you leave your necklace with me now.'

'No!' she protested angrily.

'Come now. It will be in my safe-keeping until you decide to leave.'

'Why should I not wear it because you say so?'

'That is exactly the reason: *because I say so*. I make the rules in this household and as one of the staff you have to obey them. If you do not then I will have to report you to Mr Bradshaw, and he may have to take action because of your mental condition.' Esther laughed. 'Don't look so surprised, I know about that too. Now, hand over the necklace. It will be better for all if you do. You will get it back when you leave of your own accord. Maybe you would like to think more seriously about doing that than you appear to have done since the first Mrs Bradshaw died.' She held out her hand. 'Give it me, now!'

Katherine hesitated then slowly took the jet cross from around her neck and handed it over. She realised if she defied this woman Esther would invent some plausible excuse to have her committed to a mental institution.

Esther took the cross with an expression of pleasure in achieving her aim. When she looked at it Katherine saw a covetous expression in her eyes and knew there was more behind this ban than simple opposition to the staff wearing any kind of ornament. Esther met her hostile gaze. 'And I'll have the bracelet you wear on your left wrist.'

Katherine seethed, but with the subtle threat of a mental institution hanging over her, did as she was bidden.

'That will be all, now report to Mrs Willoughby.' Esther's dismissal of Katherine lacked any warmth or consideration. She, as mistress of Ribton Hall, would always have the final word.

Katherine's body was rigid with emotion as she left the room and she fought hard to control herself, knowing that any sign of breakdown, whether mentally, physically or merely by expressing deep anger, could have a detrimental effect on her mental condition. Then Mrs Bradshaw would seize her chance to have her expelled from the house.

She found Mrs Willoughby in her room checking some household accounts.

'Ah, Mrs Westland, I have been expecting you. Do sit down. Mrs Bradshaw saw me earlier this morning and explained your position. I am sorry she has taken this attitude. I tried to persuade her otherwise but she wouldn't listen.'

'Thank you, Mrs Willoughby.' Tears were near the surface. Katherine knew that the housekeeper was sincere. She was a kindly person with a motherly air about her; they had always got on well.

'She is a very determined and bombastic woman when it comes to dealing with servants. Even I am treated no better by her than the scullery maid. I need this job otherwise ...' She left the consequences unspoken as she altered the line of conversation. 'I see she has taken your beautiful jet cross.' Mrs Willoughby's lips tightened in annoyance and exasperation. 'I could hardly believe it when she banned the servants from wearing any sort of ornament and took them all into her keeping.'

Katherine gave a little nod of despair. 'That cross was special to me. She says she will return it whenever I leave, but I have my doubts.'

'What do you mean?' Mrs Willoughby looked shocked at Katherine's insinuation.

'She noticed it the moment she was introduced to me on her arrival and since then has cast covetous eyes on it. I may be wrong but I think this ban she has imposed was a ruse to get her hands on it.'

'Surely not?'

Katherine pulled a face and shrugged her shoulders as much as to say, who knows?

'Let's hope you are wrong.'

'I hope so too, but I'll not leave here without it, no matter what happens.'

'Rightly so,' agreed the housekeeper, 'but be careful. From what I have heard about her past she can be a vindictive woman. She has got what she wanted by playing up to Mr Bradshaw and waiting for the first Mrs Bradshaw to die. She's now mistress of Ribton Hall. Mr Bradshaw has made his bed but it won't be a comfortable one to lie in.' Mrs Willoughby shuffled in her chair as if she was not relishing what she was about to say. 'I have been told to find you some employment.' She paused a moment. 'I have given it some thought and suggest you go on helping with the sewing and mending, and that I put you in charge of looking after all the linen.'

Katherine felt a certain sense of relief. 'Certainly, Mrs Willoughby. I will do my best.'

'I know you will, Mrs Westland. The first Mrs Bradshaw thought highly of you and deemed herself lucky to have found you. Now, I am also told that while the present Mrs Bradshaw is allowing you to keep your room, and believe me she couldn't do any other, she won't allow you to share any of the other family rooms as you have been used to, nor are you to use their dining-room any more.'

'That is what she told me,' confirmed Katherine.

'Then I suggest you share my sitting-room with me.'

'That is a kind thought, Mrs Willoughby, but I couldn't dream of intruding on your privacy.'

'I think I would welcome some company, especially as the new regime is not really going to be to my liking. As you know, I take my meals in a room just along from the kitchen. You can have yours with me. I will instruct the kitchen staff accordingly.'

'You are most kind. I would not want to put the kitchen staff to any extra trouble.'

'They have all been wondering what would happen to you when the new Mrs Bradshaw arrived. They won't mind when they know the circumstances. They all thought highly of you, and of course still do. So that is settled, Mrs Westland.' Her final words were delivered as a seal on the arrangement.

'Mrs Willoughby, you address the rest of the staff by their Christian names and as I am now one of the staff, I would rather you used my Christian name too.'

'But, I don't like . . .'

'Please,' cut in Katherine. 'I would prefer it.'

'Very well.' She gave a thoughtful little pause. 'And I think that, as we will be sharing a sitting-room and eating meals together, you should call me Vera.'

The weeks passed and Katherine found herself slotting into the new routine of Ribton Hall with ease. She fended off Mrs Bradshaw's criticisms of her work, jibes about the past and her loss of memory, knowing that it was done in an attempt to force her to leave Ribton Hall.

She and Vera Willoughby got on well, and in Katherine the housekeeper found a willing worker and a pleasant companion who filled what had once been her lonely leisure hours.

The rest of the staff were a little wary at first, not knowing how Katherine would fit into their way of life after she had been on equal terms with the late Mrs Bradshaw, but her easy and pleasant demeanour soon won them over. Only Martha could not get used to the fact that Katherine was no longer in a position to require her services and still addressed her as 'Mrs Westland'. She willingly helped her whenever she could escape from her new duties as personal maid to Esther. She did not like this work and readily criticised her mistress.

One day six months later the girl came racing into the linen room. 'Mrs Westland, Mrs Westland!' She panted as she tried to regain her breath.

'Calm down, Martha, calm down. What is it?' said Katherine gently, trying to ease the girl's agitation.

'Mrs Bradshaw!' Martha gulped, trying to bring herself under control.

'What about her?'

'She's wearing your necklace.'

'What?' Katherine's chest tightened.

'She's wearing the jet cross!' Martha made her voice forceful so that Katherine would have no doubt about what she was saying.

'She mustn't! It's mine.' Since the cross had been taken from her Katherine had often pondered how to get it back. Mrs Bradshaw had said it would be given to her if ever she left. Katherine had taken the promise as another ruse to get her to leave of her own accord. She would have done so if she had had been able to save enough out of the small allowance Mr Bradshaw had paid her to support herself now. As it was she must remain at Ribton Hall.

'She told me today that she is planning a small party in three weeks' time. She was trying on a new dress. Remember when she went to Hull last week? She bought a new one then. This was it. Oh, it is smart, but she said it needed some piece of jewellery to complete it. She started looking in her jewel case and produced the jet necklace I recognised as yours. She tried it on and I could tell she was pleased with the effect. I think she will wear it at the party and pass it off as hers.'

Katherine was stunned. Her anger was rising and it took a great effort to keep it under control and prevent herself from marching off to confront Mrs Bradshaw there and then. But she realised that wouldn't be wise. Esther Bradshaw would deny that that was what she'd intended and Martha would be in deep trouble for carrying tales.

'Thank you for telling me, Martha. Please keep this to yourself.'

It gave Katherine much to think about. She was sure that Martha's facts were true. They recalled for her the two occasions when she had seen Esther eye the cross with covetous eyes. Had she thought that with the passing of time Katherine would forget it? If so she was very much mistaken. It and the bracelet had stayed very much in Katherine's mind. They were links with her past and she felt sure that the cross in particular could be her key to the times she could not remember. That necklace was hers and Esther Bradshaw was never going to wear it.

Over the next week Katherine considered what she could do to get her hands on it but always came back to the same conclusion: she would have to steal it even though it was hers. She knew that Esther would have no mercy on her then and her word as the wife of the owner of the Ribton Estate would count for much more than Katherine's own denial of any theft. She knew she would have to learn Esther's plans if she was to be successful and that she would have to leave Ribton Hall before her action was found out.

A week later when Martha came into the linen room to help, Katherine put into action the key part of her plan. 'Martha, will you help me to recover my cross?'

She looked wary. 'I can't afford to lose my job, Mrs Westland.'

Katherine knew she had worded her request badly. The girl thought Katherine wanted her to remove it from Esther's keeping.

'I would like you to let me know when Mrs Bradshaw is going to be absent from the house. Apart from that, I don't want you to do anything.'

Martha looked relieved. 'That's easy. But what are you going to do?'

'Take it back. After all, it's mine.'

'But Mrs Bradshaw will find out and you . . .'

'She will, but I won't be here.'

'You'll just go?'

'Yes.'

'But where?'

'I don't know yet. I'll work something out, but it will have to be before the party. Will you do it, Martha?'

'For you, Mrs Westland, yes.'

'Good girl. You mustn't breathe a word of this.'

'I won't.'

'Good. Let me know as soon as you learn that Mrs

Bradshaw will be leaving the house for some time. Now, let us get back to work.'

When she lay down in bed that night Katherine felt a great sense of satisfaction from the fact that she had put this plan into action. Its fulfilment now depended on when Esther left the house. With this first part put into place, Katherine needed to consider all her preparations. She had few personal possessions but must have everything packed ready to leave. But where would she go? Hull? Dr Egan? Barbara? They might be sympathetic to her but, knowing her state of mind, would view her actions and story with scepticism. And they most certainly would inform Mr Bradshaw. She dare not risk that. Amelia? Certainly not after the treatment she had received from her. She would be sure to inform the authorities and have Katherine taken into custody. Roland then? He might be more kindly towards her, but his sister would certainly get to know and he would bow to her directions. It appeared that as far as her destination was concerned Katherine could make no definite plans. She had no one to go to. She would have to take whatever opportunity was presented to her and hope that the hue and cry that must follow her theft would not uncover her trail.

With every day that followed, her nervousness increased. Every time she saw Martha she expected to receive the information she wanted. When it did not come her tension heightened. She had forcibly to control her feelings lest some outward sign drew attention to her. Only Martha must know. Several times she was on the point of telling Mrs Willoughby what she was planning but instinct cautioned her not to.

'Mrs Westland.' Preoccupied with her own thoughts, the voice that called after her as she hurried along the passage towards the back stairs carrying a pile of clean sheets startled Katherine. She swung round to see Martha hurrying towards her. Katherine tensed, anticipating the news she hoped the girl was bringing.

'Yes?'

'Mrs Bradshaw is to visit Mrs Otterburn tomorrow morning. I've just informed Medwin to tell Langton to have the carriage ready for eleven. She won't be back until three.'

Excitement mounted in Katherine with every word. Her nerves tightened in anticipation of the events that had now been thrust upon her. 'Thank you, Martha,' she whispered. She started to turn away.

'Mrs Westland, I'm frightened,' said the maid, her face creased by worry. 'I don't want to get into trouble.'

'You won't. All I want you to do is to show me where the necklace is.'

'I know where she keeps it . . .'

'As soon as she goes, check she hasn't moved it. I'll keep a watch for her leaving and then meet you outside her room. You can tell me where it is and needn't be in the room when I take it.'

'But I still might get into trouble! I'm her personal maid and she'll question me. She might even think I've taken it.'

'All you need to say is that you know nothing about it. Stick to that, no matter how much she browbeats you. Everything will be all right because when she learns that I have gone, she'll realise that I have taken it.'

Martha gave a nervous nod. 'What about you? Won't she try to find you and get the necklace back?'

'That might be her first reaction but then she'll realise she's got rid of me. She'll tell Mr Bradshaw I chose to leave and therefore have no hold on Ribton Hall in any way, and she'll be satisfied with that.' Katherine paused to let the words sink in and then emphasised, 'You'll do it, Martha? You won't let me down?'

She bit her lip and nodded.

'Good girl.' Katherine gave her a smile and turned away to continue her duties. As she carried them out her mind was dwelling on the future and wondering what it had in store for her.

Chapter Twenty

Once she had finished her work Katherine retired to her room. She stood beside her bed and let the tensions of the day drain from her. After a few minutes, with her mind cleared, she directed her thoughts to the course she had set and for a moment wondered if she was doing the right thing. She chided herself for doubting her own decision. Esther Bradshaw was not going to have the jet cross that was rightly Katherine's. She strengthened her resolve and with a purposeful step went to the wardrobe where she took out a valise and started making preparations for the next morning. She must be ready to leave when the moment was opportune. As she packed she kept testing the weight of her luggage. She must be able to handle it without any hindrance. Her flight must not be impeded, for she did not know how far she would have to walk.

When she lay down in bed for the night her mind was still actively planning the route she would take. She had no definite destination in mind except that she would keep clear of Hull and Scarborough. She would not take the normal route from the Hall just in case the mistress sent pursuers to bring her back and reclaim the cross before handing her over to the authorities to be dealt with as a thief. But she thought that Esther would want to avoid any possible repercussions from the accusations Katherine might make in return. She eventually fell into an uneasy sleep.

The following morning Katherine checked that she had everything ready. She was thankful that Mrs Willoughby had taken an early breakfast and that she was able to eat on her own without any fear that the housekeeper might suspect there was something untoward about her behaviour, though she tried to keep that as normal as possible. As she made a pretence of going about her duties she hoped to see Martha but there was no sign of the girl. Nervousness crept in. Was the maid avoiding her because she had had second thoughts about helping her? Had Mrs Bradshaw directed her to other duties that would preclude her from the arranged meeting? Katherine could do nothing to ease her own mind but follow their arrangement and hope that Martha did likewise.

When the hour for Mrs Bradshaw's departure approached Katherine positioned herself at a window from which she could see the driveway at the front of the house. Impatience gripped her. Where was the carriage? Why wasn't it here? Had Mrs Bradshaw changed her mind? If she had Martha should have let her know. But supposing she had not been able to get away? Doubt churned in her mind. Then she heard the grinding of wheels on the driveway. Relief swept over her. The carriage appeared and drew up at the front door. A few moments later Mrs Bradshaw appeared accompanied by Martha. She was talking fast and the girl was nodding, understanding the instructions she was being given. After one final word Mrs Bradshaw climbed into the carriage which was soon rumbling away from the house.

Katherine saw Martha wait a few moments, as if making sure that Mrs Bradshaw did not turn back. When the girl returned to the house Katherine slipped quickly along to Mrs Bradshaw's bedroom. She was thankful to see Martha waiting for her, though she was obviously on tenterhooks.

'Thank goodness, Mrs Westland, I thought you weren't coming.'

Katherine patted the girl's arm. 'I'm here now so calm yourself. Mrs Bradshaw's gone. Where do I find the necklace?'

'In the top drawer of the chest to the left of the window.'

'Thanks, Martha. I'll be as quick as possible and away from here. I'll make it look as though someone has searched the room then she'll be less likely to blame you because you know where it is kept. So don't worry. Will you do one more thing for me after I have gone?'

Martha looked suspicious and put on a reluctant expression. 'I don't want any trouble.'

'This won't bring you that. Just tell Mrs Willoughby that I have gone and that I send my thanks to her for all her kindness.'

'Very well, Mrs Westland.'

'You need say no more than that. She'll soon realise why when Mrs Bradshaw discovers that the necklace has gone. And thank you for all you have done for me since I first came here.' Katherine startled the girl by giving her a kiss on the cheek.

'Good luck, ma'am. I wish I was coming with you.'

'Maybe I'll see you again some day. Now, off with you.'

Martha scurried away and Katherine waited until she reached the end of the passage. The girl paused and looked back. Katherine waved and received one in return. Then Martha was gone.

Katherine entered the bedroom and, after closing the door gently, went straight to the drawer Martha had indicated. She found many of the items she had seen the staff wearing and felt a sense of exultation when she saw her jet cross. She picked it up and with admiration in her eyes held it by its chain. She experienced a surge of well-being. The cross was in her hands again. She had got it back and with it was sure there was a further contact with her past she had not as yet recalled. She slipped it into the deep pocket of her dress. After a brief moment of consideration she scattered some of the other items from the drawer, opened two others and threw from them items of clothing. She went to the dressing table, opened its drawers and left them in disarray. Trinket boxes were opened as was the wardrobe.

She paused in the centre of the room, looked around and, satisfied that it seemed as if a thief had made a search, hurried from the room. She made haste to get her belongings and, with every caution, lest she meet someone who would question what she was doing, reached the back door.

Her bracelet! In the exultation of possessing the jet cross she had overlooked the bracelet. She half turned, then stopped. Dare she risk going back? It would heighten any chance of discovery. She shouldn't delay.

She unlatched the door and allowed it to swing open under her control. A quick survey of the cobbled yard told her no one was about. She slipped out and hurried away from the house without a backward glance. She half expected a call after her but none came and with each step she began to take stronger heart. Once she reached the copse, the trees would give her cover to the dip that would take her out of sight of the house.

Starting down the slope, a feeling of triumph swept over her. Her anxiety eased but she felt tension still there. She realised she must control this mixture of feelings. She certainly wasn't completely free yet, but was excited at having accomplished all she had. Beyond that she had made no decision except that she would take an old trackway Agnes had once negotiated with care when they had been out in the trap.

When Katherine had enquired where it went, Agnes had told her, 'It joins the main trackway from Hull to Malton near the hamlet of Lund. It is little used today.' Katherine had reasoned that if it was positioned between those two towns it was more than likely that stagecoaches passed down it. With no definite destination in mind she was prepared to let events take their course as long as she got further and further away from Ribton Hall.

The walk was not easy, especially as she was carrying her valise and had her reticule slung around her neck. She had been walking for about half an hour when the track became rougher. Ruts created by wheels and hardened by the sun were hazardous. Katherine realised that she must exercise caution. A false step could cause a twisted or sprained ankle that would prove fatal to her escape. To be caught and branded a thief, with its subsequent disastrous punishment, would be the end for her. She negotiated the rough ground with care but was well aware that it had slowed her progress. The concentration had tired her and once she reached more level ground and the tension drained from her, she realised how tired she felt. She must take a rest. She laid her valise down and sat on it. Her shoulders slumped. How long afterwards it was she could not be sure but she startled herself when her head jerked and she realised she had been falling asleep. She must not do that, she must keep moving. Alarmed, she stood up and set off once more.

The track, which for most of the way so far had been little wider than a small carriage, began to broaden. There must be a reason and Katherine saw that, a short distance ahead, it joined the main track she had been told about. Encouraged by this and by the fact that there had been no sign of pursuit Katherine's steps quickened.

She paused when she reached the main track, looking both ways, a little uncertain which direction to take. Seeing three columns of smoke rising lazily into the air she decided that they might be from houses in Lund. She set off in that direction, hoping she would be able to progress beyond Lund as soon as possible.

Esther Bradshaw swept imperiously up the stairs, her mind dwelling contemptuously on the weak-kneed women in whose company she had lunched. Fortunately she got on well with her like-minded hostess – control the man who earns the money and you'll find much more pleasure in life, both women believed.

When she opened the door to her room she pulled up short. The shock took her breath away. What on earth had happened here? Who had played havoc with her belongings?

She swung round and stepped back into the corridor.

'Martha! Martha!' she shouted, hoping the girl was in earshot. She was about to yell again when she stopped herself, realising she must act like the lady of the house and not like someone from the back streets of Hull.

She picked her way through the debris to the bell-pull and jerked it four times – the signal she used to call Martha from the domestic area of the house.

She had heard Mrs Bradshaw return and trembled at the thought of the eruption that would come. Hearing the mistress's shout she scurried from a room further along the corridor where she had been dusting. She clenched her hands tight, forcing herself to remember not to give anything away. Her step faltered short of the room, giving her the briefest of moments to draw a deep breath before she faced the consequences of Katherine's actions.

'Oh, my goodness!' She feigned surprise as she entered the room and stopped. 'What happened?' she gasped.

'You tell me, girl!' snapped Mrs Bradshaw. 'You've been here all the time.'

'I don't know, ma'am.'

'Did you do this?'

'No, ma'am, 'course I didn't.'

'Did you hear anyone in here?'

'No, ma'am.'

'Where have you been? What have you been doing?'

'I have been cleaning silver. I was downstairs, wouldn't hear anything up here.'

'You wouldn't be doing that all the time?'

'No, ma'am. I also sorted linen.'

'And just now?'

'Dusting in the guest bedroom.'

'So it must have happened while you were downstairs?'

'Yes, ma'am.'

Mrs Bradshaw surveyed the room. 'Someone must have been looking for something. But what? What have I got that anybody would want?' Her eyes took in a necklace hanging

334

from a drawer on the dressing table. 'My jewellery!' She was across the room swiftly and speedily, checking her jewellery, taking the items Martha was picking up off the floor. 'It's all here.' A puzzled frown creased her brow. 'Then what could ...?' She stopped mid-sentence and crossed the room to the chest of drawers. One glance brought the statement, 'It's gone! The jet cross has gone!' She swung round, eyes flashing with mingled triumph and annoyance. 'Martha, find Mrs Westland and tell her to come here immediately.'

'Yes, ma'am.' Martha hurried away, thankful to be out of the way of Mrs Bradshaw's fury, at least for a short while.

Esther Bradshaw waited with mounting irritation. 'Where has the girl got to?' she muttered to herself. Her lips tightened. She paced what clear space there was on the floor. She was not going to move a thing until she had accused Mrs Westland across this scene of chaos. Then, while she dealt with her, Martha could clear it up. 'Drat the girl. Where is she?'

A few minutes later Martha came into the room. 'I'm sorry, ma'am. I can't find Mrs Westland anywhere.'

Mrs Bradshaw's face darkened. 'Come with me,' she snapped, and stormed from the room.

Martha had almost to run to keep two steps behind her mistress as she strode purposefully to the room Katherine occupied. Mrs Bradshaw flung open the door without ceremony. It took only a quick glance to see that the room had been stripped of any personal belongings. She crossed quickly to the wardrobe and jerked the doors open with a crash that made Martha flinch. It was bare.

'Just as I thought. She's gone, after looting my room for the necklace. Did you know that she intended to do this?' She eyed Martha, doubting she would get the truth.

'No, ma'am.'

'Are you sure? If I find out you have lied, it will be the worse for you.' Mrs Bradshaw hoped her threat might make the girl reveal where Katherine was heading.

'No, ma'am.' Though she was quaking inside, Martha forced her reply to sound firm.

Mrs Bradshaw grunted and left the room. Martha glanced round her and offered up a prayer that Mrs Westland was all right and well away from Ribton Hall by now. She trotted after her mistress.

Mrs Bradshaw stopped at the door to her own bedroom and surveyed the scene once more. 'Get it tidied up,' she ordered. 'You know where everything goes.'

'Yes, ma'am.'

'Where will Mrs Willoughby be at this hour?'

'I think she'll be in the kitchen discussing the final preparations for the evening meal, ma'am.'

Mrs Bradshaw hurried to the kitchen. 'Does any of you know the whereabouts of Mrs Westland?' she demanded.

Startled by their mistress's sudden appearance, Mrs Willoughby and the cook were taken aback by the question. The kitchen maids looked at each other with puzzled expressions.

'She could be in the sewing room, ma'am,' answered Mrs Willoughby.

'She has gone,' came Mrs Bradshaw's curt reply.

'Gone?' Both the housekeeper and cook gasped with surprise.

'Yes,' snapped Mrs Bradshaw. 'Does any of you know anything about this?'

'No, ma'am,' came the answer from everyone.

'She ransacked my room and has taken a jet cross.' Esther swung on her heel and started for the door.

'Ma'am?'

Mrs Bradshaw stopped at the sound of Mrs Willoughby's voice. She turned round. 'Yes?'

'Do you want me to send Medwin for the authorities?'

Esther Bradshaw looked thoughtful for a moment or two as she considered her answer. 'No. Only the cross is missing so it is not worth the trouble. Besides, we do not know where she would go.' She left the kitchen.

As a buzz of comment broke out in the kitchen, Mrs Willoughby had her own opinion about the reason for Mrs Bradshaw's refusal to involve any authority – the cross was rightfully Katherine's and Esther would not want anyone outside the house knowing of the imposition she had placed on her staff.

It was two hours before Mrs Willoughby was able to call Martha to her room.

'Martha, you and Mrs Westland got on well. Do you know anything about her leaving?'

'Yes, Mrs Willoughby. I was just coming to see you when I got your message. Mrs Westland asked me to tell you that she was sorry she could not inform you she was leaving, and to thank you for your friendship.'

'You knew she was going to do this?'

'Yes.' Martha hesitated.

'Well?' prompted the housekeeper.

'It was the necklace ... the jet cross that belonged to her. I told her Mrs Bradshaw intended to wear it at the party. I think that sounded to Mrs Westland as if the mistress was taking it for her own. Mrs Westland was determined that should not be so and got me to tell her where Mrs Bradshaw kept it.'

Mrs Willoughby nodded. 'I guessed as much when Mrs Bradshaw said the necklace was missing.'

Alarm gripped Martha. 'You'll not tell Mrs Bradshaw?' Her voice rose with pleading.

Mrs Willoughby smiled. 'No, Martha, I'll not say a word. Good luck to Katherine. I wonder where she is?'

Katherine had a feeling of being watched as she passed between the first cottages that bordered the road through Lund. She saw faces retreat from windows when she turned her head in their direction. The sky was darkening and the first drops of rain were beginning to fall in a strengthening wind. She hoped she could find shelter. She heard a disturbing squeak and a hundred yards further on saw a hanging sign that proclaimed this building was the Creaking Wheel. Shelter! Maybe even information about a coach.

She passed below the sign and tentatively entered the building. She did not know what to expect but found herself in a passage panelled in dark oak. The flagged floor was uneven but well-swept. There was a closed door at the far end, another on her left and one on her right. She paused, wondering which she should open. There were voices coming from the one on the right, followed by a burst of laughter. She reached out gingerly for the sneck on the door, hesitated, drew a deep breath, opened the door and stepped inside. Five men turned to see who had intruded on their conversation. Immediately they all stopped talking.

Katherine sensed their shock and surprise. No doubt seeing a woman entering their sanctum had stunned them. She took in the scene at a glance. Four customers stood at a long counter and the fifth man leaned on it from the other side. The men all had glasses of ale in front of them. The room held a scattering of tables and chairs and there were also window seats.

The man behind the counter straightened to his full height. 'Good day, ma'am.' His deep voice was polite.

Katherine felt the scrutiny of every eye in the place. 'Good day,' she returned, a little nervously. 'I wonder if you could help me?'

'We'll do our best, ma'am.'

'Does the stagecoach come through here?'

'Yes, ma'am.'

'When is the next one?'

'To where, ma'am?'

'It doesn't matter. I just want to take the next one.'

The innkeeper looked a little surprised by this strange and unexpected statement. In his experience, people wanting a coach usually knew where they were going. 'That'll be in an hour.'

'And where will it be going?'

338

'It's bound for Pickering, calling at Malton on the way.'

Katherine was pleased it was going in that direction rather than heading for Hull. It would take her further away from the district of Ribton Hall.

'That will do me. Will I be able to get a seat on it?'

'I'll see you get one.'

'That is most kind of you.'

'May I suggest I take you through to my wife? You'll be more comfortable there, and she'll get you a cup of tea and a bite to eat, if you would like it?'

'That would be most acceptable, if you're sure it won't be too much trouble for her.'

The innkeeper came from behind the counter and took her valise which she had been holding all the time. 'Come with me.'

As she followed him to a door on the far side of the room she heard the conversation break out again but in lowered tones. She had no doubt the four men were speculating about her.

They entered a small passage lit from a window on the right. Opposite, stairs led to the upper floor. The innkeeper opened a door in front of them and Katherine was immediately struck by the delightful smell of freshly baked bread.

'Jenny, could you look after this lady until the coach arrives?'

'Aye.' The woman who answered was round and buxom with a ruddy face, reddened even more by the fire stoked to bake bread in the side oven. 'Come and sit down, lass.' Her voice was friendly and matched her broad smile and shining eyes.

Katherine saw the innkeeper give Jenny a wink but it was one that expressed love and understanding between man and wife.

'As you heard, I'm Jenny.' She was obviously looking for a similar response so Katherine gave it.

'And I'm Katherine.'

'Well now, Katherine, you've just beaten the rain.' She

glanced at the window and Katherine was aware that the rain had grown heavier. 'Nevertheless, you've got a bit damp, so I suggest you let me dry your pelisse and bonnet in front of the fire then they will be dry for your onward journey.'

Katherine slipped the garments off and Jenny soon had them draped over a clotheshorse to one side of the fire so that its warmth was not impeded.

'Sit yourself down.' She indicated a wooden chair beside the oak table that occupied the centre of the room. She took a kettle that was boiling off the reckon and poured the water into a large brown teapot. She took two cups, saucers and plates from a cupboard, and in a matter of moments was sitting down beside Katherine pouring out the tea.

'A slice of new bread and honey?' she queried.

'I'd love it.' Katherine smiled.

'And then a slice of my fruit cake?'

They had started into their bread when Jenny put the question that Katherine had expected would come. 'You're getting the Malton coach?'

'Yes. Your husband says that's the next one in.'

'Aye, it is. Is that where you are going?'

'I'm not sure yet.'

Jenny thought this a strange answer but was not a woman to pry into passengers' personal circumstances. She had learned better shortly after coming to the Creaking Wheel fifteen years ago. Her direct, though innocent, query of a gentleman passenger had caused an unsavoury incident which had nearly landed her and her husband in trouble with the authorities.

'The coach goes on to Pickering after an hour's stop in Malton. You can get a coach to Scarborough or York from there. From Pickering you can go to Whitby or the market town of Helmsley, though either of those will necessitate a night spent in Pickering.'

'I'm not sure what I'll do,' replied Katherine. 'I'm completely free, having just left my last job.'

'In case you decide to go beyond Pickering, let me tell you where you can find my brother Will. If you tell him Jenny sent you, he and his wife will see that you are looked after for the night.'

'That's most kind of you.'

'Well, I can't let a young lady like you be at a loss for accommodation should you need it. The coach will stop at the Black Swan. Go straight in and ask for Will Beswick. A railway to Whitby opened a couple of years ago but I don't know much about it. Will knows the coaches and carriers working out of Pickering. If you decide to stay there, he'll know where you might find employment and lodgings. He's been at the Black Swan twenty-three years so knows Pickering well enough.'

When the coach's creaking wheels rumbled into Lund many of the villagers turned out to get the latest news from Hull. The immediate bustle of its arrival calmed down after ten minutes. The passengers speedily took refreshments and twenty minutes later started to climb back on board the coach. Jenny's husband had seen to Katherine's travel arrangements and a gentleman passenger had offered her his seat, saying he would ride outside.

She said a grateful goodbye to the innkeeper and his wife and waved to them as, under the cajoling shouts of the coachman, the team of six strained in their harnesses to get the coach in motion.

Though it was not the most comfortable of rides, Katherine was grateful for every mile that took her further away from the land that had brought her both happiness and latterly sorrow and disillusion. As the distance to Malton shortened she was faced with a decision over what to do, but somehow found that it did not bother her. The decision to press on to Pickering had really never been in doubt. She was a little mystified as to why this should be so but thought no more about it, just accepted it as the natural course she should follow.

As soon as the coach pulled into Malton she had a word with the coachman about her onward journey to Pickering. He would be losing four passengers here and a quick check told him that only three new ones would be riding to Pickering.

The young men who boarded the coach were friends and once they had made polite exchanges with the other passengers, settled down to talk amongst themselves. This suited Katherine, for she felt sleepy and in a few moments was only aware of the drone of voices as she dozed. Her mind drifted subconsciously into a world dominated by a ruined abbey on a cliff top. Below it houses spilled down to a river that passed between two piers to join the sea. She saw herself walking along a quay, cross a bridge and turn into a street where she appeared to be looking for somewhere or someone.

The coach's back wheel slammed into a pot hole and out again, shaking the passengers violently. Katherine almost flew out of her seat but was steadied by the quick thinking of one of the young men who had boarded the coach at Malton. She offered her thanks and settled herself again. Now wide awake, her mind turned to the dream she had just experienced.

She recognised the scene as Whitby. Had it been recalled after all this time because of the picture she had seen at the dressmaker's? Or had it been trawled from the deeper recesses of her mind, which had always held a place for Whitby? Had this been why she had headed in this particular direction when anywhere else in the world would have done? Had it been an instinctive decision because of some special significance it held for her? She recalled that Dr Egan's opinion was that while it had some place in her lost memory, London was of a greater importance. If that was so, why had Whitby dominated her mind only a few minutes ago, albeit while she was only half awake? The compulsion to follow her course to Whitby was too strong. If that held nothing then she could turn to London in the hope she would there be able to fill the blanks in her mind.

The coach rumbled into Pickering and descended the hill from the top of which the church cast its spiritual mantle over the market town on the edge of the moors.

Katherine looked anxiously at the passing buildings, hoping to spot the Black Swan, but she need not have worried. The coach turned into the inn's yard where its arrival brought men and boys hurrying to tend to the horses, to assist the passengers and generally help with any requests or necessary jobs.

Bemused by all the bustle, Katherine was aware of being helped from the coach and then finding a youth, smart in his livery, beside her, asking, 'Your luggage, ma'am?' Katherine pointed it out to him and he soon had it in his possession.

'Are you staying with us, ma'am?'

'Er ... I'm not sure. I want to see Mr Beswick.'

'Yes, ma'am. Follow me.' The youth set off towards an open door where two maids were standing observing the hustle and bustle that was taking place in the yard.

''ere, Dolly, take this lady to see Mr Beswick.' He placed Katherine's valise carefully in an alcove beside the door. 'It'll be all right there, ma'am, till you want it.'

'Thank you.' Katherine had been fishing in her purse and found a coin which she gave to the youth who expressed his appreciation in no uncertain terms.

'Come with me, ma'am,' said Dolly, smoothing her dress at the waist.

She led the way along a corridor and turned into a shorter one at the end of which was a staircase. They mounted it to the first floor where Dolly knocked on a door and opened it when she heard a shout of, 'Enter.'

'A lady to see you, sir.'

'Well, show her in, girl.'

'Yes, sir.' Dolly stepped to one side to allow Katherine to enter the room.

As she was doing so the man snapped, 'And, girl, ain't I told you to ask the visitor's name so you can announce them?'

'Yes, sir. Sorry, sir.'

'Ah, ma'am, I am pleased to see you.' The man who rose from his chair was big and broad-shouldered, someone who had once been physically powerful but was now showing signs of flab. He was well-dressed but had been caught unawares in his shirt sleeves. With a twist of his arm he flicked a coat from the back of his chair and had slipped into it in one swift movement that made Katherine admire the speed of its execution.

'Excuse me, ma'am, I had no idea I would be entertaining a charming person like yourself.'

Katherine ignored the flattery. 'Mr Beswick I have just come on the stage, having boarded it at Lund.'

'Ah, Lund. Did you by chance see my dearly beloved sister?' he asked effusively.

'It is on her recommendation that I sought you out.'

'Then I am in my sister's debt.'

Once again Katherine ignored the flattery. 'She said you would be able to help me?'

'And in what way may I be of help?' He paused, then raised his hand when Katherine was about to enlighten him.

'Pray, do sit down. Let us discuss matters in comfort.' He indicated a chair opposite the one in which he had been sitting. As Katherine sat down he added, 'May I offer you some refreshment, a glass of Madeira or lemonade freshly made? You must be weary after the buffeting of the coach.'

'Thank you kindly. A glass of lemonade would be most appreciated,' replied Katherine.

Mr Beswick crossed to a heavy oak sideboard, picked up a jug and poured some of its contents into a glass. He brought it to Katherine who accepted it with grace. She waited until he was seated before she spoke.

'Your sister was kind to me while I waited for the coach

at the Creaking Wheel and recommended I should seek your help about my onward journey.'

'At your service, ma'am. Where would you want to be going?'

'I was going to take the first coach out of Pickering provided it wasn't going to Scarborough, but I have now made up my mind that I want to go to Whitby.'

The innkeeper was a little intrigued but, like his sister in Lund, knew it was best for his trade to ask few questions of strangers. 'Well, ma'am, it depends how soon you want to get there. You could go by train the day after tomorrow. It's a fairly new service, not the most reliable as yet. A coach will leave in three days, but if you want to get there sooner it will have to be the carrier's cart. He'll be leaving tomorrow morning about seven.'

'Then tomorrow morning it shall be,' replied Katherine firmly.

'You'll be travelling with Isaac Welburn and his nephew Ezra.' He gave a little chuckle. 'No, ma'am, they're not Jews. They are good Yorkshire folk but there's a tradition in the family of giving each new-born a Biblical name.' He raised his eyes heavenwards as if such an idea must have come from above, for what good Yorkshire folk would do such a thing? 'You'll be all right with them. There are some I wouldn't send you with.'

'Where do I find this Isaac Welburn?'

'Leave that to me, ma'am. I'll tell him to call here for you.' He added hastily, 'I suppose you will want a room for the night? I discern you know no one in these parts.'

'You assume correctly and I would be most grateful if you could furnish me with a comfortable bed and some good food.'

'That you shall have, ma'am. I'll get Dolly to fix you up.' He got out of his chair. 'I'll let you know what time Isaac will be here.'

'Thank you.' She followed him out of the room and down the stairs. His instructions to Dolly were that this lady should be given the best room in the inn. Whether it was or not, Katherine didn't care. It was nice enough for her and Dolly was most attentive in seeing that she was comfortable. That evening the maid brought her meal to her room and once again Katherine counted her blessings for the soup and home-made rabbit pie were of the highest quality.

'Made on the premises by Mrs Beswick,' she was informed.

'And all the better for that,' commented Katherine.

When she settled down for the night she recalled the dream she had had in the coach and wondered what had led her to Whitby and what she would find there.

Chapter Twenty-one

Katherine stirred in her bed, trying to drive sleep from her mind. The hammering became more persistent. She endeavoured to make sense of it as she rolled over on to her back while trying to place the unfamiliar surroundings.

'Mrs Westland, Mrs Westland.' Someone was calling her name, adding to the pounding on the door. Both sounds now penetrated her mind, bringing with them the realisation of where she was and driving away any desire to sleep again.

She sat up in bed. 'Yes?' she called.

The door sneck clicked and Dolly entered the room. 'It's time you were up, ma'am, if you want the carrier's cart.'

'Thank you, Dolly. I'll soon be down.'

The maid left and Katherine made haste. The smell of frying bacon drifted up the stairs and she realised how hungry she was. The landlord and his wife were in attendance in the dining-room.

'Good morning, ma'am,' said Mrs Beswick. 'Sit you down and take a good breakfast. There's no telling when you'll get your next meal, though I'll make you up a package that'll not see you go hungry.'

'That's most kind of you,' replied Katherine, 'and thank you for the meal yesterday evening.'

She was soon enjoying bacon and egg with thick-cut bread. She was nearly finished when the landlord informed her that Isaac should be outside the inn in ten minutes. 'He'll look after you, ma'am.'

'Thank you, and thank you too for all the trouble you have taken.'

'Ma'am, it's our stock in trade. I know the next time I see my sister she'll enquire if I looked after you, and woe betide me if I hadn't.'

Katherine laughed. 'You can tell her that I was well taken care of.'

She settled her account for the night's lodgings and was ready when Isaac arrived. She was thankful to see that the cart was covered by a hooped awning. It offered some shelter from the squally weather that appeared to be in the offing.

'Good day, ma'am,' said Isaac, touching his woollen cap. 'Whitby's a mite way off but we'll make it by late-afternoon.'

His voice was pleasant and his eyes friendly. She judged him to be in his late-forties or early-fifties, though it was hard to tell with a face beaten by the winds and rain of the North York Moors and scorched by the summer sun which could be hot even in these parts.

'This here is my nephew, Ezra.'

Katherine smiled at him and said, 'I'm pleased to meet you both and sure we will journey well together.'

'I'm sure we shall, ma'am. Ezra, take the lady's luggage and put it safe.'

He did as he was told and stowed the valise with care.

'There'll be some walking to do, ma'am. Got to ease the weight a bit for the horse on the hills.'

'I don't mind that,' she replied. 'I wouldn't want to sit all the time.'

'Would you like to walk now or would you rather ride out of Pickering?'

'I leave it to you. You know this country and where it will be necessary to walk.'

348

'Not necessary, ma'am, but where it will ease the strain on the horse.'

She inclined her head in understanding. 'I leave it to you.'

'Ride now, ma'am. Once we leave Pickering there is a long steady pull to the moors.'

He helped Katherine on to the wooden plank that formed the seat at the front of the wagon. With a final farewell to the Beswicks, Isaac called to the horse and in a moment the wagon began to roll forward.

In a short distance they turned to the left and began the steady climb away from the market town which was beginning to come to life.

The two men walked at the head of the horse with an occasional glance and remark to check that Katherine was all right and reasonably comfortable. After about two miles, Isaac dropped back to walk beside her.

'Ma'am, a little further on the track gets steeper. It would help if you would walk awhile.'

'Certainly. It will be good to stretch my legs.'

'The old seat gets a bit hard at times.' Isaac gave a sympathetic grin, drawn from experience.

'Have you been doing this journey long?'

'Best part of twenty years, ma'am, with the occasional break going to Helmsley. Customers come to expect you.'

'You've a full wagon. What do you trade in?'

'All manner of goods. I keep my eyes and ears open to assess what people are wanting but I always carry farm goods I collect in the Pickering area – eggs, butter, cheese, meat, and woollen goods spun and knitted in the local cottages.' He paused and then called out, 'Ezra, let's stop.'

'Aye, aye, Uncle Isaac.'

The wagon came to a halt with Ezra holding the horse's head.

Isaac helped Katherine to the ground. He grinned as he informed her quietly, 'He picked up this "aye, aye" business from Whitby sailors.'

They started off again. Katherine straightened her dress and removed her bonnet. She ran her hand through her hair and shook it, enjoying the feeling of freedom.

The trackway left the cultivated fields and grassland and moved into the wild moors. The land to the left began to fall away with the track coming close to the edge of the escarpment. Katherine stopped to take in the scene. A huge deep bowl had been scooped out of the hills with a narrow valley running from it in the direction of Pickering. 'What an amazing view,' she said half to herself.

Isaac who had stopped beside her caught her words. 'Aye, it is that. I never tire of it and I've seen it in all its moods: dark and mysterious when mists roll up the hillside; beautiful and tempting when the sun bathes it with noon warmth or sends its golden rays from the west and deepens the shadows.'

'You have poetry in you, Isaac.'

'Don't know about that, ma'am, but I like words.'

'Do you read much?'

'When I have time but that ain't a lot.'

'Then we are true companions, for I too could not live without books.'

'But you travel light?'

'Circumstances, Isaac. I carry one book, *Rob Roy*, a gift from a dear friend.'

'That seems to indicate you are not going home, ma'am.' He held up his hand. 'I'm sorry, I shouldn't be curious.'

'You've every right to be curious about your passenger.'

'But I shouldn't voice it.'

'I don't mind. You are right, I'm not going home. In fact, I have no home.' Katherine caught his startled look and smiled. 'It is true, but I am trying to find my past.'

'You think it is in Whitby?'

'I don't know, but I'm drawn there for some reason.'

'You have been there before?'

'Only for a few hours on my way to London by sea.'

'So what takes you back?'

350

'I don't know. I wish I did.'

'I take it you have nowhere to stay?'

'No, but I'll find somewhere.'

'No doubt you will but it could easily be not to your liking. Look, I don't want to interfere but I suggest you go to see Mrs Garner at six Cliff Street. She has bought goods from me for a number of years and occasionally takes in lodgers. I'm sure you would be well looked after there. If that interests you, I'll get Ezra to escort you there.'

'That is most kind of you and I gratefully accept.'

Katherine lapsed into silent appreciation of the magnificent scenery. Isaac respected her silence and broke it only when the track turned sharply to the left where it began a quick twisting drop down the hillside.

'Steady, Ezra. I'll see to the brake.'

Ezra knew what he had to do to steady the horse for the rough descent while his uncle applied his skill and knowledge of the surface, on which he kept a wary eye, as he applied the wooden block that acted as a brake. The track swung sharply round the spur of the hill and eased gradually to the bottom where it stretched towards the distant brow of a low rounded hill.

Katherine was surprised to find a gaunt-looking building standing beside the track at the bottom of the slope. Questions sprang to her lips but she curbed them when she saw that the men's attention was concentrated on getting the wagon to the bottom safely.

Once there, Isaac released his grip on the brake. He drew a spotted handkerchief from his pocket, removed his cap and mopped the glistening sweat from his forehead. 'Easy now, Ezra,' he called.

Ezra acknowledged him with relief. He always considered negotiating that section of the track the worst part of the journey. He had heard of nasty accidents happening there – wagons losing wheels, rolling over and crushing unsuspecting carriers; horses bolting in fright, or losing their footing in ground roughened by recent storms.

'What's this place?' Katherine asked now that the men were once again relaxed.

'The Wagon and Horses, ma'am. A very old inn. Has been used by smugglers – might still be for what I know. I keeps my nose out of such things, best not to enquire. I've heard right grisly tales of the hand of vengeance born in this inn and stretching far beyond these moors.'

Katherine could well imagine clandestine goings-on as she passed the drab building which she imagined had once been a good 'halfway house' for travellers, until it fell into nefarious ways. There was no sign of life there and the peeling sign creaked eerily in the breeze. She shuddered and was glad when they had passed it.

'You can ride for a while now, ma'am, if you wish,' called Isaac as he indicated to Ezra to stop.

Once Katherine was settled they set off again. Heather-covered moorland rolled to a distant horizon that never seemed to draw nearer. It was a large lonely land with a big sky. Today Katherine enjoyed it in the sunshine that had followed the early squalls but it took little imagination to see it as a menacing landscape in which rolling mist could easily cut you off from the outside world and disorientate your senses. Then it would be simple to become lost and never be heard of again. She had no wish to be out on the moors in such conditions nor to be there when darkness wrapped a cloak upon the land.

Ezra brought the wagon to a halt when they reached the edge of the moorland at the top of a valley.

'Would you mind walking again, ma'am?' Isaac asked.

Katherine, captured by the scene, was jerked out of her reverie. 'No, not at all.'

Isaac helped her to the ground. 'I love that view,' he commented, looking down the valley at the end of which was a distant glimmer of blue.

'I can see why,' she said as they stood side by side.

'And we can see our destination,' said Isaac. 'Though

352

we've a way to go, it does make the journey seem shorter.'

'Whitby?' There was a tremor of excitement in her question though she could not say why.

'Aye, ma'am, that's where we're going.'

'Is that the sea?'

'Aye. We drop down another sharp hill into the village of Sleights where we meet the River Esk that runs out to the sea at Whitby. We'll follow its course.'

Once they were beside the river the going was easier all the way into Whitby. The wagon was finally brought to a stop on a piece of land short of the harbour where Isaac usually stayed the night. It was a handy place from which to distribute the goods he had on order and to take the rest to the Market Place for speculative sales.

'If you don't mind waiting a few minutes, ma'am, Ezra will take you to Mrs Garner. She knows him so will understand I've sent you.'

'Thank you, you are more than kind. What do I owe you for the journey?'

'Nothing, ma'am. Your company was payment enough. You have been a pleasant travelling companion.'

'But . . .' Katherine started to protest.

Isaac stopped her. 'Say no more, ma'am. Just let me know how you get on if you stay in Whitby.'

'I'll do that.' Katherine smiled.

Ezra had already released the horse from its harness and was in the process of tethering it on a long rope so that it had a good latitude of freedom and was able to graze the rough grass.

As he chatted to Katherine, Isaac kept an eye on his nephew as he rubbed the horse down. When he saw him finish, he called him over. 'You've got the horse in fine shape Ezra. Now, I want you to take Mrs Westland to Mrs Garner's in Cliff Street.'

'Right, Uncle Isaac. Follow me, ma'am.' He took Katherine's valise from the wagon.

The road took them along the harbourside on the east

bank of the river. Ships were drawn up at the quays. Two of them lay idle, waiting to be loaded tomorrow. Labourers were hurrying to bring the last goods on board two other ships so that they would be able to sail on the early-morning tide. Sail cloth was being taken on board another vessel, ready to replace the existing sails, torn in a recent storm. The sound of hammers came from the shipbuilding yards across the river as carpenters strove to finish a job before going home.

Katherine had never imagined so much bustle and activity, nor so many people crossing the bridge in both directions. She almost lost sight of Ezra. They reached the west side of the river and took a sharp twisting climb before they turned into a street on their right. It was narrow but swept clean and the houses well-kept.

'Here we are, ma'am.' Ezra indicated a brick-built house of three bays and two storeys. Three steps led to a dark blue door with a decorated fan-light above. The sash windows were painted white and shone with the brightness of the newly washed. Ezra rapped the knocker.

A few moments later the door was opened by a small portly woman attired in a black dress that made her seem rounder. Her circular ruddy face shone as if it had just been scrubbed. The friendliness in her brown eyes was unmistakable.

'Why, hello, Ezra.' Her face broke into a broad smile on seeing the young man. She looked past him as if expecting to see another familiar face. 'Your uncle not with you?'

'We've just arrived, Mrs Garner. I left him seeing to the wagon and its load ready for tomorrow. I've brought Mrs Westland to you. She travelled with us from Pickering and is looking for somewhere to stay.'

'Good day, Mrs Westland.' Mrs Garner was quick to extend her friendliness to Katherine.

'I'm pleased to meet you, Mrs Garner,' returned Katherine. 'I'm hoping you'll be able to help me?'

'Come in and we'll see.'

She stepped past Mrs Garner, expecting Ezra to follow.

'I'll be off. My uncle might need me,' he said.

'Tell your uncle I'll see him tomorrow for my usual butter and eggs.'

'Right, Mrs Garner. Goodbye, Mrs Westland.'

'Goodbye, Ezra,' called Katherine. 'Thank you for all your help. I hope we shall meet again.'

The young man hurried away. Mrs Garner closed the door. 'Come through here, Mrs Westland.' She opened a door on the right and Katherine entered a room she judged to be the 'holy of holies', neatly furnished and so spick and span that a speck of dust dare not settle there, a room that would only be used on special occasions.

'Do sit down.' Mrs Garner indicated a red moquette armchair. 'I'm sure you would like a cup of tea after your trying journey?'

'It would be delightful,' replied Katherine.

Mrs Garner hurried out of the room without seeming to rush. Katherine could hear her bustling about in what she assumed was the kitchen. She imagined that would be as neat and clean as this room but in a working way and was probably the room in which Mrs Garner lived most of the time, for Katherine had no doubt that it would be warm and cosy – the hub of the house.

When Mrs Garner returned she brought a tray with cups and saucers and plates. 'It won't be a moment now, Mrs Westland. I always have a kettle on the reckon.'

In a few minutes Katherine was enjoying the tea and a piece of fruitcake.

'Now, Mrs Westland,' said Mrs Garner, settling back in her chair, 'how long will you be wanting a room?'

'I don't really know, Mrs Garner. I have been companion to a lady in a remote part of the Wolds. Alas, she died so I had to leave. I am now alone in the world, with no family, so am free to go where I like.'

'So you came here. Have you friends locally?'

355

'No. I know no one.'

'So why did you choose Whitby?'

'I don't really know. I took a coach for Pickering and stayed there the night. The landlord of the inn told me that the first transport out of Pickering would be the carrier's cart to Whitby and, as he recommended Mr Welburn, I decided to take it. Now here I am, not really knowing what I am going to do. I have a little money that will give me the opportunity to try and find some employment.'

'You have been open with me and I like that in a person. Besides Isaac sent you and that is a good enough recommendation for me. He wouldn't have mentioned me if he hadn't been impressed by you and thought you suitable.'

'So you'll have me?'

'Yes.'

'Oh, thank you, Mrs Garner. That's a relief.'

'I don't take lodgers on a regular basis, only now and again if they come recommended and are seeking short-term accommodation. My husband who died two years ago was a ship's captain and left me comfortably off. I take it you are a widow too?'

'Yes. My husband was killed in London.'

Mrs Garner looked shocked and offered her sympathy. 'Well, Mrs Westland, you are welcome to stay with me until you decide what you must do.'

'Thank you, Mrs Garner. I appreciate your kindness. Please call me Katherine, I would prefer that.'

Mrs Garner smiled in acknowledgement and extended the friendly gesture. 'And you should call me Emily. Now let me show you your room.'

'Emily, this will be most suitable and comfortable.' Katherine showed enthusiasm when she saw the room which was neat and homely, recently decorated with lime-washed walls and white paintwork. The bed was covered with a multicoloured crocheted spread.

356

'Delightful,' Katherine repeated.

They settled payment to their mutual satisfaction.

'I have an evening meal at seven. Please use the drawing-room as you would your own.'

'You are most kind. I am sure we will get on very well.

The following morning, blessing the luck that had brought her to Mrs Garner's, Katherine decided to explore Whitby in the hope that something might trigger a memory of her previous visit and help her fill in the spaces in her memory.

Walking by the harbour and along the West Pier, taking in the view across the river to the houses rising up the cliff-side to the parish church and ruined abbey, reminded her of seeing them from a different perspective: from the deck of a ship sailing upriver to its berth. She half closed her eyes, trying to focus the cameo of so long ago, but all she could see was herself standing on the deck beside John. Surely if they had stayed in Whitby overnight they . . . She pulled her thoughts up short. Overnight? Why hadn't that entered her mind before? Now it had come automatically and it had the ring of truth about it. So if they had stayed overnight surely she and John must have come ashore for a while? Yet, as she had walked to Mrs Garner's yesterday, and now, walking in Whitby this morning, the sights on shore were not familiar.

She fingered the cross which she always carried out of sight in her pocket. If she had been given it in Whitby maybe she could find the workshop where it had been made, but she was wary of that lest word got back to Mrs Bradshaw. She might be better off trying to find something else to jog her memory. She walked the Whitby streets time and time again, mingled with the local people as they went about their daily lives, but though she felt drawn more and more to the place, it seemed there was nothing here to impress the past on her mind.

It became a matter of some concern to her that her

357

funds were beginning to run low. She needed some source of income to bolster them and make the continuation of her present life possible. She had been with Mrs Garner two months when she voiced her problem to Emily.

'I realised you were getting worried but did not voice any observation for fear you'd think I was wanting rid of you. Far from it, Katherine. You and I have got on so well I don't want to lose you, though I know some day it's inevitable. You cannot spend your life in your present situation. You are still young and should be leading a fuller life than you are. For that you need some means of support.'

'I have given it a lot of thought and as I have gone about I've kept a lookout for something that would suit me. But I'm afraid if I do not find something soon I must turn to anything.'

'Don't rush into it, my dear. And don't worry about your rent. If that becomes impossible for you then I shall wait until you do find something. I know there are not many opportunities for young women of your station in life. I will prod some of my friends in case they know of anything. Don't worry,' Emily added quickly, 'I will not reveal your situation.'

'You are too kind to me, but I would be grateful if you do hear of anything.'

Two weeks later Emily returned from afternoon tea with a friend who had also invited four other ladies.

'It will be all tittle-tattle,' she'd said with no small measure of disgust on going out, but returned in a state of great excitement. She cast her outdoor clothes to one side in the hall and hurried into the drawing-room where she found Katherine reading. 'News, Katherine! Good news, I hope.'

Katherine looked up, startled by her friend's exuberance. Before she could say anything Emily went on, 'Mrs Foulser ... gossipy old battleaxe, but it's just as well ... she had heard that the Glossops of Farndale House ... nice place in its own grounds on the outskirts of Whitby ... are looking for a governess who can teach their ten-year-old daughter. I immediately thought of you but did not say anything. I probed a little and added what I gained to my own knowledge of the Glossops.'

Emily's excitement spilled over on to Katherine with the mention of the word governess. She was immediately all attention and swept up in Emily's enthusiasm as she went on.

'They are a well-respected family in Whitby. Mr Glossop's grandfather and father made money through the whaling trade. He formed a trading company on the back of that wealth and has done very well. According to Mrs Foulser he is expanding by opening a London office and because of his reputation has already made a number of deals with shipping firms operating out of the capital. That business is likely to take him to London on a number of occasions. His wife will accompany him but they don't want their daughter to be pitched from one tutor to another and see the ideal answer as a governess who will live in at Farndale House.'

'Emily, that sounds wonderful. It would just suit me and be the answer to my problem. Thank goodness you went to that tea party. I know you were a little reluctant to do so.'

Emily gave a little chuckle. 'So I was. Ah, well, let's hope something good comes of it.'

'But what can I do? Will they be advertising the position? I can't just go marching up to the front door saying, "I've come for the job of governess".'

'Why not? I know if I was wanting a governess for my daughter and someone like you turned up, I would think my luck was in. I would be saved all the bother of trying to find someone.'

'You really think I could?'

'They are good people, devoted to each other by all accounts. I don't think it's idle gossip that they are very kind to their staff, both at the house and in his workplace. If you could get that post, I think you would be extremely happy there.'

By the time she rose the next morning Katherine had firmed her resolve to do as Emily suggested.

When she voiced her determination and asked for directions to Farndale House over breakfast, Emily was pleased and immediately began to organise proceedings.

'You will not walk there and arrive like someone needing a position. You must arrive with a little flair and ceremony. You will travel by carriage.'

'But ...' Thinking of the expense, Katherine started to protest.

'No objections, I will send the maid to hire one.' With that Emily rang the bell and when the maid appeared, instructed her to hire a carriage to be here in half an hour.

'As you will be arriving unexpectedly, without an appointment, it will look better if you are chaperoned, especially as I am a Whitby woman and you are not.'

'I bow to your judgement, Emily, and thank you for your thoughtfulness.'

'Best of luck, my dear, though I'm sure you don't need it. Your presentation will be all you need,' enthused Emily to inject confidence into her as the carriage turned into the drive at Farndale House.

It was an imposing building, set back a quarter of a mile from the trackway running inland out of Whitby. Katherine could see that whoever had chosen the site had done so because of the views it afforded across the town to the old abbey on the East Cliff. It may catch the wind but when they neared the house she saw that its solid construction would withstand anything the elements could throw at it. The large stones were formidable and, though there were plenty of windows from which to take in the view, they were equipped with wooden shutters that could be swung into place if ever a storm threatened to be particularly vicious. Though in some ways the grey stone and slate roof gave it a dour appearance, Katherine felt comfortable with this house. She put it down to the fact that any starkness had been eliminated from it by the use of ornamentation on some of the stonework and by the turret construction at one corner of the building.

The coachman jumped down to help the ladies from the carriage. Four shallow steps led on to a low terrace spanning the front of the building.

Katherine licked her lips nervously and offered up a silent prayer for help as Emily tugged the bell-pull. She gave Katherine a supportive smile and whispered, 'Everything will be all right. Just be yourself.'

The door opened and a neatly dressed maid looked queryingly at them.

'We would like to see Mrs Glossop,' said Emily firmly.

'I will see if she is receiving visitors,' replied the maid. 'Please step inside.' When she had closed the door she asked, 'Whom shall I say is calling?'

'Mrs Garner and Mrs Westland.'

The maid hurried across the hall to a door on the right, knocked, paused, then opened it and entered the room. When she reappeared she held the door slightly ajar and motioned to the callers. 'Mrs Glossop will see you now,' she said quietly, and opened the door wide for them.

Katherine did not have time to take in her surroundings but received an overall impression that the room was big and elegant yet comfortable, taking in more as the minutes passed. For now she was drawn much more to the striking delicate beauty of the lady seated in a chair close to the window, her arm round the waist of a little girl standing beside her, reading from a book on her lap. There was a serenity and composure about the scene that soothed Katherine.

'Rebecca, run along now while I talk to these ladies.'

'Yes, Mama.' She gave her mother a kiss on the cheek

361

and ran from the room, giving Emily and Katherine a friendly smile as she did so.

Her mother watched her until the door was closed and then turned her gaze to the newcomers. 'Ladies, please do sit down,' she said gently, indicating chairs close by her.

'Thank you, ma'am,' said Emily, 'and thank you for seeing us.'

'You, I think, must be Mrs Garner. I have heard of your work for the widows of men lost at sea. You were once pointed out to me when my husband and I attended a memorial service at the parish church for some members of a crew lost in the Arctic.'

'I am flattered you should remember me, ma'am.'

'And you must be Mrs Westland.' Though the woman's eyes were gentle Katherine realised that they were taking in every detail of her appearance and forming an initial impression of her.

'Yes, ma'am.'

'What can I do for you ladies?' Mrs Glossop's eyes flitted from one to the other until Emily gave her reply.

'I hope we are not being presumptuous in coming here with a particular enquiry. I have heard that you could be looking for a governess for your daughter?'

Mrs Glossop gave a wry grimace and raised her eyebrows. 'My, there are some gossips about.'

'I am sorry if I have ...'

'No, no. I mean no criticism of you, Mrs Garner. I am just surprised that word has got out so quickly. It is only three days since my husband and I decided on this course. Do please go on?'

'Well, I have brought Mrs Westland to meet you. She is wanting employment and I think she might be just the person you are looking for.'

Mrs Glossop turned her eyes back to Katherine. She gave a comforting little smile, trying to eliminate the nervousness she saw rising in Katherine after her remark about gossips. 'Tell me something about yourself.'

362

'I am originally from Newcastle. I have recently been in employment as a companion to a lady some years older than me.'

'Where was this?'

Katherine had feared this question might come up but as Emily knew the answer could not hold back.

'Ribton Hall in a remote part of the Wolds.'

'Your reason for leaving?'

'My employer died.'

'I'm sorry. Did she have children?'

'They were grown-up, married and living in the south of England.'

'And yourself?'

'None,' she replied, not wanting to explain the suppositions and doubts that had haunted her.

'Your husband?'

'He was killed in London.'

'That must have been a great shock to you.' Mrs Glossop, not wanting to dwell on the subject, added with a touch of doubt in her voice, 'You have no experience with children?'

'I will be honest with you, ma'am, I have none but believe I can offer something to a girl of ten. I was brought up by loving parents who gave me a good education which I feel capable of passing on to someone like your daughter. I love books and reading and would encourage her likewise, although I notice you must be guiding her on that path already.' She indicated the book Mrs Glossop was still holding.

She smiled. 'You are observant, Mrs Westland. I too love books and would certainly hope that Rebecca gains the same love. They are a window on the world and can enchant for many hours. Have you anything else to add about yourself? What brings you to Whitby, for instance, and to Mrs Garner? I take it that indicates you have no family or relations here?'

'Quite right, Mrs Glossop. When I left my last employment I was free to go anywhere. I had no particular reason for coming to Whitby, but here I found myself. Mrs Garner was recommended to me as being a likely person to provide me with a room. Although she does not take people on a regular basis, and when she does it is more for companionship than anything else, she befriended me.'

'No doubt, like me, she liked what she saw and was prepared to go on first impressions.' Mrs Glossop smiled. 'I was going to suggest I should get references from Ribton Hall.' Katherine's heart missed a beat here. 'But that would take time. I couldn't guarantee I would receive an immediate reply and can't afford to wait. I want someone settled in here with Rebecca soon as my husband and I will be going away in ten days' time. You have pre-empted my advertisement. I will go on my immediate impressions and trust them. The position is yours Mrs Westland, but shall we say for a probationary period of six months at the end of which you or I can terminate the employment with immediate effect? If after that time we are both satisfied, new terms can be negotiated.'

Relief flooded over Katherine. The tension that had built up in her, especially at the mention of Ribton Hall, drained away.

'Thank you, Mrs Glossop. That suits me. I am most grateful to you and will do my best for Rebecca.'

'I'm sure you will. My husband leaves the employment of staff and the running of the household to me, but as regards a salary he will make the arrangements. I can assure you he will be more than fair. Now, I think we should tell Rebecca and will do it over a cup of hot chocolate.' Mrs Glossop had risen from her chair, placed the book carefully on a table beside her and crossed to the bell-pull by the fireplace.

A few moments later a maid appeared. 'Ella, please tell Rebecca to come to see me and then bring us four cups of hot chocolate.'

'Yes, ma'am,' replied the maid brightly.

364

When the door next opened Rebecca appeared. 'You wanted me, Mama?'

'Yes, darling. Come here.' She held out her arms to her daughter. 'I have something to tell you,' she added as she hugged her. 'These ladies are Mrs Garner and Mrs Westland.' The girl smiled at them as her mother indicated who was who. 'Mrs Westland is to be your new governess.'

'Oh, good!' Rebecca cried excitedly. 'I liked her when she first came in.'

The adults laughed at the child's perception.

'I'm looking forward to getting to know you, Rebecca,' said Katherine. 'I'm sure we'll get on very well together and have a lot of fun.'

'Do you like reading? Drawing? Walking? The garden? The sea?' Questions came thick and fast and Katherine barely had time to keep up with a nod for each.

They only came to a stop when two maids arrived with the hot chocolate.

Mrs Glossop calmed her daughter down, and in the course of the next half-hour employer and employee got to know more about each other and both were satisfied with what they learned.

'I suggest that tomorrow you come back and meet my husband and then arrange to come here permanently the following day. That will give all of us time to get to know each other before my husband and I leave the following week.' Mrs Glossop and Rebecca saw them to the door.

When Katherine paused to say goodbye, Rebecca said, 'I'm so glad you are coming, Mrs Westland.'

'Thank you, Rebecca. I'm looking forward to our time together.'

As the carriage drove away, Emily smiled and patted Katherine's hand. 'There, I told you it would be all right. They have certainly taken to you, my dear, and it's no wonder, you being you.'

Katherine squeezed her hand. 'It's thanks to you I got the position, I will be eternally grateful.'

As she made that comment Katherine wondered what the future held for her now. Her life had taken a new turn but would it lead to her filling the gaps in her memory that still haunted her? Did her feelings for Rebecca stem from a maternal instinct and love she had once felt for someone else?

Chapter Twenty-two

The following morning Katherine could hardly contain her excitement. The carriage that they had hired the previous day arrived on time. Emily wished her good luck and Katherine was on her way.

When she was shown into the drawing-room her heart missed a beat when the man who was standing looking out of the window turned round. He was the handsomest Katherine had ever seen, and with his wife beside him she thought what an attractive couple they made.

He was tall, maybe a couple of inches over six feet. His elegantly cut clothes emphasised a slim athletic build. His dark thick hair was brushed back at the temples, giving him a debonair look. There was a determined set to his jaw but that was mellowed by gentle dark-blue eyes with an alertness about them that indicated he would miss nothing.

'Good morning, Mrs Westland.' He extended his hand as he came forward.

'Good morning, sir.'

'Let us sit down. I have heard about you from my wife. Don't worry, I don't want to know any more. I trust Isobel's judgement entirely. She and I have talked things over. What we require from you is that you should give our daughter affection, a good education, and some training in etiquette that will make her a sound and likeable person with no airs and graces.'

'From the little I saw yesterday I think that you and Mrs Glossop have placed her on that road already. I will do my best to continue it and give her all the love I can. I do assure you she will be well-protected under my care.'

'Good. Now, I understand that you are going to move in tomorrow?'

'If that is still convenient?'

He looked for confirmation to his wife.

'It is,' she replied. 'What time would you like to arrive?'

'Would eleven o'clock be suitable?'

'Ideal. Before you go today I will show you round the house, the room you will occupy, and let you meet my staff.'

'That brings me to another important point that my wife and I have discussed. You will be spending a lot of time with Rebecca and so will be in close contact with us as a family. Therefore we think you should live as one of us.'

'But, sir, you will want your privacy,' protested Katherine.

'As, no doubt, will you, but I am sure we will all find time for that.'

'That is most kind of you, sir. I do assure you that because Rebecca and I will share so much and a certain love and respect will naturally grow between us, it will not intrude on the love she has for you nor on that you have for her.'

'We could see that as a potential problem and I am grateful you are aware of the possibility. Now, if you are to live as one of us, I think it best if you and my wife use Christian names.'

'If that is the way you prefer it then I am only too glad for it puts relations on a pleasanter footing.'

'Good. I think that settles everything. No, it doesn't. You will be paid generously in cash the last day of every month.'

Though he did not mention a specific figure, Katherine

did not question this. They were taking her on trust so she would do the same. To appear mercenary could sour the relationship right at the start and she did not want that. She considered herself lucky to have found such a position. She did not want to spoil things.

'Thank you.'

'Do you need anything before the end of the month?'

'Oh, no.'

'You can take over now, Isobel.' He rose from his chair. 'I look forward to meeting you tomorrow, Katherine.'

'And I you.'

As he left the room Isobel stood up and Katherine did likewise. 'I'll take you to the room you will occupy.'

They climbed the wide oak staircase that was lined with landscape paintings.

Katherine paused halfway up to view one that had caught her eye. 'That is particularly good. What is the subject?'

'It is the Cornish coast. It was painted by my mother.'

'She is very talented.'

'Was, I'm afraid. I think of her every night as I pause to look at that picture.'

'Do you paint?'

Isobel gave a little laugh. 'No, I'm hopeless. Mother's talent was never passed on to me but I think it might be coming out in Rebecca. You will be able to judge that. I am pleased you have an eye for a picture and for artistic talent.' She started up the stairs again. Reaching the top, she turned to the left. The corridor was lit from a round window at the end. There were two doors on the right and two on the left. Isobel paused. 'The two end doors on either side lead into rooms for your everyday needs. Richard has had the latest plumbing devices installed. Each of those rooms is also accessed from the room next to them, that is Rebecca's on the right and yours on the left, so that you are both independent of each other and of the rest of the household.'

369

Katherine had never heard of such luxury before. 'That is most thoughtful of your husband. He must be a farseeing man.'

'He looks into all the latest gadgets, sometimes causing great upheavals with them, but Rebecca and I and the staff know his ways. Now, let's find her.' Isobel knocked on the door and opened it. 'Rebecca, Mrs Westland is here.'

'I know, I was watching for her from my window. Hello, Mrs Westland.'

'Hello, Rebecca.'

'I'm going to show Mrs Westland her room, take her round the house and introduce her to the staff. Do you want to come with us?'

'Oh, yes, yes.' The girl scrambled to her feet from the rug on which she had been sitting, abandoning her pencil and paper as she did so.

'May I see what you were drawing?' asked Katherine.

Rebecca picked up the paper a little reluctantly and showed embarrassment as she passed it to Katherine.

Her eyes widened at the sight of two well-drawn horses in a field lined on one side by trees. She cast Isobel a quick glance. 'Rebecca, this is wonderful. I am very impressed.'

'You can keep it if you like?'

'Thank you. I'll put it in my room.'

Isobel led the way across the corridor and when Katherine saw her room she was speechless for a few moments. It was simply furnished but with the most attractive oak furniture: a bed, chest of drawers, wardrobe, dressing table, desk and armchair. The curtains and cushions were of the same matching, flowered material and the bed was covered with a deep red quilt.

'Do you like it?' prompted Rebecca.

'It's beautiful.'

'And you have a good view out of the window,' said Rebecca, running to it.

Katherine went to join her. Fields rolled away before

climbing towards the moors, a vast landscape that would mesmerise with the ever-changing light and weather. 'It's breathtaking.' She turned round, her eyes damp with appreciation as she thanked Isobel.

They set off on a tour of the house which was much bigger than Katherine had imagined when she had first seen it. The turret rooms, upstairs and downstairs, were used as sitting-rooms, the upper one affording a wonderful panoramic view of the coast.

As they made their way to the kitchen and staff quarters, Rebecca said, 'If you get lost, Mrs Westland, I'll show you where you are.'

Katherine laughed. 'Thanks, Rebecca, that will be a great help.'

Isobel took her first to meet the housekeeper, Mrs Dyer. Katherine realised Isobel had already informed her of the appointment, for she received a warm but cautious welcome. The introduction of a governess who would live as one of the family was a new situation for the staff of Farndale House.

Katherine extended her hand in friendship. She was facing a tall thin woman whose severe features might be off-putting but Katherine felt sure that behind the exterior lay a warm-hearted person. If she was not, she was sure Isobel would not have had her in the house.

'Mrs Dyer, I am sure we will get on well.'

'There is no reason why we should not. If there is anything you wish to know about our routine here at Farndale House, please don't hesitate to ask. Now, if you would like to come with me, I'll introduce you to the rest of the staff. They will all be in the kitchen at the moment.' She started for the door.

Rebecca skipped beside her. 'Isn't it exciting, Mrs Dyer, having a governess?'

She smiled at the girl's enthusiasm. 'I'm sure it is, Rebecca.'

Katherine was quick and pleased to note the depth of

371

affection for the girl in the housekeeper's eyes, and realised that so long as she had Rebecca's welfare at heart she would have an ally in the housekeeper.

Isobel allowed Mrs Dyer to make the introductions to Mrs Ryan, the cook, to the two kitchen maids and three other maids. Katherine greeted them all with the same warmth, then Isobel stepped in with an explanation for Katherine. 'Mrs Dyer organises the household routine as she sees fit. None of us has a specific maid at our service but all of them are familiar with what is required in the household.' She then addressed the whole staff. 'As Mrs Dyer has no doubt told you, Mr Glossop and I are employing Mrs Westland as governess to Rebecca and she will be living as part of our household. I am sure you will all do your best to make her life here as pleasurable and easy as possible.'

When they returned to the hall Isobel said, 'Mrs Westland will be coming to live here from tomorrow, Rebecca. Run along to your room now. I want a few more words with her.'

'See you tomorrow, Mrs Westland,' Rebecca cried with obvious anticipation, and raced off up the stairs.

'Sit down for a few moments, Katherine, there are one or two other things to explain,' said Isobel as they entered the drawing-room. 'We do a certain amount of entertaining of friends and you will be included. In certain circumstances Rebecca is allowed to participate until eight o'clock. On those occasions you will see her settled in bed and then if you wish you may return to our company. If Rebecca is allowed to be with us, the evening meal will be earlier than at the times she is not, so that in neither event will your meal be interrupted. You must be free to go and come as you please without neglecting her. We have two carriages, two coachmen and a groom. If those vehicles are not in use you are free to use them, but get one of the men to drive you.'

'That is most kind of you. I will use them with discretion. They will enable me to introduce Rebecca to the delights of the countryside and the coast.'

'If you have any more questions do ask me or Mrs Dyer, though I have no doubt that Rebecca too will be ready with an answer.' Isobel rose from her chair. 'Until tomorrow at eleven.'

On the way back to Cliff Street Katherine was filled with joy at her good fortune. Mrs Garner was waiting to hear her news and was swept up in Katherine's enthusiasm.

'And it's all thanks to you,' she concluded, giving Emily a hug of appreciation.

'I did nothing really but latch on to a piece of gossip.' She gave a little laugh. 'It's a good job I have a keen pair of ears. I hope everything works out for you.'

'It will if I have anything to do with it.' Katherine wondered if that would include filling the gaps in her memory but was determined not to let that thought deter her from the splendid stroke of fortune that had befallen her. If her position as governess brought such a result then so be it; if it did not she saw that she could make a full new life with the Glossops.

Mrs Garner was determined that it would not be a tearful goodbye, no matter how much she knew she would miss Katherine. So she waved her friend a heartfelt farewell in the morning, with both of them making a promise that they would keep in touch.

As Katherine walked into Farndale House she felt she was walking into a new life and that filled her with determination to make it succeed. Gone were the days of anxiety. She had been happy for most of the time since she had been found barely alive on the shore at Robin Hood's Bay, but there had been moments of deep despair. The good times she would remember, the others she would shut out.

She settled in quickly and by the time Mr and Mrs

373

Glossop were to leave the following week had established an easy-going relationship with Rebecca but one which the girl would not abuse. Katherine mapped out a routine that was flexible enough to take into account the vagaries of the weather, impulse decisions, particular interests and out-of-the-ordinary situations. The ties of friendship between the governess and her pupil were nurtured and grew quickly but Katherine was careful not to let it get out of hand, nor to impinge on the daughter-parent relationship which she saw as the bedrock of life at Farndale House. This in its turn derived from the love that was clear between Isobel and Richard Glossop. Witnessing the special affection between the two of them stirred Katherine's thoughts and made her wonder if such a relationship had existed between her and John. She supposed it must otherwise she would not have been aware of his presence or have heard his voice at Ribton Hall. In the quiet of her room, with such thoughts assailing her mind, she yearned to know such a love again.

'Katherine, you have been with us six months, are you satisfied with Rebecca's progress?' asked Isobel when they were enjoying a cup of hot chocolate one morning while Rebecca was completing some work Katherine had set her in her own room.

'I am. She is a quick learner with wide interests, a delight to teach and a lively companion. But it is really you who should judge her progress.'

'Richard and I were discussing it last night and I must tell you that we are highly delighted with what Rebecca has achieved and the way she is developing. She is much more willing to learn than she was, and we believe that is due to you.'

'It is kind of you to say so but I think she has a good example in her parents.'

Isobel gave a little shrug of her shoulders. 'She is much more willing to talk to us and share her experiences than

374

she was. Now, you yourself, are you happy with us?'

'Extremely. I will be ever grateful to you for taking me in as one of the family.'

'Good. Friends who were naturally curious about your arrival have all been charmed by you, telling us we have found a gem and that they are in no doubt Rebecca will benefit greatly from your teaching and influence.'

Katherine blushed. 'They are more than generous in their assessment.'

'Richard and I think not, so let's say the probationary period is over and I know that he will adjust your remuneration accordingly.'

'That is most generous but there is no need. I am perfectly happy with the present arrangement.'

Isobel raised her hand. 'Say no more. Richard has settled it. Now, talking of friends, he wants to give a special party in a month's time so that it is something you can look forward to. I tried to dissuade him but he insists.'

'Then I take it that there is an occasion to celebrate?'

'Well ...' Isobel hesitated. 'It will be my birthday.'

'Then it is something special and I agree with him that it should be celebrated. What is he planning?'

'He leaves the details to me but insists we are to have a special dinner for about forty guests, the meal to be followed by dancing.'

'Then you must let me help with the organisation.'

'It is more a matter of putting everything in motion. Mrs Dyer and Mrs Ryan are unstoppable from then on.'

'Do let me help.'

'There will be invitations to send. You could help me with those. I was planning to do them tomorrow.'

'We could do it together and involve Rebecca. Does she know about the party?'

'Yes. I mentioned it last night just after she had gone to bed, but told her not to breathe a word until I had spoken to you about it.'

'I thought she was excited about something. I'm sure she

would like to help with the invitations. I'll tell her when I check the work she is doing now.'

'You're bursting to tell me something, aren't you, Rebecca?' Katherine teased, having kept the child on tenterhooks while she scrutinised her essay.

'You know? Mother has told you? Isn't it exciting?' Rebecca's voice rose with every word.

'Yes,' laughed Katherine. 'Tomorrow your mother and I are going to write the invitations and you can help.'

'Oh, good.' Rebecca clapped her hands.

'And there is one other thing. As it's your mother's birthday, I think we should go into Whitby and find a present for you to give her.'

'Oh, yes, yes!'

'Good. But say nothing to her.'

'A surprise for her?'

'Yes. I think she would like that.'

'When shall we go?'

'I'll see when I can arrange the carriage.'

A week later Isobel stood on the steps of Farndale House to return her daughter's enthusiastic wave as the carriage pulled away. Though Katherine had said this was an educational trip to the abbey, Isobel had guessed what lay behind Rebecca's enthusiasm but, not wanting to spoil it, had said nothing.

The child could hardly contain her excitement as the carriage started its descent into Whitby. She took in all the activity, with people jumping out of the way of the carriage as it progressed across the bridge to the east side, and gazed wide-eyed at the ships, some anchored in mid-stream, others moored at the quays. She liked the noise after the solitude of Farndale House: the shouts of passersby, the hub-bub of conversation, the rumble of carts, the screech of the seagulls and the lapping of the water along the timbers of the quays.

Langton took the carriage into the yard of the White

Horse. 'I'll be here whenever you return, ma'am,' he said dutifully as he helped Katherine to the ground. Rebecca jumped down beside her.

'Thank you, Langton. I'm not sure how long this will take,' she replied. She took hold of Rebecca's hand and left the yard. They turned into Church Street and into the flow of people.

'Now, Rebecca, what do you think we shall find?'

'Oh, I don't know, Mrs Westland, but it has to be nice.'

'I'm sure we'll find something suitable.'

They took up a leisurely pace, pausing to look in shop windows, considering this and that but not feeling enthusiastic about anything in particular even though at certain stores they were cajoled to buy by the shopkeeper viewing possible customers from his doorstep.

When Katherine realised that there were a considerable number of jet workshops in this part of Whitby her mind drifted back through the years and she wondered if it was in any of these that she had been given the jet cross that nestled in her pocket.

'What about a piece of jet?' Katherine suggested.

'Do you think Mother would like it?'

'I'm sure she would, and it would be something for her to wear and remember you by every time she did so.'

'All right.'

They went into the first jet workshop they came to. It was small with six men working at benches, each at a different stage in the processing of the final item that would be put on sale. A man came forward and touched the brim of his bowler hat.

'Good day, ma'am, what can I do for you? And you, miss?' He gave Rebecca a fatherly smile.

At their request he produced a number of pieces which he spread out on a bench for examination. As Rebecca looked at them, Katherine's mind was trying to span the years, hoping that being in a jet workshop might rekindle some knowledge of her last visit, but this one did not

377

conjure up scenes from the past except that there were men working at benches.

'There's nothing I really like.' Rebecca's voice drew her back to the purpose of their visit.

Katherine looked apologetically at the man. 'I'm sorry. It has to be something special for her mother's birthday.'

They left the workshop and in the course of the next hour visited six more without success. At each of them Katherine hoped something would spark off her memory but nothing did.

'It's hopeless,' groaned a despondent Rebecca. 'We'd better think of something else.'

'As you wish.' As she was agreeing Katherine had taken a few more steps. 'Wait a minute. There's another here, we may as well make one more try. There's a window.'

They went to it and gazed at the ten pieces laid out with care so that they showed to the best advantage. Obviously someone with an artistic eye had set out the window.

'That one!' A note of triumph had come to Rebecca's voice and her eyes shone with anticipation of making the bracelet her gift to her mother.

'It is rather nice,' agreed Katherine. 'Should we go and have a look at it and see what else there is?'

'Oh, yes.' Rebecca was already starting towards the door.

The workshop was almost half as big again as the others they had visited. Six men were carving and etching round a central bench and others were at the wheels used to mill, clean and polish pieces of jet. Three of them wore blue jackets the fronts of which were streaked with red, no doubt from the powder they were using on the jet. A man who occupied a bench with a youth in one corner of the room rose from his seat when he saw Katherine and Rebecca.

'Good day, ladies,' he greeted them with a friendly smile.

Katherine smiled to herself when she saw a tremor of

satisfaction run through Rebecca at being regarded as grown-up. It prompted her to request: 'Please may we see the bracelet that is in the window?'

'Certainly, miss.' He half turned and called, 'Robert, the young lady would like to see the bracelet in the window.'

The youth laid the tool he was using carefully on the bench before crossing the room to gain access to the window display.

'Thank you.' Katherine smiled at him as he reached the table beside which they were standing. She received a warm smile in return from eyes that were attentive, eager to please. At eighteen he was tall, with a confident and friendly air.

'I'm Mr Harris and this is my son Robert,' said the man by way of introduction. 'The piece you are interested in was carved by him.'

Katherine's attention was directed to the bracelet which Rebecca was already examining. 'It is beautiful,' she commented. 'A work of art. Did your son set the display in the window?'

'Yes.'

'He has an artist's eye. It must appear in all he does.'

'Thank you, ma'am,' returned Robert, with colour rising in his cheeks.

'Is this a whale?' asked Rebecca, glancing over her shoulder at him.

'Yes, it is.' He crouched down beside her, picked up the bracelet and turned it round slowly. 'The scene goes all the way round and depicts more whales in the distance. I made that wavy pattern round the edge to represent the sea and to make a frame for the picture.'

'You did all that yourself?' the girl asked in wonderment.

'Yes.'

'You're clever.'

'I'm sure you are too.'

379

Rebecca cocked her head. 'Oh, yes, I am. I draw.'

'I would like to see your drawings some time.'

'One day I'll bring them to show you.'

'Would you like to see some more pieces that Robert has made?' His father broke in to stop the exchange getting out of hand.

'Yes, please,' said Katherine quickly. She did not know why she said this when it seemed obvious that Rebecca had set her mind on the bracelet that lay in front of her.

Robert left them to go to a display cabinet.

'Your son has talent,' praised Katherine.

'He has developed quickly but in this trade you can always go on improving.'

'And he has charming manners. You must be proud of him.'

'Yes,' came the reply without further comment.

Robert returned with six pieces of beautifully carved jet and laid them on the table. Katherine examined them with interest but though Rebecca cast her eyes over them her mind was already made up. The bracelet was bought and they left the workshop.

Rebecca was delighted with her purchase. 'Wasn't Robert nice?' she said with an eagerness that would brook no disagreement.

Katherine had no intention of doing so. 'Yes,' she replied thoughtfully.

In the quiet of her room she reflected on the reason she had requested to see more carvings and realised it was because, for some unknown reason, she had wanted to spend more time there. Had that workshop something familiar about it, or was it Mr Harris and his son who'd stirred something in the depths of her mind?

As he and Robert walked home Stephen Harris's mind turned to the lady and the little girl who had visited his workshop. There had been something attractive about them. He could not put his finger on why they had had this effect

380

on him except that they seemed like decent people. It was as if he had met them before, but he would have remembered if he had. Robert's chatter broke into his thoughts and he dismissed them from his mind. He would probably never see them again.

Chapter Twenty-three

With the day of the party drawing near, excitement pervaded Farndale House. Though preparations went smoothly there was a sense of bustle everywhere. The kitchen staff and their additional help, brought in for the purpose, put their hearts and skills into making the buffet one to remember. The dining-room was laid out so that the guests need not be kept waiting, and with doors giving access to the terrace space for the guests was enlarged. Seating in the ground-floor room in the turret and in the second drawing-room above was arranged into groups while that in the main room, which also had access to the terrace, had been cleared to leave the floor clear for dancing.

Katherine was drawn into the excitement and Rebecca was going to be allowed to stay up later than usual.

Soon after half-past six guests started to arrive and within half an hour everyone who had been invited was in conversation with friends or making new contacts. From the landing overlooking the hall Rebecca pointed out the people she knew to Katherine and they enjoyed exchanging comments about the ladies' dresses, revealed when their cloaks and pelisses were taken by the extra maids who had been engaged for the evening.

Isobel glanced up from the guests she had been greeting on their arrival and signalled to Rebecca that she wanted her to come down. Rebecca waved back in acknowledgement and ran down the stairs to her mother. Katherine saw words pass between them and laughter come to Rebecca's eyes. She skipped away, stopped, turned to look back at her mother who gave a slight shake of her head. Rebecca smiled and then started off again towards the drawing-room at a leisurely walking pace. A few minutes later the quartet that had been engaged for the evening started to play gently so that the music drifted through the house soothingly. Later the tempo would alter when the dancing started.

Katherine came slowly down the stairs thinking of the transformation in her life since she had come to Farndale House. Maybe she shouldn't worry any more about the gaps in her memory, merely accept the present and see the life into which she had been accepted as her future.

She reached the bottom of the stairs just as another guest, possibly the last one, arrived. He shrugged himself quickly out of his overcoat and handed it and his hat to one of the maids. Then, with a broad smile and his arms held wide, he came to Isobel. He kissed her on both cheeks as his hands took hers, whispered something in her ear which brought a trill of laughter to her lips and merriment to her eyes. He turned to Richard then and Katherine saw the deep friendship in the eyes of both men as they shook hands and exchanged greetings.

The man who had just arrived held himself erect, seeming to add to his six foot two. He was handsome in a rugged sort of way. There was nothing to retreat from in his open friendly face. In fact, quite the contrary, Katherine felt drawn to it. She started, realising she had been staring. She started to turn towards a door leading to the terrace.

'Katherine.' Richard had seen her and called out. She turned back. 'Come, meet our dear friend.'

Richard and Isobel escorted the stranger. 'This is Jack Palmer,' said Isobel. 'You would have met him before now

383

at one of our dinner parties but he has been away. Jack this is Katherine Westland, governess to Rebecca.'

'I am pleased to meet you, Mr Palmer,' said Katherine, and held out her hand.

He took it, and as he bowed slightly raised it towards his lips, but his eyes never left hers. 'It is a pleasure and one I wish I had had sooner. I regret I was out of Whitby.' Katherine blushed.

A maid appeared by their side with a tray of drinks. They each took one and when Isobel and Richard left them to have a word with two other guests, Jack said, 'Governess to Rebecca, do you enjoy that?'

'I do. She is an easy child to deal with and the fact that she is interested in most things makes life easier for me, Mr Palmer.' Katherine's words came faster than she'd intended but they seemed, though they were not, an escape from the soft eyes that held hers still.

'Ah, yes. Now, Mrs Westland, this is a relaxing, care-free evening and I hope you and I are going to find mutual interests and become friends, so should we not dispense with formalities? You call me Jack and I'll call you Katherine.'

Though she was taken aback by this approach from someone who was a complete stranger she could take no offence, in fact she agreed with every word he said and felt a sense of satisfaction as she did so.

Pleasure kindled his eyes. 'Good, that is settled. It is a pleasant evening, should we take a turn along the terrace?'

As they made their way there she noticed the number of greetings that passed between Jack and his fellow guests. Whoever he was, he was well known and liked.

'From previous remarks, I take it you have been away from Whitby for a little while?' she said.

'Yes, for most of the past year.' He offered no reason for his absence. Though she was curious she knew it would be impolite to question him. Besides he directed her away from the subject when he added, 'But I don't live in

384

Whitby. I live near the river, upstream at Sleights. And you, I detect from your accent, though it is not marked, do not come from this area.'

'No, I was born in Newcastle but have spent some time in London.'

'What brought you here?'

'My husband was killed there and I . . .'

'I'm so sorry. I shouldn't have . . .'

'It's all right. I decided to leave London but had no family to go to and somehow ended up here.'

'And that is our gain. I can sympathise with you, for I lost my wife in childbirth two years ago.'

'Oh, I am so sorry. The baby?'

'Lost as well.'

'What can I say?'

'Nothing, please don't try. That was one reason I have been away for nearly a year. I thought I could face my loss here but eventually I went to friends in Cornwall. They helped me enormously.'

'You had no family in Whitby?'

'Oh, yes. They were a great support, but as time passed I found they were too close. In spite of all their good intentions they were smothering me. I suppose that was only natural, seeing that I am about ten years younger than my two sisters. I just had to get away. I've been back only a fortnight and now I can cope with their kindness and they have realised what they had been doing. Now we are closer than we have ever been.'

'So some good has come out of tragedy?'

He gave a wan smile. 'I suppose so.'

'Well, I don't know what it was that brought me to such a wonderful family as the Glossops, but I'm grateful for it.' Her voice brightened. 'As you said, this is supposed to be a pleasant evening. Let's talk only of happy things.'

He laughed. 'You are quite right, but it has at least enabled us to learn a little about each other. If you are going to stay as Rebecca's governess we will see more

385

of each other. Through business Richard and I have become good friends and visit each other's homes frequently.' He glanced round and saw some people making their way to the dining-room. 'Would you like something to eat?' He disposed of her empty glass and led her to the dining-room where they made a selection from the tempting buffet.

As they turned from the table someone caught Jack's eye and he excused himself but made her promise to keep some dances for him.

Katherine strolled into the drawing-room and exchanged greetings and conversation with those people she had previously met. Strangers introduced themselves and were pleased to make the acquaintance of Rebecca's governess. Katherine relaxed in an atmosphere conducive to friendliness. She was on the terrace when Rebecca came rushing up to her.

'Mrs Westland, you must come.' She grabbed Katherine's hand and started to lead her away. 'I'm going to give Mama her present.'

'Wouldn't you like to give it to her on your own?'

'No, no.' Rebecca shook her head vigorously. 'You must be there. You helped me choose it.' She led Katherine into her father's study where she had told her parents to wait for her.

'Now, Rebecca, what is it? We really shouldn't leave our guests like this,' chided Richard.

'I know, but this won't take a minute. And I wanted Mrs Westland to be here.' She produced the package from behind her back. 'Happy birthday, Mama,' she said, eyes sparkling as she handed the parcel to her mother.

'Oh, Rebecca.' Isobel showed her surprise. 'Thank you, my love. What is it?'

'Open it and see,' cried the child excitedly.

Isobel carefully unwrapped the paper and raised the lid of the box. 'Oh, my goodness,' she gasped, her eyes widening with surprise and delight. 'It's beautiful.' She

386

bent down and hugged her daughter tearfully. 'Thank you, Rebecca, and thank you for being so thoughtful. When did you get it?'

'Mrs Westland took me into Whitby. Remember?'

'Of course. The day you went to the abbey.'

'Yes, but it was really to get you a present. Mrs Westland helped me pick it.'

'That is wonderful of you, Rebecca.' Her father gave her a hug. 'Now, we must get back to our guests.'

'One moment, Richard.' Isobel slipped the bracelet on to her left wrist and then held her arm at full stretch so all could admire it. 'Now we should get back.' As they went into the hall she said, 'Soon be time for bed, Rebecca. If you want something else to eat, go and get it now.'

'Then can I watch the dancing for a few minutes?'

'All right. For half an hour.'

'I'll find you,' said Katherine.

Rebecca ran off. Richard saw someone with whom he wanted a word.

'Thank you for helping Rebecca choose my present. You have brought her a lot of pleasure. I hope you are enjoying the evening?' Isobel said.

'Very much.' Katherine wondered if she could learn a little about Jack Palmer. 'I found Mr Palmer a charming man.'

'He's delightful,' replied Isobel. 'He and Richard came together through work and struck up a great friendship. Jack's an attorney and handles Richard's legal work. He was devastated when he lost his wife but seems much better since he has been away. I think he will be able to face life now. I sincerely hope so. He's in good spirits this evening.'

They had been strolling through the house and when they reached the terrace Jack saw them and excused himself from the group he was talking to.

'May I take Katherine from you, Isobel? She promised me a dance and when the band is playing so beautifully it is a pity not to take advantage.'

387

'Of course, Jack.'

He smiled and took Katherine by the elbow. 'And I want to dance with you too, Isobel.'

'I look forward to that,' she replied, and added as she glanced at Katherine, 'He's a good partner.'

'She flatters me.'

Katherine soon learned that Isobel was right. Jack was light on his feet and expert in guiding her. Her head whirled and she felt lost in time, a heady experience she had not felt for so long. It seemed as if she existed in another world. One dance followed another and Katherine wished it could go on forever.

She saw Rebecca sitting quietly as if she hoped she would not be noticed and told she should go to bed. She was tempted to let the child stay a little longer but her parents had made a stipulation regarding time and it should be adhered to.

The third dance with Jack came to an end. 'I really should take Rebecca to bed now,' she said reluctantly.

'I saw you look in her direction so I was expecting you to say that.' He smiled. 'While you do I'll fulfil my obligations to my hostess and maybe oblige one or two other ladies who have been looking at you with envy.'

'Oh, my goodness, have I been monopolising you?' She was flustered. 'I'm sorry.'

'Don't be. It was my pleasure, and I hope you enjoyed it too?'

'Delightful,' she returned with a smile.

'Don't be too long and we'll dance some more. You certainly must save the last one for me.'

'I look forward to that.' She hurried round the room to Rebecca. 'Sorry, love, I think we had better do as your mother and father say.'

Rebecca's lips tightened in disappointment but she gave a little nod.

The music started again. Couples moved on to the floor but then held back when they saw their host and hostess start to dance. All conversation stopped, only the strains of the music drifted round the room. Richard and Isobel glided in unison to its beat. They were lost in each other. No one else mattered. This was their time, a time to remember long into the future, for this was their tune, one that epitomised their love for each other and meant so much to them both.

Rebecca's eyes widened. She had never seen her parents with such an aura. 'Aren't they lovely?' she whispered.

'They are,' Katherine returned quietly. She took Rebecca's hand in hers and wondered if her son would have said the same about her and John.

She was relieved when at that moment Isobel, still dancing, looked round the room and signalled to others to join in the dance. As people moved on to the floor the spell was broken.

'We'd better go now.' Katherine saw Isobel look in their direction. 'Wave to your mother and father.'

Rebecca smiled and gave a vigorous wave. Isobel said something to her husband and they both hurried over to their daughter. 'Goodnight, love.' Isobel hugged and kissed her. 'Thank you for this wonderful present.' She turned her arm so that they could look at it together. 'People have been admiring it.'

Rebecca's eyes lit up with pleasure.

Richard kissed her and said, 'You're the most beautiful person here.'

'Not as beautiful as Mama.'

He adopted a serious expression and pursed his lips in mock thoughtfulness. 'Well, maybe not, but you are second to her. Now, off to bed, young lady.'

'Have you had a good time?' asked Katherine as they went up the stairs.

'Oh, yes. I love to see all the beautiful dresses, and people are so nice to me.'

'So they should be. You are a special person.'

'Isn't everyone special?'

'I suppose we are in different ways.'

'Is Mr Palmer special?'

'Yes.'

'You seemed to enjoy dancing with him?'

'I did. It's a long time since I danced.'

'Poor you. Well, now you can make up for it. I'm sure he'll ask you to accompany him if he's asked to another party.'

Katherine blushed with embarrassment. She felt the child was reading her mind for that was exactly what she'd hoped. Out of the mouths of babes ... Could Rebecca be right? But all she said lamely was, 'Oh, I don't think so.'

Rebecca's eyes were heavy with sleep brought on by all the excitement when Katherine tucked her up in bed. She left the room and walked slowly along the landing and down the stairs, deep in thought.

'What lies behind that thoughtful expression?'

Katherine started but quickly composed herself and smiled at Jack. 'Nothing worth bothering about.'

'You looked so serious. This isn't an evening to be serious so may I bring you back to the frivolity and ask you for another dance?'

With her wishful thinking gone Katherine allowed herself to be swept up in the jollifications that went on until the early hours of the morning.

As Katherine lay down in the softness of her bed she thought sleep would come immediately but it did not. Her mind was full of the dances she had had with Jack. She could still feel his strong arms around her waist yet they'd exerted only the lightest of pressures as they'd guided her through every step with an expertise that seemed natural to him. She could still hear the softness in his voice, still see those wonderful sparkling eyes that expressed so much. His final, 'This has been a most pleasant occasion, made more so by your wonderful company. Good night, Katherine, I hope we shall meet again before long,' kept running through her mind. Were those words really heartfelt or were they courtesies that came naturally to him?

She chided herself for doubting him. Jack Palmer couldn't be like that, there was too much honesty about him. Katherine scolded herself again for thinking like a love-sick girl and finally fell asleep, only to find that a tall handsome man strode through her dreams and carried her off to a new life.

Over the next three months Jack's visits to Farndale House became more frequent on various excuses that he needed to see Richard about some aspect of his business.

'Jack, we dealt with this problem last week,' Richard pointed out one day. He gave a little smile as he eyed his friend. 'Come on, you don't fool me. I'm merely the excuse for you to see Katherine.'

Jack gave a small embarrassed grin. 'Was it that obvious?'

'Well, I notice you always manage a turn on the terrace with her. Isn't it time you invited her to accompany you to dinner or whatever? I presume that's what you would like to do?'

'I find her interesting and attractive.'

'So what holds you back?' Richard saw him hesitate with his answer so precluded it. 'It's Jenny, isn't it? You think she wouldn't want you to. Look, Jack, we have our lives to lead. Jenny would want you to live as you would like. Your feelings for Katherine do not mean you think less of Jenny. You shared happiness together and that will always be a precious memory to you, no matter what you think of Katherine or how devoted you become to her.'

Jack looked thoughtful for a moment when his friend had finished. He glanced up and met Richard's searching eyes, filled with concern and understanding.

'Thanks. But it will interfere with her duties here.'

'Jack, something can always be arranged. Isobel and I aren't always away, and if we are at home there is no reason why Katherine can't take advantage of that.

Granted, we are her employers but we regard her and treat her as one of the family. If you can find pleasure, and maybe more than that, in her company, then I for one would be pleased for you and I'm sure Isobel will too.'

Just at that moment she walked into the room and caught Richard's last remark.

'What would I be pleased about?' she asked, looking from one to the other.

Richard explained, and when he had finished Isobel turned to their friend. 'Jack, I would be delighted for you, and I know Jenny would be too. She and I were close. If anything happened to me, I would hope that Richard found happiness elsewhere, without forgetting me and the love we shared.'

There was satisfaction in Jack's smile. 'Thanks, both of you. Tell me, what do you know about Katherine?'

'We find her a wonderful governess and Rebecca loves her. She is most considerate for Rebecca's welfare, and that our daughter's love is always first and foremost for us. She is very careful and tactful about that,' said Isobel.

'What about her past?'

'Now, aren't you being over-cautious?' queried Richard, raising an eyebrow.

Jack grimaced with doubt and shrugged his shoulders.

'We like what we see in Katherine and that is all that concerns us,' said Isobel. 'Ask her yourself if you want to. We have never probed into her past but we do know, as I'm sure you do, that she is a widow. She comes from Newcastle and came back north when her husband was killed in London. Beyond that we know nothing and don't need to know more. She fills the position of governess to our satisfaction and does not take advantage of being treated as one of the family. I imagine that if you do get serious with her you would like to know more. Only she can tell you that and I suggest that you ask no one but her.'

'Thank you for your wise words. You are good friends.'

*

392

Katherine was aware of the deep friendship that existed between the three and that Jack was always welcome at Farndale House. But this did not account entirely for the ever-increasing frequency of his visits and for the fact that on every occasion he was able to spend time with her. Not that she objected; in fact, she began to look forward to his visits. She found him attentive, considerate, interesting, with a wide range of conversation. Though a rapport and empathy developed between them, she sensed he was a little reticent to make their relationship any closer. From little things that had been said she knew he was still in love with his late wife and accepted that that was as it should be. Seeing and feeling that love, she began to feel a new closeness to John, and that began to revive memories of him. He became clearer to her. She began to remember things they had done together and recalled the position he had taken up in London. If nothing more developed from her relationship with Jack she would be ever grateful for what he had done to restore these small gaps in her memory, though he would never know how he had helped her.

'Katherine.' Jack stopped when they reached the end of the terrace one day. 'Would you do me the honour of dining with me at the Angel in Whitby on Wednesday evening?'

'I would be delighted. I will have to see if someone will be here for Rebecca, though.'

He gave a wry smile. 'I've already checked with Isobel. There's no reason why you can't be free that evening. She will be at home.'

'You were sure I would say yes? What if I had said no?'

'Then I would have been deeply disappointed.' His eyes were fixed on hers and she had the sensation of being drawn into a pool from which she would not want to escape, for there in its depths would be the life she longed for, one of love and devotion. His hands came to her waist and he drew her to him as his lips met hers, gently at first then lingering a while.

Katherine made a special journey into Whitby to buy a new dress. When she returned, Isobel and Rebecca were excited to see it and she took little persuasion to put it on so that they could have a preview before the night she was dining with Jack. It was of light blue broche silk with a floral pattern. The bodice came to a point above a plain pleated skirt. The neckline across the top of the shoulders was trimmed with blue lace as were the full-length sleeves. She had chosen a white shawl to wear loosely round her shoulders.

'Exquisite,' applauded Isobel. 'It's just right for you.' She realised that Katherine had gone out of her way to make an impression.

'You look lovely,' praised a wide-eyed Rebecca.

'Doesn't she?' agreed her mother. After a few minutes more she added, 'Run along, Rebecca, I want a word with Mrs Westland.'

When the door closed behind the departing figure, Isobel said, 'You look special and have a radiance that speaks to me of love. Do you love Jack?'

Katherine hesitated and then said with slow deliberation, 'I don't know. At times it is an overwhelming yes, but then caution dulls my enthusiasm. Should I let this happen? He is still in love with his wife.'

'There is nothing wrong in that and if you love each other it need not be an obstacle. In fact, the devotion he still has for Jenny could strengthen his devotion to you. I knew her very well and know she would not resent you. She would welcome any happiness you can give Jack.'

Katherine gave a considered nod and said, 'Thank you, Isobel, your words are a comfort to me. But we are getting ahead of the situation.'

'Better to face these facts now than later and be hurt. And remember, you are the only one who can tell if and

394

when you are truly in love.' She altered her serious tone. 'What matters for now is that you enjoy yourself on Wednesday.'

When she got ready that evening, Katherine was tempted to wear her jet cross but decided against it as she did not want to detract from Rebecca's present to her mother. Instead she slipped it into the pocket of her dress.

Jack called for her in a carriage he had hired. She realised he had planned the evening carefully when, after being greeted effusively by the landlord of the Angel, they were escorted to a table discreetly placed in a quiet corner of the dining room. There were a number of people already seated at various others. She was aware of eyes on them and of whispered conversation, no doubt commenting on her attire and the fact that the eligible widower, Jack Palmer, was accompanied by a lady.

The meal was leisurely, the food succulent, the wine complementing it and kind to the palate. The atmosphere was relaxing and their conversation flowed among amusing and serious topics. They were awaiting coffee when Jack leaned forward, resting his forearms on the table, and looked her firmly in the eye.

'I know little about you, Katherine, except that you are a widow. You were born in Newcastle, your husband killed in London. You came north after that. Beyond that I know nothing except that you were a companion to someone, that you came here as a governess to Rebecca, and that Isobel and Richard think highly of you.' He stopped and let his eyes make an enquiry.

'There is little more to tell,' she replied quickly, but knew he was expecting more.

'How long is it since your husband was killed?' he prompted.

Katherine's mind raced. How much should she tell him? If she admitted it was fifteen years ago he would want to know what had happened in the intervening years and that might lead her to have to reveal her loss of memory. Such information could shatter the closeness that was developing between them. She did not want that. Would she be able to convince him that she was normal except for the few gaps that had not been closed? So, unseen by him, she crossed her fingers as she replied. 'About the same time as you lost your wife.'

'You did not want to stay in London?'

'Too many memories and I had never really liked living there but it was John's place of employment. It meant promotion for him if he went there.'

'And the dutiful wife went along?'

'I loved him.'

'I'm sorry,' he hastened to say when he saw her eyes dampen. 'I shouldn't have probed.'

She reached across the table and touched his hand. 'That's all right, Jack. I do still love him but don't let that be a barrier between us. I suspect you have the same feelings for your wife.'

He nodded. 'I do. I am pleased we understand each other, and if you want to go on with our relationship it holds much promise.'

'I would not want to miss that.'

From that moment they enjoyed each other's company more and more. Whenever an invitation to some function was issued to Jack it always said 'and guest' and the host and hostess knew he would be accompanied by the charming widow, Mrs Katherine Westland.

'Gossip is beginning to fly about us, Katherine,' he pointed out one day when they were walking on the cliffs above Sandsend. 'I think it is time I introduced you to my family before they hear the rumours and get the wrong idea.'

'I would love to meet them,' she replied.

'Very well, I'll arrange it for next Sunday if that suits you?'

'Admirably. Isobel and Richard are taking Rebecca to see some friends at Ugthorpe.'

'Then Sunday it will be. I will arrange carriages for my two sisters and their husbands to arrive at my house at three. I will call for you at two.'

'Tell me a little about them before I meet them?'

'Elizabeth is married to Stephen who has a jet workshop in Whitby. Mary is married to Harry Mulgrave who comes from a family of fishermen in Robin Hood's Bay.'

Fear tightened the pit of her stomach. Robin Hood's Bay! Would Mary and Harry recall the shipwreck? Could they possibly link her to it? She must control her raging thoughts. The likelihood of their doing so was remote. It was so long ago and she had not been there long. Should she tell Jack her story now? But that would force her to reveal things she did not want him to know now, if ever, unless her memory was completely restored. She tightened her determination to follow her present course and face whatever came when it did.

'Have they any family?' she asked.

'Mary and Harry have two sons, both married and keen fishermen like their father. Elizabeth and Stephen have one son who will follow his father into the jet trade.' He saw no reason to enlighten her further about them at this stage.

'You get on well with all of them?'

'Yes, but I don't see as much of them as maybe I should. The gap in our ages, ten and eleven years, always seemed to make a different and led me to make friends of my own age. Representing Whitby merchants legally took me away on many occasions. But they have always been supportive, especially when Jenny died.'

'Thank you for that information. It makes them seem less formidable than they might have been, though they are bound to view me with a critical eye.'

'You needn't worry. They are easy to get along with.'

'I hope so because I will be under scrutiny. Who has our

397

brother found? Will she measure up to Jenny?' She eyed him seriously. 'Was she a favourite with them?'

He stopped, turned her to him and looked at her with a serious expression that meant what he was about to say was serious. 'Yes, she was, and I think that is why they swamped me with their sympathy and attention. But you need not worry, you will charm them just as she did. They're Yorkshire folk and they'll not let preconceived ideas get in the way of their good judgement.' He ran his forefinger along her furrowed brow. 'Wipe that away.' She smiled. His lips met hers. 'I have fallen in love with you, Katherine Westland.' He kissed her again but this time his lips lingered, emphasising his words and feelings.

The following morning Jack called on his sister in Whitby.

'Well, dear brother, what brings you here so early in the day? Must be something urgent. After all we have seen little enough of you since you returned from Cornwall, and even less in recent weeks.'

'Elizabeth, for that I apologise,' he replied. 'Certain things have occupied me.'

'No doubt.' She smiled to herself. She knew her brother and had recognised his usual nervousness when he was about to announce something of family concern. 'Would you like a drink? A cup of chocolate or something stronger?'

'Maybe a brandy, if you have a drop?'

'A brandy it shall be,' she replied, and went to a cupboard from which she took a bottle and a glass. 'So you need fortifying?' she said as she placed the items in front of him so that he could help himself. 'You must have something serious to say.' Her eyes twinkled with amusement. 'Something to do with the odd whispered word that comes to us?' she teased.

He looked up sharply from the brandy he was pouring.

She laughed at the alarm on his face. 'Don't look so shocked. Rumours do come our way even if you think they don't. So, who is she?'

Annoyance made a fleeting appearance. 'I had hoped to mention her before you heard gossip.'

'Well, you've been too slow,' was his sister's retort, 'so get on with it now.'

He took a gulp of his brandy. 'Elizabeth, she's a wonderful person.'

'I'll be the judge of that when I meet her.' It was said in a teasing manner, for he knew that where affairs of the heart were concerned she would not interfere.

'That's what I've come about. I want you to meet her on Sunday. I'll send a carriage for you at quarter-past two.'

'Very well, Stephen and I will look forward to that.'

'Bring Robert if you wish.'

'I'll leave that to him. Now tell me a little more about her?'

It was almost the same scenario at Robin Hood's Bay, but Jack found it easier having been through it once already.

'Bring Crispin and Martin and their families, if you wish.'

Mary gave a shake of her head. 'I don't think so, Jack. We'll not overwhelm your lady at our first meeting. That can come later if things work out.'

He smiled. 'Oh, they will, Mary. I'm sure she will charm you all.'

'Sincerely, I hope.'

'Katherine could not be otherwise.'

As she watched her brother walk away from the house, Mary said to herself, 'My, Jack, you *are* in love. I hope nothing happens to mar it.'

Chapter Twenty-four

Jack smiled as, with Katherine beside him, he watched from the window of the drawing-room two carriages coming up the drive to his house by the river in Sleights. His tone was amused as he said, 'I thought that would happen.'

'What?' she queried.

'My sisters arriving together. They've contrived it between them. Neither would want the other to meet you first.' He took her hand. 'Come, let's go out and greet them.' He led her into the hall, where she stopped and looked round.

'I think this is a wonderful entrance,' she commented. She had been entranced by it when she had arrived with Jack earlier in the afternoon. And the same impression of enchantment had remained with her as he had shown her round the house, containing every evidence of a man who had got on well in the world. Jack was a man of taste, evident in his furniture, books, decorations, and especially in the art works that were displayed throughout the house. She was gratified that success had not spoiled him. That became obvious in the way he greeted his sisters and brothers-in-law.

Katherine, without appearing shy or apprehensive, hung back a little as he welcomed them. The two ladies, having made their greetings, moved past him and came towards her while Jack turned to welcome the men.

'I'm Mary Mulgrave and this is my sister Elizabeth Harris.'

'I'm Katherine Westland, and I am pleased to meet you.' She shook hands with a warmth and friendliness which was enhanced by her amiable smile. 'I trust you have had a pleasant journey?'

'Indeed we have,' both agreed.

Katherine knew she was coming under close observation and was thankful that she had chosen a fairly plain dress with no pattern to take away from its attractive light blue. The only ornamentation was the lace collar around the high neck and cuffs. They had both studied it with a critical eye and Katherine was pleased to see a flash of approval. The first moment had passed in her favour. She hoped the rest of the afternoon continued to do so.

The men had reached them. 'Katherine, these are my brothers-in-law, Harry from Robin Hood's Bay and Stephen from Whitby, and this is Stephen's son Robert.'

'We have met,' said Stephen courteously. 'You came with a little girl to my workshop a short while ago and bought a bracelet. In fact, the little girl chose it.'

'I remember. The nice lady,' put in Robert.

Everyone laughed at his enthusiastic remark.

'Thank you, Robert. Yes, I brought Rebecca Glossop to find a birthday present for her mother. I'm her governess.'

'I hope she liked it?' said Stephen.

'She did indeed. She, like me, thought it exquisite.'

He glanced at his wife. 'It was a piece Robert made.' He knew she would be pleased at the praise.

'You have a talented son, Mrs Harris,' said Katherine.

'Thank you.' Pride glowed in her voice and smile. 'And, please, it's Elizabeth.'

Katherine turned to Robert. 'Have you been busy making more bracelets?'

'Yes, and other things,' he replied. 'You must come and see them some time.'

'I would like that.'

'You would?'

'I'm sure I would.' She saw his eyes lighten and was drawn by his friendly enthusiasm. It was as if he had an empathy with her and wanted to know her better. The spell that was woven around them was snapped when she heard Jack saying, 'Let's go inside.'

In the hall two maids took the outdoor clothes from the guests and Jack led the way into the drawing-room.

'A glass of Madeira for you all. We'll have tea later,' he offered as everyone found a seat. 'I think you'll find the cook has some lemonade in the kitchen for you, Robert, run and fetch it.'

When he had left the room Stephen looked at Katherine and said, 'The day of your visit, Robert spoke of you all the way home.'

'And when he came in I had to hear all about it,' said Elizabeth. 'He took you on that visit to the workshop, but never expected to see you again. What a coincidence you should know Jack so Robert meets you again.'

'It is my pleasure also. He was charming to us when we were looking for the present,' said Katherine.

She was aware that Harry had been watching her closely but was still taken aback when he said tentatively, 'Katherine, have we met before?'

Her mind reeled. Harry was from Robin Hood's Bay. Surely he had not seen her then? She was there but a few days and it was so long ago ... 'I don't think so. I'm sure I would have remembered if we had.'

'You mean, once seen never forgotten,' laughed Jack over his shoulder from the sideboard where he was pouring the Madeira.

'There was something at the back of my mind.' Harry tried to brush aside the reason for his question.

'Must have been someone else. You've never been to Newcastle or London, and Katherine has not been in Whitby long.'

402

She was thankful that Jack made such an observation. It set the seal on the matter and she hoped Harry would not probe further.

The rest of the day went well. When the time came for the guests to leave, they all departed saying how pleased they were to have met Katherine.

'I can see you have been good for my brother,' whispered Mary as she went to the carriage arm in arm with Katherine. 'I know Elizabeth feels the same. She managed a quiet word with me and asked me to say so in case she did not get the opportunity.'

'I'm so pleased. Thank you for your kindness in understanding that I do not mean to be an interloper or a stealer of his affections.'

'I don't think it is in your nature to be that.'

'Thank you. I look forward to meeting you all again.'

'We will make it frequently. It will be nice to see more of Jack, and of course you.'

Jack and Katherine made their goodbyes and raised their hands in farewell as the two carriages drew away. They laughed when Robert poked his head out of the window, shouted 'Goodbye! Goodbye!' and waved enthusiastically.

They strolled back into the house. 'You made a conquest there,' commented Jack.

'He's a nice boy. They are all good people.'

'I'm glad you like them. They certainly like you.' He gave a little chuckle. 'I have their permission to go on seeing you if you will allow me.'

Katherine pursed her lips doubtfully. 'Well, I'm not sure.' The twinkle in her eyes teased him.

He swept her into his arms and kissed her passionately. 'Does that sweep your doubts away?'

She leaned back against his arms around her waist and looked into his eyes. 'It surely does Jack Palmer. But, you know, after that, you'll have to go on sweeping them away.'

*

403

Katherine found life more and more idyllic over the next few months. She was happy teaching Rebecca whose work was showing much promise. She knew that the child's parents had discussed their daughter's future education, for Katherine had voiced doubts about her ability to widen Rebecca's knowledge and ability as she thought the child deserved. But nothing would be decided in a hurry.

Isobel and Richard were pleased by the deepening relationship between Jack and Katherine. Knowing the governess would not jeopardise her commitment to Rebecca by abusing any privileges, they complied with Jack's desire to see more of Katherine. Because he wanted her to be truly accepted by his sisters and their families, visits to them became more frequent. The more they saw of her, the more attuned they became to the idea that their brother might have found a partner to take Jenny's place.

Elizabeth and Stephen were more than delighted that Robert seemed to have taken to Katherine. He was always full of life when she visited, loved her to call in at the workshop so he could show her his latest creation. He liked nothing better than when they walked by the harbour and on to the West Pier where he would expound his knowledge of the ships and the sea. She saw he was a popular figure among the sailors, but she, like Elizabeth, was ready with warnings of what the sea could do, though she never revealed her personal experience of it.

There were times when she thought she caught Harry or Stephen looking at her oddly, as if trying to grasp something from the deepest recesses of their minds. At such times she'd try to revive her own memory. Stephen was a jet worker. Had he given her the cross? Surely she would have remembered him if he had but her recollections, which were still hazy, were of an older man than he would have been at the time. And had Harry been among the men on the beach at Robin Hood's Bay? She dare not ask, for that would reveal a part of her life untold to Jack which in its turn would disclose her loss of memory. She thrust such thoughts from her mind and instead let herself

404

be absorbed in the happiness she was experiencing. The past did not matter, it could be lost in the love she had for Jack. The future, where she hoped nothing could overcome the love they shared, could take care of itself.

A year after her first meeting with Jack's family he took her to dine again at the Angel. It was a calm night without a cloud in the sky. The darkness was pricked by a myriad stars and a bright moon sent its silver rays sparkling across the tranquil sea.

Katherine did not demur when Jack suggested that they took a circuitous route back to Farndale House. The track took them along the cliff top towards Sandsend before turning inland. He pulled the carriage to a halt at the highest point. It afforded them wonderful views of the sea and the coast which dipped and soared beyond Sandsend to huge cliffs, dark and menacing as they contested the silvery sheen of the moon. They sat, taking in the beauty and enjoying the sensation that they were alone in the world. The hiss of the waves breaking gently on the sand below seemed only to add to the silence enveloping them.

Jack slid his arm round Katherine's shoulders. She felt safe. Nothing could upset her world now. She snuggled closer to him.

'Katherine ...' his voice was low, barely above a whisper, as if he should not be breaking the silence at all. 'Will you marry me?'

For one moment she was so entranced by the quiet beauty around them she thought she had not heard him properly. Then the sense of his words penetrated. She twisted round, eyes wide with pleasure and surprise.

'I love you, Katherine, marry me?'

'Oh, darling, yes.' She tilted her face upwards and he met her lips with a kiss that spoke of the deep love he felt for her. She responded so fervently there was no doubting her love for him.

*

They gazed across the moonbeams on the water, absorbed in the joy of being together.

Hardly daring to break the mood, Katherine asked, 'When will you tell your family?'

'Let's keep it a secret from everyone for the time being,' replied Jack, wanting to savour the joy of her acceptance before anyone else shared his elation. 'We'll have a party for my family and a few special friends. Give them all a surprise by announcing it then.' He paused a moment and with the light of mischief fading from his eyes added, 'Unless you think otherwise and would rather make other arrangements?'

'No, no.' Katherine was quick to reply. 'That will be perfect.'

Jack, wanting to grasp her acceptance as quickly as possible while paying some attention to the rules of propriety, added, 'I don't think we should have a long engagement. We'll fix a date and announce that at the same time.'

'That will take them doubly by surprise,' chuckled Katherine.

'Then you agree?'

'Oh, yes.'

'We'll talk more about that tomorrow. I have to come to Farndale House on business. For now . . .' He said no more but drew her closer.

She felt safe. The troubles of the past no longer held any significance for her. If she never filled the gaps in her memory it would not matter. Anything she could not remember would have no bearing on her future life. That was now to be shared with Jack, and in her heart she knew John would approve. She tilted her head towards him. 'I love you, Jack Palmer.'

'And I you, with all my heart. I thank you for bringing me a joy I'd thought never to experience again. You are good for me, Katherine Westland.' His kiss confirmed his words and she responded to the love that shone in his eyes and trembled on his lips.

It was two o'clock by the time Richard and Jack had

concluded their business which they had conducted throughout lunch, leaving Isobel and Katherine to have theirs with Rebecca.

'I'm taking Rebecca for a walk, Richard,' said his wife when the two men came into the hall. 'It'll do you good to come with us after being cooped up all morning.'

'Right,' he agreed. 'Coming, Jack?'

'He has other things to see to,' commented Isobel quickly before Jack could answer. She knew he would have accepted out of politeness.

'Oh, has he?' There was confusion in Richard's voice but almost immediately he realised what his wife was hinting at – leaving Jack to see Katherine. 'I'll get my coat.'

As Richard went to the closet Isobel winked at Jack and, with an inclination of her head, indicated the downstairs turret room.

He gave her a knowing smile of thanks and was into the turret room before Richard returned.

Katherine turned from the window when she heard the door open. 'Jack.' Her eyes shone and her smile was filled with all the pleasure she felt at seeing him. She held out her hands to him.

He took them and was thrilled by her touch. 'You look wonderful!' He drew her closer, slipped his arms round her waist. Their lips met and lingered in a moment charged with longing.

'I love you,' she whispered as their mouths parted.

'And I you,' he returned. 'You've not had second thoughts about what we said yesterday?'

'No.'

'Then we'll start planning.'

Katherine's face was radiant with anticipation.

Plans were made, dates fixed and the guest list compiled. When these were settled Katherine asked, 'Who will be your best man?'

'Richard, of course. Do you approve?'

407

'Emphatically.'

'What about bridesmaids?'

'I'd like Rebecca. We'll ask her at the party after we've made the announcement.'

'Good, I thought you might. She'll be so excited.'

'I might ask another friend, but I'll think about it and let you know.'

'Very well. Oh, there is another thing for you to consider. Since my return from Cornwall I have never got around to thinking about a housekeeper. My cook has supervised. Now we shall certainly need a personal maid for you, and as we will be doing more entertaining, which will probably mean more staff, I think we should engage a housekeeper to oversee everything under your direction.'

'If you are sure, I think I know exactly the people who would suit. Let me write to them and if they accept we can discuss them later.'

Jack, being eager to please, said, 'If that is the way you want it.'

After careful thought, two days later Katherine wrote two letters.

Dear Mrs Willoughby,

I was sorry I did not see you before I left Ribton Hall. I hope you received my message from Martha and that you understood my circumstances.

Now, to the purpose of my letter. I am getting married on 30 July and would like to offer you the position of housekeeper at my new home. I would also like to engage Martha and would ask you to put this to her. If you accept I will arrange for you to travel to Whitby with a friend from Hull, and will send you the details later.

I would suggest you keep all this to yourself and when the time comes need only tell Mrs Bradshaw you are leaving.

I am sure you will like the house which is a few miles outside Whitby. I hope you and Martha will accept the positions. I look forward to hearing from you.
Yours sincerely,
    Katherine Westland

Dear Barbara,
I hope you will be delighted to hear that I am getting married to a wonderful man on 30 July. I want you to be my bridesmaid and would be honoured if you would accept.
    If you do, I would ask a favour of you – namely that you escort two friends to Whitby for me.
I am in good health and gloriously happy.
Ever your dear friend,
    Katherine

Chapter Twenty-five

Katherine took special care with her preparations for the party. She wanted to look her best and bought a special evening dress for the occasion. As she stood in front of the mirror making a final assessment of her appearance she realised that a finishing touch was needed, something round her neck to enhance her dress and yet be attractive in its own right. She stood for a few minutes wondering and was still doing so when she automatically went to her coat, hanging in the wardrobe. She felt in the pocket and lovingly withdrew the jet cross. She stood looking at it in her hand. She had kept it hidden for so long, fearing what might happen if it was seen, but now chided herself for such a negative view. Besides, time had passed and who would ever learn how she had retrieved what was rightfully hers? She slipped it round her neck and viewed it in the mirror. 'Perfect,' she whispered, feeling elated that now she would wear it again.

She travelled to the party with Isobel, Richard and Rebecca. Jack greeted them when they arrived and, as the maids took the coats from the new arrivals, directed his friends to the drawing-room, saying, 'The family are in there.' He took Katherine's hand. Hearing a rumble of wheels approaching the house, he added, 'Wait with me and greet the rest of the guests.'

The hall hummed with greetings, brief exchanges and

laughter. Missing Katherine when the Glossops had entered the drawing-room, Robert came out into the hall. Seeing her, he hurried over to greet her. 'Hello, Mrs Westland,' he said with a warm smile. His eyes immediately settled on her jet cross. 'That is a lovely piece of work,' he said enthusiastically. He reached out to finger it, then hesitated.

She smiled. 'It's all right, Robert, you can touch it.' He took it carefully in his fingers and turned it over. When he let it go and it hung in just the right place, he added, 'I haven't seen it before. Where did you get it?'

'Oh, I don't remember. I've had it a long time. Before you were born.'

'It's beautiful,' he said, and turned away as other guests arrived.

Katherine watched him for a moment, wondering why she had said 'before you were born'. It was true enough, but why had she said that? Her attention was then swallowed up by new arrivals, the last of the guests.

'Father ...' Robert drew Stephen to one side when he returned to the drawing-room. 'I've just seen Mrs Westland. She's wearing the most beautiful jet cross, you must see it.'

'I'll keep a look out for it. Have we a rival? Did she say where she got it?'

'No, she said she has had it a long time.'

Stephen's eyes were on the cross as soon as Katherine came into the room, for all jet work interested him, but it was not until some time later that he was able to examine it more closely. He and Katherine had got into conversation in one corner of the room and, seeing that everyone else was engaged, he took the opportunity of commenting on the cross.

'I treasure it,' she said in reply.

'It is very beautiful indeed. May I take a closer look?'

'Of course.'

411

She held it out for him and he took it with the loving care of someone who truly appreciated jet work. He scrutinised it carefully without making his concentration obvious, turned it over and let her take it back.

'If I may ask, where did you get such a wonderful piece?' he asked cautiously, for he had noticed a special mark – his mark – the one he had used for the first time on that particular cross and on all the pieces he had made since.

Katherine could not understand why her heart started to race when he examined the cross. Now her nerves tightened. 'I can't really remember but I think it must have been in Whitby many years ago when I was on my way to London.'

'A present from your husband most likely?'

'I don't think so. I'm almost certain it was a stranger who gave it me.'

'A stranger? That's curious.'

'Someone I think we met on the ship . . .'

Stephen's mind was racing as the information, vague as it was, was presented to him. He saw nervousness in Katherine's troubled eyes and decided that to press further would not be advisable. He could sense some relief in her when, at that moment, Jack came and took her away to meet two of his friends. Stephen watched them thoughtfully. What had worried Katherine? Had she something to hide? Could it be connected to the jet cross? He saw them reach Jack's friends. She half turned and glanced back at him. In that brief moment a germ of an idea was sparked into life. Since the time when she was introduced to the family he had had a feeling that he had seen her before, but had always dismissed that as extremely unlikely. Now . . . the glimpse he received in that brief instant carried him back to a certain other moment in time and he realised then how she came to have the jet cross he had made so many years ago. Mr Simpson had given that cross to a young lady on her way to London with her husband. Katherine had just related similar facts, though she had seemed strangely unsure as to their veracity.

He strolled on to the terrace, deep in thought. Jack had met her at the Glossops' he knew she had been in London, that her husband had been killed there, but what else did he know about her? There seemed to be a big gap in the chronology. Did that hold secrets he should know of before going through with a marriage that on the surface seemed born in heaven? Should Stephen himself confront her and gauge her reaction?

'You're deep in thought.' A voice startled him and he looked up to see his brother-in-law Harry observing him from the doorway. Stephen did not answer immediately as he tried to order his own confusing thoughts. 'Come on, out with it,' Harry prompted.

Stephen took his arm and led him away from the doorway. 'Ever since we met Katherine I have thought I'd seen her somewhere before but deemed it impossible. Now, I've just remembered where. I made the jet cross she is wearing when I was still working for Mr Simpson. It has my mark on it.'

'What?' His expression of surprise carried doubt too. Stephen went on to enlighten him quickly.

When he had finished Harry's expression was pensive. 'It's interesting you have been wondering where you had seen her before because I have been doing the same thing.'

'You? But how could you have met her before?'

'I can't be sure that I'm right but I have a feeling I once saw her on the beach at Robin Hood's Bay.'

'What? You can't have done.'

'You remember the terrible storm of '35?'

'Of course. How could I ever forget the awful tragedy it brought, and the unexpected blessing that followed soon after?'

'As you know, there was one official survivor whom Dr

413

Bennett afterwards took to Scarborough. When I found her on the beach she seemed to know nothing of what had happened and suffered a total loss of memory. The lady was wearing a jet cross but I took little notice of that. It was her bracelet that was of more concern for on it were the names Katherine and John.'

'What?' Stephen was astonished. 'Are you sure? It was such a long time ago.'

'The names haunted me for quite a while. I often wondered who they were and what had happened to her since then.'

'But this is too much of a coincidence, for Jack's Katherine to be the same person!' Stephen pointed out. 'She does not wear such a bracelet.'

'She could have lost it or maybe prefers not to wear it now. But you have the evidence of your jet cross.'

Stephen nodded. 'What has happened to her in the intervening years? Loss of memory could mean she was put into an institution. Maybe she is still unstable.'

'We've seen no evidence of that. She seems normal enough to me.'

'But you never know. Shouldn't Jack learn what we suspect? Shouldn't he know what those missing years entailed?'

'Yes, but we had better tread warily. We should be sure of our facts.'

'Then let's tackle Katherine.'

'Now?'

'It is better cleared up right away before it becomes harder to do.'

Katherine glanced round the drawing-room. For a moment she was on her own. She saw that everyone was occupied in conversation so slipped into the hall. She needed a few minutes' quiet reflection. With family and guests here the significance of the step she was taking suddenly weighed heavily on her. Maybe a few moments alone would settle her mind and she could convince herself that the commitment she had made to Jack was justified. If she had any lingering doubts whatsoever she could withdraw before anyone else knew of it.

She was concentrating hard on her own preoccupations as she walked towards the terrace but was aware of agitated muttering coming from a small room used to receive solitary guests. She wondered who it could be and what they were doing there. The door was ajar so she pushed it tentatively. It swung back noiselessly. Robert was standing in front of a mirror that hung over a mantelpiece on the left-hand wall. He seemed agitated as he brushed his hand against some unruly hair on the crown of his head. His lips were set into a line of annoyance.

'Trouble, Robert?' she asked quietly.

Startled, he swung round. His embarrassment at being discovered quickly disappeared when he saw Katherine. 'This hair won't go right for some reason. I've never had trouble with it before.'

'Let me see.' When she reached him he turned round with his back to her. 'It's this piece here. You've been taking it the wrong way.' She parted the hair so that she could put it in the right place.

She suddenly stopped what she was doing and froze. A chill gripped her. She stared at him. Picture after picture flashed through her mind. The past hit her forcibly. A baby cuddled in her arms. A toddler laughing at play. A child clinging to her in fright as a tempest tore around them. Then a mighty wave snatched him from her. She cried out as she tried to grab him but he was gone.

She gazed in disbelief at the diamond-shaped birthmark on Robert's head. It would not normally be visible but parting his hair had brought it to her notice. She had never seen it before ... But she had! The years rolled away. More gaps in her memory were filled until only a little of her past remained unattainable. A doctor and midwife, concerned to point out a diamond-shaped birthmark on the

415

head of a child she had just brought into the world. Robert's birthmark was exactly the same and in exactly the same place as that of the child she had borne who had been snatched from her arms by the raging sea! Katherine felt weak at the knees.

'Is it right now?' Robert's voice broke into a mind dazed by the implications of her discovery.

'Yes.'

'Thanks.' He started for the door. 'Are you coming?'

'In a few minutes.'

There was something about the way she said it that told Robert she wanted to be alone.

When he closed the door behind him she sank on to a chair. Could this be true? Could two people have an identical birthmark in exactly the same place? The fact that she had once had a son was evident from the pictures of him that had come back to her with the further restoration of her memory. Had James survived the shipwreck as she had done? Her mind was in a daze but through the confusion came a voice: 'Don't mourn our son.'

'John?' She half whispered his name.

'Don't mourn our son.'

Had she misinterpreted his words when she had first heard them? She had taken it that John was trying to ease the pain of her loss. But had he meant that there was no reason to mourn because their son was alive? Her mind thundered. Had John led her to this room, when Robert needed someone, so that she could learn the truth?

But what should she do? She ached to hold him in her arms as a mother would a son, to love him with a mother's love and receive in return a son's love for his mother. But could she? Robert knew Elizabeth as his mother so was it likely that he would ever accept her? But why not, when he knew the truth? They had got on so well, it was as if there was a natural empathy between them, its origin unsuspected. Or would Robert's life be shattered by the revelation? And what of Jack and their marriage? Could he accept Robert as his own son when his sister regarded him as hers?

She shook her head, trying to clear her thoughts, and was left with what could be the only solution – forego marriage and leave Whitby, taking Robert with her to a new life. It was the only solution if she revealed what she suspected. No, not what she suspected but what she knew to be the truth. People would be hurt but what joy she would experience when she held her son in her arms. 'Oh, John, help me.' The cry remained silent on her lips. With his help she must come to a decision quickly. People would be wondering where she was.

A knock on the door interrupted her. She brushed the dampness from her eyes and called, 'Come in.'

The door opened and Stephen and Harry looked in tentatively.

'Robert said we would find you here. If we aren't disturbing you, can we have a word?'

She signalled them to come in even though she did not want company at this moment.

As they came further into the room, concern clouded Harry's face. 'Katherine, are you all right?' he asked automatically for the pale, drained face before him brought back a vision of just such a face lying on the beach at Robin Hood's Bay so long ago, a face he had never been able to dispel completely from his memory. He was now convinced that Katherine had been that person.

She looked at them enquiringly.

Stephen drew a deep breath. 'Katherine, when I examined your jet cross earlier this evening I recognised it as my own work.'

'Yours?' She looked puzzled.

'Yes. I always mark my work, a sort of trademark. It is on that cross – the first time I'd used it. You said you had had it a long time and that it was given to you. I believe I know by whom.'

417

'But a stranger gave it to me . . .'

'No stranger to me. I worked for him. Mr Simpson. You came to his workshop after meeting him on a ship from Newcastle bound for London. He must have taken a liking to you and your husband for he let you choose any piece you liked from the shop.'

Katherine's mind was rocked as further gaps in her memory were filled. 'He told us that he was going to leave his business to his foreman.'

'That's right. To me.'

'You had your son in that workshop, a nice boy . . .'

'Who thought you a nice lady.'

'But it was Robert who said that?'

'True, but Peter said it first, many years ago.'

Katherine shook her head as if she was trying to understand.

'Where is he?'

'He died in the Whitby lifeboat going to the aid of a ship that was wrecked south of Robin Hood's Bay. He was only eighteen.'

'About the same age as Robert is now,' she said, but thought, 'As James would have been.'

'Yes.'

'I think you were in that wreck and survived it,' put in Harry. She looked at him in a daze but the desire for explanation in her eyes made him go on. 'I was among those who found a survivor on the beach. She wore a bracelet with the words "Katherine and John" on it. When Jack first introduced you, your face stirred something in my mind. I was never quite certain until the moment we entered this room and I saw that same ashen look. It was so like the face I saw on the beach. You are that person, aren't you?'

She nodded. 'Yes.'

'So long ago. Does Jack know? And does he know where you have been since and what has happened to you?'

Alarm came into her eyes. 'No!'

'Why not? Shouldn't he do so in the light of your close-ness? Why haven't you told him?'

'I was afraid that if I did, he would want nothing more to do with me.'

'Why?'

'The trauma of the shipwreck caused a loss of memory.'

'You have been in an institution?'

'Not in the sense you mean.' She explained briefly what had happened to her. 'My memory returned gradu-ally but there were still gaps when I met Jack and, as I say, I thought he would turn away from me if he knew. Those gaps have now been filled, some in these last few moments. Only the truth of one needs verifying.' She hesitated.

'And that is?'

'I was never sure if I had had a child. That I had has just become clear to me.'

'How?' Harry looked at her with curiosity and not a little apprehension in his eyes.

'My memory was sparked and I remembered my son had a birthmark on his head.'

'What exactly jolted your memory?' Alarm rang in his question.

'I heard someone in here and when I looked in Robert was having trouble with his hair. I put it right for him and saw a birthmark identical to my son's.' The exchange of glances between Harry and Stephen was not lost on her. 'Am I right in believing my son was not lost in that ter-rible storm?'

There was hesitation from both men until Stephen said, 'We'll have to tell her, Harry.'

He nodded reluctantly, realising there was nothing else they could do. Between them they told her how the child had been found and the decision they had made about his future. She listened without a question and sat in thought-ful silence, regretting all the years she had not known her son. Tears streamed down her face.

'What will you do?' asked Stephen.

She wiped the tears away vigorously and said defiantly, 'Don't you think I have a right to my own son?'

'I suppose you have. But think of the devastation it would cause,' said Stephen. 'Elizabeth would be shattered to lose another son.'

'He *isn't* her son.'

'She regards him as such, always has. She's given him all her love, as have I. And what would it do to him? Robert thinks of us as his parents. Suddenly to find he is not . . .' Stephen left the implication unspoken.

'If you cannot see it that way, what about you and Jack?' Harry took up the plea. 'Wouldn't it shatter any hope of a happy future together? If he took Robert as his son, would it not drive a wedge between him and his sisters? Robert's love for our families would be breached and the damage to him and to them would be irreparable.'

'I have a son,' she whispered harshly.

'You have,' agreed Harry with resignation.

The two men realised they could say nothing more. What had had to be said was in the open. The future lay in Katherine's hands.

'Think on it,' said Stephen, quietly and without malice. He and Harry left Katherine to her thoughts.

Her mind was far away, roaming through the past that was whole and illuminated for her now. So much ran rapidly through her mind, but most of all she saw her son and that brought joy to her heart. She could have that again. He could be hers, to love, to hold, a son whom she could tell about his father and with whom she could share so much. She stood up, stiffened her spine and tugged at her dress. She had people to face but first she must see Jack. She glanced in the mirror, pinched her cheeks and patted her hair. Satisfied, she went into the hall.

'Ah, Katherine, there you are. I was just coming to look

for you. I think we should make our announcement now.'
He had just come from the drawing-room.

'I was ...' She let the words fade away. He looked so
happy. Could she deny such happiness to the man she
loved? But could she deny herself the love of a son?

Jack opened the door to the room. 'Ladies and gentlemen.' His voice, charged with joyous excitement, caught
everyone's attention. Silence descended on the gathering.
He half turned and, with an adoring smile, held out his
hand to Katherine.

Her mind was in turmoil. Decision after decision and
their likely consequences flashed before her eyes as she
stepped towards him. She felt his hand grip hers and heard
his frantic whisper, 'Are you all right?'

She could not meet his eyes but gave a small nod.

'Ladies and gentlemen,' he repeated, 'I have an
announcement to make.'

Katherine's lips trembled with a desire to stop him but
no sound came. It was as if someone had gagged her.
'John?' she silently implored.

'Katherine has been gracious enough to accept my hand
in marriage.'

A buzz of chatter and exclamations of joy rang out on
every side. Katherine saw apprehension on the faces of
Stephen and Harry.

They knew she had not had time to tell her story to Jack.
Was she intending to go through with this engagement and
then claim the boy as hers?

There was a movement behind them and Robert pushed
his way to the front of the crowd of onlookers. His face was
bright with excitement. 'Now I can call you Aunt
Katherine!'

She looked straight at him. She could sense the tension
in Harry and Stephen. She hesitated then said, 'Yes, of
course you can.' Her voice was steady and strong, and she
held out her arms to him. 'We'll spend a lot of time
together,' she said as she hugged him to her. 'And I'll tell

421

you about your Uncle John,' she added silently, as she saw grateful thanks on the faces of Stephen and Harry who came forward to add their own congratulations to those showering down upon the happy couple.